Red Shoes

A Riverhaven Novel

By

Satyros Phil Brucato

Quiet Thunder Productions • Seattle, Washington

Red Shoes

Red Shoes

A Quiet Thunder Productions Book

ISBN 978-1-953203-01-4

Cover Illustration by Cora Ocean

Cover and interior design by Sherry Lynne Baker

Typeset by Quiet Thunder Productions, Inc.

Quiet Thunder Productions

625 North 143rd Street

Seattle, WA, 98133

USA

Printed and bound in the USA

∾ ∾ ∾

For
Asha, Bryan, Damiana, Danielle, Dragon, Francesca,
Inanna, Inky, Isyllt, Ivy, Kate, Kitty, Sooj, Tempest,
and Lady Snow Leopard.

And to the beloved memories of
Raven Bond and Coyote Ashley Ward.

∾ ∾ ∾

So I danced in stillness
And I felt the city move

WAS ALL THIS FOR REAL?

∿ ∿ ∿

B lue was dancing like mad when she burst into flames.

It didn't happen suddenly. She'd been busting chaos-angel moves on stage when I'd noticed smoke rising from her hair. Blue's feet flashed and spun beneath her jingling skirt. Sweat shimmered on her tattoos. Her eyes rolled back till all I could see were the whites. Her pale skin began to glow.

"How's she *doing* that?" Ashley whispered.

"I have no idea," I whispered back.

Flames flickered from Blue's scalp, then swept across her skin. Her black vest caught fire in a sudden puff, the flames shining on the tiny mirrors woven into it.

"Holy *shit*," Ash hissed.

We launched ourselves at the stage.

For dancers, fire is *bad*. Modern bellydance gear tends to be full of artificial materials, which often melt on contact with flames.

Lots of us – especially the ones who dance with fire – stick to cotton garb when dancing for just that reason. Blue's gear had Lycra, Spandex, and lots of other things that don't like fire. And it was melting to her skin.

She didn't scream. Not once. Aside from the sound of the flames, she was totally silent.

Still dancing, too. Dancing like flames.

Booming over the sound of those flames, "Maiden Goes to Bollywood" set up a counterpoint to the horror show on stage. Ash grabbed two glasses of water off nearby tables and threw them both on Blue. The water hissed and spit across the fire.

I whipped my head around, frantic, looking for something to roll Blue up in to smother the blaze. Nothing. Ah, hell – I leaped onto the stage, sprinted to the bundle of clothes and stuff I had set off to the side behind the curtain, and grabbed the leather jacket my last ex-boyfriend, Karl, had given me for Christmas.

Blue whirled around the stage like a flaming dervish, still utterly silent. Ashley tried to tackle Blue and roll her on the floor, but the heat kept her leaning in and then pulling back out of sheer self-preservation.

The audience – realizing this wasn't part of the act – freaked out. Yelling, pushing, chairs and tables scattered, knocked over... a mosh pit at the bellydance party.

Blue's skin crackled. Her hair blazed. I yanked my jacket from the pile of crap backstage and dashed over to where Ashley and Blue were weaving back and forth like MMA fighters too scared to throw the first punch.

FWUMP! I threw my jacket over Blue's flaming back and slammed her down. Our feet skidded on the water-splashed stage, and all three of us fell on top of each other – me on Blue, Ashley on me.

Blue never made a sound.

I heard thumps nearby as some vague shapes hopped up on the stage with us. Ash was screaming in my ear. Blue stayed quiet. Her skin kept burning around the jacket as I rolled us around trying to put the fire out. I felt the heat from her body through the leather. If my jacket had been cheap-ass leatherette, it would've melted to my hands.

Someone pulled Ashley off me. Someone else had a fire extinguisher. He blasted us with the extinguisher. The whole thing seemed to be going on somewhere way outside my reality, which is a good thing because otherwise I'd have totally lost my shit.

My best friend Meghan says that in times of shock, your mind disassociates from your present circumstances. And so, as Ashley flailed around in the grip of some big dude I'd never seen before, and the guy with the fire extinguisher hosed us down, I felt myself looking at the whole scene through the length of a long mental tunnel. *Oh*, said that distant part of my brain, *I hope this doesn't mean I'm gonna pass out.*

I didn't.

All around me, I felt people moving: Inky and Caroline from our troupe, Arcana Darque. Chalice and some other dancers from different troupes. Tabi, the owner of the Hearthstone. Other folks I didn't recognize.

And right there, under my jacket, my friend Blue, who wasn't moving anymore.

It didn't look like Blue. It didn't look like *anyone*.

That's when I passed out, halfway through throwing up everything I'd eaten for the last week.

PIECES

LITTLE NAKED ME

∾ ∾ ∾

The thought hit me as I was digging myself out of the barf-encrusted black pit I'd fallen into. *Blue! Was she…?* I breathed in fast, and choked on… um, oh fuck, I breathed in… *her*.

I almost threw up again but coughed my head off instead.

The coughing set off an artillery barrage in my skull. I squeezed my eyes shut against the pain, so hard that stars exploded behind my eyelids. My puke-burned throat kicked up round after round of fresh agony. The more I coughed, the more it hurt.

A guy with very strong hands pulled me away from where I'd been laying.

"Hey," said a soft male voice. "Um… you okay?"

I tried to reply but couldn't catch my breath.

My wet legs tangled in the soaked folds of my skirt. My nostrils blazed with a hot swamp of fresh vomit, fire-extinguisher foam, and burnt smells I didn't want to think too much about. My coin-bra had ripped apart and spilled itself down my chest.

I wrapped my arms around my ribcage to keep the entire world from seeing the goods, shivering with pain and shame and disgust. I couldn't even breathe, much less open my eyes. Sloppy chunks of everything I'd eaten that day slipped across the skin on my arms and chest. Coughs kept booming up my throat, squeezing my chest and shoulders tight. I hugged myself so hard I thought my ribs might break. The dark behind my eyelids strobed with flashing colored lights.

But I was better off than Blue.

Oh, *Blue.* Jesus...

I wanted to look, but knew I'd have nightmares forever if I did.

Cold blackness opened up inside, and I fell into it for a while.

Raised voices and stomping footsteps surged around me in a tide of sound. I felt bodies push past me, their words garbled into noise. The stage beneath us creaked and bowed under the weight of our chaos. And through it all, "Maiden Goes to Bollywood" still thumped through the room, shaking loose the last pieces of my composure.

I finally managed to stop coughing long enough to breathe.

"Hey," the guy behind me said again. "You all right?"

"Please," I whispered through the graveled puke-track of my throat, "tell them to turn that *Fucking. Music. OFF.*"

"Uh... right." His hands lingered for a second on my shoulders – not pervy, just concerned. "Um, you gonna be...?"

"I'm gonna be fine," I lied. "I just need to glue my head back together."

The unseen guy let me go. I felt his boots thump across the stage. My own boots – a pair of badass New Rock Reactors – were still in my pile of stuff backstage. So while my Good Samaritan clumped offstage to turn off the music, I kept my eyes closed, pushed myself up to a trembly semblance of my usual height, wiped off the worst of the slimy mess on my skin, and shambled blind over toward where I thought my stuff was heaped.

Not far off, I heard sirens. I finally opened my eyes. Good Sam had someone turn off that goddamned music. The houselights went on, blinding me for a second but providing a remarkable improvement over the glaring red and green. At the sight of smoke in the air – *Blue* smoke, my brain had to add, ha-ha – I felt my guts throw down another gauntlet at self-control.

I value my snarky sense of calm. It's gotten me through some prime breakdown real estate. But me and sanity were going to have a nice long chat when this mess was sorted out, and I was not looking forward to that discussion.

I did, however, manage not to puke again.

Back on the stage, in the weird glow of house lights and the stage-lights overhead, the guy with the fire extinguisher tried to CPR a smoking slab of nothing. Tabi, the other dancers, and a stunned-looking bunch of audience people hovered around them, some of 'em shooing away the others with a worthless chorus of "*Give them some air, give them some room!*" Thick curls of smoke hovered like lazy ghosts above the stage. Eyes watering, I dug around in my gym bag for a towel and the T-shirt I'd brought with me to the gig.

Blue wasn't moving.

Blue wasn't *Blue*.

A certain bellydancer was never gonna breathe again.

Not ever.

It hit me then: a sledgehammer of recognition carved out of sheer finality.

Blue wasn't gonna laugh at Ash's shitty jokes anymore.

Blue wouldn't be showing up at my place again with a *got-beer* grin or smudged makeup from her latest breakup.

We would not be grabbing venté lattés at Java Saints, trading bad-date stories in the little-girls' room, texting each other with news of the latest whatever in our lives.

There was a block of burnt meat on the stage and a thick mess of charbroiled human smoke hovering over it, just waiting to catch on to what it means to be dead.

And suddenly, halfway through slipping off the broken bra, I just curled up and dropped into a soggy crying-jag where the only certainties involved darkness and hurt and a place in the middle of my chest where Blue was never gonna be again.

Eventually, I pulled myself together enough to shrug off the rest of the coin-bra, wipe myself as clean as possible, and pull my shirt on before some asshole stared taking pictures of me on his phone. Deliberately *not* looking at the place where a bunch of EMTs were strapping something Blue-like onto a gurney, I swiped the dirt off my feet, dug my socks out of the boots, strapped on my pouch-belt, and put myself more or less back in order. The headache kicked around in my skull as I dragged some tissues across my face. Behind me, I felt a creepy prickle across my back. Assured that I wasn't a walking wardrobe malfunction, I turned around to blast whoever was looking at me.

No one *was* looking at me, though.

Instead, Ashley was standing behind the dude who'd pulled me off of Blue. He had his back to me, like a gentleman who didn't want to intrude. Chalice had her back to me as well, though something in her posture suggested she might have been the one whose gaze I felt. A whole mess of people I didn't recognize were huddled around on the stage, and Ash had a tall woman whose aura screamed *COP* standing right next to her. I hadn't had much experience with cops, thank everything that might remotely be considered a god, but I didn't need a *Hey where's your ID?* to know a cop when I saw one who was as much a cop as this lady was.

Still dressed in her dance-gear, Ash had her arms crossed so tight against her chest that the coin-bra looked like a gleaming silver toothpaste tube. In total lockdown mode, Ash looked my way. "Hey, Genét," she said, the rhyme sounding as though it'd been dragged behind a car for an hour or two.

"Hey, Ash…" I corrected myself, "uh, Ash*ley*." Yeah, everyone calls her *Ash*, but that was the wrong time and place to use that word. "You… um… okay?"

Her face crushed up a bit inside, but she nodded. "Yeah. Yeah, I'm cool."

"Yeah," I echoed in that way you use when there's no set of words that fit the situation. "Yeah, me too. I guess. Kinda. Maybe."

The guy turned around when he heard me talking. Big dude, short blond hair, shy and sweet-looking as a puppy who'd been punched a couple times in the face and isn't sure what to make of that. "M…miss?" He stammered, uncertain, over that one word.

I nodded to him. "I'm good. Hey… thanks."

We all just sorts stared at one another for a few seconds, wondering what the fuck to even *say*.

"Miss Shilling?" Ms. Cop stepped forward just a bit. "I'm Detective Fallon."

"Hey," I sighed in her general direction. My Snappy Patter switch had definitely been flipped somewhere along the line. Since I felt like an idiot sitting there while the three of them cast shadows over me from the light of the stage, I pushed myself up standing.

Which is how I first noticed that my hands were kinda burnt.

Not *bad* burns, fortunately. Mostly like I'd touched a hot stove with both my palms. But red and sore and a bit puffy.

"Huh," I said, regarding them. Lady Eloquence was nowhere on the premises.

Detective Fallon looked my hands over from a distance. "Do you need to get one of the EMTs to look you over, Miss Shilling?"

"No… um, well… maybe yeah." I didn't want to go anywhere near them, though. Or, really, I didn't want to go anywhere near the blackened spot on the stage that used to be my friend. My boots stayed welded to the floor while I looked at my red hands and tried to sort out the chaos in my head.

Shock, as Meghan said. Total fucking shock.

"I'll go get one," Ashley said. She slid off behind Detective Fallon and Punched Puppy Dude, shaky but starting to get the grip on herself that I seemed to be losing on my end.

My bones shook. My hands burned. The less said about my throat, my guts, and the inside of my head, the better. That wet skirt still pressed against my legs, and I found myself breathing as little as possible. Each breath tasted like...

"Oh, fuck this," I muttered. "I am *not* throwing up again."

"Would you like me to get you anything, ma'am?" Punched Puppy looked like he might get punched again.

"Nah." I told him. "thanks. That's okay." I looked back over at the detective. "Um... I guess this is the part where you tell me you need to ask me some questions, right?"

"Pretty much," she said. "Yes."

DON'T ASK QUESTIONS
YOU DON'T WANNA KNOW

∿ ∿ ∿

By the time the long night finally wound down, I found myself back in my car, heading home in my jeans while my burnt-smell skirt awaited a sad date with the garbage man. Detective Fallon's card, which I'd stashed in my pouch-belt, nagged at me. Something, I realized, was creeping through the fog in my head.

I'd answered all her questions as accurately as I could: No enemies I knew of, no stalkers, no psychos. Blue had *exes* and *rivals*, sure – everybody does – but no one I could imagine showering her with gasoline and setting her on fire. No, I hadn't seen anyone go near her just before she went up in smoke. The Hearthstone stage is pretty small, and there's no catwalk or anything that someone could hide on while dumping stuff onto the stage from above. Honestly, I'd been kinda dumb leaving my stuff on the stage like that… but it's not like there was anywhere somebody could have run to if they'd grabbed my bag and tried to make a break for it. No one could have been behind Blue or attacked her without being seen.

Besides, Blue hadn't ignited from an outside source. That fire, from where I'd been sitting, looked like it'd come from *inside*.

At least it didn't seem like she had suffered.

Ashley was about as calmed down as anybody *could* be after what had just happened. Once we'd changed back into normal clothes, we hugged and cried and then her friend Aaron came to pick her up. Chalice and those other dancers were long gone.

Yeah, we made an impression. I didn't blame Chalice for not sticking around.

They'd all been in the audience when things started, though, so it's not like any of the other dancers could have set Blue on fire even if they'd wanted to. And I couldn't imagine why they'd *want* to. It's not like Chalice was Queen Bitch of Stephen King High.

Everything had seemed *normal* until it wasn't normal anymore.

As Aaron and Ash drove away, I found myself wishing that Meghan was still in town so she could just pick me up and I could go fall apart somewhere in private. But Meghan was on tour with her band, my roommate Kristen was at work, and I just really didn't feel up to explaining things to anybody else. By the time I left the Hearthstone, cops and TV cameras and other idiots had pretty much shut the place down for the night. Maybe it's selfish, but I was hoping this whole thing wouldn't put the Hearthstone out of business. Rising rents had already done enough damage to every decent place in Riverhaven. I didn't want to lose anything else that night.

It was close to 10:00 o'clock when I softly shut my car door, laid my head on the steering wheel, and just cried for a while. By the time I wiped the snot and mascara off my face, it was almost

10:30. I'd steamed the windows up something fierce, and so I rolled 'em down once I hit Route 246 and headed back toward Ashland U.

The cool air off the river pulled the worst of the smell off my clothes and skin. I wasn't sure I'd ever get it out of my head. Heavy clouds and hints of rain hid the moon and reflected back the city lights as I raced traffic back toward home. Hallucinogen's "Jiggle of the Sphinx" blasted out of my speakers when I turned my sound system on, but after the night I'd had, I just wasn't in the mood so I just turned the damn thing off and let the rush of night air be my soundtrack for the drive.

My head is never a quiet place. No one's really *is*, I guess, but I'm especially sensitive to my own internal podcasts. One of the most insistent voices in my mental space is something I call Trivia-Locker Brain: That part of me that's always stashing away trivia and puzzling out patterns that might or might not fit together. Trivia-Locker Brain catches things I might miss otherwise. And as I sorted out the horrors in my head, that little voice kept chiming in: *Hey, Genét, aren't you missing something?*

"You mean like the fun night out with my friends I was *expecting* to have?" I snarled out loud. Yes, I talk to myself. Deal with it.

I mean like that detective.

"How so?" Again, out loud.

How'd she know your name?

I felt my mouth do that little half-open thing I sometimes do when I've suddenly noticed a puzzle piece falling into place.

I hadn't told her my name. Hadn't even *met* her yet. But she called me "Miss Shilling," and then – during our interview – "Jennifer." *No one* calls me "Jennifer" except my parents and relatives, and I'm slowly breaking them of that habit. Anyone she'd have asked about me at the Hearthstone would've referred to me as *Genét*.

So, she'd known who I was before she came to talk to me. And she knew more about me than she should have known.

That realization gave me new and interesting things to ponder as I drove home from watching my friend die right under my hands.

PICK THEM UP AND
CRASH THEM DOWN

～ ～ ～

I was tempted, for a minute, to just drive home to my parents' house and have a nice big breakdown. It's not like that's far away – just another fifteen minutes or so, traffic willing, from my apartment off campus. I mean, it's not like it's some terrible admission that you can't handle life if you go visit your parents right after you see a friend die.

But I'm stubborn like that. And I wanted space. And before I saw anybody else, I wanted a nice long hot shower.

By the time I'd hit the Riverford Road exit, a slight rain had misted the windshield, so I closed the windows and hit the AC. Up here in the Appalachians, we're essentially a rainforest region, and especially seeing as how we're built around a river, rain's a pretty frequent occurrence. I felt a strain of tears starting behind my eyes again, but by then I was more or less cried out. Beneath those tears, I was *pissed*. And when I'm pissed… well, let's just say that I'm not someone who just sits back and lets stuff go.

In hindsight, I see that I was pushing back against a tornado of grief. I mean, it's not like we were besties or anything like that, but Blue had been funny and kind and silly in a way and just a little bit mean to people who deserved it and then she was… just… *gone*. The more that realization started creeping in along the edges, the harder against it I pushed. "The best thing about anger," my mom says, "is that it's a great way to forget what's really going on until you can do something more than just get mad about it." I'm not sure we process anger quite the same way, Mom and I, but that night I was furious, and processed it by going into puzzle-solving mode…

…which is how I figured out why Detective Fallon knew me by my legal name.

My family has kind of… a history with the law. My brother, my half-sister, even my dad. And so, Dad keeps an old friend of his on retainer – one of the best lawyers in town, maybe in this part of the whole South. I hadn't been in any trouble myself, but word gets around when cops are involved, and so it's not too surprising that a cop I'd never met was at least familiar with my name.

There were other possible reasons, too.

Most cops handle mundane cases: robbery, rape, murder, the sort of stuff we hear about on the news. A lot of stuff, though, never *makes* the news. It winds up on the internet, and in those weird-ass newspapers they used to have in checkout lines back when I was a little kid – the Bat Boy updates and Elvis sightings and other crap that you're more likely to see on a T-shirt than on real news sites.

I'd seen stuff like that before.

Back a few years ago, some seriously weird shit went down in our high school. Meghan had been at the nexus of it all, and certain authorities had no choice but to get involved. I'd done my best to leave that high-school shit in the past where it belonged, but *my* name was probably dashed across a police report or two. And if Detective Fallon was who and what I thought she was, then she would have read those reports by now.

Lots of weird shit happens that folks never hear about… or that we hear about as "urban legends" and conspiracy theories. Cops know better, though; they see more weird shit in a month than most folks imagine in a lifetime. And so, "off the blotter" as they say, most police forces have cops assigned to handle the weird-shit cases. I don't know the details, but I remember that when the shit went down with Meghan, the cops who came to take her statements, and mine, were not ordinary cops.

If my hunch was right, then Detective Fallon wasn't ordinary either.

Now, I've always been pretty good with puzzles. Dad was buying me 1000-piece jigsaw puzzles before I hit middle school. Instead of band posters or cute kitties, I've got Josephine Wahl and Stephanie Law jigsaw puzzles sprayed with fixer and stuck on my walls. Where other folks see pieces, I see patterns. When I'd started my car, I had a handful of pieces. While I drove home, patterns started to appear.

A lot of puzzles – especially the complicated ones – feature pieces with nothing but a solid color that matches the solid colors on other pieces that fit together. Until you start feeling out the edges and laying them next to one another, the pieces all look similar. The earliest part of working out a puzzle involves seeing how those one-color pieces seem slightly different… and then how they're related… and then how their similarities make them fall into place.

As the windshield wipers smeared rain across the glass, I pictured blobs of color cut into asymmetrical bits. Then I started spotting edges and fitting them together in my head. That's usually what I look for: colors and edges and the ways they fit together. You start at the edges and work inward, snapping together all the bits that look like they might be related. When the edges and images start coming together, you know the solution is just a matter of time, patience and perception.

Humid thickness swooped in as I opened the car door and traded my AC for the sticky delights of southern mountain rain. That rain picked up some intensity by the time I'd grabbed my gym bag and headed inside. Once out of the car, I realized just how badly I stank of smoke and… no way was I going down that dark ugly side-street again, so I hunched my shoulders and crossed my arms as the rain plastered my T-shirt to my skin. Without my jacket, I looked like a wet cat at a frat kegger. Thankfully, the rain had cleared the streets. I made it to my building without hearing a single rude remark. Count that as a Win in an otherwise loser night.

The Aberdeen – my building – is a converted brownstone with six units, two on each floor. The windows to my place were dark, so Kris was probably still out at work. My New Rocks clumped up the empty hall to the stairway. My headache had settled into a dull thud that matched the heavy tread of my boots. Our hall was empty, thank God, and so I didn't have an audience as my shock-shakey hands fumbled for my keys.

The ghost of sandalwood incense welcomed my shivering ass through the door. I clomped across the floor, offering silent apologies to our downstairs neighbors, dropped my gear in my room, and ditched the stinky clothes in a plastic bag that I stashed at the bottom of my laundry basket. Elfin faces glowed from the puzzles on my walls, but my head had other puzzles to deal with as I grabbed a robe and headed toward the shower. As I sorted through the pieces of tonight's atrocity, I started looking for the ways they'd fit together, and what I could do with them when they did.

The hot shower helped tone the headache down. I scrubbed myself so clean my skin hummed by the time I turned the water off. The pieces I had in my head so far looked something like this:

• One cop who knows my legal name, and who maybe also knows about my family, Meghan, or both. Mentally, I colored that one dark blue.

• At least three local cops who work outside the box with regards to crimes and investigations. Again, dark blue.

• One friend dead of apparently impossible causes. This piece I was indigo – still blue, but not cop-colored blue.

• One restaurant-slash-performance-space with a kid who died on its stage. Okay, that one's Hearthstone gray.

• One tribal fusion bellydance troupe. Given our name, our color obviously was black.

• And one me, who'd already been near Ground Zero in some local weirdness, and so who knew not to dismiss things that seemed impossible. I colored myself purple, because I like dying my hair purple.

This wasn't much to work with, but I doubted there were 1000 pieces I needed to sort through before the picture emerged.

And what would I do if and when it *did?*

First off, this was probably murder. Old movie references aside, people don't just explode. Not like that, anyway; from what I'd read, spontaneous human combustion *is* a thing but it's usually a *private* thing. Okay, first thing's first, I'd need to start looking up incidents of spontaneous human combustion online and see what I could sort out from there.

Second, if it *was* murder, then I needed to have some way of moving the pieces into somebody else's hands. I'm not a moron; people who'll kill one person will kill another. I was *so not* gonna paint a nice big target on my chest. Once I caught sight of the whole picture, I was going straight to the police with it. Detective Fallon had given me her card, so when the time came, I was gonna use it.

A faint mewing in the hallway put me on notice: Inanna knew I was home, and thus it was my sacred duty to make sure she got a treat. I toed her out of the way as I opened the bathroom door and let all the steam out. A perpetual kitten, Inanna was almost ten years old but still tiny and cute and loaded with attitude. She recoiled with feline disdain from the opening door and the clouds of shower steam, looked up at me, and unleashed a drawn-out, eyes-closed *Meeeeeeeeewwwwwww* aimed straight at my ailurophile heart.

"Yes, Mistress. Right away, Mistress." I dodged Inanna's dainty scrambles as she led me to the kitchen by force of cuteness and elemental will. She'd apparently been sleeping when I first got home, or I'd have been tripping over her when I came in the door. Kristen clearly wasn't home, and the cat-bowl held less kibble than the floor in its vicinity. I reached up to take some bonito flakes from the cabinet, pinched a scatter of them, and dropped them in front of Inanna's eager face. The sheer normalcy of the daily routine pushed the evening's events into a background that began to resemble sanity.

After paying tribute to our little household goddess, I went back to my room and closed the door. If Kristen *did* come home soon, I didn't want her spotting some undoubtedly graphic slices of human pot-roast on my screen and pondering just *why* she'd agreed to share house-space with a serial killer. That went double for her girlfriend Celeste, who I wasn't 100% certain about myself. Nice girl on the surface… but then, isn't *everyone* nice when they stand a chance of getting in your pants? Celeste, at least, treated Kristen well, which was a damn sight better than the last few dudes and ladies to tromp through our humble abode. If she was going to be a long-term proposition, though, then Celeste didn't need to any reasons to doubt *my* sanity. I've lost bigger friendships than this one over some sweetheart or other, so I had no great desire to push the matter with my choice of midnight reading.

Car tires hissed through the rain outside my window. Chilly little love-taps clicked off the glass. Through half-closed curtains, I watched the breeze shift some branches in the streetlamp light. *So,* I thought as I tapped my mouse and brought up a vivid screenshot of the Taj Mahal, *do you really wanna do this?* Did I seriously plan to spend the next hour or so staring at articles about people who set themselves on fire? Why not just leave this shit to the police?

Soft paws padded an insistent *Let me in!* on the closed door to my room. Rain and cars and tree limbs shaped a symphony of night outside my window. Sitting in my chair, I felt the evening settle into me with black-hole gravity. *Y'know,* I thought, *maybe I SHOULD just leave this to the cops.*

A few taps later, I'd made up my mind: *Check Facebook and go to bed.*

But life is like a hangnail you just can't leave alone. And when you watch life take a sudden header off a flaming cliff, its irresistible momentum pulls you after it.

Don't forget to bring back my green pashmina, you wretched girl! ;)

See you tonight!

Huggles <3

Blue. My last Facebook message from Blue. From earlier today.

Seven hours old, give or take.

And I felt everything under my ribs take a 20-mile freefall straight into black cold oceans.

I didn't cry. Like I said, I was all cried out by then.

I just sat there looking at the screen with Inanna on one side and the rainy night on the other.

And then I brought up my browser and went to work.

DESPITE ALL MY RAGE

∾ ∾ ∾

By the time I heard Kristen's key in the lock, I'd given myself several months' worth of nightmare fuel and learned more than I'd ever wanted to know about spontaneous human combustion. Apparently, it's a real thing, although *how* real a thing it is depends on who you ask.

The theories I ran across ranged from the scientifically plausible to the happily demented. Aside from one case where a baby (oh my God, a *baby!*) in India ignited from apparently unknown causes, the people listed in various internet articles were almost always old people, usually alcoholics, typically bedridden or something close to it. One dude going by the charming handle GnosticWarrior had a bunch of articles claiming that SHC was a self-inflicted form of hell: a chemical – or rather *al*chemical – moral disease in which the victims turned themselves into human IEDs by "wallowing in vice and perversion" until their bodies erupted into flame in order to cleanse their self-pollution. Yeah, if *that* were true, half the football players on earth, and pretty much all the rock stars, would have gone napalm by now. Still, given all the other lame explanations I could find – smoking in bed, people stumbling around drunk till they lit themselves on fire, something called "the wick effect" in which human fat, under certain rare conditions, could function like a giant candle – the alchemical idea seemed to make more sense than most.

Okay, I admit that the first few images I found were enough to make me wanna shut down my browser and go read up on leprosy or something. After a few minutes, though, I got used to the ashy bones and severed legs sitting in the middle of otherwise unburnt living rooms. Somehow, my brain had the good sense to disconnect those pictures from what I hadn't wanted to see onstage. The pictures of screaming people with flames coming from their mouths and eyes were a little harder to take. Those, though, were obvious faked – artists' interpretations of human combustion, not the real thing. I *did* manage to snag some real images of burnt corpses and that monk who set himself on fire in Vietnam or something, but I left those little doorways into pixel-hell as thumbnails on my screen. The real thing was more than enough for me, thanks, and I had to sleep *sometime* this century.

Oh, yeah – did you know that spontaneous human combustion usually leaves the legs unburned? Yeah, most of the photos from actual cases of SHC had one or both legs sitting alone in piles of ash. A couple featured severed hands as well. The articles I read speculated that the extremities didn't burn because the source of the fire came from the torso, and the cooler temperatures in the legs and hands left them intact while the rest of the body burned. That didn't make much sense to me, especially since one of the legs *did* burn up in several of the pictures. Those lonely legs, discarded like broken doll-parts, sent icy little spiders running up and down my own legs and arms. Most of the pictures, thank God, were black-and-white; somehow, though, that made them seem worse, like sad frames from ancient horror movies or weird videos from '90s rock stars.

Kristen broke the trancey abyss I had been staring into for the last two hours or so. She'd been trying to be quiet, but our steel apartment door couldn't be silent if all our lives depended on it. *Your lives DO depend on it*, whispered Trivia-Locker Brain. *In this fucked-up world, two little girls and a cat need all the protection they can get.* I shrugged aside the lovely thoughts *that* thought kicked off inside my head, and called out "*Hey, Kristen,*" loud enough for her to hear without being so loud that it freaked her out.

"*Hey, you,*" she called back, obviously tired. No wonder – it was almost 2:00 a.m. I was going to hate life at work tomorrow. "What are *you* still doing up at this hour?"

"Binging on porn and heroin."

"Save some for me."

I love my roommate.

Outside my door, I heard Inanna setting up the *Mama-feed-me* chorus. "Hello, little queen," Kris soothed as she set down her stuff and kicked off her shoes in the living room. I stretched out the kinks, tightened my robe, and got up to say hello. "Are you decent?" she asked as I opened my bedroom door.

"Never."

"Good. I need a few laughs."

She flipped on the living-room light as I opened my door. Even though I'd been staring at the computer screen for hours, the bright contrast with our dark apartment made my headache flare back up again. On reflex, I squeezed my eyes shut. "You okay?" she asked.

"Nothing that a nuke and a few handfuls of arsenic won't cure." I opened my eyes again and shuffled out to give her a hug.

Kris smelled like a sports bar with a few too many side-orders of beer. "Long night at work?"

"Is there any other kind?"

"Not really, no." I gestured to our couch. "*Sit*."

"Yes, m'lady." Kris looked paler than usual. Even her grin seemed tired.

As Innana jumped up into Kristen's lap, I headed to the kitchen to get treats for them both. "Milk for you," I called back, "or something stronger?"

"Just water, thanks. I've inhaled enough booze to keep me drunk for a year."

"Tough night."

"Yeah, no *shit*." Kris stressed the profanity with an emphasis that would make Scarlett O'Hara's ghost twist itself into knots of indignation. Proper Southern Ladies we ain't.

I poured water for Kris and pinched some fish-flakes for Inanna as my two roommates consoled one another – Inanna for Kristen's hard night, Kristen for Inanna having to endure endless hours without our company. "So," said Kris as I headed back into the living room, "how'd the show go tonight?"

My face said more than my words might have.

"Wow," she breathed. "That bad, huh?"

"Worse than you can possibly imagine."

"I can imagine some pretty bad shit."

So I told her.

"*Okayyyyyy,*" she said after a pause that would have swallowed Godzilla and had room left over for snacks. "Congratulations. You have added to my capacity for awful."

"Yeah." I sighed with every bone and muscle in my body. "Mine too."

"Seriously," she said, setting Innana's protesting kitty-form aside. "Honey, I am *so* sorry." She got up to give me a hug, and I leaned into it without another word.

We stayed that way for a while before I broke the mood with a mock-gruff "Sit *down* already, girl. You've been on those feet all night."

"Yeah, tell me about it," she replied, extracting herself from the hug and collapsing back into the couch.

I sat down too, finally. I'd been pacing as I talked, and my legs were killing me. Kris and I leaned in to one another on the couch, not bothering to fill the space with words.

I would take a bullet for this woman. Or a tank-shell. Or a nuke.

Kris and I met right after I graduated high school. We'd both been in this boffer-fighting sorta-medieval live-action roleplay thing, and our shared sense of obnoxious humor connected us pretty much immediately. Meghan had been making noises about hitting the road by then, and I guess I was looking for another BFF to fill the void when she inevitably left. A blonde bundle of attitude and heart, Kristen practiced archery while I preferred sword and shield. During spars and battles, we had one another's backs. And when we both ran through our inevitable games of Boyfriends & Breakups, we had each other's backs there too. Kris has the dubious distinction of knowing more about my sex life than anyone has a right to know, including me. And so she was the obvious choice when I moved out and got my own place away from home.

The summer all this stuff went down, Kris and I were between our sophomore and junior years at Ashland U. Kris was majoring in business management but had been looking at switching to vet school. I remained undeclared, taking business classes, art classes, dance and psychology and a couple of computer programming classes too. I'd had my eye on a career in computer game design, which – given my inclinations toward puzzles and fantasy-stuff – seemed like a natural choice. Still, my parents wanted me to have a strong foundation for other careers, and I agreed with them.

Given where I came from, I could have gone anywhere in the country. I grew up in Shooter's Ridge, and while we're not exactly mansion-rich, my parents do pretty well for themselves. They didn't come from money, though. Mom was a track-star jock in high school, and Dad was a computer geek. They'd both been divorced once by the time they met, but if there were any cracks in their marriage now, I'd never noticed any. I think I'm the only person I know whose parents are still together, and they're disgustingly PDA even though they're a kinda old for that shit. I'm the baby, and sort of the good daughter too. My brother Rick is a total fuckup, and Lisa, my half-sister, isn't much better. They both got a bit too used to our parents' money, and so I took that as my cue to be as self-reliant as I could. I can't say that broke Mom's heart… or Dad's either. They both respect the fact that I want to make my life, my way, on my terms, with as little help as I can manage. From the time I was a kid, Mom showed me around her real-estate job while Dad showed me how to work with computers and indulged my obsession with puzzles. I didn't *need* to go to Ashland U; I didn't *need* my own apartment, or my job. But I *wanted* to show everyone I could do it, but not go *too* far from my nest. Not yet, anyway.

So yeah – Kristen, bullet, me.

And we both needed sleep.

Eventually, we scooped ourselves off the couch and headed to our respective bedrooms with a hug and a promise to knock on the other one's door if the boo-scaries came calling in the dark. Kris had bad night-terrors on a pretty regular basis, and I'd woken up more times than I wanted to remember to the sound of her screaming in the next room. I wasn't really prone to nightmares myself, but I expected a few that night for sure.

Thankfully, I was wrong.

I don't know what I dreamed about that night, but burning people wasn't one of them. Thank God. Thank *God*.

YOUR GIRL IS
PASSING STRANGE

∿ ∿ ∿

How *you?*

The text from Meghan was waiting for me when I woke up around 10:00 the next morning. I hadn't heard either the ringtone or my morning alarm. Thankfully, I wasn't due in to work until 3:00, but 10:00's a lot later than I usually sleep until. I still wanted to hit the gym before going in to work, but if I was gonna have time to eat, work out, shower, and head in to Fullerton Heights, then I needed to get my ass in gear.

Bad night last night, I texted. *Gotta workout. Then work.*

A moment later, Meg's reply came in:

<3 hugz sorry about bad night

My vision blurred a little. *Talk later?* I texted. *Miss you.*

miss u 2

I couldn't resist: *You miss U2?*

fuck no. U2 blows goats with a straw

The laughter felt good.

When is good to talk? I typed.

gig tonight. maybe after midnight my time

What time-zone are you in?

Denver

So around 1:00 a.m. my time. The way I was feeling, I wasn't sure I could handle two late nights in a row. Still, I texted back *Working tonight. Might crash after. Call me anyway?*

will do hugz

Slay 'em dead, bardic badass.

always

<3

The morning felt slightly better then. Not much, but a little.

An hour later, I was taking my frustrations out on a heavy bag in Warrior Fitness. The pain from my burnt palms just gave me one more thing to throw against the bag. I guess it's predictable that a wannabe superhero like me would work out in a Mixed Martial Arts training gym, but I picked up a lot of habits from my retired-jock mom. She had me taking tae kwon do almost as soon as I could walk, and while I'm not really disciplined enough to be a serious martial artist, I like being able to punch boys and not get arrested for it. "If you're going to train," Mom told me back when I'd said I wanted a gym membership, "then find good trainer and a serious gym. I'm all in favor of you getting in shape, but don't waste your time and our money going to some show-off so-called 'fitness center.'" Yeah, Warrior has the word "fitness" in the title but the heavy smell of the place comes from sweat, not body spray, and the guys and girls who work out there hold a respect for hard work, not poseur antics.

"Yo, pretty lady," came a voice too full of himself to take seriously. "Your boyfriend forget your anniversary or something?"

Okay, not *many* poseur antics.

"Not in the mood, Childers," I growled. "Get lost."

Eric Childers went to Crow Creek with me and Meghan. He was a douchebro there, and three years later he still hasn't grown up much. You'd think he would have gotten tired to trying to get a rise out of me after four or five years, but I guess hope springs eternal. Childers is like the little boy that people say is "just teasing you because he likes you." Problem is, he's my age, and if you haven't grown out of that shit by the time you're 21, you're probably not ever going to.

"Pretty good swing on that left, Jenny," he said, mangling my old name in the most annoying way possible. "Your follow-through's a little weak though – not bad, but you'd get more leverage if you– "

I threw a spinning heel-kick into the bag.

"Not bad," he repeated after a moment. "If you want, I could show you– "

"The only thing I want," I replied, not looking at him, "is for you to go look at yourself in the mirror..." *JAB*. "...and ask yourself seriously…" *KNEE*. "…why your mouth and your brain…" *SHIN STRIKE*. "…were separated at birth."

Oh, stellar.

The bag was not impressed. Nor was it much moved.

My comeback would probably have been more effective if I had actually been strong enough to have some impact on the bag. In my head, I've got this badass image of myself. Reality keeps falling short of it. One of the reasons I work out the way I do is because I want to bring that badass self into my real world. Especially with Childers grinning that Cheshire Asshole grin of his, I wanted to perform some jaw-dropping feat of cinematic prowess.

Instead, he just looked at me, then at the unmoved bag, then back to me. "Keep at it, Shilling," he said as if he was some sort of coach. "Keep at it," he repeated, "You're showing improvement." And then he walked away.

Dick.

I proceeded to picture Childers' face on the bag as I pounded my knuckles, shins and elbows into aching rainbows of glorious oblivion. I threw a few other faces on there as well, even adding faces for guys whose actual faces I had never seen.

Okay, look – I like online gaming, too. I don't live my life around it or anything, but it's fun and my 78th level Blood Elf rogue didn't get that way by accident. I channel my imaginary hero-self through a combination of real-life workouts and online badassery. Some days, though, I wonder why I fucking bother. It's not like I score much encouragement from the guys online… unless, of course, you count dick pics as validation. And I don't. It's just gotten worse over the last few years, so I've been spending more time in the gym and less time on the games. Hard choice, I know. When real life offers more rewards and less abuse… well, there are only so many hours in a day, and I knew which way I preferred to spend them. If I'm gonna catch shit from douchebro dicks, I'd rather do it somewhere where I can at least kick a few of them in the face.

$$\sim \ \sim \ \sim$$

"Ow."

"You all right?" Our trainer Jacqueline eyed my hands with concern. I'd worked off every ounce of energy I had left, and my hands sang with exquisite disapproval.

"More or less," I said, unwrapping my hands and wrists. Thankfully, the MMA style of wrapping leaves your palms free for grabbing and blocks. My burns sizzled here and there where the wrap scraped against them, but it wasn't like I'd wrapped up my entire hands or anything. Sweat seeped little salty trails into the edges of my eyes and plastered my hair into a spiky wet halo. Back behind me, Childers was sparring noisily with Ricardo. Certain people show off even in a serious gym.

"Kinda intense out there." Jacqueline followed me as I snagged my towel and headed toward the showers. "More so than usual."

"What can I say?" I shot over my shoulder. "Life's intense sometimes."

She shot me a look of her own. "Just don't break yourself."

"I'm good. Thanks." My tone was the driest part of me.

"You better ice those hands when you get home," she added as she left me to my silent rage pity-party. "You're gonna need them for more than punching sandbags."

She was right, too. Work sucked that evening, and it was my own damn fault.

I still haven't entirely decided what I want to do when I grow up. Computer-game design is sort of a dream-gig, but it's not the only option. Nasty field, from what I hear, where the turnover is unreal. And did I really *want* to subject myself to 24/7 rageheads for whom the very *concept* of a gamer with boobs was grounds for an internet hate parade? Probably not. I'd done a coding-and-security internship at Dad's company in Raleigh-Durham, so that was an option, sort of. I'm too restless for a cubicle job, though – even one that pays big bucks. And so, I soon found myself working at a high-end clothes shop named Crash, where unhealthy amounts of my paycheck were coming home to my closet afterward. Still, Rose – the franchise manager – paid pretty decently. Given Crash's prices, they could afford to. I was sort of Rose's unofficial assistant manager, so that helped. Still, retail was not a career path, not even for a career nomad like me.

My parents, thankfully, usually support my indecision. Dad, after all, had taken two years off in between high school and college to bum around Europe and India, and Mom worked a bunch of different jobs before settling in real estate. As Dad says, "I never heard of someone on his deathbed wishing he'd spent more time at work." So, even though work *is* important (to me if not always to my brother and half-sister), I was pretty much raised with the idea that life doesn't begin and end at the office.

Still, by the time we closed up at Crash that night, my legs were ready to dump me and go home, and my hands were cursing me in six different kinds of sign-language. If you haven't had the pleasure, let me advise you that spending a five-hour shift on your feet (plus another hour to close up and put stuff away) is not exactly an ideal way to conclude a day filled with kickboxer training and redirected grief. My burnt palms hissed at me with every hanger hung and every box unpacked.

When I took my dinner-break, my phone had a text from our dance-troupe leader, Vivienne:

Troupe meeting 8:00 Can u come?

Can't, I typed back. *Working until 10:30 or so. Sorry.*

I guess her phone was off at that point, because I didn't get a reply before I had to go back on the floor. The text woke up that tornado of grief again, and for a few seconds I felt like falling over into a big sobbing heap. After a few more seconds of squeezing my eyes shut so hard my head hurt, I wiped my face, fixed my makeup, and went back into the fight before I lost my shit for good.

Work was busy enough to keep my body occupied, while still giving me enough time to move puzzle-pieces around in my head. Still, I didn't have *enough* pieces to start forming any kind of picture. Blue had not fit the profile of most SHC victims, and unlike almost any other case on record she had not been alone when she burned.

Another common element in every case of human combustion I could find was that there were no direct witnesses. Aside from the baby in India – who, as I knew from both the article and from my Dad's stories about his time in India, had probably been exposed to toxic chemicals – people who burst into flames for no apparent reason were found afterward, more or less turned to ashes with a few spare parts left over to remember them by. Blue had caught fire in front of over a dozen people; there were no apparent chemicals involved, and no open flames either. Locking my emotions behind the *Can I help you* smile known to retail monkeys everywhere, I kept forcing myself to look back at Blue in the seconds before and after she caught fire.

Clearly, I was missing *something*.

But what *was* it that I missing?

Like some fucked-up video you can't look away from, I kept watching her dance, watching her start smoking, watching the smoke curl around her scalp as her skin began to glow – first with exertion, then with heat. Her eyes rolled back, her mouth half-opened in the ecstatic smile of a horny saint, her body flowed like liquid skin.

It hit me then: *She'd been trancing out.*

The fire began when Blue hit a trance-state.

Anyone who dances seriously, or who goes to raves or surfs in mosh pits, knows that you often hit a state of trance where your mind, body and soul – if you believe in such a thing – blend and warp and run together. You blur into what Meghan calls "the world between the worlds," where the usual rules of physics don't apply. Weird shit can happen when you hit that sort of trance. Had Blue hit that level of a trance onstage? And if so, was that the first time she'd done it, or was this part of a bigger pattern I didn't know about yet?

"Earth to Genét. Come in, Genét."

Oops.

"Sorry, Rose," I said, shaking off my own trance. The store was half-full of costumers, and one of them was glaring an *Are you ready yet* bitch-face at me. Her manicured hands held enough clothes to cover my paycheck two or three times over, so I stashed my thoughts behind a smokescreen of customer-service zeal.

Still, I had some new pieces for the puzzle, and they'd begun to form a picture.

YOU'D BEST DANCE

∾ ∾ ∾

A little past 11:00 p.m., I found myself unstrapping my New Rocks by the door as Inanna proclaimed how bored she'd been all day. Her indignation could be soothed only a significantly generous offering of fish-flakes, delivered with all mortal dispatch by Surrogate Cat-Mama #2. "Come on, little queen," I urged as I skritched her fuzzy black head… not that Inanna *needed* urging, mind you. The question of who was leading whom to the kitchen was resolved when our tangled procession ended at the cupboard. Inanna got her offering, and I half-skated across the hardwood floor in my socks, glad to be home and knowing that my night was not quite over yet.

After dumping my gear and stripping off my socks, I pulled out my yoga mat and did a few quick stretches in the living room. Weary cramps were beginning to set in by then, and I felt so tired that I physically hurt. I pinged Meghan with a `Home now` text, but figured that she wouldn't get it until after she came offstage and broke down the band's gear. Considering that her current band had keyboards and a cello, a bass player, and a drummer named Thunderdome, that breakdown could take a while. I didn't expect to hear from her until after one o'clock, and wasn't 100% sure I'd still be awake by then.

Part of me kept waiting for the text from Blue that would say this was all just a horrible joke. Special effects, wanted to get a rise out of y'all, ha-ha. I willed that text to arrive, knowing it never would. Underneath that wanting stretched a pit that I was trying to build a bridge over with whatever bits of sanity I could grab. Anger and denial grabbed each other's throats and wrestled up and down that bridge. In the dark at the bottom of it was the sight I never wanted to see again. So I found myself looking everywhere but there.

On the drive home, I'd been laying out my puzzle and adding the new pieces to the mix. The dance-trance piece was new, and it brought a few more potential pieces to the table with it. Mentally, I'd colored the trance-piece green, to distinguish it from the blue, indigo, gray, black and purple pieces I'd already spread across my mental puzzle board. During my post-yoga shower, I sorted the various colors out and added a few new ones too:

• The trance suggested a connection to GnosticWarrior's alchemical explanation for human combustion. I colored that piece gold, after the goal of alchemy.

• Obviously, Meghan wasn't involved in any of this. She understands weird stuff a lot better than I do, though, especially when it comes to music, so she might have had some insights I could use. I added a blond-wood piece to my collection – a piece the color of Meghan's favorite guitar.

• In the center of that mental puzzle, Blue's piece provided the indigo nexus of the design. The black of our troupe and the purple piece for me were connected to her by… I added another piece, red, for dance in general. That red provided a bridge to… hmmmm, to quite a few things, actually. There was still too much space and too little connection to make a coherent puzzle yet. A kind of gravity, though, seemed to pull them towards each other. The orbits and connections weren't quite clear, but I could work with that.

After drying off and pulling on some sweats, I padded out to the living room to give Inanna some attention. Kris was apparently working late again, so I had time to think as Queen Purrhead curled up in my lap and butted her face against my hand. Kitty-therapy had its desired effect, and I let half an hour or so go by where I drifted into a Zen state between all my earthly concerns.

Eventually, I fished out my phone and texted Vivienne: *How did the meeting go?*

A minute or so later, my ringtone played the intro to the Violent Femmes song "Dance Motherfucker Dance" – the ringtone I'd assigned to Vivienne. "*When I say dance,*" sang my phone, "*you best dance, motherfucker!*" Typically, I answered the phone before the ringtone dropped the MF-bomb on unsuspecting ears. Alone, though, I tended to let it ring through, if only for my childish amusement. Meghan introduced me to that song in middle school, and we used to crank it up and dance around when no one else was around to hear it.

I answered. "Hey, Vivienne."

"Hi there, Genét. How you… how are you doing after last night?" When she's not having to go all drill-sergeant on some errant dancer, our troupe leader has a deep voice, rich with laughter. You never get the feeling that she takes *anything* lightly, but still she usually manages to avoid the self-important bitchiness I've noticed in a lot of other dance teachers. Then again, Vivienne was always less of a "teacher" than a den mother. Now one of her cubs was dead, and the pain I heard in her voice helped me *not* tell her how very sick I was of hearing people ask me that question.

"I'm good, more or less," I lied. "How are *you?*"

She barked a bitter laugh. "Honestly? I feel like charbroiled shit."

Even knowing she couldn't see me over the phone, I nodded on reflex. "Makes sense. I get that."

We talked out awkward stabs at comfort for a minute or so. "So," I asked her, Does anyone know what happened yet?"

A long pause. I could picture her trying not to cry. Or maybe not even trying not to.

"We don't know yet."

I nodded again. It's funny how often we forget that nonverbal cues don't work too well over the phone. Not knowing what to say, I made a sympathetic sound in my throat.

"I heard you got burned too," Vivienne said. "Are you okay?"

"Pretty much, I guess. How's Ash?"

"Not good. She never showed up tonight."

Damn. I didn't convey *that* sentiment over the phone.

"So…" I could hear Vivienne trying out different phrases in her head before finally asking me, "Do you think we should continue now?"

"With the troupe?"

"Yeah."

"*Yes.*" The emphasis I put on my answer made it clear I meant it.

Another pause, not quite as long.

"Thank you." The words came out so low I barely heard them.

"It was an accident," I told her, not entirely sure myself just how much of an accident it was. "It's not the troupe's fault." I thought for a moment, then added, "And not yours, either."

Vivienne hadn't been able to come in the night Blue died. It was a work-night for her, and she'd passed the mantle off to Ashley for the night. No wonder Ash was taking this so hard. She'd been standing there while I tackled Blue with my jacket, and if her head was anything like mine, she'd been replaying every second of those few minutes back to herself over and over and over…

God, what a mess.

"What happened," I continued, "could not have been stopped. It was something with Blue, not with the venue, and not with us."

Another really long pause.

"What," she said, "do *you* think happened?"

That was the question, wasn't it?

"I don't know yet," I told her. "But I'm gonna find out."

There it was: an admission – a promise, even – that Genét was gonna get to the bottom of this mystery. After a second, I started laughing at myself. Maybe I needed a pedo-van and some Scoobie snacks, too.

My laughter had a freaky edge to it. I guess that's not surprising.

See, I always kinda wanted to be a hero – to be Buffy or Black Widow or maybe even River Tam. That's why I like gaming: the chance to be something bigger and better than just another American kid with more money than she deserves. Having a best friend from a poor family in a rotten neighborhood really brought it home to me that most folks don't have it as good as I do. And so, yeah – I wanted to be a hero. In a weird sort of way, my off-the-cuff remark was sort of a mission statement for that desire.

"What's funny?" Vivienne's voice had that sort of bend to it that folks get when they're not sure whether or not they're supposed to laugh along with something you just said or just call the police on you.

"Oh, sorry. I was sorta laughing at my hero-complex, that's all."

She decided to laugh along with me after all. "So," she said after we'd shared some distinctly nervous hilarity. "What are you doing? To find out, I mean."

"I don't know yet. Just looking some stuff up. Seeing what makes sense."

"Mmn." That uncertain tone came though the phone again. "Well," she said after a long moment or two, "let me know what you find out then, okay?"

"Uh… sure. I guess. I *will*, yeah."

Making some hasty excuses, Vivienne bailed.

"Well," I said to Inanna, who was looking up at me with an *Are you done yet?* expression, "*that* was odd." So saying, I went back to petting our household goddess in the manner to which she had become accustomed.

Kris came home about a half-hour afterward. I'd been dozing with the cat in my lap, and when the keys rattled in the lock Inanna abandoned me for Cat Mama #1 and the treats that would inevitably follow. We said our usual hellos and goodnights, and then I headed in to my room to wait for Meghan and see if I could draw any more conclusions from that whole alchemy /trance /fire connection.

My slumbering computer reminded me that it had been almost a month since I'd last logged in to *World of Warcraft*. Wow, who'd have thought that having a real life would cut into dungeon-crawling, right? I fought the urge to log in and see who was online, and couldn't bring myself to deal with Facebook at the moment. Blue's last message there had cast a sort of hangtime spell on that particular social medium, and I wasn't prepared to see how fast the rest of the world had moved on past her. I'd left the browser open to those spontaneous human combustion links, and after brushing off some invisible angst-spiders, I went back to the essays by GnosticWarrior and looked them over for references to trance-states and fire.

Nothing. Lots of ranting about sin and purification, and some half-correct body-chemistry connections between sulfur, alcohol, and mustard gas; nothing, though, about inducing human combustion through frantic activity like dance.

…the way she moved, the smell, the glow of her skin, the shine behind her eyes as they rolled back in her head…

Ugh. I had to shake the memories out of my skull.

Something nagged at me from the back of my mind, but I wasn't able to pick it out of my general state of confused uneasiness.

I knew that voodoo dancers could perform physically impossible feats when they tranced out. Dervishes, too. I decided to Google *trance fire voodoo dervish* and see what I came up with.

"*I am not a pretty girl…*" sang my phone. Meghan. I adopted her Ani DiFranco ringtone as a way of keeping her close to my heart after she left. She actually *is* a pretty girl… and an angry one, too… but Meg refuses to see that girl in the mirror, and I can kinda understand why. Her family has more issues than People magazine, and so she's got a vested interest in not seeing what's obvious to everybody else.

"Hey there, rock star," I said, with more energy than I had felt up until that point. Like I'd said, I missed my friend. "How's the road treating you?"

"*God*, Genét," she said. "What are you still doing *up*?"

"I was bored enough to talk to you."

She chuckled. "Must be pretty fuckin' bored, then." Meghan's voice is kinda low and deep for a chick, especially for one her size. She's three or four inches shorter than me, and looks even shorter than that because she's usually slouched behind her guitar. Tonight, she sounded throatier than usual. Must have been a wild show.

"God, Meg – what's with the Henry Rollins impression, huh?"

"*Doooode*," she purred, "So. Much. Magic. Tonight."

The word sent a chilly slither up the back of my neck. To cover, I said, "Well, *tell* me about it then, dumbass."

Meg chuckled again as she recounted some especially tasty moments from the night's festivities. Apparently, she and her bass player /on-again-off-again boyfriend Tucker had been arguing all day. Again. Max, the band's keyboardist /cello player, had been doing a slow burn (again), and the tension had finally been broken by their drummer – one Karl Edgar Jamerson, aptly nicknamed Thunderdome – totally going off on them both. Again. Sounds like fun, right? I guess for musicians on the road that *is* what passes for fun, though, because according to Meghan, the show that night went better than usual. Really well, in fact. "We took it all to the stage, and rawked that fucker *down*, man!" She laughed a glass-gargled laugh, and I heard the others laugh with her.

I *so* do not understand musicians.

"Cool," I told her as her story wound down. "And seriously, it's good to hear from you."

"Good to hear you, too." The girl I've known since fourth grade came through the rock-star façade. Meghan hates sounding vulnerable, but she'll still let down that wall for me. "I've missed you lots. It's weird not having you here."

I almost went on tour with her too. She offered, and I was tempted. But the thought of living in a van with Tucker, Meg, Max, their gear, and Thunderdome set off "*Oh, FUCK no*" alarms in my head. I hardly liked Tucker under the best of circumstances, and Max... well, Max is cool herself, I guess, but I've just got this little jealousy thing going on that's not really *about* her, exactly, and I want my friendship with Meghan to last, not to crash and burn on the road.

"Well," I assured her, "Riverhaven will still be here when you get back. So will I. That's not changing." Optimistic words, I know, but I had to say that.

"Riverhaven," she said, "can die in a fire. You better not."

I shivered.

"No plans of that," I said, trying to keep the shake out of my voice. "I'm staying away from that shit."

"Good. So how *was* the show last night?"

The tone of her voice was totally innocent, but she couldn't have hit the nail on the head harder if she'd tried.

"Um…" I let my voice trail off. How did you say something like this, anyway? "Not so good, actually."

"Why? What happened?"

At first, I tried to talk my way around the incident. And yeah, that's how I was trying to phrase it for myself: "The *Incident*." But then, I saw Blue's eyes roll back in her head and watched the smoke start to rise into the spotlights and felt her rolling underneath me and then I just totally fucking broke.

Meghan listened for a while, offering some soft, wordless reassurances and a few "It's okays" when it seemed like I needed to hear more than sympathetic sounds. If she could have climbed through the phone and hugged me, she probably would have.

"God," I told her in between sob-ragged breaths, "it hurts so *BAD* not to have you here right now. I'm sorry, but that's true."

"You don't have to apologize to me," she said. "Not ever. You've got nothing to be sorry for."

"But I want you to be happy playing music and stuff on the road," I told her. "And there's still some selfish part of me that wants my friend back."

"Shhhhhh…" she soothed. "It's okay. That's not selfish…" Her voice picked up some of its usual snark… "…and if it *is*, then bitch, I'm selfish as fuck too. 'Cause I miss having you having my back." She softened her tone again: "And I miss my best friend."

"God," I said, trying to sound cooler than I felt, "I never want us to wind up like all those high-school friends that go off to college and then never know what to say to each other again afterward."

She barked a rough laugh. "Girl, *you're* the one who went to college! I just went off to become a worthless musician like my dad."

"*No.*" My tone sharpened. "*Never* like your dad. You have *NEVER* been like him."

"No shit," she replied. "I'm actually *doing* this shit with my life. He just sits around dreaming."

"Yeah," I growled. "And don't you ever, *EVER* disparage that, Meg."

"Ooooo, listen to *you*, college-girl," she said. "'*Disparage*,' yet. Wow. When'd *you* start eating dictionaries for breakfast? Folks'll think yer all *smart* 'n' shit." That's kind of a running joke with us. Meghan has a Class-A vocabulary, but she covers it up with slurred words and swearing so that people don't think she's too smart for her own good. I don't usually try to seem less intelligent than I am, but I think that's another luxury of having rich parents who aren't insane.

"I'm serious, Meghan. Yeah, I miss you, but I am *so* glad you're out there doing what you want… hell, what you *need*… to do. You've got a gift, kid. Don't fucking waste it. And don't sell it short by trying to act cool. Especially not with *me*, bitch." I laughed. "I know where you *live!*"

"First you gotta *catch* me, bitch," she shot back. "I'm goin' *mobile!*"

"Who-song references now, Meg?" I laughed again. "That's fucking *prehistoric!*"

"Hey, you *got* that reference! Who's prehistoric now?"

"My Dad was a DJ. I've got an excuse."

"Your father wouldn't be caught dead playing the Who."

"True enough." Dad told me that when he was in college radio, someone had been doodling a hangman game on the bathroom wall. He wrote underneath it: *Last WKIW deejay to play the Who.*

"You sound better now," Meghan said, suddenly serious. We've always been able to do that for each other – bring the other one out of a mood like that.

"Yeah," I admitted. "Thanks."

After bits of small-talk about Inanna's feline rulership and Eric Childers at the gym, I brought up something we could really only talk about long after dark: "So Meg – that musical-trance thing you do sometimes…"

"Ye-*ahhhhhh…?*" Her voice took on a wary tone.

"Um… I don't know how to say this, exactly…"

"Spit it out before you choke on it."

"Okay… The fire last night. Blue…"

"Yeah?"

"I think she was trancing out. When she caught fire."

A long pause.

"Meghan?"

"Shit."

That quiet syllable held volumes of significance.

"What is it?"

"Okay." The tiredness had returned to Meghan's voice. "All right… so, there are supposed to be songs that – if you sing them – set you on fire."

"You're shitting me."

"Nope. Hindu myth. The Dikpa Raga, I think it's called. There's a bunch of metaphysical lore about the deeper powers of music. And some of those powers are distinctly unpleasant." This was the Meghan people didn't usually see or hear: the girl who could talk music theory with a classical pianist, or discuss specifics of electrical technology with a sound engineer. Back in high school, she'd begun studying metaphysics with some of her stranger friends. So if there was anyone who might know why a trancing dancer would go up in flames, Meghan would at least know who that person was and what the reasons for that impossible act might be.

"How so, Meghan? And what sort of 'powers,' exactly?"

"Well," she said, settling into the role of my mystic advocate, "the theory is that everything that exists came from a primal cosmic sound. You know that whole *om* thing people do in yoga class?"

I nodded, then remembered that she wasn't in the room. "Yeah," I said. "Go on."

"That's supposed to be an echo of the cosmic sound – *the* Om, like the real one. The universe is supposed to be the echoes and refractions of that sound, running throughout the universe in infinite frequencies. If you tap into those frequencies, you can change the laws of physics and manifest things that science says are impossible."

"This is a weird-ass conversation, Meg," I said, trying to joke off the eerie crawl up the back of my neck. "You sure we're not dreaming right now?"

"If we are," she said with a flatness that turned that crawl into a full-force shudder, "then it's a dream I've been living for most of my life."

There's so much that even best friends don't know about each other.

We talked for a while after that – about GnosticWarrior's alchemical theories, sublime musical frequencies, legends of Chinese phoenixes and the nine perfect tones. Through it all, I watched puzzle-pieces form in my head and start to move together in something like an image. It still didn't make a coherent picture, and parts of it sounded unreal. More than once, I felt myself drifting, our words becoming a sonic ribbon stretched across the emptiness of reason. If even a third of the stuff she said was true, then logic and science are colored tissues spread out to cover the Abyss.

But my hands were burned, and Blue was gone, and that Abyss was looking pretty fucking logical by then.

Closing the door on this meant closing the door on what I already knew was true. And it meant closing the door not only on Blue but on Meghan as well.

And there was no way I was gonna do any of those things now.

It was almost 3:00 a.m. when I realized that Meghan's words were blurring in my ears. "Meg, I love ya," I told her, "and there is no way to tell you just how much I appreciate what you've been telling me just now…"

"But you're falling asleep," she finished.

"But I'm falling asleep," I confirmed, "and I need to be something like functional tomorrow at work."

"Then go to *bed*, bitch," she said, slipping back under her usual snarky armor. Meghan laughed just to let me know she didn't mean it (much…), and then added, more seriously, "And for fuck's sake, Genét, if you're going anywhere near this stuff, be *careful.*"

My mind caught a whiff of burning Blue. "Oh, trust me," I told Meg, "I *am.*"

"My guess is," she said, "that your dancer friend had no idea what she was doing. Maybe she opened the wrong gate at the wrong time and let something nasty out. But…" She paused to underline what she said next: "*Something nasty IS out there.* And it might not have gone back in its bottle when it finished things with Blue."

And oh, gee – what a cheerful thought *that* was.

FALLING

THEY WERE ALL
MY FRIENDS

~ ~ ~

I'd been hoping for another dreamless round of sleep. And I wound up disappointed. My subconscious wasn't crass enough to replay "the Incident," or otherwise fill my dreams with burning bodies, but I spent the night running through mazes, fighting families full of serial killers, and facing a stack of necessary purchases while my bank-card kept coming up DECLINED DECLINED DECLINED.

Fuck you, subconscious. Fuck you and the nightmares you rode in on.

I woke up shaky from lack of rest, a yawning pit in my chest where my heart should have been. My brain began spiraling through doubts and fears and possibilities before I'd scraped myself out from beneath my blanket and dropped myself into my AC-chilly room. My desktop still showed the results of my various Google searches – a spew of esoterica and fantasy-gaming wikis that added up to a headache's worth of digging. Some of them I'd printed out as Meghan and I had talked last night; most were still open in an array of windows that would have crashed a lesser system. I'd scrawled out a pile of notes, too, as we'd talked, mostly words or names that I'd check out later.

Aside from my troupe-mates, I had no real inclination to even *look* at most of those people on the list, much less talk to them about something as personal as this situation. Meghan's choice of friends had certainly become bizarre since our high-school days, and I'm not even sure she'd consider most of the people she named to be "friends" at all. After crossing off the names of the obvious weirdoes, I wound up with Ash, Caroline, Inky and Vivienne, plus three friends of Meghan's from a music store called the Silver Key: Corwyn, Dia, and Dervish… none of whom I looked forward to talking to in person. Just the idea of doing that made me want to crumple that list up, throw it out, and go back to bed.

Clearly, I was in a real mood that morning. The late nights, nightmares, and suppressed shock was doing a number on my head. Top it off with a pre-dawn conversation about scary metaphysics – a conversation that dredged up a lot of stuff I'd been trying not to think about too hard for the last five years or so – and I was off my game, big-time.

Okay, look: I love magic in the abstract sense, when it's fireballs and dragon CGI, or when I'm reading about it in a book. Some of the things I'd heard from Meghan these last few years, though, had begun pushing me toward corners where magic was a real thing, and that scared the piss out of me. Much as I'd made an effort to listen to her with an open mind when she talked about some of the stuff she'd seen and done, it was some pretty weird shit even by my fantasy-junkie standards. I'd like to think I was just being a good friend by listening to her – kind of the way you'd nod and smile and change the subject when someone you've known since grade school takes an evangelical wrong-turn and starts talking about Antichrists and prophecies and shit. Seriously, though: How good a friend is someone who humors you about your most important beliefs? And how good a friend could I be to Meghan if I refused to accept things that were part of her everyday life?

Once that door was opened, I had to look at what *I* really believed in too. Dad's sort of a passive Buddhist atheist, and Mom's never been someone who cared about church one way or another. My brother pretty much believes in himself, and Lisa converted to Catholicism but never makes a big deal of it. Until things got weird back in high school, I had never asked myself what I believed in; after that, I didn't want to look deep enough to ask. Part of my cranky morning mood came from the realization that I had been living out a serious case of denial. And part of the shock that hit me when Blue died was the shock of having that denial blown into a pretty cloud of dust. Waking up that morning didn't just mean getting out of bed. It meant accepting a lot of stuff I had been trying *not* to accept for years. I'd been drunk on denial, and now it was time to purge it from my system.

Sure, I could just tear up the list of names I got from Meghan, and then go off to work and dance practice, and the gym, and back to class when the semester started up again next month. I could tell Meghan that I talked to those people when I actually hadn't, and I could find some way to act satisfied by whatever official explanation got plastered over Blue's "incident." I could keep pretending that people didn't actually burst into flames Because Magic, and keep punching pixels and practice bags when I knew that real monsters were right outside my door.

I could do that. Most people do.

And I'm not most people, so to hell with *that*.

"Okay, darlin'," I told myself as I stared down the haunted chick in my mirror. "It's time to stop *playing* hero and start *living* hero."

And that thought scared the living piss out of me.

There's a reason people don't take all the weird shit in this world *seriously*, and it's because the Abyss stares fucking back at you and it won't take No for an answer.

Part of a hero's journey, as I learned in lit class, involves stepping away from the safety of home and walking into the Dark Woods that good little girls and boys are supposed to stay away from. And if a wolf eats you, or a devil takes your soul, then at least you'd die knowing you faced down something magical, not just staying safe at home dreaming about what might have been if you hadn't been so fucking scared.

That's when it hit me: *Fairy tales.*

The thing that had been nagging in the back of my mind suddenly exploded, throwing a new set of puzzle pieces all over my board:

Dancing.

Fairy tales.

Fire.

Red shoes.

I'd come across the phrase "red shoes" in my Google search. I had ignored it because it looked like a dead end. Suddenly, I remembered that Cinderella's evil stepmother – before Disney and the Victorians had gotten hold of her – had been forced to dance to death in red-hot iron shoes. Another fairy tale featured the Devil giving a pair of red shoes to a girl who began dancing herself to death in them. Dorothy had ruby slippers on her Yellow Brick Road, and she'd gotten them off the corpse of a witch she'd accidentally killed; Dorothy killed that witch's sister by throwing water on her, which suggested a connection to fire as well. All the alchemical stuff I'd been reading about the previous night started to make a lot more sense. I threw myself into the desk-chair and began looking stuff up.

I was deep in my web-search when Kris tapped on my door. "Genét? You okay?"

"Rhyming and everything," I replied from behind my keyboard. "Hi, Kris-Kitty. Yeah. Thanks."

"Can I come in?"

"Sure." Wrapped up in my robe and sweats, I was as "decent" as I was gonna get.

She opened the door and Inanna rushed in too, jumped up on my bed, and announced her presence by purring her head off at me. "Hey," said Kris, "how you doing this morning?"

I laughed a little. "People keep asking me that."

"It's really not *that* surprising, is it?" She sat down on my bed and began petting Inanna. I reached over to pet Inanna too.

"No, it's not," I admitted. "And thanks for asking. I do appreciate it."

"Who were you *talking* to at 3:00 a.m.?"

"Meghan. Sorry – I didn't mean to keep you up."

"You didn't. I was reading."

"Couldn't sleep?"

She grimaced. "Fucking nightmares."

"Again? Oh, sweetie…" I reached over and squeezed her shoulder. "I'm sorry. I didn't hear you."

"I didn't…" She glanced down at the bed. "I don't usually scream in my sleep. Those are just the really bad ones."

"Wow." If Kris has "really bad ones" that often, then I don't wanna think about what her usual nightmares are like, or how often she must have them. "I'm sorry," I repeated, leaning over and opening my arms to offer her a hug.

She took me up on the offer, but more stiffly than usual. Kristen's a pretty physical person, so if she was holding on to something that hard, it had to have been a bad night for her.

At least we had the cat, who promptly shoved herself between us like she was due All The Snuggles and needed to remind us of that fact.

Kristen has some pretty bad abuse issues in her past. Nasty stuff. Nightmare fuel. Somehow, she managed to get out of that mess with a strong mind, a loving disposition, and a wicked sense of humor. The ghosts keep coming back at night to haunt her, though, and while she goes to campus counseling when she can afford to, no one has managed to banish them just yet. I've learned not to push the closeness, especially not on a physical level, so when I want to show sympathy and support, I let *her* choose how close it gets.

People can be such haunted houses, and even the best friendships have many closed doors.

"You working tonight?" I asked her.

"No, thank God. Celeste and I are going out to a movie, I think."

"Oh, good." I added a brief squeeze to the hug and then let her go. "That place has been running you flat." I smiled at her. "Pretty soon, you won't have to unlock the door – you can just slide right under it."

She laughed. "Inanna would turn me into confetti."

I skirtched that cat's head. "Our little Goddess of the Underworld."

"That was Eriskigal. Inanna's sister,"

"I knew that."

"Did *not!*"

"True." If I was gonna be digging into fairy tales for clues to Blue's demise, though, I was going to have to keep my mythologies straight.

Back when Kris and I moved in together, she'd told me that Inanna had been named for a story about a Sumarian goddess who presided over pretty much everything: beer, sex, war... sort of a frat-party of divine providence. At some point, she got bored and decided to drop in on her sister, the Goddess of Death. By the time she got to the underworld, she'd stripped herself of everything that made her special – at which point her nasty bitch sister ripped her skin off and tossed it on the wall of hell. Her handmaid and uncle managed to free Inanna through a couple of flying balls of dirt whose names translated into Hope and Compassion. Kris told me that her little black cat was essentially her ambassador out of the underworld of her shitty home-life. Given how protective the little furball could be when Kristen was upset, I figure there was more truth than poetry about the name she possessed.

"So how about *you?*" Kris asked, poking me in the shoulder. "On the phone till God-knows-when with your rock-star friend." She dropped into a more serious mode. "I wasn't trying to listen in or anything, but that sounded like a serious conversation, judging by the tone in your voice. You okay?"

"Yeah…"

Kris jacked her face into a *Don't bullshit me* glare, and looked me dead in the eyes.

I nodded. "Okay, yes – I'm hurting. That shit the other night…" I sighed. "Man, was that really two nights ago already?"

Now it was Kristen's turn to hug my shoulders. "Oh, honey."

"Thanks," I said, hugging her back and slightly pulling away. "It's… really hard to explain."

"Well, *yeah*. Your *friend* died. That's not a simple set of emotions, doofus." She half-grinned, then continued with a more serious expression. "Did anything like this ever happen to you before?"

The familiar chill ran back down from the base of my skull. "You mean, like what? Like a friend dying?"

"Yeah. Like that."

"Actually, it has. Yeah…" Brenda Cummings, the girl on our street who got hit by a car when I was six. Shenni Trudeau, who committed suicide my sophomore year of high school. My teacher Ms. Lund, who died of cancer the year I graduated. My Gramma and two Grandpas and a few really distant relatives. Dad's friend Anwar. Rick's friend Scott. Yeah, I knew a few "people who died," as that old song said. This was the first time, though, that I'd seen it happen in person.

"Messes you up, doesn't it?" Her face slid toward an expression that suggested she'd had more first-hand experience with death than I did. "I remember…" and then she shut that thought down before it went further.

"It does." I filled the space left by another passing ghost. There seemed to be a few too many of those here already.

"Have they figured out what happened yet?" she asked. "The news just mentioned an accident with fire."

The news. Oh, shit! I'd forgotten about the news.

"Not really," I said, reaching for my phone. Yep, there were messages. I'd had my ringer off during work, and turned it back off again after talking with Meghan last night. One message from my Dad, three from my Mom, and a handful from Inky, Caroline, Tabi, and Detective Fallon. And I had work tonight. This was looking like a busy day for me.

"Lots of calls," Kris said, noting the messages.

"Yeah," I replied. "I still haven't talked to my folks about it." Inwardly, I kicked myself for bringing up my essentially functional family when hers had been such a horrorshow.

Kristen didn't seem to notice. "You should probably give them a call, then," she said. "I bet they're worried about you."

I nodded. "Probably are, yeah." Club, dance, fire, death… yeah, just what every parent wants to hear about in connection with their daughter.

Dad and Mom give me a lot of latitude. They had both been pretty independent when they were kids, and they hated the whole helicopter parent thing that lots of parents from their generation have. "If I'd had to live with that kind of supervision when *I* was a kid," Dad sometimes said, "I would've been bouncing around in a padded cell by the time I hit puberty." Mom had been a tomboy, so she didn't smother me either. We had our rules, of course – I'd had a curfew until my 18th birthday, and wasn't allowed to close my door when a boy was in my room – but they let me have a lot of freedom when I was a kid, and give me privacy when I need it now.

Still, yeah. I figured I should call them.

After another hug, Kris scooped up Inanna and she closed the door behind them. I decided to get dressed, so once I'd sorted out a presentable outfit for interviewing weirdoes, I put my ringer back on and dialed Mom's cell phone. Rule #1: *Always call Mom first.*

Mom answered on the third ring. She'd probably been at work. "Hola, Kidling," she said. "You doing okay?"

"*God*, Mom," I huffed, "*everybody* keeps asking me that."

"Well…" she said with a leading edge, then finished it up: "Honey, I'm so sorry. About your friend."

"You sound like my *roommate*, Mom," I said. I tried to laugh, but it got stuck somewhere south of my mouth.

"How *is* Kristen?"

"She's good. She told me I ought to call you."

"Smart girl."

"Sorry. My ringer was off. I forgot to turn it back on after work." What *is* it about parents that they can make you feel like a kid again without even trying to?

"It's not a problem, Kidling," she said. "I just wanted to make sure that you were okay after the other night." A pause. "But honey, I'm not expecting you to be 'okay' after something like that, either." Her voice held warmth with professional brevity, like she was between clients or meetings at work. "Do you want to come over later this evening?"

"Thanks, Mom," I told her, "but I'm working tonight. Maybe Sunday, for dinner?" Sunday's usually the most relaxed time to drop back by home. Dad would still be in Raleigh-Durham that week, but Mom and I could go get dinner at Maxfield's or – now that I was drinking age – even grab a beer.

Boy, that thought felt weird. But really nice as well.

"Sunday sounds good," she said with the tone of someone who needs to get back to work. I appreciated that. Now that the economy was doing better than it had been a few years earlier, Mom was busy selling and renting properties all over Shooter's Ridge, Fort Franklin, and Peter's Church – some of the higher-end neighborhoods around town. At those prices, she often told me, her clients expected perfection… not, as I mentally added, a daughter whose friend had caught fire during a bellydance performance.

A few pleasantries later, I was leaving a message for Dad and getting back with Ashley, Inky, and Caroline. Ashley sounded sedated, which wasn't too surprising. Inky had her snarky-armor in full spike-mode, and Caroline was talking about quitting the troupe. Her voice had a catch to it that snagged on my radar – just a hint of hesitance that suggested guilt. I pressed on that hint to see where it might lead.

"How do you mean?" I asked her.

"About what?" A wary note slid into those two words.

"Well…" I played innocent. "You just said you told Blue to keep her head on straight. What'd you mean by that?"

"I didn't say that." I saw blast-doors starting to close.

I pounced for the opening: "Well, *why* wouldn't Blue have her head on straight, Caroline?"

"Well, it was…" *Mayday! Mayday! Mayday!* "She was kind of, um, nervous and stuff about her routine…"

"Yeah…?" Half-conspiratorial, half-questioning.

"She'd… she was… seeing stuff, I guess."

"You *guess?*"

"Um…" I could practically see her edge her thumb toward the screen of her phone. "Caroline," I said, "this could be important. *Please.*"

Silence. Then…

"I've gotta go."

"*Please,*" I repeated. "What was going on that night? I need to know."

"Dammit." Caroline's voice held an angry edge. "Why couldn't she have just saved that shit until *after* the damn show?"

Score one new ugly-colored puzzle piece.

"Saved *what* shit until after the show, Caroline?"

"Um, I don't know." Her voice slammed shut on everything but that lie.

"*What* shit, Caroline?" I repeated, reaching for that sympathetic tone I'd had a few words earlier.

"Nothing."

"Oh, come on…" My voice started to get an edge too.

"There's *nothing*, Genét. Drop it."

"Okay," I said. "Sorry, I was just trying –"

She hung up.

I had officially failed Interrogation 101.

But now I had some more pieces to my puzzle. And the cold recognition that I was probably looking at a lot more than I'd expected to find.

BUT NOW I TRY
TO BE AMUSED

～ ～ ～

How *did* people research stuff before the internet? I spent the rest of the morning and about an hour after lunch looking up and cross-referencing everything I could find about the Dikpa Raga, Hindu music metaphysics, alchemy (which I discovered went a lot deeper than that stuff about turning lead into gold), fairy tales, spontaneous human combustion, and all the various side-streets I found myself linking through while I read up on the rest. It was a strange way to spend half a day but it beat the numb blackness I felt rolling around in my chest.

My headache from the other day was beginning to reemerge when I realized I needed to get my ass in gear if I wanted to grab a parking space near work. The rain had come back with the intensity of a southern summer storm, and I had no desire to work seven hours in an air-conditioned store while soaking wet. I didn't think Rose would approve of that either.

I held off on calling Tabi or Detective Fallon back. Tabi probably wanted to make sure I wasn't gonna sue her over the burns on my hands – which were feeling much better by that point – and her message told me that she wanted to give me her insurance information, just in case. I wasn't anywhere near ready to go to Detective Fallon with the half-baked mess I had cooked up at that point. She might be walking the paranormal beat, but Fallon was still a cop and I didn't need to be laughed out of the station, rushed off in handcuffs, or buried wherever they put people who start to know too much. Maybe once I had something more solid about the stuff that Blue had apparently been on lately, I would call back the Detective and lay it out for her. My instincts, though, said I had too many pieces and too little puzzle. There were still a lot of questions I wanted to look into first.

Oh, and then there was the prize. While I was looking into fairy tales – which, I soon realized, should really be spelled *F-A-E-R-I-E* tales to set it apart from that Disney crap – I ran across what might just have been my smoking gun:

Red Shoes.

Apparently, some designer drug in the local raver club scene was going by the name Red Shoes. I hadn't even known there *was* still a raver club scene; it sounded pretty '90s to me. But from what I found online, this drug made people dance like maniacs and see things that weren't really there. A few articles and posts claimed that it raised your body temperature, although how anyone could *tell* that if they'd been dancing hard in a packed club was kinda beyond me. Even still, the ties between alchemy, wild dancing, faerie tales, creepy mysterious figures and mystic punishment were way too strong to ignore. If Blue had been taking drugs before she danced, that would explain a lot even if those drugs didn't include Red Shoes.

Another constant pattern in almost all of the SHC cases I read about is that they usually involved substance abuse – usually alcohol, but sometimes other drugs as well. One theory insisted that the victims had gotten fucked up and then lit themselves on fire; others speculated that the drugs themselves had caused chemical reactions, and my buddy GnosticWarrior claimed that the abuse of drugs was part of the chain of sins that led people to create their personal hells out of alchemical reactions that burned them from the inside out. If Blue *had* been doing drugs, I can't say I was surprised. It's not like most drugs are a big deal anyway, and our crowd tended to prefer acid or ecstasy over, say, meth.

Personally, I stay away from most of that shit. Yeah, okay, I've smoked a few joints here and there, and I did mushrooms with Stacia just before we graduated high school. Big deal. I hate hangovers, though, so I don't drink like a college kid. Been there, done that, had to throw out one of my favorite blouses when I couldn't get the puke-stains out of it, *and* I wound up on YouTube, too. Thanks, but no. You can throw that party *wayyyyyy* over there. I'll watch. And probably laugh at you too.

It's not like I'm blind, though. Most of the folks I know smoke pot, a few trip on a more or less regular basis, and rolling is so common that half my friends carry water bottles around. Blue probably *was* on drugs that night... and knowing her, they were probably a bit more hardcore than pot and ecstasy.

So... Red Shoes. I was gonna have to look more into that when I got home from work.

I thought for a moment about asking my Dad about that too. He *was* a DJ in the '80s, after all, and had been around the block a few times, especially by the standards of an old-school computer geek. But Red Shoes, from what I could dig up, was new stuff, still pretty underground. I'd pulled up a few references to homebrew recipes for the drug, but they were mostly darknet stuff, and I didn't want those kinds of fingerprints on my computer's search history. So this whole designer-drugs thing was sort of new territory for me, but not necessarily for Dad. Still, if I could avoid having an even *more* awkward conversation with my parents than I was already going to be having about the whole *How do you feel about your dead friend?* thing, I'd rather steer clear of it than put my foot in it.

Now, I can talk to my parents more or less about anything: school, depression, drugs, even sex if I needed to (yeah, *that* conversation was awkward). *Magic*, though… no, that shit was off the table as far as they're concerned. My parents are pretty cool, all told, but everybody's got secrets and that was staying one of mine.

My headache faded soon after I hit work. The next seven hours seemed to fly right by. I guess the rush of digging up clues had washed away most of the tiredness I felt from the previous day's workout. My wrists ached a bit but most of me felt fine… *better* than fine, actually. I realized, after I'd found a space not too far off from Crash, that I was feeling especially energized that day. As I opened my umbrella and headed into the store I felt kind of like a knight putting on her helmet and riding off to kick some dragon's ass… or better yet, to ride him into battle with some darker villain boss.

Work that night was a total turnaround from work the previous evening. I felt like I had all the answers, my customer-service mojo was running in high gear, and Rose complimented me on how I looked that night. We racked up some impressive sales and closed up earlier than usual. "Good work tonight, Genét," Rose told me as we locked up shop. "Have a nice weekend."

I should have taken her advice.

BECAUSE THEY TOLD ME
THAT I'D FIND YOU HERE

∿ ∿ ∿

The Silver Key sits at the bottom of a stairway that drops you below street level and brings you to a maze of shops buried under Abernathy Place, near Raven's Park. Bigger than it looks when you first walk in the door, the shop curls around through nooks and crannies and pillars and posts. Instruments hang everywhere: guitars of all kinds, arrays of percussion, brass and wood. Two soundproofed practice-rooms sit off in a corner under a sign that reads *Please let us assist you with the cords and instruments.* Meghan calls it a secret shrine to music, and (as usual) she isn't wrong.

A black-tiled floor contrasted with warm wooden walls as I entered the shop to follow up on Meghan's contact list. The blond wood soaked up the faint sunlight shining in from the street-level windows that crept across the top of the walls, granting a bit of access to the land above this space. I thought of those faerie tales where magical people live "under the hill," hidden from the mundane world in a land where they can be themselves without too much mortal interference. Adventurers go into this "underworld" (and there was that word again: *underworld*) as part of their quest away from home and hearth. In Lit class, Ms. Hopkins pointed out that the "hero's journey" that Joseph Campbell talked about finds its way into popular media all the time; from *Star Wars* to *Dungeons & Dragons*, certain archetypal symbols appear over and over again. The underworld was one of them, and I wondered as I headed toward the counter – willing myself to be calm and cool – if I was gonna need my own Hope and Compassion dirtballs to get me out of here intact.

The thought was stupid. Meghan had worked at the Silver Key for years, and I'd been here dozens of times already. Unless I was buying a present for Meghan, though, it wasn't the kind of place I'd have gone into without her there. Walking through those familiar doors all by myself underscored just how much things had changed for me since she left… and, for that matter, since the night Blue died.

Had it already been *three* days? Had it *only* been three days? My life since that night had been an odd fugue-state, despite the everyday realities of work, home and the gym. I'd gone and worked out at Warrior Fitness for an hour or so that morning before leaving for the Silver Key, figuring that maybe I'd feel more like a hero if I did. Of course, as Ms. Hopkins also pointed out, Joseph Campbell was a sexist product of Edwardian academia, and women had no place in his "journeys" except as guides, distractions and rewards.

Well, one of my guides was standing behind the counter: Dervish, a tall, inked guitar-chick with dyed black hair, purple tights and a matching purple scarf, a ratty black Utilikilt, Army surplus combat boots, and a crop-top Iron Maiden T-shirt that looked older than me. Meghan often jammed with Dervish before she'd gone on tour, and so I'd met Dervish several times before. She seemed manic even by my standards, though, and so I often used Meghan as a buffer for that excessive energy. Older than me by a good five years at least, and taller by an inch or so, Dervish was a fixture in the local bellydance scene as well. She danced with Hands of Fate and Labyrinthine, but I'm not sure she actually belonged to either of those troupes. She hooped, too, and spun fire, and was by several degrees of magnitude far cooler than I am. I'm not normally insecure but going up to talk to Dervish made me feel like a little kid again.

It's funny: I'm generally the one with the social skills and Meghan follows my lead. But this was Meghan's world now – all magic and music and tall girls with more tattoos than God. Okay, Dervish doesn't *actually* have all that much ink, and I've got two tats and some piercings myself. But like I said, she always seems comfortable at the grown-ups' table, while I usually feel like some gawky girl making her first trip away from the little kids' one.

"*GENET!*" Dervish cried, dashing out from behind the counter to give me a bone-crushing hug. What had I been worried about? She seemed happy to see me. "How you *doing*, girlfriend? I haven't seen you since before Meghan left!"

"I'm good, pretty much," I said, hugging back. Dervish isn't a Mack truck or anything, but she has a way of taking up a lot of space. "Meg says hello. She told me to come see you."

"*Awwwwww!*" Everything Dervish said seemed to be capped off with exclamation points. You could almost hear them in the air by her head. "She's such a sweetheart! And how's the tour?" She grinned. "They having fun storming the castle?"

"They didn't wind up calling themselves that," I reminded her. Meghan had wanted to call her band Little Plastic Castle, but I told her that folks might think they were an Ani DiFranco cover band. Thunderdome suggested MSG, for Meghan Susan Green, but Thunderdome is kind of a goof. They settled on the name Black Swan, partly because Meghan loves that movie, partly because it sounded cool, and partly because she wrote a song called "Black Swan Blues." A "black swan," she told me, is supposed to be a strange occurrence that undermines peoples' expectations. That expression fits Meghan and her band, so they went with that name in the end. Still, Dervish had favored the Plastic Castle name, and few people in our little corner of the world can keep from quoting *The Princess Bride* in casual conversation anyway.

"I know," said Dervish, pouting with exaggerated disappointment. "But hey, how are they *doing?*"

"I think it's going well," I told her. "If nothing else, they still haven't killed each other yet."

"That's the trick with bands," she said. "It's rare that you find folks you click with musically who *aren't* complete flakes. And when you wind up stuck with them in a van or a bus or..." She paused, clearly recalling an awkward memory. "Somebody's *car*, and you wind up sharing beds or sleeping on the floor in a big heap, and... arg. You also wind up wanting to kill each other whenever you're not on stage. And eventually when you *are* on stage together, too!"

"So I hear."

"Speaking of hearing," she said, her voice dropping from its usual hyper octave, "aren't you in Arcana Darque?"

The bouncy mood popped like a porcupine's balloon. "Yeah," I said, sighing. "I am."

"Oh, man," she said with that sympathetic tone I was getting *seriously* sick of hearing. "I'm so sorry. Were you there? I heard you were."

"News travels," I said with a little more edge than I'd intended.

"It does." Suddenly, Dervish seemed more like the adult she chronologically is. "And I totally understand how fed up you probably are at this point about people bringing it up."

"I kinda *am*, actually."

"I get that. That makes sense." She stepped back to give me a little more space. Even then, her sheer presence radiated back at me like a physical force. "So, do you want me to leave that alone and get back to why you came in today?"

I sighed again. "That pretty much *is* why I came in today."

"You mean, not to see my shining face?" Her kidding half-smile helped unkink the tension in my jaw.

"It's always good to see you, Dervish," I said, reaching into that vortex of energy to pat her on the shoulder. "But I came to ask you some stuff. Meg… Meg*han*… said I should talk to you, or Corwyn, or some of the other folks here." I'm the only person allowed to call Meghan "Meg." She bristles like a wet cat if other people do it.

"What about?" she asked, pulling over a stool made of that same blond-toned wood. "And here – sit down if you want."

"Thanks." I did. My morning workout was beginning to catch up with me. Everything was. "So…" I began, glancing around. "This is kinda weird."

She laughed. "It's cool. We do a lot of 'kinda weird' around here."

"I got that impression, yeah."

"How much did Meghan tell you?"

"About her working here?"

Dervish nodded, her own eyes glancing around to make sure we were alone. That early in the day, we were.

"She said… you and Corwyn, Dia and Max had been… um, sort of *training* her in stuff other than just music."

"Yeah." Again, Dervish had snapped back into adult mode. "It's connected to music, but yes. Yes we were." She got a wary look. "How much about all that has she told you?"

"I was there when the weird stuff went down back in school."

"Okay," Dervish said. "Just needed to make sure I wasn't telling tales out of school, as it were."

I shook my head. "You're not."

"Cool." Her dark brown eyes looked into mine like she was searching for something in there behind them. "So what do you need to know about?"

"Hard to explain," I said, even though I guess it probably wasn't so much hard to explain as just hard to say out loud.

I took a breath. "It's about Blue." Another breath, deeper this time. "And…" I glanced around the store. "About Red Shoes."

Dervish's eyes closed, shutting me out. "Fuck," she whispered. And then she opened them again. "*Please* tell me you're not doing that shit too."

"Oh, *hell* no."

"Good." Her grin snapped up like an electrocuted Pinocchio. "Because if you were, I would have to bash your brains in with a tuba and bury your body underneath the parking lot."

"Um…" I leaned away from her. "Okay, so that's kind of… *intense*."

"Sorry. Kidding." The adult was back in place. "I'm sort of the dictionary definition of intense."

"Got the update." I shook the dryness out of my voice and angled for common ground. "Meghan kinda warned me about that."

According to Meghan, Dervish was a rich kid from Manhattan whose parents didn't have the slightest idea what to do with her. They threw money in her direction every so often, so they probably loved her in some fashion. Meg's impression, though, was that they found her embarrassing, and so they let Dervish follow her dreams as long as they led away from the family's reputation and didn't take her over a cliff.

"So," I pressed her, "I get that you're not a fan of Red Shoes. What do you *know* it about it, though?"

"Not much," she said, her eyes back to searching mine for clues. "But enough to know that I don't want it anywhere near me. Or the store."

"I just found out about it last night," I assured her. "I was reading about it online, but I heard stuff that leads me to think Blue might have been on Red Shoes the night she died."

"Shit." Dervish growled the word with several layers of feeling. She looked down, glanced around again, and said – in a much lower voice – "We *seriously* should not be talking about this in the store."

"Wow." I nodded. "So this is stuff even the *rock stars* don't wanna talk about in public?"

She laughed again, but this time it sounded more harsh than amused. "I don't know that anyone would call us 'rock stars' around here, but no… it's not something we should talk about in a place of business. Especially one that already has cops sniffing around it on general principle."

"Seriously?" I asked. "Why?"

Now her laugh sounded more amused. "Sweetheart, we're *musicians.* Cops hate us on general principle. Every time some freak fucks an eight-year-old or ODs on some shit or other, the cops come looking for him in here. A cop might love listening to music, but when it comes to 'the usual suspects' we're the first people they come looking to round up."

"Even here?" The store seemed too clean and orderly to get on anyone's Most Wanted list.

"*Especially* here," said Dervish. "Like you know, we're not exactly Casteridge Music or Music Center." The places she'd named were more upscale, "respectable" stores where the school bands sent their students to get instruments. "Once the cops get done shaking down the pawn shops, they show up here looking for the answers they didn't find over there."

"What fun."

"Always." Like magic, her manic grin popped back into view. "Corwyn and Dia are out of town at the moment. They sort of left the place in my oh-so-capable hands for the duration, but maybe

I can help you out a little. Let's meet up somewhere else that's *not* the store, after I get off work tonight."

"Sure," I said, rising from the stool. "I'm already off work tonight."

Our timing turned out to be perfect; some dude with a Rasta hat, green cargo pants, and a sleeveless brown vest walked in just as the bell chimed over the door.

"When and where is good?" I asked her as I glanced over to the dude. He nodded to me with a half-smile as he headed over to the acoustic guitars and picked an Ovation off the wall.

Dervish came over, holding a business card with a number scrawled across the bottom in red ink. "Here's a number you can reach me at."

"Oh, crap," I said, remembering my prior engagement. "Lemmie check in with Vivienne first. We were supposed to be having a troupe meeting soon, about what we're gonna do from here."

"Y'all thinking of disbanding the troupe?" Rasta-boy was murdering Bob Marley's ghost in the background. I'd noticed some faint music when I'd first come in – a serpentine cover of the Stones' "Gimmie Shelter" – but whatever music was playing now had been drowned out by jangling guitar butchery.

"God," I whispered to her, "how do you *stand* that all day?"

Dervish snorted. "Comes with the territory. And most of the folks who come in here are actually really *good*. I guess that makes up for it. A little."

"I hope so." At least he wasn't playing "Stairway to Heaven." I fucking hate that song. "But no, we're not talking about breaking up. Not yet, anyway. Vivienne's feeling kinda rough…"

"I can imagine."

"But I told her to hold off for now. *Especially* right now. I don't want her making any decisions like that this close to…" I couldn't say it. "*Stuff*," I finished. Lame.

"Yeah," she agreed. "Don't make any quick decisions. That's too easy to do when you're grieving." There was that adult side of her again. Dervish seemed to switch back and forth between modes that way.

"Thanks." I reached to give her a hug as Rasta Boy began singing as badly as he played. "And *now*, I am out of here before my eardrums go on strike."

"Take me with you?" she said, only half-joking.

"You can always tell him to stop."

She grinned that shocked puppet grin again. "I could always brain him with a tuba!"

"You could."

"But that's so much *workkkkkk!*"

"Suck it up, sister," I told her, feeling far more comfortable with Dervish than I had when I'd first come in. I guess I didn't need Meghan with me to feel welcome here after all. "That's why they pay you the big bucks."

"I *wish*." She sighed, rolling her eyes for emphasis.

As I headed out the door, I saw Dervish walking back to the acoustic guitar section. I suspect she was going over to offer some instruction to Rasta Boy. If she'd had a tuba hidden behind her back, I couldn't see it from where I stood.

THE SWEET MORNING FOG

∾ ∾ ∾

Since I was more or less in the neighborhood already, I figured I would drop by the Hearthstone again and check in with Tabi about insurance and all that stuff. If nothing else, the news that I wasn't planning to sue her would probably brighten her morning. So I angled my car down South Port Road and headed toward the water. If I recalled correctly, the Hearthstone was open for breakfast, so I'd probably catch them right between the breakfast and lunch periods, when Tabi might have time to chat.

From what Mom has told me, Riverhaven started off as one of several ports along the Cherokee Ridge River. A series of warehouses had been constructed, and a small marina remained operational. The current runs too fast in that section of the river, though, and so the commercial ports and marinas moved down to the Basin, where the Whalbarton district, Fort Franklin, and Cherokee Ridge converge on the east side of the city. For a while, as I understand it, the South Port district became a slum, especially in the 1970s, when Riverhaven went through what's euphemistically referred to as "an economic downturn." The '90s, though, brought money to the city in the form of a booming

IT community. That much I know because Mom and Dad were part of it. And so, thanks to low rents and real-estate prices, Riverhaven got gentrified. Mom was part of *that* project too, and she'd made serious swag for her now-former bosses before getting tossed out on her ass during the most recent "economic downtown. These days, South Port tilts on that axis between boho chic and budding slum. I guess that's why Tabi could afford to deck out Hearthstone the way she has.

I parked my car in the small lot assigned to the Hearthstone. Yesterday's rains were evaporating in a humid cloud of sunlit haze. Running down from the heights of the Smoky Mountains, the river stays cool even in the summer, which in turn keeps Riverhaven cooler than most of North Carolina, and I am perfectly okay with that. Most summer mornings, the collision of cool water and hot sun creates fog along the Cherokee Ridge coast. And so, breakfast at the Hearthstone starts with fog and ends in sunshine. That's one of the reasons I love the place.

Arriving shortly before noon, I'd missed the breakfast menu. Too bad; one of Terrance's omelets would have gone down nicely after my morning workout. Tex was on now, though, and he grills some killer burgers. They'd managed to air the place out since I'd last been there, thank God, but the sight of the police tape across the stage still dropped a sick lump in my stomach. The sunshine through the windows lit the room up cheerfully, but each time my eyes swept the room, they kept getting snagged on that goddamned stage. I forced myself to look for a black smudge where Blue had died. The stage, so far as I could tell, was unscarred. It looked as if "the incident" had never happened at all.

Despite the warm morning, chills trickled down my back.

From the other end of the room, I could see how small we probably looked in that long hot moment… and it's not that big a room, either.

It hit me then how intimate death is for the people in the middle of it, and how small it gets from not *even* that far away.

"Morning, Genét." Tabi's voice startled me.

"Or pre-lunch rush, anyway." My rigid smile felt like I'd caught a bit of Dervish's shocked-puppet fever. "Looks good in here today. Nice and busy." *Marvelous*, I thought, *you not only LOOK like a lunatic now, you SOUND like one too.*

Tabi looked as though she hadn't slept nearly enough. Not surprising. Her voice sounded tired too. "How are…?"

I held up one hand. "*Please* don't ask how I'm doing."

Tabi nodded. "Fair enough." She motioned to the one empty booth. "Want to sit down?"

"That sounds," I told her, "like a wonderful idea."

I sighed as my butt hit the wooden booth. My workout was catching up with me. "You said you had some stuff for me to fill out," I said. "Insurance forms?"

"Yeah," she replied. "I can get them from my office."

I reached out and stopped her. "Sit down for a minute. You look like you could use it."

Tabi recoiled from my hand. Something distant passed across her face – a discomfort deeper than simple tiredness. "No, that's okay."

That something hung there between us for a long, quiet second.

"Thank you, Genét," Tabi added. "But like you said, we're just about to hit the lunch rush."

"Yeah." I dropped my gaze to the wood grain of the table. "Sorry. Bad timing. I didn't mean to interrupt business."

She laughed at that. To me, at least, that laugh seemed brittle. "It's okay. There's no such thing as *good* timing when you run your own business. Every day's just one big five-alarm fi–"

Tabi cut the word off but we both heard it anyway.

Awk. Ward.

"Oh, God," she whispered. "I'm…"

"It's okay," I said, letting us off the hook stuck in the air between us. "I know how you mean it."

"I need to get back to work," Tabi said. "I'll go fetch them for you. You can fill 'em out here or take them home and bring them back later. Grab whatever you want to eat – it's on me." Tabi held up her hand as I started to protest: "No, it's my treat. Get what you want."

"Thank you, Tabi."

"Not a problem." She turned back toward the kitchen. "Good to see you again, kid," she said over her shoulder at me.

"Good to see you too," I said, my best *Don't call me kid* smile plastered across my face… with humor underneath it but also a bit of real impatience. At her age – or mine, maybe – the whole Treating Me As An Adult thing apparently comes and goes.

I wound up ordering a blue cheeseburger, onion rings, and homemade chai. A server I'd never seen before brought them out to me, along with Tabi's insurance papers. I'd planned to fill them out at the table but realized I had overstayed my welcome at the Hearthstone. Leaving a $10.00 tip for the server, I got up and headed toward the door. My one attempt with server work taught me what a rough job it is. Other kids from Shooter's Ridge might take good service for granted. I would never be one of them.

The last of the fog had burned off by the time I got outside. I still had bits of burger in between my teeth. My phone chimed at me while I stood next to my car with my tongue wedged in an unattractive spot: "Code Monkey," by Jonathan Coulton – my ringtone for Dad.

Dad was one of those dudes who helped get the world hooked on Kate Bush, R.E.M. and the Police. His own tastes, though, are a lot less mainstream: Elvis Costello, Killing Joke, that sort of thing. Some of it I like, a lot of it I don't, but at least I didn't grow up thinking that the sun rose and set on That Week's Fucking Pop Star. If nothing else, he cultivated a love of music in me… and a sense of humor about the ways you could put songs to use. He loves to talk about how he'd begin his shows with stuff like "We Want the Airwaves" by the Ramones, "Wake Up (It's 1984)" by Oingo Boingo, or – when he was in a bad mood – "Holiday in Cambodia" or "We've Got a Bigger Problem Now" by the Kennedys. For a guy who's essentially a backpacking computer-nerd hippie, I guess my Dad's mostly pretty cool.

"Hello, sweetheart," he said when I answered. His voice sounded a bit more Forced Casual than usual.

"Hi, Daddy." I heard a note of sad-kid desperation slide into my own voice.

It's always like that, isn't it? You *try* to show your folks how grown up you are, but the truth kicks your best intentions right in the shins. It must be a genetic thing.

"I heard you were a badass the other night," he said. Dad knew better than to ask me how I felt. "I'm really proud of you."

I had to laugh. "Even though I wrecked a $400 jacket?"

"*Especially* because you wrecked a $400 jacket. I saw the video. You were magnificent."

I cringed. "There was a *video?*"

"These days, there's *always* a video."

"Nice," I said, spotting a bitter note underneath that word. "Me and Ash are up there trying to put Blue out, and some fucker's *filming* it instead of helping us." My parents don't care much if we swear in front of them so long as – like Mom used to say – we could use the words intelligently in a sentence.

Dad signed. "It's easier to *look* at the world than it is to live in it."

"Tell me about it." I hated the way my voice broke on that remark. I couldn't help it, though, and Daddy would understand.

He said some comforting stuff that I really don't remember, and it must have done the trick because I didn't actually cry this time. Dad always had a better way with us kids – or at least with me – than Mom did. I think it's the jock in her. Or maybe she just got sick of raising kids because my brother's such a shit. Anyway, Dad helped me get sorted out without ever asking me about my feelings or giving me the *I'm-so-sorry* talk. In the Kingdom of Computer Geeks, my dad is king, if only because he's not blind regarding social skills.

"Do the police know anything yet?" he asked when I'd dug myself out of the emo debris.

"Not yet," I told him, "but one of the detectives wants to talk to me."

"Do you want Frank present?" Frank Chambers, Dad's enthusiastically overemployed lawyer-friend.

"No, I don't think so. It's not like anyone thinks I was involved in anything."

"That's good," he said. "Still, it might be a good idea to at least have him on hand in case things go in directions you don't want to talk about." Dad's trust for cops is about average for punk hackers who've gone respectable… which is to say that he really doesn't have any.

"Maybe," I said, my mind spinning through the possibilities. There was a lot of stuff I didn't really want Mr. Chambers or my parents knowing about: Red Shoes, alchemy, and the bottomless pit of weirdness that could be involved if even half of what Meghan said was true. Detective Fallon might be clued in to the stranger elements of my life, but I'd kept the stuff with Meghan quiet for a reason. Sure, my parents are cool about a lot of things, but magic was not on the table as far as I was concerned. And that went double for their lawyer.

"All right, Genét." Dad was the first one in the family to respect my wish to not be called Jennifer. "I'll trust you on this. Still, I'll text you Frank's number in case you change your mind."

"Thanks, Daddy," I said with genuine gratitude.

"Don't let the cops get near the rubber hose," he joked. "And if anyone says 'National Security,' *run*."

"I will," I told him, laughing.

"Even if you don't take him with you," Dad said, his voice more serious, "let him know where you are, and give him the names of the officers you're talking to." He paused. "Do that *before* you go in. I'm serious."

"I hear you, Dad. And yes, I will." I meant that seriously, too. Dad had seen a few friends go into "friendly chats" with the police and not come back out again for a few months… or a few *years*. That's why Mr. Chambers is part-lawyer, part-friend, and part-bodyguard.

My phone gave me that little sound-blip that lets you know you've got a new text. "I've got it, Daddy," I said. "Thanks."

"Got what?" He sounded puzzled.

"Your text."

"I didn't send it yet."

"Oh." I checked my incoming texts. One from Caroline. Huh. I'd have to read it when I got off the phone. "Yeah," I said. "It's from someone else."

I could hear his smile on the other end of the line. "My popular girl."

"Yeah, well…" I had to smile too.

I always *had* been kind of popular, too. Not fast-track popular, but the kind of girl who was usually on the guest-lists for parties and stuff. Paradoxically, because I really didn't *care* about being in the In Crowd, I was sorta there by default without stressing about it. My friend Scharlotte said it was because the popular kids thought I was too cool to *try* and be cool, and so therefore I *was* cooler than the folks who kept trying to be cool. I can't honestly say that my parents' money *didn't* have anything to do with my popularity, but I had never been one of those dicks who held money over other people's heads like some rich kids do. My best friend was a poor kid who never wore shoes, so by rights I *should* have been an outcast… except that I wasn't. Go figure. Worrying about that stuff always seemed kinda stupid to me.

Once I'd wrapped things up with Dad, my curiosity had begun to buzz. Getting back in my car, I checked the text.

`can u meet me n ash at the bottle tonite? meeting there @ 8`

Caroline still hadn't gotten the memo about texting in real English. Kids these days, right? As I texted back `Sure. See you there,` I thought about bringing Mr. Chambers-style backup, just in case anything went wrong.

That may have been the smartest thing I'd done all day.

WHEN YOU'VE GOT
SOMETHING TO LOSE

∾ ∾ ∾

I left one message with Mr. Chambers, another with my backup, and then called Detective Fallon. As I expected, I got her voicemail, so I left her a message about coming in to talk that weekend or maybe late morning on Monday. Traffic was almost nonexistent, especially for a Friday afternoon, and the sun brought out the sweetest flavors of my town. Riverhaven sits in the hallow between a range of mountains, with Route 40 running just past us and the river running more or less through the center of town. On sunny days, the mountains catch the light and glow with gray-green majesty. Nearby Asheville might be more famous, but as far as I'm concerned, Riverhaven's the prettiest city in our part of the world.

Not all of Riverhaven, though, looks as nice as downtown or Shooter's Ridge. Off to my left as I swung back home along Route 246, the bleak shadows of Dagger Woods and the Stone Fort "barrows" tossed a gloomy cold shoulder across the northern part of town. The mountains above them keep that part of Riverhaven dark during most of the day, even in high summer. The winters there get nasty, and so the lowest-income neighborhoods in Riverhaven stretch from the far side of Hagar's Hollow to the fringes of Ashland, where I live. The worst of that stretch gets called "the Burn," mostly because that's exactly what it did back in the '90s. While the rest of Riverhaven blossomed, the Burn has remained more or less a scar where no one with a bit of sense goes unless they're blind, desperate, or incredibly stupid.

On the seat beside me, my phone played a snatch of "What the Water Gave Me" – my generic ringtone for calls from people I haven't already assigned a ringtone to. I glanced over at the screen, which told me that Detective Fallon had gotten my message. Since I couldn't pull over and I was *not* about to answer the phone at 60 MPH – two friends of mine have been hurt by people who were drive-texting – I let it go to voicemail. I'd call her back when I got home.

Besides, I was thinking about Caroline's meeting at the Bottle, a sketchy-cool art space that sits in Shady Creek, on the inner side of Route 246 across from Stone Fort and the Burn. That's not a *bad* part of town, necessarily – Meg walks through it all the time, and I used to walk through it with her before I got my car. Still, Shady Creek is not exactly in my comfort zone after dark. Arcana Darque usually rehearsed at the Bottle too; given all the weird shit from the last few days, though, I wasn't exactly looking forward to a return trip this evening. I half-wished Rose had put me on the shift-schedule for Crash that night. It would have given me a good excuse not to go to whatever it was that Caroline had planned.

Recognizing my unease, I made a mental note to call someone else from Meghan's list. I'd feel better if he had my back.

As I pulled off onto Galahad Road, I ran a checklist of stuff to do when I got home:

• Call Detective Fallon, my backup, and Mr. Chambers.

• Check social media pages for some of the people who were starting to seem significant. See what I could learn from them.

• Grab a nap. It looked like it might be a late night.

Inanna greeted me at the door as usual, and received her usual *someone's home now* tribute. Leaving my door open in case she wanted to join me, I got myself comfortable and made a few calls. Ten minutes later, I had a Saturday afternoon appointment with Detective Fallon and a firm "maybe" from this evening's would-be backup. Now that I had a meeting-time with the police, I gave Mr. Chambers' office a ring.

"Thank you for calling the offices of Archer, Chambers Law Group," said the receptionist. "How may I direct your call?"

"Hey, Peggy," I told her. "It's Gen… I mean, *Jennifer* Shilling."

"*Genét!*" Peggy seemed delighted. That's one of the things I like about our family attorney: Mr. Chambers values the human touch. "Your father *told* me you might be trying to get in touch with Mr. Chambers."

I laughed. "Yep. Is he around?"

Her voice dropped to a serious note. "You're not in trouble or anything, are you?"

"Oh, no," I assured her. "But something went wrong with a friend of mine, and I was a witness and the cops want to talk to me about it—"

"And your father thought it'd be a good idea to have Mr. Chambers present for the interview," she finished. "That makes complete sense."

"You're good," I told her.

"It's all those cop-shows I watch," she said, then laughed. "Oh, *wait* – no, that's right. It's my *job*."

I laughed with her, and we caught up for a minute or so before she put me on the line to Mr. Chambers. Thankfully, he was in his office instead of in a meeting or at court. Timing seemed to be on my side today.

"Hello, Genét." His deep voice flowed through my phone's crappy speaker. It's no wonder he does so well with juries.

"Hello, Mr. Chambers."

"I hear you might need a chaperone for a date with the police?"

"Pretty much," I said, then added "Not that I'm in trouble or anything…"

"If not, then you'd be breaking a long family tradition," he replied before rolling out a luxurious carpet of a laugh. "When your father called me, I figured that you were taking up where your brother and sister left off."

"*God*, no."

"Or him. Did he ever tell you how we met?"

"No," I said, intrigued.

He laughed again. "Then *I* won't."

"Attorney /client privilege."

"Exactly."

"Cute," I said, a little peeved that I'd let him set me up like that.

"That's why my clients trust me, Genét – your father included."
He paused. "Besides, I was making a point. Do you know what it
was?"

"I'm not sure," I told him. "I can think of a few."

"Good," he replied. "That's one of the things I've always liked
about you, Genét. You don't accept the *obvious* answer as the *only*
answer."

"Thank you, Mr. Chambers. And thank you for using the name
I prefer."

"That's common courtesy, I think: To let a person dictate
how they'd like to be defined. Our parents – and this may sound
like heresy coming from your family attorney, but it's true – don't
always know who we truly are inside. Or who we see in the mirror
when we look back at ourselves." He let that sink in. "I also think,"
he continued, "that it's important to recognize that part of a person,
whether or not I'm working on a case for them."

No wonder Dad kept him on retainer. Or why they'd been
friends for at least as long as I've been alive.

"So, *which* point were you making to me, Mr. Chambers?"

He chuckled. "You're an adult now, Genét. And if you secure
my services, then you are my client too. Your family may be paying
me, but I would be *your* attorney."

"And that means," I said, "that what I say to you is protected."

"Even from your parents," he concluded, "if you want it to be."

"Thank you. But is that cool with Dad? I mean, he *does* pay the bills, for the most part anyway."

"He *insists* upon it, actually. Unless I know something that puts your family at significant legal risk, or which suggests that a member of his family is in serious imminent danger, he has always insisted that you should all enjoy full confidentiality with me when you reach legal maturity."

Damn, I love my dad.

We spent a few more minutes discussing the pending interview, set up a meeting-time slightly before the talk with Detective Fallon, and exchanged a few more pleasantries before signing off. "Thank you again, Mr. Chambers," I said. "I really appreciate this."

"*Frank*," he told me. "I'm working for you now, Genét, and so I'm Frank." He chuckled again. "And I *will* be frank with you, too."

"Good," I said, smiling loud enough for him to hear it. "That's exactly what I want."

I felt a stabby punch of guilt in my gut after hanging up. *Girl,* I thought, *This isn't anything to laugh or smile about.* Grief, I've realized since then, is like that. It makes you feel guilty just for being alive.

∾ ∾ ∾

I dealt with my guilt the way I deal with most things: By throwing myself at the problem and trying to fix it through sheer stubbornness.

My social media quest turned up a few hints about the sad state of Arcana Darque. Vivienne was posting about Blue, accepting condolences, and swatting a few trolls who popped up to make cruel jokes at our expense. (What the fuck is *wrong* with those people, anyway?) The troupe's webpage had a memorial note about Blue, also probably from Vivienne. Apparently, a lot of people had seen the video too. Wonderful. Vivienne refused to answer any questions about the cause of the fire, and a few open-ended comments on the threads suggested that people were responding to other comments that had been deleted. I was glad to have missed that freakshow, but felt bad for having left it all in Vivienne's lap, too.

Ash had been vaugebooking about "times of transition" and "taking hard looks at her life," so I assumed she was quitting the troupe. Great. So apparently Vivienne *had* gotten everything dumped in her lap. Way to be a *leader*, Ash. Inky's only comment had been to post a cryptic *I'm sorry if I'm being a hermit again but my friend died and I need space right now. Hugs to everybody, unless you're a dick, in which case you can go eat a barrel of shit.* Caroline had remained silent – no posts from her at all, on any platform, since before the show. That afternoon, she'd posted and retweeted a note: *Come see me and my Sisters in Darqueness enchant the multitudes at the Hearthstone, 8:00 p.m. Sisters in Darqueness? Enchant the multitudes?* Fucking *please.* I'd known Caroline was drama queen, but *seriously?* And since then? Total dead air. A rain of comments ran down her Facebook page but she hadn't responded at all.

Jesus, did we even *have* a troupe anymore? It was beginning to look like not.

It's not like I was devoted to the art of dance or anything to begin with. I mean, dancing is fun and all. I enjoy it, and was beginning to learn some of the more serious applications of dance from my various classes, wishing that maybe I'd been more into the ballet lessons Mom and Dad had set me up for when I was a kid. The tribal-fusion bellydance thing suited me better, though. It's not traditional enough to feel confining, but not as *what the fuck ever* as twirling around a club or dancing like a hippie. I didn't need a million years' worth of training to feel good at it, it's kinda vaguely tied in with the Greek side of my mother's family history, and it integrates elements of yoga and tai chi in ways that felt more comfortable than going *en pointe* or that sort of shit. Every so often, though, I felt that deeper pull of something *more* within the dance. As I read the Facebook posts, I felt a growing sorrow because I hadn't really treasured our group up until it look like it was gone. Okay, so I wasn't the most devoted tribal bellydancer in town. Not even really the most devoted one in the troupe. But I kinda *liked* dressing up like Edward Scissorhands' hawt little sister and throwing down some moves to Dead Can Dance remixes. If nothing else, I'd liked the sense of community we enjoyed together, practicing techniques for two or three hours and then hitting Saffron Tiger or Persian Palace for garlic naan or some serious hookah time. Underneath that sense of funtime, though, I felt *connected* to something even deeper. To a sort of sisterhood, if that makes sense. In its original forms and cultures, bellydance hadn't been put on for dudes' amusement. It was something that women shared between each other, a type of communion just for us. And as I read the comments and posts, I felt that sisterhood slipping away.

Giving in to another tidal-pull of loss, I laid down for a nap with Inanna curled up on my back. But although I dozed a little bit, sleep ducked out the door each time I reached in its direction.

Three hours or so later, I had confirmed my interview with Detective Fallon and let her know that I was bringing my attorney.

"You *know*, Jennifer," she asked, "that you're not being charged with anything, right?"

"Yes, detective," I assured her. "It's just a formality."

"Of course," she replied with a chilly forced cheerfulness. Oh, *this* was just gonna be a *joy*.

So, I'd texted Caroline, `are we practicing tonight?`

no, she replied. `just talking`

Yeah, *that* didn't raise my hackles at all. `What about?`

`wether or not to dissolve AD.` *AD* being textspeak for Arcana Darque.

`Vivienne and Inky coming?`

`inky maybe not heard back yet from viv`

Annoyed and a bit suspicious, I texted back `Kind of a big discussion to have without the troupe leader.`

A pause.

`we no`

Unsure whether to take that response as Caroline's shitty spelling, an intentional reference to their negativity, or a Freudian mixture of both, I texted `Usual practice space?`

`yiss`

`Why not at Saffron Tiger or Persian Palace?`

`we've payed for space might as well use it`

Not even considering an alternative. Yeah, this was feeling better and better.

Not sure I can make it.

U quitting too?

I can't tell you what it was about those three words that made me change my mind. Maybe it was the idea of leaving Vivienne without an advocate. Or just plain curiosity. It could have been the sneering tone I heard behind that text, like a needling echo of that old meme *U mad bro?* I'd like to think it was something noble in me but it was probably my refusal to let someone assume I was a quitter.

No, I texted. *See you at 8:00 p.m.* I took snarky pleasure at spelling the text in grammatically correct English.

So, I *was* going, then. But I was *not* going alone.

THE TRUNK YOU
KEPT YOUR LIFE IN

～ ～ ～

Before I left, I also texted Vivienne about the meeting. Partly, I was curious about whether she'd even *heard* about it, and partly I wanted to give her a heads-up in case the troupe was walking out on her behind her back.

You think they're out? Vivienne's tiredness came through in text form. This had to be a *terrible* week for her. She hadn't actually told me whether or not they'd told *her* about the meeting but she seemed to expect it anyway.

Maybe, I replied. Not sure. *Going to find out.*

Thx, Genet.

I'm not out, I told her, *unless you want to dissolve AD.*

Not yet, she texted. *I want to save it if I can.*

Good, I replied. *And I want to help you if I can.*

<3

See you there? I asked her.

Not sure yet. Will try.

So there it was, then. I was committing myself to something I hadn't really taken too seriously up till then. Whatever happened, I was probably gonna wind up taking Ash's place as second-in-command of Arcana Darque. This week was just full of surprises. *I have got*, I thought as I strapped myself for the coming battle, *to be out of my fucking mind.*

~ ~ ~

"You owe me for this, Genét," he said. "You owe me big-time."

"*Seriously?*" I quirked one eyebrow at him. "That's the best line you could come up with? I know you better than that, buddy, so call in a script-doctor before I get seriously pissed."

Taunting a guy like Roland Castille, aka Rol, would probably be courting an ER visit for the average person. Rol's big the way a Harley-Davidson is big: thick, heavy, and powerful as fuck. Rol's not loud, though – pretty much the opposite *of*, actually. Still, most folks wouldn't dare to bust his balls, especially not if he was doing them a favor. Rol's friends, though, know that busting his balls is usually the best way to get him on your good side… provided, of course, that you've earned the right to do that in his book. And I *have*.

Rol and I both went to school with Meghan and Tucker. He and Tucker go back pretty much forever, and he and Meghan hit it off when she pulled her kitty-in-the-Doberman's-face routine on him back when they first met. It took me a while to get past Rol's hulking-slab-of-meat façade, but when I did I found a profoundly *kind* person hiding from a seriously fucked-up life. If anything, Rol owed *me*, not that either of us would ever admit that to one another's face. And so, as he took up most of the passenger's side of my car, he narrowed his eyes at me and said "Anyone who's headed for the Bottle in off-the-rack Ganni jacket needs to have a talk with her wardrobe department."

"I deserved that."

"You totally did."

Rol and I have spent the last few years bonding over watching movies and tearing them apart for fun. It shows in the way we communicate: Like a comments section but with less misogyny and fewer queer jokes. I wonder what I'll do when he gets a boyfriend. I hope that dude's the understanding type. If there's something we can pick apart about a movie, Rol and I *Riff Tracks* the hell out of it.

By the time I'd picked him up and headed toward the Bottle, the sun had pulled its nightly disappearing act behind the mountains. Summer or no summer, we had a stiff breeze coming off the west, and so we'd both slung our jackets in the back seat of my car: mine a beat-up Ganni bomber jacket, his a no-name piece of battered biker armor. Both of us, I think, were dressing for effect. But where my jacket was more or less bravado, Rol's was part of his daily personality. It's not easy being the only orphan of a dead guy and his equally deceased former wife. It's even less so when your gay Dad died of AIDS, you're adopted by his lover, and you've concluded that you're probably gay yourself. Now, Riverhaven's cool in some ways; it's still part of the South, though, and being gay still ain't healthy 'round these here parts. Being big and scary is part of Rol's way of reminding folks to mind their manners and keep their bullshit to themselves.

I'd always kind of avoided Rol throughout most of school – not because I gave a wet fart about the gay stuff, but because he was a big bald surly dude who radiated *Fuck with me and die.* I got over that, though, my last year of high school, after he'd taken up for a bullied kid in my geometry class. I don't even remember the kid's name, and I'm not sure Rol ever even knew it to begin with. But when some guys were giving him the school-bully beatdown, Rol stepped in and showed them what a beatdown really looked like. As the boys scraped themselves off the floor and walls, and school security came to drag Rol off to his newest suspension, Roland picked up the poor guy's backpack, handed it back to him, and told the dude, "They give you any more shit, man, you tell me about it. It'll be the last time they ever do." Rol made sure the bullies heard him say that, too. As far as I know, they never bugged the kid again.

I spoke up on Rol's behalf with the school administration, and Meghan did as well. I organized a student rally to keep Rol from getting expelled, with Meghan and I using every bit of social clout we had. Rol and I got to be kinda buddy-buddy after that. There've been a few times when one of us needed the other one's back, and we've been there for each other every time. And while that's totally a brother /sister caretaking thing, I know that Roland Castille would not let someone hurt me without going through him first.

Hence, him taking up most of my passenger seat on our trip out to the Bottle to deal with who-knows-what.

"So you don't trust your friends anymore," he asked me.

"I'm not sure," I replied.

"Not sure you can trust them anymore, or not sure they're your friends anymore?"

"Yes."

"Why're you going, then?"

I frowned. "I guess I need to know where things stand right now." My headlights passed over a stripped and abandoned car as I pulled my own car over onto Hallgate Road.

"Well, for starters," he said, "you're batshit stupid to be bringing a fucking *Prius* out to Shady Creek. Someone's gonna wreck it on general principle."

He had a point. Generally, I rode over to practice with Blue. She had suggested it when I first joined the troupe, and now I knew why. I hadn't stopped to think of what my car would look like out in this neighborhood. It's not like I'm *totally* blind to the resentments that people have against folks with my family's income, but I can be clueless about it at times, especially when there's other stuff on my mind.

I pulled over. "You're not wrong," I said, "for once."

He twitched a corner of his mouth in what I'd come to recognize was his smile. "And fuck you, too."

We ended up parking my car back a few miles, near Riverside Road. It meant a walk, but I was up for it. And with Rol beside me, no one was gonna say a fucking word.

~ ~ ~

"Don't talk so much."

"Huh?"

"You talk a lot," Rol said as we approached the Bottle. "If you want to figure out what's going on in somebody's head, *let* them do the talking."

"How so?"

"Just be quiet and look at people. Better yet, *don't* look at them. It makes folks nervous." Our boots clopped across cracked pavement. "I learned that from my uncle: Nervous people say things they didn't mean to say. So keep quiet, and let 'em spill their guts to you."

"Thanks," I said. "Good advice, I guess."

Rol didn't say anything, just looked straight off toward our destination.

"I see what you did there," I told him.

He still didn't talk but I think I saw him smile.

It was full-on dark by the time we spotted Ashley outside the main entrance, pacing around and texting on her cell phone. Music rumbled from the building, a wash of sounds colliding and running together into a tuneless surge of sonic sludge. Faint light from the windows illuminated a trashed-up parking lot, occupied by a handful of old cars and clusters of chatting Bottleites.

I think the Bottle is technically considered abandoned. Somebody, though, brings in enough money to keep the lights on and the water flowing. No heat or anything, but I suspect that the realtors involved are accepting cash under the table rather than simply boarding the place up and taking their chances with the neighborhood. Keeping this space *empty*, after all, would be more trouble than it's worth. *Every* city has squatters in its abandoned buildings – hell, the Burn is Squatter Central. The Bottle, though, hosts a self-contained community, with its own economy, leadership council, utility-providers, and even a collective to handle litter, bathrooms, and other chores. And so, the "abandoned" Bottle is a pretty jumping place.

Folks call it *the* Bottle but actually it's got two of them. On each of the front corners of this block-long, block-wide warehouse space, a huge dirty-white milk-bottle tower rises up to just above the level of the roof. These two tacky towers hold the building's best studios and living areas. Most of the rooms are smaller – wood-and-brick rectangles with hard-worn hardwood floors. A few ramps and sagging stairways, broad enough to haul machinery up and down between floors, run up through each of the building's four corners. Lots of folks live there full-time, while other groups – like Arcane Darque – just rent space. Everyone with a brain keeps strong padlocks on the doors to their rooms, and lots of people avoid the basement.

As I soon realized, there were *very* good reasons for that avoidance.

This section of Shady Creek is mostly warehouses and empty storefronts. A section of train-yard runs off into the darkness beyond the parking lot. The Bottle sits surrounded by an asphalt no-man's-land lit mostly by moonlight, the building's windows, and spillover from the few streetlights that aren't broken yet. It is not, for obvious reasons, the safest place in town. And that sense of danger makes it a perfect spot for ten thousand little rebellions and an edgy sense of cool.

Rol and I cruised with silent authority through the parking lot. I followed my friend's lead of being quietly impressive, saying nothing, meeting no eyes, and retaining an animal awareness of our surroundings without acting wary in the process. Ash, by the door, scowled at her cell phone, shoved it in her bra, and then noticed us coming her way. Ash is pretty tall – taller than me by a good two or three inches – but still short in comparison to Rol. From her expression, I judged she was none too thrilled to see I'd brought an escort.

Despite the thick humidity and lingering summer heat, Rol and I both kept our jackets on. I can't speak for Rol, but mine felt like armor and I needed armor right then. Ash, by contrast, wore a tank-cropped Motörhead shirt, ladder-shredded black jeans, and battered black Docs. Her pale hair hung like pasta across her face, like she hadn't showered in a day or so. "Hey, Genét," she said, glancing up at Rol like she wanted to give me a hug but wasn't sure that he wouldn't eat her if she tried.

"Hey, Ash," I said, giving her the sought-after hug and noticing the extra cling of tension in her arms. "This is Rol," I said, pulling a somewhat graceful dismount from the hug. "He's cool. He's a friend."

"Uh… hey, Rol," she said.

Rol said nothing. Simply nodded his head once.

"Where are the others?" I asked.

She gestured with her head. "Upstairs in the practice space." She looked at Rol. "You coming too?"

He nodded.

"Oh," she said. "Cool." Whatever sincerity she might have intended got lost between her brain and her voice-box. Ash hauled open the heavy wooden door set into the north-sided bottle-tower, and Rol stepped through first, still silent and moving like a boss.

The long hallway gaped like a cavern of amber-yellow light. Music rumbled vibrations through the soles of our boots. Graffiti murals reached from the concrete floor to the wood-beamed ceiling, broken by tall doors on hinges and occasional tracks. Behind those doors – some open, most not – we could hear people talking, joking, partying, fighting, fucking, listening to music, and otherwise passing their time in a space outside the mundane world.

"So yeah," Ash said once she'd closed the door. "Caroline's upstairs, setting up the space."

"What about Inky?" I asked her. "And Vivienne?"

Ash half-froze. "Vivienne had to work." She tossed the words out like meat for a watchdog. "I don't know about Inky yet. I think she's coming. Maybe she's not."

I said nothing.

"I'm not sure," she said. "Let's go up."

Man, Rol was *right* about that whole silent-treatment thing.

Ash spilled awkward small-talk all over the stairs as we headed up toward the third floor. I gave her enough encouragement to keep her talking, but Rol said not one single fucking word. We hauled ourselves up the broad yet stifling stairways as their wood creaked in cranky disapproval. Echoes from the rooms spiraled up the stairwells, their specifics baffled by the brick walls and wooden steps. Sticky smears of *god-only-knows-what* stuck to my boots, and dense humidity closed in as we approached the third floor.

It's not like I'd never been to the Bottle after dark before. Hell, most of our practices happened after work and school, so night has been our default time since pretty much ever. That night, though, I felt marked and targeted – out of place. In the company of "friends," I should have felt secure. But Rol was wary and Ash was giving off vibes like a trapped cat looking for a face to claw off on her way out the door. And so I kept my mouth shut as we plodded up the steps, feeling the wood buzz underneath my boots.

The Bottle has a certain *smell*: a hovering miasma of spray paint, sweat, aging wood and mildewed brick. That smell gets heavy in hot weather, and although cool air had swept down from the mountains as it often does, the Bottle kept the day's heat… well, *bottled up* in that darkened sweatbox. By the time we hit the third floor, my damp shirt clung to me like paint beneath my jacket.

"Oh, *dude*," Ash spat into the dimness. "*Pants*, please!"

A bone-thin naked guy sitting on the top steps grinned at us, his skin shining in faint yellow light. "Evening, ladies," he said, totally unconcerned. "And *gentleman*, too."

"Stash the cock, weirdo," rumbled Rol – his first words since the parking lot. "No one here wants to see it."

Nekkid Dude shook his white-boy dreads. "So don't *look*, man! It's too fucking hot in here for clothes." He looked up at my big looming friend – either too brave, fucked up or crazy to care about Rol's size. "This is free space, man, so I'm being free. *You're* free, too." He gestured the hallway past him. "I'm not in your way, so don't get in mine either."

I give the guy credit for balls, anyway, even though I had no desire to see them.

"Whatever." Ash dismissed him, striding past me, Rol, and Nekkid Dude. "C'mon, guys, let's do this already."

"So," I ventured as we headed towards our practice space, "what *are* we doing here tonight?"

"Telling our future, I guess," she said as she knocked. "*Yo, Caroline,*" she shouted at the door. "It's me. They're here."

"Who's 'they'?" said Caroline's voice on the other side of the door.

"Genét and a friend of hers."

"Oh," said Caroline's voice.

A few seconds later, the door squealed open on rusty tracks.

Okay, so imagine a Cheshire Cat on meth, his spirit trapped in the body of a Suicide Girl. That was Caroline, grinning with manic intensity as she hauled the door aside. That grin froze tight to her face as she eyed Rol. "*Come on in,*" she cried with cubic zirconium cheer. I hadn't been quite sure just *what* to expect but Manic Pixie Caroline was not it.

Caroline had been part of Arcana Darque since before I joined the group. She'd always struck me as being kind of a mopey drama queen. Oh, she's hawt, I guess; as with Dervish, I lagged light-years behind her level of cool. But where Dervish struck me as a basically decent person on caffeine overload, Caroline was far moodier – quick to blow up at Vivienne, herself, or other people if something didn't feel right to her. I wouldn't have been at all surprised to learn that she was bipolar or something like that. If she *was* bipolar, though, then this was Caroline in a manic state. Her curly purple hair glowed in the dim light, backlit by a collection of candles she had placed all over the room.

Unlike the rest of us, Caroline had dressed in her tribal dance garb: coin bra hung with turquoise and peacock feathers; tattered fishnet sleeves over her tattoos, bare feet, full jewelry, a horned headdress, and overlapping layers of a shredded black skirt. She'd decked our practice room out with dozens of candles, a cooler, and a makeshift altar. A large goblet and a bottle of Hidden Legend mead sat in the center of the altar, next to a photo of Blue and a statue of Hekate or Lilith or something like that. Branches, flowers, and a scarf that I recognized as Blue's completed the memorial setting. A thin sandlewood haze drifted in the restless air, the humidity barely touched by fingers of breeze coming through the open windows. An ancient boombox pumped out a bass-heavy Niyaz track that bounced off the walls and got lost in empty space. Caroline held the door open as Ash, Rol and I stepped through, then slid it closed behind us all with eerie finality.

"Hi, everybody," she gushed, setting a chair in front of me. "I'm glad y'all could make it here tonight." She looked up at Rol. "Hi, gorgeous. I don't know who you are but you're with Genét and so you must be cool." Before he could respond with anything other than his patented glare, she wrapped herself around him in a nuclear bear-hug. Even Ash seemed to be surprised by that.

"Where's Inky?" I asked as she flung herself at me as well. I hugged her back but with considerably less enthusiasm. I'm all in *favor* of hugging when everyone involved is cool with it, but Caroline hadn't bothered to ask either one of us, and Rol didn't seem cool with it at all.

"Oh," Caroline replied, "she couldn't make it tonight."

"Vivienne either?"

"Vivienne had to work." She hurried over to turn down the boombox, which had pushed our voices past the comfort-zone. "That's better," she said. "Sorry – I kinda like it loud, and it's so fucking *crazy* in here on a Friday night in here to begin with."

"Yeah," I said, flashing back to Nekkid Dude and wishing that I hadn't. "I got that memo."

Ash wandered over to the altar, glancing back at Rol to catch his reaction to all this. For his part, Rol seemed to take the whole thing as a given. He picked up a chair and moved it over by the door. "That's Rol," I said, motioning to him. "My friend. He offered to walk me over since I had to come alone." His mouth quirked a little at that last part, but he didn't contradict me.

"God," Caroline breathed, "he's *cute*."

I tried not to snort. Rol is many, many things, but "cute" is not on the list.

"You should *totally* join the troupe," she said, going over to him and running her hand along his jacket sleeve. "I'll bet you dance like a god."

"Did she mention," he replied, "that I'm a fag?"

"So what?" She shrugged. "*I'm* bi. Ash is bi. Half the dancers in town are queer. You'll fit right in."

"So, Caroline," I added, "do we need to have the 'socially appropriate' conversation again?" We'd never actually had one *before*, but she was totally creeping me out. This was *not* the Caroline I'd shared a troupe with for the past six months or so, and while that one wasn't exactly the life of the party, I vastly preferred her over the one we were in the room with now.

"Shit," she hissed, "I'm just trying to be *nice* to your friend here. *Jeeze.*"

"I *get* that," I told her. "But grabbing folks you don't know isn't cool."

"God, Jen-*AY*, stop being such a *virgin!*"

"Y'know what?" I said. "*Fuck* this." I headed towards the door. "C'mon, Rol. I'm done."

"*Wait.*" This voice sounded totally unlike the Caroline of two seconds ago. All the manic bravado collapsed into a single pain-filled syllable, and I stopped in spite of myself.

"I'm *sorry*," she said, and her expression was pure misery. If I'd smashed her grinning face in with a hammer, the change could not have been any more drastic. "Genét, Rol – I apologize."

Ash looked at Caroline with only slightly less surprise than I felt.

"I'm kinda fucked up," Caroline went on, "about Blue… and… and I was just trying to make it better." She reached out toward me but I pulled back. "I was wrong. I overstepped. You're *right*. I'm sorry."

I glanced up at Rol. He pressed his lips together in a way that suggested that I stay quiet and let her keep spilling.

"Okay, I admit it. I had some mead before you came in." She gestured to the altar. "I got it for us so we could celebrate Blue – have some kind of wake or something." She stepped back toward the altar. "but *Inky* couldn't come and *Vivienne* couldn't come and I wasn't sure *you* would come and… well, me an' Ash would just be left here on a fucking Friday night with a bottle of mead and some fucking photographs and *that* would be fucking *that.*"

She sat down in one of the chairs. "And y'know, I just wanted something *more* for her than that. So yeah, I fucked up. I'm sorry."

I wish I could say I was enough of a bitch to walk out anyway.

But I wasn't.

Instead, I gave her a hug, pulled off my jacket, and draped it over the seat I pulled up next to her. "Okay," I told her, "I'm willing to stay if you're willing to chill out."

"Thanks." The hurt look she threw at the floor was more like the Caroline I was used to. "And hey," she said to Rol, "I was out of line. I'm sorry."

Rol did that corner-quirk thing with his mouth. "No problem," he muttered. I wondered if he meant it.

Ash came over and pulled up a chair as well. "It's too damn hot up here to stand, anyhow."

Rol sat back down again in his chair by the door. "Did you want to come over here?" Ash asked him.

"Nah," he said. "I'm cool over here."

"You sure?" she said, lifting a pack of plastic water bottles. "You want something to drink or anything?"

"I'm good."

"Okay," she said, putting them down.

"I'll take one," I told her, and so she handed me a bottle. Between the long walk and the hot room, it tasted especially good.

Caroline hovered right around the verge of tears without actually falling over it. Instead, she eyed the dusty footprints we'd left during practice on Monday night. "Jesus," she said, so softly

I could hardly hear her over the music and surrounding noise, "it doesn't take much to change a lot of things, does it?"

I started to answer her but shook my head instead.

"It's weird," she continued after a long not-quite-silence, "I almost didn't go that night. I felt like crap, and Blue talked me into going anyway." She scuffed at the floor with the ball of one foot, her arms closed tight against whatever she was feeling. "She didn't even get much of an audience, y'know?"

"It was on YouTube," I added.

"*Fuuuuuuck.*" The word grated itself up through her throat. "I heard about that. Did you watch it?"

Again, I shook my head. I had stared at the link back in my room the night before but could not bring myself to actually watch it.

"It's fucked up," Ash added. "People just *filmed* it while we were…" An ugly sound strangled whatever else she might have said.

"And then they posted it," I finished, "on goddamned *YouTube*." I had glanced at the comments the previous night. The top one said *Gee, that's gonna leave a mark.* The next one was worse. I couldn't read them beyond that.

And then I felt the invisible fist slam itself into my ribcage and I just kind of fell into myself.

The footprints on the floor showed where Blue had stood and walked and danced. I remembered her wearing the scarf around her shoulders, tied just enough to keep it from sliding off. I heard her chuckle over a cup of chai at Jezebel's, sliding out her bank card to cover the check for dinner. And then the room was too tight, too close, too hot to look at and so I let it all mist over as I closed my eyes.

"How fucked up," Ash was saying, "do you have to be before you could even *think* that was funny? A person burns to death and all you can think to say is '*epic fail*'? Her voice held enough ghosts to host its own Halloween party. "I just can't stop *smelling* her," she whispered. "I can't stop seeing her eyes. It's like she... like *Blue*... got inside of me somehow and won't go away."

Eyes still closed, I reached out to squeeze Ashley's shoulder. "Not your fault," I told her. "It's not your fault."

"I was in *charge*," she insisted. "I was *responsible*."

"You didn't set her on fire," I said.

I felt her shoulder clutch as she folded up inside. The ragged sound she made seemed like self-strangulation. A hurt animal cry welled up behind that sound and hung in eerie counterpoint to the music in our room and the joyful chaos beyond it.

We all moved in then – even Rol – to hold her as she cried.

Without moving further, we all fell into a vast and lightless pit where the only touchstone was our sense of loss.

That night, I understood why folks get drunk at funerals. Or laugh. Or fuck when they think that no one's looking. Because the awful immensity of death – *real* death, not that shit on TV or games or movies where Superman wastes half a city fighting with a dude from Krypton, but *REAL DEATH* where the people who lost that person have to live without them – has a way of getting past your armor and busting up everything inside. It sets up shop in your chest, in your eyes, in your guts, and every so often it kicks you right where the blow hurts worst just to let you know that it *can*. And so, the four of us just lumped ourselves together in a black ball of hurt and clung to one another like nothing else existed. Because for us, right then, nothing else *did*.

The boombox cycled through two or three songs before Caroline pulled away and asked "Who else wants some mead?"

"I do," Ash said from between our arms.

"I'll take one," Rol rumbled.

"Yeah," I finished, "I'll have one too."

So Caroline poured the mead into the goblet – some ceramic handmade thing with a pentacle on it – and she held it up like an offering. "Blue and I," she said, "used to go to this shitty summer camp when we were kids."

"I didn't know you'd known her that long," I said.

"Oh, yeah," she answered, staring off somewhere past the wall. "She told me about Vivienne and dance and invited me to form the troupe with them. But back when we were kids, we weren't… y'know, the most *popular* kids at camp."

"I have *no* idea," said Ash, "how that feels. None."

Rol made an affirmative sound.

"So anyway, they had horseback riding at that camp," Caroline went on. "'Camp Cherokee' – how's *that* for cultural appropriation?" She waved the cup in a mocking salute, then took a drink. "Blue and I wanted to ride the horses but the other girls wouldn't let us. They said we were too small and too stupid, and one of the fucking counselors agreed with them. And then they said that we had to earn the right to ride the horses by mucking out the stalls. That fucking counselor – Jeanie, or something asinine like that – told us they were right. And so she showed us how to clean up horseshit and change the hay and do the other stuff they were actually supposed to do. I guess Jeanie figured she'd put off her share of the chores on us and we'd be too stupid to know better.

"Anyway, we did it. I actually *learned* something doing that, y'know, and so me and Blue kinda got to like it. Not cleaning up the shit or anything but getting to know the horses and feeling like we were doing something productive. I mean, the older girls got to ride on the horses and stuff but *we* got to see how the horses actually *lived*. But Jesus *Christ*, we smelled bad. I mean, y'know, we smelled like people smell when they clean up stables, and the older girls started calling us names and shoving us around, and that first night after we cleaned up the stables, they locked us out of the cabin because they said we smelled too bad to be allowed to sleep there. 'Go sleep in the stables,' one of them yelled through the door. 'Go sleep in shit where you belong.'

"So I start to get all furious and I start banging on the door and screaming threats and stuff, and then Blue – Monica…" She stopped for a second. "Did you guys even know her name was Monica?"

Rol shook his head. So did I – Blue's Facebook profile just listed her as Blue Palisade. Ash nodded. "Yeah. I used to work with her at Farm Fare when were in high school." *Weird*, I thought. I'd known Blue for years too, but the only name I'd ever known her by was *Blue*. Giving her more of a name seemed to somehow make her even more real.

"So, Monica…" Caroline went on, still staring at the wall as if she was watching her life play out there. "She says 'Shhhhh…'

"And she's like 'I have a better idea.' And so we go down to the manure pile, and we get a bucket, and we carry a bucket of the ripest-smelling shit we can find back up to the cabins, and we go into the big common bathroom, and we dump the shit into every toilet, shove it up every faucet in every sink, and we grab a stool and stuff it into the heads and the drains of every shower except one. And then we took turns washing up and showering off before we stopped up *the very last* sink and shower-head. And then we just fucking *left*. We ran off down the camp trail in the dark until we got to a road, and then we hitched a ride off this dude who was *seriously* freaked to see two wet little girls on the road to nowhere in the middle of the night. He took us in to the police station, where we told them about being abused at the camp, and so of *course* the cops called our parents and the camp got in serious trouble, but the part we never heard about..." Caroline stopped to laugh. "Was what had to have happened the first time those fucking girls, or those shitty counselors, or stuck-up Jeanie and her two-faced elitist ass tried using a sink or taking a shower..." Caroline put down the cup and mimed a prissy little princess flouncing up to a sink and trying to wash her hands, and squealing "*OMIGODDDDDDD!!!*" as imaginary liquid horseshit flowed out all over her hands.

We all laughed, and Caroline took up the pantomime, mincing her way to the imaginary shower and squeaking up a storm of horrified obscenities until the rain of imaginary turds flew down in her face and hair, and I guess you had to be there to get the full effect but we laughed our asses off in schadenfreude heaven as Caroline finished her act, picked up the cup, proclaimed, "*Here's to Monica, here's to Blue, here's to the Shower Goddess of Everlasting Poo,*" and we all applauded as she took a long drink, turned to the rest of us, and said, "Okay – who's next?"

Ash went next, telling a story of how she and Blue had faced down some dudebros who'd been hassling them on the street. At the end, she took a big drink to honor "*Blue the Warrior, Blue the Friend, Blue the Badass Who Never Backed Down.*"

I went next, telling them a long gaming story about how Blue and I had gone to GenCon two years earlier and wound up whomping the crap out of some dicks who thought "chicks can't play *Warhammer 40k*." For my drink, I celebrated "*Blue Xavia, the Tyranid commander with No Pity and a heart of steel.*"

"I didn't know her," said Rol when his turn came, "but I'll drink to her anyway." And so we went through the rest of that bottle of mead, and a bunch of other stories, and when that bottle was empty Caroline took out another and the stories continued until all of the mead and most of the water was gone.

And that burning ghost behind my eyes became a shining bright sister-geek who took no shit and did no wrong.

The mix on the CD in the boombox ran through, and Ash grabbed the iPod and plugged it into the box. "Music for sorrow," she asked us, "or music to dance?"

"Dance," said Caroline.

"Dance," I agreed.

"Fuck it, let's dance," said Rol.

And so Ash cued up a playlist that started – no shit – with "People Who Died," by the Jim Carroll Band, and we launched into a drunken cyclone of flailing feet and swinging arms. Out of habit with this space, Ash and I had ditched our boots and socks. My jacket hung from the back of the chair. We spun and leaped and smashed into one another with glorious abandonment of sense.

Furniture went flying and we didn't give a single fuck. Anything but the altar was fair game. I threw myself against Rol. He threw himself into me. The room became a bone-jarring blur. The raw impact of leather, wood, bones and skins became a celebration of everything we'd lost, everything we'd shared, everything we would all lose someday when the carnival closed up shop for each of us and headed off down the road without us. We screamed and we cried and we danced ourselves sick.

I don't know how we wound up in the hallway, but we did. And then in another room. And then in another, bodies crushed against us in a neon smear. In each room, we grabbed more people, and dragged them with us to another room, and the whole Bottle became one mad wild hunt, crashing from party to party until the wood beneath my feet became concrete and the stairs kept going down and down and some part of my brain lit up at last when I saw the faces blur from humanity to monstrosity and a shrieking shred of self-preservation finally woke up like a siren in the back of my head.

I was dancing.

I was weeping.

I was burning.

Not with fire but with sweat, steaming in the flashing dark. Crushed in a moving press of madness and heat.

In the basement.

The fucking *basement*.

Where *no one* went in their right mind.

And where all of us suddenly *were*.

'CAUSE I SWEAR IT'S FUN

∾ ∾ ∾

Hell was a hot slam in a dark basement filled with faces that never belonged to any human thing.

Hell was knowing that I *should* stop moving but being *unable* to stop moving.

Hell was the flash of strobing horror that passed for light in a crush of sweating bodies who'd slid straight past sanity and into some unknowable abyss.

And hell was realizing all of this and not being able to do a fucking thing about it.

Pounding beats slammed my body into spasms of activity disconnected from my mind. My bones sizzled with pulsing heat. Pulpy scents and acrid nose-burns stewed in coruscating fog. Each sensation plowed into, under, through every scrap of conscious thought. My brain kept slipping on molten grease, burning on contact, skidding into joyful terror ecstasy. Every constant, every handhold for coherent thoughts, got pulled off and shoved out into an endless vortex of increasing speed.

Faces and bodies reached out to me through the blur: an eyeless ring of fangs and tongues. A whipping mass of ectoplasmic thorns. A shrieking blond tornado of hair with uncountable eyes in the face underneath. I watched two impossibly skinny girls carve strips of flesh off a laughing teenage boy. Rol bounced off a living pillar of stone and steel. Caroline threw her head back, laughing, bright red tears pouring from her eyes. Gray human shapes with too many arms and legs writhed in hardcore hentai sex. Red war-Buddhas blazed with incandescent light. Arcs of lightning surged through dark-wrapped chaos. Pulses of hot and cold energy blasted through my veins in hyperkinetic washes of implacable sensation. The beat blasted every molecule of my integrated self, and if none of this sounds coherent it's because none of it *was*. My brain kept churning word-salad from impossible sights, stringing them together with bright dementia.

Dashes of crazy blasted through my mind. All of it *looked* real but none of it *could* be. I thought I saw Chalice blazing like a barefoot faerie queen, lit from inside by bright red strobing lights. A shining red scarf rippled across her shoulders. A cadaverous glowing-eyed *thing* puppeted behind the sound board like an Iron Maiden T-shirt come to life and spasming like Frankenstein's Monster fucking endless lightning bolts. The red war-Buddhas hovered cross-legged in crimson smoke. Between them, dancers writhed and howled, their voices lost in thundering beats and the screams ripped from the bottom of my lungs.

Like I've said, I'm no innocent. I've smoked pot, done 'shrooms, got puking drunk, and flung myself into various mosh pits at various shows. This was beyond anything I had ever done before, light-years past any experience I'd ever had. The heat under my skin seemed to boil and cook. If I stood still, I felt like I would burn.

Is this what Blue felt like before she died?

That thought stuck. Like a barbed harpoon, it came sailing through the chaos and punched through the delirium and fucking *held* an anchor-line in place. Mentally, I grabbed for it, hung on, and tried to pull myself out of the storm. My body, though, kept moving, pounding my feet raw against the concrete. A snatch of ancient lyrics ripped through my brain: Donita Sparks shouting *You and me till the wheels fall off!* I shoved back against the urge to self-destruct. My body fought my brain, and everything between them screamed.

Ash crackled through flickering light, her hair a slash of bright-colored blades. I threw myself at her, trying to knock us both out of the dance. She sidestepped me, if she'd even been there at all, and I crashed hard against the concrete floor. Instantly, I found myself tangled in a sea of legs and feet, kicking me, stomping me, dancing around me, soaring off into the bright /dark void of faces and fire. Impact punched me halfway out of the trance-state I'd been sailing in. The sticky-wet floor gave me something solid to hang on to.

The wall of legs pulled away from me. A wall of blackness reached down and wrapped itself around my waist. I kicked and punched at it until the darkness shouted "*KNOCK IT OFF! I'M ROL!*" and lifted me off the floor. My view went even more skewed and bent as I guess he threw me over his shoulder and hauled me up and out of the crowd. Rol or no Rol, I kept flailing until he finally yelled near my ears: "*YOU DO THAT ONE MORE TIME AND I'M FUCKING LEAVING YOU HERE!*"

I can't honestly say it sobered me up, but I *did* stop trying to kick his ass. As if such a thing had been possible with me hanging over his shoulder.

My bones still kept trying to burn through my skin. The room still skittered and sizzled with bright /dark intensity.

From my vantage point hanging down by Rol's meaty ass, I watched the impossible carnival boil and pop. But the solidity of Rol's bulk and his nicotine-thick jacket gave me an anchor to cling to as he shoved a path through the thundering mess of not-quite-humanity. Around us, the faces melted and merged: wizened critters, sleek seducers, amorphous nightmares whose skin seemed to bubble with leprous worms… I think I saw it all as we pushed through the crowd: fanged hippies and bat-faced girls, all dancing through a glowing fog of impossible darkness and shattering light.

Pro tip: Never hold a drunk girl over your shoulder, especially not if her belly and the epaulets of your biker jacket happen to share some breathing room. Because if you *do* do that, then you're liable to make the wonderful discovery that Rol and I both made as we headed up the stairs… which is this: Hot mead makes a *magnificent* party-favor, especially when it's pumped up the throat of a chick who's slung across your back.

Thankfully, Rol dropped me to my feet just as the second bolt of boiling stew surged up my throat and bent me over in the traditional posture of Saturday-night ritual. Yeah, I threw up on my bare feet and the cuffs of my jeans, but at least I didn't puke down the back of his jacket. *That* might have tested our friendship even further than everything else that happened that night.

One vigorous bout of retching later, I was hunched over the steaming remnants of lunch. On the plus side, though, I could more or less sort out the warring sensations in my head. Rol kept his distance from me while also making like a wall to shield me from everybody else. The heat under my skin bubbled and snapped but I had a more coherent picture of where we were and what was happening to us.

Broad concrete stairs ran from the gloom above us to the lightning pit we'd left behind. A handful of spectators gaggled and necked on those stairs, but the real action was below. Caroline and Ash were lost in the crowd. A metal handrail marked the edge between solid steps and empty air. I grabbed that handrail and pulled myself half-standing. My belly felt like a Warrior Fitness amateur after a few rounds sparring with Ronda Rousey. My throat felt even worse.

Rol placed one hand on my shoulder. "*YOU OKAY NOW?*" he shouted above the noise.

"*OKAY IS FUCKING RELATIVE,*" I shouted back, "*BUT I CAN STAND AND I CAN WALK, SO LET'S GET OUTTA HERE.*"

Rol still seemed pretty fucked up himself but we both managed to hold ourselves upright as we leaned on the walls all the way back up to the third floor to fetch my boots, socks and jacket. We saw a few folks here and there along the way; the real party, though, still seemed to be going down in the basement.

"I thought nobody ever *went* in the basement around here," Rol said when we could speak in more or less our normal voices again.

"I guess they save it for special occasions," I replied, my throat one long expanse of red-hot gravel. "Did *you* see how we wound up down there?"

"Not really, no," he said. "But that wasn't just *alcohol* we drank."

"No," I said. "It sure as hell was not." The real picture began to form in my head, and it did *not* make me happy.

Thankfully, Nekkid Dude was probably down in the basement or something. The third-floor hall was empty, our mix still booming from the open doorway to our room. Also thankfully, no one had run off with either the boombox or my things. I used Caroline's T-shirt to clean off my feet, as I wasn't feeling terribly charitable right then.

Rol went over to the altar, but didn't touch anything. "Hey," he called over to me, "you mind seeing if there's anything on this altar besides the obvious?"

"How do you mean?" I asked, each word a bit of barbequed roadkill dragged up the back of my throat. Grimy fingernails greased with pure *Wrongness* slid up and down my skin, under my clothes, across my bones.

"I know some people who can do some pretty weird shit," he said, still swaying from the effects of whatever the hell we'd shared earlier. "I just want to make sure that I'm not gonna get blasted into next week by a protective spell or anything like that."

"I sort of doubt it," I said, shoving my socks inside my boots. Now that he'd *mentioned* it, though, the idea didn't seem far-fetched at all. "I don't think that's Caroline's thing."

He pointed at the pentacle on the goblet, and the goddess-statue beside Blue's picture. "You don't *think* so, huh?"

"Point taken," I said, grabbing my boots and jacket. Rol stepped back, and I checked it out. As far as I could tell, nothing was terribly unusual about the altar. The *goblet*, though, was another story. So were both bottles of mead.

"Um, Rol?" I asked. "Do *you* see this too?"

"See what..." he asked as that second word trailed off into a new word: "Oh."

"So you do."

"Yeah." His voice hardened. "That fucking bitch."

The goblet – or, more accurately, the bit of backwash *inside* the goblet – held a faint red sparkling glow. A cinnamon bite flowed through the honey-scented alcohol. The bottles held a bit of that glow too. I didn't need Detective Fallon to tell me what it was, but I grabbed the bottles anyway.

"Why didn't we notice that sooner?" Rol said as we headed for the door, then towards the stairway at the far end of the hall… the one we *were* least likely to run into Ash and Caroline on if they decided to come looking for us.

"From what I've read about this crap," I told him, pitching my voice low and leaning in toward Rol, "it's not visible unless you've had some of it first."

"Well," he said, glancing at the walls, which now glowed with weird arcane designs, "that explains a lot about this place."

"It does." I stopped at the top of the stairs to pull my boots on. I'd had enough barefooting for one night in the Bottle. For one *lifetime*, really. Troupe or no troupe, I didn't plan on coming back.

Because Rol was glowing a little bit too. And I *wasn't*.

And I didn't know what to *do* with that, except get the hell out of Dodge and try to sort through the puzzle-pieces later.

I wish I could say we had a peaceful walk back to the car, sobered up, and headed home. But that is *so* not what happened.

I JUST MIGHT SHOVE

‿ ‿ ‿

Rol puked up his own share of glowing red slime halfway down the final set of stairs. He'd been getting steadily *un*steady since we left the practice room, and by the time we hit the top of the last stairs between the building and the parking lot, he was glowing with a stronger shade of red.

"Hey, Rol," I whispered, afraid to be heard in the echoing stairwell, "have you looked at yourself lately?"

"Yeah," he breathed. "I'd kinda noticed that."

"You ever see it before tonight?"

"Nope."

"Wonderful." I headed down the stairs, still clinging to the handrail. I was far from steady myself. "I wonder what that means."

Rol bolted forward, and I kinda screamed like a little girl. But instead of grabbing *me*, he grabbed the handrail and this spectacular shower of shimmering goop burst out of his mouth as he sprayed the stairwell with what looked like pulped fairy juice under a black-light glow.

I heard voices at the top of the stairs. Near the bottom of them, too.

The music still pounded through the building's halls. Now, though, it seemed to carry a distinctly menacing air. Those voices sounded less like *voices* than like echoing chitters and childlike cries. Flapping, skittering, clacking sounds oozed from the hallway at the bottom of the stairs. "Um, Rol," I urged, "not like I want to hurry you along or anything, but our visa in this place may have just expired."

Rol hunched over, still clinging to the handrail.

"C'mon, buddy," I muttered, stepping up under his free arm, and taking on some of his weight. "You can throw up all over the parking lot but we really need to get out of here now." If things got bad, I had a hand-stunner and some mace in my jacket. How I had been stupid enough to leave them behind earlier was something I needed to sort out once I got us out of the Bottle and back to something remotely resembling safety. As we dragged ourselves down the remaining steps, however, I needed both hands to keep Rol from falling on his face. And given Rol's titanic mass, Mistress Gravity had become my least-best friend.

He'd begun to sweat glowing red crystals too, and Rol's skin was hot to the touch. His legs twitched as I manhandled him down the stairs. Above and behind us, the voices and sounds grew. I thought I heard boots and feet scuffling down both hallways toward us, and hissed affirmations that they'd catch up with us soon.

"Never leave a man behind," I kept repeating. "Never leave a man behind. Come *ON*, Roland – I am *not* leaving your saggy butt in this hellhole. Get a fucking *move* on, soldier, or I'll kick it all the way home."

"That," he mumbled, trailing some sparkly crimson drool, "would be *awesome*. I could use the rest."

"You're not getting out of PT *that* easily, boy." We were almost to the bottom of the stairs. "Now drop and give me 20."

"*Fuck* you, sir," he said, clearing his mouth with a resounding spit.

I watched the glittering red arc of spit hit the wall and congeal, my brain lacking a smart-ass response.

"What's coming for us?" he asked as I darted my head around back down the hallway.

That was a very good question.

From the sounds behind us, I had envisioned a horde of hellbeast critters, clacking their mandibles in preparation for their feast.

What I saw down the hallway creeped me out even more.

Aside for a few opened doors and some Bottleites chatting about God-knows-what, the hall was more or less empty.

In a material sense.

But in a shimmering haze that drifted on some plane I could tell was *not* part of material space, I saw a tangle of limbs, eyes, mouths, and other appendages out of an anime porn collection. The tangle sparkled with what I could tell was the *absence* of light, and the tendrils of grasping unholiness wavered in and out of my vision, flickering like the strobes downstairs through an array of dimensions that defied scientific classification.

And in a few of those eyes, as they looked at me, I thought I sensed something even more appalling than the thing itself:

Recognition.

My lizard-brain rolled up in a big ball and began to cry.

After what felt like a very long pause, I think I squeaked out something along the lines of "It's nice to see they didn't skimp on the special-effects budget this time out."

Then I grabbed Rol and we started trying to run.

∿ ∿ ∿

I did say *trying* to run. That's not exactly what we *did*. If you've ever been punched in the gut five or six times and then tried to do anything but crawl, you know what I mean. Oh, we *wanted* to run but our bodies did not cooperate. So we both tripped down the outside steps, hit the sidewalk, shoved ourselves into crouching balls of pain, and then lurched into the darkened parking lot with whatever-the-hell-that-was right behind us.

And in that grand betrayal of gravity and grace, I dropped the goddamned mead bottles, which shattered on the pavement.

Thank whatever gods happened to be having a laugh at our expense that night, neither one of us faceplanted in the broken glass. But my chance at getting the liquid analyzed, or of turning it over to Detective Fallon, went spilling as we stumbled upright and ran for our lives.

By that time, several more cars – a dozen, maybe, probably more – had been added to the parking lot. A few of the ones we had passed earlier were gone. Many of the spaces closest to the doors were full, and so Rol and I ducked behind those cars and weaved like heroes in an action movie, waiting for that pandimensional horror to bust through the door and start upending cars or something.

And nothing happened.

So we dodged behind some more cars, putting both bulk and distance between ourselves and that terrible *thing* we'd seen in the hallway.

And nothing happened.

Y'know how in a movie, there's always that moment where you expect something to happen and then it doesn't happen, and so the heroes relax their guard and *that's* when it happens?

We know that scene. Rol and I always see it coming when we watch a movie. So we did *not* relax our guard.

And *still* nothing happened.

So we started looking over our shoulders into the pitch-dark parking lot, lit on the fringes by the streetlights from a dozen blocks away and the faint sheen of starlight that makes everything look slick and shiny yet impenetrably black. We let our eyes adjust to the darkness and we motioned to one another and neither of us made a sound beyond our labored breathing and the muted scuffle of our boots.

And something happened.

I damn near screamed when a sudden buzzing stung my hip. Slamming my hand over my mouth, I realized that my cell phone – which I'd set to vibrate before we got inside – was processing messages. *Lots* of messages. At least eight from what I could guess once I figured out what the buzzing sensation was. Rol noticed me looking down, and shot me a *You okay?* look. I nodded and pointed to my belt-pouch, then mimed a cell phone by my ear. He nodded back, and then turned as the door to the Bottle opened and let the light spill through.

We both tensed, but it was just a group of laughing Bottleites coming through the door. Then we tensed again and started looking over our shoulders because of course *that's* when the monster gets you, usually from behind while you're looking at the distraction in front of you.

But even *then*, nothing. Not even the floating haze that we'd seen inside, oozing past the people in the doorway who now lit up joints or cigarettes and began smoking as they bullshitted about things we couldn't really hear.

And so, when the cramps in our bellies and legs and backs got to be too much to deal with, we scuttled off as far as we could go, stood up warily, and then headed back toward my car with as much forced casualness as we could manage.

Hazy dawn had started to trickle across the cloudy sky by the time we hit Maynard Street and returned to the welcome glow of streetlights and porchlamps. "Holy crap," I whispered, still not quite ready to talk louder than that, "we must have been down there a lot longer than we thought."

By now, Rol's glow had faded and we were both walking more or less like usual – a bit stooped over, thanks to our respective cramps, but able to stand up and move like two people who *hadn't* just spent a night in hell. I didn't know about Rol, but *my* energy was seriously depleted and my body protested vigorously about all the crap I'd just put her through.

"You check your phone yet?" Rol asked, his whisper rumbling in a subwoofer bass.

"Not yet," I replied, reaching for my pouch. "I don't think I really wanna know what time it is." At least we were both essentially sober by that point. The last thing we needed to top this night off was a drunk driving charge on the morning of my interview.

Fuck. The *interview.* I groaned. "I'm gonna need to get home once I drop you off, take a quick shower, and then go meet my lawyer to discuss things before we both meet up with Detective Fallon."

"I can't believe I'm saying this after last night," he said, "but you need more backup?"

"Nah," I assured him. "It's cool. Thanks."

"Good," he said, and left it at that.

I pulled my phone out of my belt-pouch. Turned it on. And stopped.

The world seemed to drop out from under me.

"What?" Rol asked, also stopping.

"No," I said. "This can't be right."

A wave of panic hit me and damn near knocked me over.

I tried to breathe, but my chest wouldn't move.

I felt my jaw fall open as I stared at the screen.

Yeah, there were reasons all those texts and messages had piled up.

It was almost 6:30 a.m.

Two days later.

DRINKING THOSE MOMENTS

∽ ∽ ∽

I don't normally do purses. Not since tenth grade, when I made the mistake every woman probably makes at least once in her life, and left my purse behind when I got up to do something and returned to find that it wasn't there anymore. Oh, sure, I *own* a few purses, but I don't use them unless I'm dressing up for something where a wide belt filled with pouches won't go down too well. Besides, what self-respecting action-heroine wears a *purse*, for God's sake? Does *Wonder Woman* have a purse?

Don't answer that.

Like I mentioned earlier, I wear belts with pouches on them. Get most of 'em from Crash, from Mata Hari Dancewear, or from places I shop at on the internet. Some are brown, most are black, and one's a deep dyed blue leather that goes beautifully with half my wardrobe. Right at that moment, there on the street with dawn starting to tinge the sky, I was *very* damned glad I'd worn my belt instead of a purse. Who knows what might have happened if I'd left a *purse* sitting in an open studio in the Bottle for two goddamned days.

Two goddamned days.

When had it happened? When did time slip out from under us and go running off on its own merry way, probably giving us the finger as it went? Did it happen when we drank the mead? During our wake for Blue? During the dance? In the basement? Did that thing in the hallway take us out of the normal flow of time while we stood there for what only seemed like seconds before running out the door? Was *the whole freaking Bottle* in a time-warp? And that thing we saw: Did it recognize me? Had there been more than one of it? Did it come up after us from the basement, or did I hear one behind us on the stairs as well? *Did EVERY FUCKING FLOOR have one of those things too?* Were they *always* there? Had they been *watching* us? Watching *me?* Watching us dance at practice, watching us hang out, talk, arrive, leave? Cold chills ripped through me: Had they watched us in the bathroom? I'd never *showered* there, but hey – everybody's gotta… I started shaking, and almost dropped my phone.

"What *is* it?" Rol insisted. "Genét, what's *wrong?*"

I hadn't told him yet.

How *do* you tell your friend that he just lost two days of his life for you?

My brain tipped over and started screaming down a corkscrew slide. All the puzzle-pieces in my head got swept off my mental table by a big black arm made of concentrated nothing. For some sense of solidity, I guess, I started fumbling with the pouches on my belt, making sure that everything was there. Car keys? Check. Wallet? Check. Phone? Obviously. Breath mints? Spare tampon?

I dropped my phone and the back cracked open and the battery went flying and I couldn't stop shaking and my stuff started jumping from my pouches like little suicides and hitting the ground and I couldn't stop digging and Rol was right near my face yelling "*GEN-AY! Reality check. What the hell is WRONG?*"

I knelt down to try and put my phone back together. He knelt down next to me. "Genét," he said, much softer but with a shiny edge of terror, "you're kinda freaking me out here. What did you see on your phone?"

"Oh, *Rol*," I groaned. "You better check yours, too."

He pulled his cell out of a pocket while I snapped the battery back in my own, closed it up, and clenched it tight, willing my hands to stop shaking. "Damn," he said. "The battery ran down. Knew I should have charged it before I left."

Crouching down, I put my head between my legs and forced air in and out of my open mouth. I tried to do some three-part yoga breathing but my body shook too hard. Inside my head, Trivia-Locker Brain was running around bashing into things, trying to make sense of the clearly impossible.

"*Underhill*," I heard myself say out loud between breaths. "We went Underhill."

For those of you who *haven't* spent most of your life reading fantasy books or thinking that faerie tales are cooler than cable TV, "Underhill" is an element of classic faerie tales and myths. In many stories, a hero goes literally underground in order to face some great challenge. Time stands still down there, or moves at a different rate than it does in the everyday world. It's the whole Rip van Winkle thing, except that instead of falling asleep and waking up years later, you go somewhere else and then come back from it days or months or even centuries later. I guess we were lucky to have only lost two days but that was still freaking my shit out.

It's one thing to read about that crap happening to Thomas the Rhymer, and another thing to have it happen to you.

"What are you talking about?" Rol asked. By now, that shiny edge in his voice was starting to glow. Rol *himself* had stopped glowing but he was clearly starting to pick up my freak-out in spite of his best efforts.

I turned my phone back on, and it did its little boot-up song-and-light show before going into start mode. By that point, I could breathe a little easier. "Rol," I told him eye-to-eye, "I am *so* sorry. I didn't mean for *this*."

"Mean for *what?*" Rol's voice dropped down to a barely audible rumble.

I took a deep breath. Held it. Let it go.

"Spit it out," he said.

"We were in there a long time."

"I noticed." By now, then dawn was obvious.

"I mean *long*."

"*How* long?"

I swallowed. "Two days."

Time hung there for few more seconds while he processed that.

"Two days?"

I nodded.

"You are shitting me." It was not a good sign, that voice, that expression. Rol didn't blink and there was no question-mark in those words.

I didn't blink either. Just looked him in the eyes.

So, kind of an important thing about Roland Castile: anger management is not among his superpowers. Anger is, though, and he's got lots of it to work with. Back during an especially bad scene in high school, I even thought he might have hit me if he'd had a shred less self-control. Instead, he'd bashed his knuckles bloody against a brick wall. And right then, outside the Bottle, there were no brick walls in sight.

I love Rol. As a friend, I mean. And I trust him. Usually. Right then, though, I was having visions of Black Widow in the Helicarrier right before Bruce Banner lost his shit.

"You. Are. Shitting. Me."

Very softly, I shook my head.

"*FUCK!!!!!!!*"

The shout knocked me back on my ass.

Rol was suddenly a million feet tall, towering over me, his arms locked in rigid angles, his head thrown back so far that all I could see was his throat and jaw as he screamed "*FUCK! FUCK!!! FAAAAAAAAAAAAAHHHHHHHHHK!!!!*"

"HEY! *SHADDAP*" some dude yelled from a nearby house. "*It's six o'clock in the goddamn morning.*"

"*FUCK you!*" Rol shouted in the general direction of that voice.

"Rol…" I said, trying to get to my feet.

"*Fuck you TOO, Genét.*" He spun down in my direction so fast I tipped over and fell back on the pavement again. "*Jesus fuck, TWO DAYS.*" He stamped his boots dangerously close to my own. "Uncle Tim is gonna *kill* me. My *boss* is gonna kill me! I'm probably gonna get *fired*, and *YOU…*" He lunged in again, and I swear I felt a fist whoosh past my face, but my eyes were closed and I couldn't tell for sure. "You fucking owe me, fucking *owe* me, fucking *OWE ME.*"

"*GREAT!*" Now it was my turn to yell. Before I even realized what was happening, I was up on my feet, eyes open, my face a few inches from his own. The adrenaline slam threw me into fight mode. If he was gonna hit me, I was gonna go all Warrior Fitness on his ass. "*Great,*" I repeated, "I fucking *OWE you.* So what, you gonna *hit* me, hero? You lost two days and you're gonna take it out on me? *I* lost two days *too,* motherfucker, and if you don't get out of my *face* about it, I'm gonna kick you into next *week!*"

"I'm calling the *cops,* you little psychos. Calling them right *now.*" Lights were on in windows, I noticed suddenly, and I saw several shapes behind the curtains, looking out.

Rol held himself in check with everything he had left to give. My heart pounded out a speed-metal double-kick inside my chest. My fists were ready to go, and Trivia-Locker Brain suggested a few minor adjustments to my stance, just in case one of us took a swing.

But neither one of us did.

"Police are on their way," said a calm woman's voice from a nearby window. "And you hit that young woman, kid, I'm gonna kick your ass myself."

"I'm not hitting *anybody,*" Rol said, lowering his arms like he was setting down two cars he'd been holding up.

I eased back, rippling with adrenaline shakes, still shifting my weight in case Rol or someone else made another unexpected move. In my entire life, I'd never been so close to that edge before. Sure, my brother and sister and best friend have tempers, but *never*, until that moment, had I seriously thought I would get hit by someone who could hurt me outside of sparring or a mosh pit. Rol's anger scared me. *My* anger scared me more.

"Let's get outta here," I told him, "before this whole thing gets any worse than it already is."

By the time I'd collected my stuff off the pavement and we'd both walked off enough adrenaline to get anywhere near one another, I had apologized to Rol about a dozen times and he'd apologized once or twice to me. The shapes still lingered near their windows, but no one else yelled or made a move as we vacated the premises and speed-walked into the rising dawn.

I didn't hear sirens, for which I was profoundly grateful, although a cop-car *did* slide past where we would have been if we'd stuck around to chat.

The rest of the neighborhood woke up and got ready for work while we walked the remaining distance to my car in silence. We didn't see any more cop cars, and no one stopped to question us.

Monday morning. Damn. I needed coffee, a shower, and a new life.

I had a lot of calls to make. Lots of excuses to make, too.

As we walked, I ran through the list, tried to decide what to tell them, and came up blank.

NOT LIKE I NEED
TO DEPEND UPON ANYONE

ꙮ ꙮ ꙮ

Over his objections, I drove Rol home. We didn't talk much at first, although we still managed to snap at each other about whose fault the whole mess was.

"You knew it was a trap," he said. "So why'd you go there at all?"

"I *didn't* know," I insisted.

"You *thought* it might be. That's what you called me for."

"And you were supposed to have my back."

"I *did* have your back. Who got you out of that basement?"

"*After* we both got plastered and did God-only-knows what."

"I still got you out of there," he huffed, his arms crossed tight across his chest. "Had to haul you over my shoulder *and* you almost puked down my fucking back."

"Well," I said, glaring straight ahead into Monday morning traffic, "don't fireman's-carry the drunk girl."

"How the fuck *else* was I supposed to get you out of there?"

I banged the steering wheel in frustration. "*I don't KNOW.* Why did we even *get* that far in the first place?"

"'Cause you were fucking *ripped.*"

"*You* were fucking ripped *too.*" I turned to face him, which might not have been my wisest move. "Why were *you* drinking, Rol?"

He crossed his arms tighter. "*I* don't know. It seemed to be the thing to do at the time."

I snorted and turned back to the road – a good thing, too, given how close one car almost came to sideswiping us. Leaning on the horn felt good. "Stupid fuck," I snarled at the departing car.

"Don't worry," he said. "I'm not doing anything like that for you again."

"*Good,*" was the only thing I could think of to say, which was stupid and childish and we both knew it.

"I'm sorry," I said about a block later. "I'm being a total bitch to you, and you don't deserve it."

"You're right," Rol said. "I *don't.*"

"You don't."

"And," he said about a block after that, "*you* don't deserve me acting like a total ragehead dick. I'm sorry about your friends, and I'm really sorry about me back there."

"It's okay."

"Thanks."

"So," Rol said about two blocks after *that*, "did we just have our big bonding scene back there, or what?"

"Probably."

"There's *totally* a theme-song going right now."

"No question."

"It better not be Nickelback."

"It's *totally* Nickelback."

"Fuck you."

"Fuck you too."

By the time we got our anger out of the way, we'd both realized that each of us had lost sight of the plan after we got in the room with Ashley and Caroline. "They played the hell out of us," Rol insisted, and while I was willing to be a bit more sympathetic to Ash's pain, Caroline had spiked the goddamned mead and gotten us to join her. Ash probably *knew* about that too, and didn't stop either us or Caroline from doing what we did.

I swear, I was gonna kill them both.

Between the walk, the traffic, and us working out our stuff, it was nearly 9:30 when I dropped Rol off at his uncle's place and headed back home myself. I had yet to return those phone-calls and texts, because I knew it would take hours and I was dreading every minute of them. The sheer weight of tiredness pushed me down in my seat. That restless sensation of Wrongness continued to crawl under my skin. I hurt just to *think* about how much I'd put my body through that week, and although my brain was functioning on an essentially rational plane, the things I had on my mind were anything *but* rational.

As I drove, I tried to sort out the pieces and then gave up. Too many of them kept changing shape and size and color when I looked at them too hard. Somewhere along the line, reality as I knew it had been warped. I couldn't figure out exactly how or where, but Red Shoes, the Bottle, and that weird scene in the basement had been parts of it.

Was our group-hugs moment in the studio *supposed* to have been a trap? Were Ash and Caroline sincere? Did Caroline dope those bottles of mead – maybe even the water too – to muddy up the trail back to Blue's OD? Or was all of it meant as a sincere tribute to Blue, however warped it might have been? God, had *all three of them* been doing Red Shoes without us knowing about it? And gee whilickers, let's just open up the paranoia door and ask ourselves if Inky and Vivienne were doing it too. Was I the only one in Arcana Darque who *wasn't?* Was *that* why they drugged me? Were they trying to kill me before I could talk to the cops?

God, another headache was setting in. As I eased myself out of my car, my belly cramped again as I stood up and closed the door.

I did some mental calculations. My period wasn't supposed to start for another week or so, and so even with the two-day loss, the cramping couldn't come from *that*… I hoped. I thought about Rol spewing up the glowing goop on the stairwell, and kicked myself for not asking him why *he'd* been glowing too. Did that junk have a half-life in our bodies… and if so, then how *much* of one? *Crap,* I though, *would it show up on a drug test?* And if so, what would it show up *as?* The more I thought about the whole mess, the messier it became. And none of that was handling my phone-calls, a shower, or my first meal after a two-day fast.

Piece by piece, I told myself. *Sort it out piece by piece. You don't need to finish the whole damn puzzle right now. Take care of what needs taking care of most.*

And so, I tromped up the stairs to Inanna, our apartment, a shower, and my bed.

One sandwich, one shower, and a multitude of petting later, I was texting Mom and Dad to let them know I was okay. *Lost weekend,* I told them both. *Will explain later.* Exactly *how* I was gonna explain that remained to be seen, but I had other urgent business to attend to. A quick phone-call to Crash settled things with Rose. *Sorry,* I told her, *I was so sick that I literally fell asleep all weekend and missed my alarms.* No, not partying – a flu or something. I didn't think I had been contagious on Thursday night, but if she or anyone else on the floor started feeling woozy, then get thee to an urgent-care clinic and I'll probably see you tomorrow. Yes, I'll call if I'm still feeling sick, and yeah I might still need a day or two more to recover. Grateful that I didn't have an ogre for a boss (especially now since I might have had a better understanding of what an ogre might actually *look* like in real life), I hung up and took a deep breath as I scrolled to Frank's number and returned his three calls from the weekend.

"Thank you for calling the offices of Archer, Chambers Law Group…"

"Peggy, it's Genét."

"Oh, my *God,*" she said, pitching her professional veneer out the office window, "I'm glad to hear your voice. Mr. Chambers will be glad too." She paused. "*Please* tell me you're not in jail."

"Nope," I admitted, "although this morning, that was kind of a near thing."

"Do I want to know?"

"I'm not sure how to explain it just now. Is Frank around?"

She laughed. "So it's *Frank*, now. He *must* be working for you."

"Just honoring a family tradition, or so I hear."

"He's *not* here, unfortunately. Court this morning, and another case this afternoon."

I grimaced. "I sort of figured that. Oh, well. Could you please let him know I'm all right, I'm not in trouble… not yet, anyway… and I'll be *very* glad to talk to him when he has time available for me?"

"I will," she said. "Stay *out* of trouble." The smile I thought I heard on that last bit was only half joking, and I knew it.

"I'm trying," I told her even though I was lying and we probably both knew it. "Thank you, Peggy. I appreciate it."

"It sounds like you need some sleep," she said.

"God." I laughed. "That obvious, huh?"

"Get some rest, Genét."

"I have that somewhere on my schedule. And thanks again."

"No problem, kiddo. Have a nice nap."

Okay, time for Detective Fallon.

Stalling for time, I left a note for Kristen on her door. I had already texted her as well but wanted to leave some proof that I was home and safe. Holding Inanna's purring little form, I paced around our living room, trying to sort out just *what* I was gonna tell Detective Fallon that wasn't going to start World War III. If I came clean about the Bottle, she'd have a SWAT team up there, ready for God-knows-what, and who knew what kind of a shitstorm *that* would turn into? Did the Bottleites have guns? If they *did*, would they use them against cops? And what about the dimension-floating horrorshow Rol and I had seen? The thought of cops facing down that thing from the hallway… or worse, having to face down *four or five of them*… on *my* say-so, no less… made me bury my fingertips in fur and snuggle for dear life. I felt the shakes in my shoulders again, and willed myself to *not* crush the poor cat in my nervousness. For Inanna's part, she simply closed her eyes and purred. Our little goddess of the Underworld.

And *then* there was the basement: the Underhill where I… and *Rol*, too, I reminded myself… had left two days of our lives behind. How could I even begin to explain to Detective Fallon that time worked differently there – maybe differently in the whole Bottle, for all I knew. Thinking back on it, I realized that my cell phone had not vibrated until after we reached the parking lot. So did that mean that time hung suspended in the Bottle? That *couldn't* be true, though. We had been practicing there for ages, and while I could see an hour or two moving differently, we would have *noticed* something more drastic than that. So probably the basement, then. Okay, so was it *what* we did, *when* we did it, who we did it *with*, what we did it *on* when we did it, or some weird combination of the above? And why did the people who run the Bottle let those *things* loose to do who-knew-what? Did they even know about them… and yet, how could they *not*, especially if Red Shoes was their common drug of choice? Did they make Red Shoes in the basement? Was that time-slip a by-product of the process, like explosions in a meth-cooker's place? Why did it *glow?* Why didn't we see it glow *sooner?* And why was *Rol* glowing too? God, where did I even start to figure out what I *could* and could *not* tell Detective Fallon? Just thinking about it made me want to lie down and sleep till it all went away.

Topping off the shit-sundae was Rol, my friend whose understandable anger issues nearly caved my face in. *Did* he try to hit me? I wasn't sure. If his fist *had* connected with me, though, I'd be in an ER if not the morgue. Stepping back from the big guy who essentially liked me, Rol was a huge, angry, dangerously unstable dude whose innate decency did not mean he wouldn't put me in a coma and feel bad about it later. If he *had* hit me… I didn't want to think about what that would translate into in terms of foot-pounds per square inch and their long-term effects on me. Or on *him*, for that matter. Pixels may bleed, but they don't go to prison or spend the rest of their lives eating through a straw. I'd been taking my safety, and Rol's stability, for granted. I couldn't do that anymore.

Oh, and just for extra flavor, my brain tossed in the reality that I had just lost two days – *two goddamned days* – that I would never see again, without even realizing I had lost them. If I was the get-drunk type, I would really have wanted a drink.

After that night, though, I wasn't sure I would ever drink again.

My thoughts chased their tails for at least an hour when the irony of losing more time over the experience of losing time hit me between the eyes. *Okay, Jennifer,* I thought, *if you just had an inexplicable and apparently supernatural experience, and you don't know how to explain it, or who you can talk to about it without getting laughed off or touching off a catastrophe, who do you call to talk to about it?*

Meghan. Solid choice.

So I did.

BE THE CHILD WHO
SPEAKS THE TRUTH

ᔕ ᔕ ᔕ

Hola rock star! How goes the open road?"

"Hey, Nay!" One of Meghan's many nicknames for me involves rhyming something with the second part of my adopted name. "What's *up*, danger-girl?" I'd caught her in a good mood, then – bantering, not sullen. With Meg, you're not always sure which side of her you're gonna get.

"Oh, *Gohhhhhhd*." My groan grated like a rusty hinge. "It has been unbelievable. *Literally* unbelievable."

"I kinda figured that," she said in a more serious tone. I could hear the whooshing sound of air around the frame of the Black Swan: an appropriately painted Safari that served as her band's transport, lodgings, and mobile argument facility. Someone else had to have been driving, because Meg doesn't risk the Swan or her spotty driver's record by chatting on the phone while she's at the wheel. "Anybody give you a hard time?"

"You have no fucking idea."

"Who was it? Who do I need to kill when I get back?" It was always that phrase: *when I get back*. Not *when I get home*. She already *was* home. Riverhaven, for Meg, is "back," not forward.

"No one," I assured her. "No one on your list, anyway. The ones I spoke to so far have been helpful, mostly." I paused, a mild surge of PTSD shaking my head at the memory what might have been Rol's fist hissing past my face. "Especially Rol," I added to be fair to what he *had* done, and what he'd given up, in order to help me so far.

"Good." She barked a laugh. "I'd have to hurt him otherwise."

The image of tiny Meghan hurting massive Rol would be funnier if they didn't both have such awful tempers.

"*Hey, Genét.*" Thunderdome's jovial roar came from somewhere off to Meghan's side, muffled by the distance and my friend's thick curtain of hair. "Do I need to fire up my dad's woodchipper yet?"

"Not *yet*, Thunderdome," I said, loud enough to be heard through the speaker. "Though I'm sure I can arrange something by the time y'all get back."

"Eyes on the *road*, T," said Meghan. She's got a funny way of ordering around guys who could break her in half, and they have a funny way of listening when she does.

"Sure, Boss." I heard the car accelerate, and sent the proverbial silent prayer that their road would be clear of cops. "Later, Genét," he yelled. "Be good!"

"Never," I responded. In the background, I could half-hear greetings from Tucker and Max as well. "Tell everyone," I told Meg, "I say hello back."

She did, then returned to me and her serious tone. "So what happened?" she said.

And again, I told her. All of it, especially the parts I wasn't sure I believed.

"Wow," she said when I'd finished. "That's… *wow*."

"Uh-huh," I agreed. "Any ideas what I'm supposed to *do* with all that? Especially the part that involves talking to a detective who probably comes with her own techno-cosmic bullshit detector?"

"*That* is a *very* good question," she said, clearly thinking through the various awful possibilities. "So, how much do you trust your lawyer?"

"He's been with my family since pretty much ever. I know he's gotten my dad out of some really nasty situations." Yeah – with Homeland Security, the FBI, Microsoft and Disney, for starters, and through more encounters with the Riverhaven PD than either of my siblings would be willing to admit in court.

"Yeah, but can you trust him with *this?*"

"I honestly don't know, Meg." Like I said earlier, magic was kinda off the table as far as my parents were concerned. There's cool parenting, and then there's wrapping your kid up nice and snug while the nice folks from Psycho Services come to pick her up for you. Could I trust *Frank* with this stuff? Arg. I wasn't sure I wanted to test the boundaries of "serious imminent danger" where my family might be concerned.

I think she heard the stress in my voice, 'cause Meg's voice dropped to just low enough to me to hear. "It's cool, Genét. It's cool. We'll figure it out." She paused. "Hey, I just thought of something."

"Yeah?"

"Did you see that hentai-thingie in the hallway actually hurt anybody?"

I thought about it. "Um, no."

"Did it touch anything? I mean, like knock anything over or open doors or anything like that?"

"No. Definitely not. We kept expecting it to come after us, but it never went through the door."

"So what if you *didn't* see it?" Meghan said. "What if it was the shit in your system, or some kind of illusion, or maybe even a watchdog sort of thing – y'know, just set up to *scare* people into leaving?"

"That's…" I thought about it. "I *hadn't* thought of that, actually."

"I'm not saying it *was*," she put in. "I mean, it *could* have been some eight-dimensional killer beast. But if it didn't hurt anything, and it didn't chase you, then the odds are good that it wasn't actually a physical threat to you."

"So it's basically harmless."

She laughed. "I didn't say *that*, dummy! There's all kinds of stuff out there that can fuck your shit up forever without ever touching you physically."

"Comforting."

"Yeah, I know. *Especially* when there's magic involved, which I have no doubt there is." She chewed on that for a second. "Did you get hold of Corwyn and Dia yet? They know a lot more about this stuff than I do."

"Out of town. Will Dervish do?"

She chuckled "Dervish would do fine."

"What do *you* think it was, Meghan?"

"Huh." I heard that whooshing sound in the background as she considered it. Thunderdome and Max were debating where to stop for dinner. Dinner? Crap. Okay, I realize that Meg was in a different time zone, but still time was slipping past me a little too fast for my comfort. Or sanity. Or whatever. I glanced at my phone. 2:45. Damn. And I hadn't even taken a nap yet. How the hell was I still on my feet? Even *without* the two-day time loss, I'd still been awake for over 24 hours, body-time. No wonder I felt so fried.

My phone buzzed. Incoming call. I checked the number: Detective Fallon. *Fuck.*

"Um, Meg? I've got an incoming."

"Who?"

"Detective Fallon."

"Don't answer it yet."

Adrenaline began surging in my chest again, locking everything down and speeding everything up. "I can't just keep blowing her *off*, Meg. What if she's got people watching my house?"

"Your parents' house?"

I slapped my head. "*No.* I mean my apartment house. What if they *know* I'm home and she's calling to *check* on me because *she knows I have to answer?*" My voice was rising just a little. Like as in, actually a lot.

"Shhhhh…" Meg's voice soothed me through the phone. "It's *okay*, Nay. You're *fine*. You're cool. You didn't do anything *wrong*. She's not watching you."

I closed my eyes. The phone buzzed some more. "God, I'm really going paranoid, huh?"

"Kinda, yeah – but you've got a right to."

She talked me down a little more as the call went to voicemail and my heart slowed down to somewhere approximating a vigorous run.

"Okay," Meg said eventually, "Here are some ideas. Now, I have no idea how right or wrong I actually am. I'm no expert on any of this."

"You know more than I do."

I heard her smile. "That ain't much."

"*Tell* me about it."

"I will."

She did.

According to Meghan's best guesses, Rapey McTentacle-Thing might be one of several different what she called *manifestations*:

Maybe it was exactly what we thought it was: Some sort of whack-ass demonic thing from an H.P. Lovecraft fever-dream. In that case, we were well and truly fucked, and *very* lucky to have gotten out of there with our sanity and health intact.

On the total flipside, it could have been a delusion brought on by Red Shoes, hard dancing, mind-fatigue, and several days' worth of lost food and sleep. In which case, it never existed to begin with.

In between those possibilities, it could have been a few other things: a cross-dimensional entity with no physical substance but an existence on a plane (or series of planes) that only certain people could see, and maybe then only certain conditions; a living warp in time and space; an illusion whipped up to freak people out if they'd been naughty as far as the folks in the Bottle were concerned; an essentially non-aggressive critter conjured up to protect the place; a seriously elaborate holographic projection; a *psychic* projection of the place itself, bred by the mental energies of the people who lived and partied in the Bottle; or… well, *Other*, in which case we had no fucking clue what it was.

Oh, and those possibilities were not mutually exclusive, either.

Joy.

"How do you *live* with this, Meghan?" I asked her when she got done running through the list.

"Live with what?"

"With the idea that the things you just told me could be real."

"Because I *had* to, Genét. Because they *are*." Her voice got that sad, stubborn tone she has when she talks about her asshole dad or her missing mom, or the way club-owners will fuck over a band if and when they can get away with it. "I've been living with it most of my life, and you've *seen* some of that first-hand."

"Yeah," I admitted. "Does it help if I say I've been trying to forget that part?"

"Not really, no," Meg said, her own voice a little tighter than I think she might have meant it to be. "It doesn't go away just because you want it to. Believe me, I tried that door already." And I knew *that* part already, too. She and I had talked a lot about some of the weird trips her head would go off on sometimes. From the tone in her voice, though, I got the impression there was still a lot she'd never told me.

Does it make sense that that realization kinda hurt my feelings? But then, I reminded myself, how good would I have been at listening if she *had* told me that stuff before now? If I was having trouble accepting it when the proof was splattered all over *my* life, how could I have possibly accepted it when it was only splattered all over *Meg's?*

Wow, I thought, *I'm a really shitty friend.*

I think the tears came from me being so damn tired. Seriously, I do.

"Okay, Meg," I told her once we'd gotten my head screwed back together again, "I need to go grab some food, and you need to get back to your band and go grab some food yourselves."

By that point, we had an action plan: Contact Detective Fallon and let her know that I was okay but needed to report being dosed. I wasn't thrilled about the idea of narcing out Caroline and Ashley, but Meg convinced me that *not* reporting it would make me look like I was covering for them. Rol should be left out if things if possible. He had a record, and things wouldn't go well with him if and when the cops came calling. All the same, I shouldn't lie about him either – that would go even worse. If I could get hold of Frank before the interview, great. I might wind up being implicated in Blue's death, especially if they told me to take a drug test and found Red Shoes in my system. That's the *other* reason I needed to come clean about being roofied: chances were good that the cops already had autopsy results, and if there was Red Shoes in Blue's system (which was pretty much a given), then there's no way I *wouldn't* look bad if I didn't report getting dosed with the same junk without my knowledge or consent.

Have I mentioned yet how Caroline and Ash were *so* at the top of my shit list?

Okay, leave out dimension-crawling demons unless I was specifically asked about them. As for the two lost days, well… I'd been dosed and there wasn't anything metaphysical about losing two days to *that*. *Oh, God*, I thought, *they're probably gonna want me to take a rape-kit test too, if they think I got drugged and lost time as a result.* That idea appealed to me about as much as the thought of facing the Hall-Thing with a toothbrush and some spit, but it was probably inevitable and not entirely a bad idea. By that point, I hadn't had consenting sex with anyone in months, and if I'd had *un*consenting sex recently, then I would damn sure want to know about *that*, too.

"And now," my friend told me, "go and get some food and sleep. But don't forget to make those calls first."

"You too, Meg. And hey…"

"Yeah?"

"Thanks for putting up with my clueless ass."

She chuckled. "Thanks for all the years you put up with *mine*."

"Friends are *for*," I said.

"Friends are *for*," she agreed.

My feet were kinda raw from dancing on the concrete, so I slipped on some furry mocs as I went into the kitchen for late lunch. Inanna got her usual offerings, plus a little extra for having played the part of my furry worry-beads. In the process, I called Detective Fallon back.

"Hello, Detective," I said, keeping my voice as light as possible.

"Genét," she said, her own voice even. "Good to hear from you. I was starting to get concerned."

CAGED BY FRAIL AND
FRAGILE BARS

∾ ∾ ∾

Cops speak in capital letters. Even when they're not actually talking, police officers cultivate an aura of authority. I get that – I mean, with their jobs, that authority is literally a matter of life and death. Officer Friendly can't *afford* to be your friend, y'know? And so, when I heard Detective Fallon's voice on the other end of my phone, I heard Capital Letters and Cultivated Authority in all its glory. I'm not saying that she was being mean or cold or condescending or anything like that; if anything, her voice was kind. Even so, her kind voice radiated Capital-A Authority, and I wound up apologizing before she'd given me a reason to apologize. "I'm sorry to have not gotten back to you sooner, Detective Fallon. I was just…" I caught myself. "Things came up."

"I had figured as much," she said, her voice offering a sort of faux-maternal softness. "What happened? Are you all right?"

"I'm…" I tried to picture this conversation as a puzzle, with every sentence forming a piece fitting into the right place to create a picture of *my* choosing, not hers. That's harder than it sounds, especially when you're making it up off the top of your head and the consequences of getting things wrong are pretty much unthinkable. "I'm more or less okay," I finished. "I'm still trying to sort it all out."

She made a soothing sound. "You've been through a lot, Jennifer."

"Genét," I told her. "I prefer to be called Genét."

"As in Jean Genét, the French absurdist playwright?"

"Oh, you're good."

She laughed. It's weird, hearing a cop laugh like that. "*The Balcony* is an old favorite of mine. I had a teacher in high school who favored avant-garde theatre, so we learned about Genét and Ionesco and Albee and so on." Detective Fallon let loose with a low, shadowed chuckle. "Ms. Marx probably should have been fired for the stuff she taught us, but I thought it was wonderful."

Fired teacher. I wonder if she'd intended to open that door for me. Probably had, yeah. Several of our teachers had gotten fired during the bad old days in high school. Detective Fallon had to have known about that, so I wondered if I was being offered a great big hook wrapped in a pretense of confidentiality. If I was *right*, that told me a lot about who I was dealing with.

"I know that feeling," I said, laying down that piece to see what the picture looked like. "I had a few teachers like that. One of 'em even got fired for teaching us a little too much."

"What did that feel like, Genét? To have him fired like that?" Now she's talking like a therapist? I felt like she was switching the game from puzzles to chess.

"It didn't feel like anything," I lied. "He wasn't my teacher." I let her hear me smile. "And I hadn't said anything about the teacher being a 'him.'"

A slight pause. Then, "Not bad, young Jedi. Not bad at all." A geek-culture reference, too. Detective Fallon had done her homework on me.

"Am I a suspect, Detective Fallon?"

"Should you be?"

"No. And the video should tell you as much." I heard myself getting annoyed in spite of my effort to stay calm. "So why are you treating me like one?"

"How do you mean? We were just talking."

"Detective Fallon," I said, more self-righteously than I really wanted to sound. "If you've done as much checking up on me as you're trying to show me you've done, then you know I'm not stupid."

"That's true, Genét. You're not."

"And so I have to assume that you're dropping little clues to me to find out just *how* stupid I'm not."

"Very astute."

"So *why?* Why, if I'm not a suspect, are you testing me like this?"

This time, I think she let me hear *her* smile. Kinda like a shark, or a cat with an especially fat and stupid mouse. "Because, Genét, if you're as smart as you seem to be, and you've watched as many cop shows as I suspect you probably have watched, then you know that *everyone's* a suspect and every bit of information matters."

We both let that sink in for a moment.

"And *that*," I said, "is why I want my lawyer present when we meet up."

"That's wise," she replied. "Not because you're in trouble, but because we have no ideas where these sorts of conversations will take us."

"True." All of a sudden, I felt so cold that the one little word was all I could say. The ramifications of every potential wrong word seemed to rush in to tackle me. I needed to get hold of Frank again.

"So…?" she continued. "Have you contacted your lawyer again since 'things came up'?"

"I have, yes." This time, I kept my tone as level as I could. "He's in court right now, but I'll let you know as soon as I have an answer about his availability."

"Thank you," she said. "And in the meantime, Genét?"

"Yes?" I felt layers of meaning behind her half-question.

"Don't try to find out any more answers on your own. I don't want to be investigating *your* death, too."

After a terse sign-off with Detective Fallon, I made sure my door was locked and then stretched out on my bed. Outside the door, Inanna mewed with boredom, but as much as I wanted to snuggle up with a furball about then, I also needed to feel safe and secure *somewhere*, and nowhere felt quite safe.

If this had been a movie or something, I'd have had dreams filled with burning bodies, floating clouds of eyes, or something else of great significance.

But I didn't. I just fuzzed out to the sound of Inanna mewing, and was out of commission until long after dark.

∿ ∿ ∿

I'd turned my phone's ringer off so that I'd be able to sleep. As usual, though, I left it on vibrate and set my hand on top of it, which is why I finally woke up right around 9:00 p.m. to the insistent buzz underneath my hand. "Hello?" My voice cut a rusty rasp through my remaining sleep. "Who's this?"

"Genét," came Kristen's voice. "Oh, good – you're okay. I was just checking in."

"Where are you?"

"In the living room, where I've been for the last few hours, hoping you were okay in there behind that locked door."

"Huh?" I said, trying to piece my foggy brain back together. "Oh, yeah... sorry. I just really needed to sleep."

"I figured that." By now, I could also hear her voice echoing up the hallway through my door, a weird stereo effect where the physical soundwaves reached me a little bit after their electronic simulations. "Well, when you're ready, we have pizza."

"Oh, cool," I said, belting a robe on over my T-shirt and underwear. Kris and I are casual, but not *that* casual. "Thanks for grabbing that."

"No problem," she said as I stepped through the door and got both the electronic voice and the physical one at roughly the same time. "I thought you'd need some food whenever you'd had your beauty sleep."

"Sleeping Beauty," I said to her in person, shutting off the phone and unable to resist the faerie-tale reference after the last few days of weirdness. "That's me."

A large Garlic Jim's meat-lover special turned our living room into an olfactory substitute for a girls' night out. My mouth immediately informed me that a substantial tribute was owned to my taste-buds and stomach for three days of deprivation, minus one quick sandwich and a scattered late lunch. Kris and I dug in while I hashed out a mouth-filled summation of what had happened, withholding the part where Rol might have tried to deck me. I didn't want Kris to feel unsafe with Rol if and when he wound up coming over again for movie night. Besides, I sort of thought that losing two days of your life to a friend's weird errand might actually be an understandable justification for trying to take said friend's head off at the shoulders. I was gonna have to keep an eye out for more of that sort of thing, and drop Rol hard if I needed to, but in that one case I thought maybe he deserved a little slack from me. So I left that moment out of the account. The rest of the story, though – including the bit where I saw Hastur Jr. floating after us – I left intact.

"Well," she finally said as we picked at the pizza bones, "I will never accuse you of having a boring life, Genét. *Ever.*"

"You're taking this remarkably well."

"No, I'm kinda freaking out inside. I just know how to keep a straight face while I do it."

"What about? The time-eating monsters part?"

"No," she said a bit more forcefully. "The part where my roommate gets roofied by her friends and winds up seeing understandably weird shit during a three-day bender at the Bottle." She leaned forward. "And you are *so* not going back there again. If I have to sit on you and tie you down, you're *not*."

"No," I said, waving her back down. "I'm not. Right now, I'm just trying to figure out what I *am* doing."

"Well, first off, you're telling the detective that Caroline and Ashley dosed you. That's some serious shit. It could have gone a lot worse than it did." She frowned. "Are you sure you didn't have… um… that you weren't…?"

"Molested?" I added. "Yeah, that had occurred to me." Given the skeezy sensations rippling all over my skin even now, I wasn't 100% sure I *hadn't* been. "But no, I really don't think it happened, thank God."

She looked distinctly relieved. "You're sure?"

"Um… *ish?* I wasn't missing any clothes. My belt was still on. No one took anything. I checked. Phone, money – everything's the way I left it. Hell, no one even stole my jacket while the studio door was open…" I frowned too. "That's weird."

"What's that?" she asked.

"The studio," I said, sitting up and arranging pizza crests so that I had something to do with my hands as I talked. "Ashley left the boombox playing. It was still playing when Rol and I got back there."

"Was it a CD? Maybe it was set to repeat."

"No. It started out with a CD, but then Caroline hooked up her phone to it."

"So it was a long playlist. Or she just set it to play everything on her phone."

"No." I shook my head. "It *was* a playlist – I remember that much. And still… Kris, have you ever *been* to the Bottle?" I realized as I said it that I'd noted a few stray pieces falling into place. "I mean, it's not exactly Larceny Central, but I just can't see a room standing open for *two whole days*, with music playing and a boombox and cell phone and a jacket and a bunch other of stuff just sitting there in plain sight and *nobody* coming in to steal it… hell, not even to mess with it."

"Well, you said they were all still in the basement, right?"

"Not *everybody*. Lots of people, sure, but not every person in the building. Not for two whole days."

"Yeah." She sat back, thinking. Inanna butted her head into Kris's hand, and Kristen stroked our little fuzzball's face. "That *does* sound weird, even for that place."

"I saw a few people out in the hallways when we left," I went on. "And nobody seemed interested in the open door. Other doors were open, too, and no one was sneaking around trying not to get caught."

"Maybe they know better than to fuck around with other people's stuff." Kris grimaced. "I mean, if there's a gang running the Bottle, it would make sense that there's also a big '*Hands off or else*' rule in place over there."

"True…" Something else was nagging at me. Then I got it: "The *candles*."

"What candles?"

"The ones in the room." I got to my feet and started pacing. "If we'd been gone two whole days, then the candles would have burned out long before Rol and I got back to the room. But they didn't – they were still burning when we got back. Melted down a bit, I mean, but they hadn't gone out. And in two lost days, they *would* have!"

"Maybe Caroline replaced them. I mean, there's a *lot* you don't remember."

I thought about it, then shook my head. "No. Like I said, everything was all where I remembered it being. If we'd been in and out of the room over those two days, things would have been different just because we'd been there."

"How do you know they *weren't* different?" Kristen's head swiveled to keep track of me. "I mean, you're smart and all, but last I knew you don't have a photographic memory."

"I think if four intoxicated people were living in a room for a day or two, that place would look a *lot* different than it did."

"Than you *remember* it looking."

"Point taken. Still…" I sat back down again. "It doesn't *feel* like that's what happened."

"Are you sure," Kris said with a softer and more sympathetic voice, "that maybe you just don't *want* to think otherwise?"

"*Jeeze*, Kris – I thought you were supposed to be my *friend*."

"I *am* being your friend," she said, leaning forward to touch my arm. "I just want to make sure you're not making some sort of *X-Files* episode out of being drugged at a party."

I shot a side-eye in her general direction. "*X-Files*? Retro, much?"

She gave me the patented Kris-Kitty Glare. "You know what I meant."

"Yeah," I admitted. "And thanks. I'm just trying to sort it all out in my head."

"That's not surprising." Kris got up, looked to me for approval, then came and sat down next to me, squeezed me tight, and then let go and sat back where she'd been sitting. "That's fair. I'm just looking out for my girl."

"I know. And I appreciate it." We both looked at the pizza box and its pillaged remnants of delicious bonding. "This is a lot to sort through."

We made a decent amount of non-crucial small talk for another hour or so while Kris confirmed that I wasn't in denial about being raped and I assured myself that I wasn't out of my fucking mind. Eventually, we hugged our goodnights and headed off to our respective dens, Innna trailing Mommy to her room.

I wanted to grab some extra sleep, but the various pieces of puzzle kept spinning around in my head, trying to reorient themselves into a pattern that made more sense than a time-stopping drug-haven where people caught on fire if they weren't being eaten by pandimensional cloud-critters.

I texted Caroline and Ash. To exactly zero of my surprise, neither one answered.

I texted Rol too. *You OK?*

More or less. Didn't get fired.

Good.

Uncle Tim's pissed. If I was younger, I'd be grounded.

Sorry, Rol. I apologize for getting you into that.

In bed now. sleep.

Uncertain about whether he was saying that he was asleep or that I should go to sleep, I took his advice. *Night,* I texted him. He did not text back.

Outside, I heard rain start up again as my thoughts slowly chased themselves to sleep.

ADRENALINE NIGHTSHIFT

～ ～ ～

I woke up around 4:00 a.m. Outside, the rain seethed against the trees, walls and windows. Inside, I felt like I was vibrating against my own skin, my bones and muscles humming to strange music I couldn't hear. The shadows of my room coiled with smoky menace. Yep, the last few days were really fucking with me. I had to get up and get moving or I was gonna explode.

My bed lamp banished the worst of the shadows. My body kept buzzing, though, so I did some yoga stretches to give it something better to do. My floor creaked with every move I made. Much as I tried to stay quiet, I found myself issuing silent apologies to our downstairs neighbors. Y'ever notice how much louder everything seems in the middle of the night, when everybody's sleeping except you? Yeah, I've noticed it too. Especially that night.

After I'd stretched my body into a grudging semblance of cooperation, I tried pacing back and forth in little circles. No good – the damn floor creaked too much. I'd have loved to go outside and just walk it off, but I've seen too many horror movies to be one of those girls who walks outside alone at night and becomes the next meal for Snacky McMonsterpants. Hell, who needs monsters for that kind of shit? Warrior Fitness training or no Warrior Fitness training, I wasn't stupid enough to tempt fate that badly.

My computer-chair beckoned. So did my sleep-key-blackened screen. It'd been weeks now since I'd delved into *WoW*, and I felt the draw of heroic pixels slashing simple solutions through a simpler world. For a second or so, I felt the ghost of that familiar track-ball and the rush of flashing my fingers across the keys as enemies exploded into experience points. Mimosatia, my 87th level blood-elf rogue, was itching for a fight. *C'mon*, I heard her whisper, green eyes and purple hair vivid in my mind's eye. *Let's go kill some shit*. And y'know, it was tempting. I hovered near the chair, half-reaching for the keyboard that would wake the system up and take me somewhere brighter than my bedroom and the dark mess of possibilities in my head.

But no.

I think maybe I was way too restless to go online just then. Besides, I'd need to function once morning hit, and bringing up the internet was a good way to make sure I'd never get back to sleep. More than all that, though, I think I just didn't want to give up and escape. Gaming is fun and all, but I'd needed to have the *Real World vs. Fantasy World* chat with myself a few times over the last few years (and my folks had needed to have it with me a few times before that), and as bad as things were looking in Genét's Headspace, Population Me, there was nothing that would be made better, and a lot that might be made worse, if I ditched out on the Real World now. Especially since the lines between Real World and Fantasy World were getting blurrier than usual about that time.

Not now, Mimosatia, I told the cartoon rogue in my head. *Maybe next time.* This time out, I needed to get my hero on without the benefit of pixels.

Reaching for my phone, I thought about calling Meghan again. *Nah,* I figured – *she's probably sleeping too.* Or arguing. Or driving. Or fucking. Or maybe all of them at once. You never can tell with some people, and Meg is one of those people. I texted her with a simple `Hey you - you up?` When I didn't get a text back, I gusted out a great big breath and decided to grab a Pop Tart or something to take my mind off the insomnia… and better still, off the visions in my head behind that lack of sleep.

Easing my bedroom door open, I slipped out into the living room, walking on the balls of my feet in order to put as little weight as possible on the goddamned squeaky floor. Kristen keeps her door open when she sleeps, partly so Inanna can come in and out when she wants to, and partly so I can get in quickly when Kris is having terrors. The only times it's closed, for the most part, are when she's got Celeste over or when she's on the phone with someone and doesn't want to share the call. I know better than to walk into her room without calling or knocking first (assuming she's not having screaming terror-itus, anyway), so it's not like she needs to shut it when she's getting dressed. Because she keeps it open, though, I have to be extra careful if I'm up and about when she's still asleep. My roommate's got enough horrors in her head without me adding strange noises to the mix.

Heading out to the kitchen, I managed to get across the floor with as little squeakiness as possible. Our living room /dining area features a pretty decent rug to muffle the chairs, TV, and our occasional bout of roommate yoga. Still, I winced with each step, mentally apologizing to anyone I happened to rouse at Why the

Fuck Aren't You Asleep O'Clock. I made my way to our fridge by feel, the rooms vaguely illuminated by the streetlamps outside our windows, fuzzing through the curtains to wrap our apartment in soft half-light. The refrigerator light blasted my eyesight white for a second; by the time I'd gotten myself a glass of milk and shut the door again, my eyes had adjusted to the light, and the resulting darkness left me blind.

The scream made me drop my glass.

For a second, I froze into that full-body ice mode that I hit whenever Kristen has her terrors. It's something you never get used to. By the time I bolted for her room, Inanna had come flying out the half-open door, knocking it full-open for me so it wouldn't slow me down. Just the same, I rapped on the open door a few times, calling out to Kristen. *Never* go busting into someone else's room unannounced, especially not when you know how terrified they are before you enter.

The shrieks from the darkness blew ice through my bones as I knocked our traditional one-two-three-times pattern. Given my last few days, the fear cut deeper than usual, and I had to root my feet to the floor and scrape the words up past the gravel in my throat. What if this time things were *worse* than night-terrors? What if that time-twisty tentacle thing had followed me home and was busy staging its homemade version of *Urotsukidoji* on my friend? "*Kris?*" I forced my voice to a loud half-whisper. "*Kristen!* It's *me*. It's *me*, hon – you're okay. I've got you." Having satisfied our usual protocols, I shouldered the door aside and shoved myself past the terrors in my own head.

Twisted up in a tangle of sheets, my roommate threw her head back screaming. If she'd heard me, I couldn't tell. Kris's eyes remained squeezed shut so hard my own eyes hurt just seeing her.

Straining against invisible arms, she thrashed in muscle-locked contortions as I leaned in over her bed and called her back into this world. When her eyes cracked open, I held out my hands to her. "It's *okay*, honey – I'm here. You're okay. It's *me*. I'm here."

"Oh, *fuck*," she growled, shutting her eyes again. "*Dammit*, Genét, I'm sorry."

"Love," I told her, "you have nothing to apologize for. *Nothing*."

She leaned into me as I slid onto the bed and held her as she cried a while.

My roommate had been through sixteen kinds of hell, but it didn't follow the usual patterns people come to expect from this sort of thing. That's not my story to tell, and I won't. Let's just say that girls can be every bit as cruel and vicious as boys, and some kinds of violation don't show up on a rape kit. That's one of many reasons I'm so damned protective of her. No one else was ever gonna hurt Kristen again. Not on my watch.

I won't lie, though: as I held my sobbing friend, I scanned the darkness for tagalongs from my weekend party at the Bottle. Even with a little bit of leftover creepy-sight, though, I saw nothing supernatural. All the horrors in that room came from human sources, nothing more. And really, that was bad enough.

Eventually, Inanna came back into Kris's room and snuggled up against her mom, purring in that comforting way cats instinctually know. I held Kris and rocked her for a while as the three of us curled into an insulating ball and waited for dawn to wash away the night. By the time I'd tamed the burning hunk of hatred in my heart down to a dull ache of vengeful chivalry, I realized I was fucking *done* with people who abused folks I cared about.

Whatever was going on, wherever it led, I wasn't gonna sit things out.

Sorry, Mimosatia, but I had to up my hero game.

And pixel-killing wasn't gonna fix things that happened in the real world.

NOTHING TO HIDE,
NOTHING AT ALL

~ ~ ~

Police stations are designed with to make sure you never, ever want to go into one again. I recall my mom referring to their style of architecture as "brutalist," and although I'm not sure they all look that way, the downtown precinct house at South Carver and Middlevale certainly does. Okay, I think the architect might have been trying to give the place an Old World type of charm or something. The result, though, looks like a factory tried to swallow a castle and threw it up halfway through the meal.

Granite flagstones stuck on top of concrete blocks for the first story, topped off with red brick braced with yellow edging stones that probably looked a lot better a century ago… the structure may have once *meant* well, but it really hasn't *aged* well. Clasped shutters block any view you might glimpse of the world inside that building, and the arched stone around those windows – topped off, over the main doorway, by a big brass cop-badge type of shield – reinforce that fortified impression. Okay, technically that's not brutalist in the architectural-style sense. The impression given by that building, though, is brutal enough for me.

That day, I was having second thoughts, third thoughts, a whole math exam's worth of thoughts that involved turning around and heading back home. The previous night's heroic resolve had hardened into a blot of apprehensions, most of which involved saying the wrong thing to the wrong person and winding up stuck in a cell somewhere in the belly of that beast. *Everyone's a suspect*, Detective Fallon had said. Had she been speaking rhetorically, or *was* I a suspect too? Even if I wasn't before, would I become one if or when she found out about the whole mess at the Bottle? The more mental pieces I looked at, the worse the picture became.

My lawyer met me outside that architectural monstrosity, dressed a tad more casually than his usual court attire: smoke-gray Ralph Lauren sports coat, black slacks, crisp off-white business shirt, and a pair of shiny black wingtips.

"No tie, Mister Chambers?"

His grin spread up past his eyes and into what's left of his tight-cropped graying hairline. "What'd I tell you, Genét?"

"Oh, right – it's Frank now." I gave him a quick hug, if only to settle my nerves with contact. Frank's a solid guy, not so much in that flabby way older guys get, but with some definite middle-weight and a build that suggests occasional visits to a gym. He's older than my dad by at least a decade, but like a lot of other Black folks I've known, he's aged better than most white folks do, I guess. My family never went in for all that "Say hi to Uncle So-and-So" stuff that a lot of families use when little kids meet friends of their parents. He's been hanging out with Mom and Dad for longer than I can remember, but around our house, to us kids, he's always been "Mister Chambers." Until now. "So," I couldn't resist asking, "are you 'Frank' to Rick and Lisa too?"

He laughed. "Oh, *God* no." Something sad seemed to cross behind his face. "Not anymore, anyway. They used up that privilege." His glance back at me didn't require an explanation.

"I won't, Frank. I promise."

Frank laughed again, more freely this time. "Never say 'I promise,' Genét. It's like a *Kick Me* sign for God."

"Got it." My own smile felt like a rubber band pulling across my lips. "And thank you for using the name I prefer."

"You're an adult now, girl. And adults should be able to define the terms of who they are."

"Even if they're 'girls'?" I tried to make it sound more playful than it felt.

Frank's smile looked more sincere than mine did. "Point taken. Old folks have old habits. I'm sorry." He looked me over, noting my more-business-than-usual attire. "Blouse? Suit slacks? Shoes, not boots? Looks like you even took a few of your piercings out. Not sure I recognize you like that, Genét."

"Hey, at least I didn't dye my hair brown or something."

"At least."

I glanced past him at the stone artifice we stood in front of. "I remember you telling Lisa that walking into court looking like a rock star was a good way to wind up on the judge's smackdown list."

"Not sure I phrased it quite like that," he said, amused. "And you're not going into court. Still, it's a good thing to remember, no matter what you're dealing with, if you're dealing with the law."

He shook his head. "You would not *believe* some of the stuff I've seen people wear into court. And not just kids, either – people who should have known better by that point in their lives."

"So," I asked, squeezing the word out past the tightness I felt closing up my throat. "What can I expect in there?"

"You're not a suspect, are you?"

"Not that I know of, no."

Frank scrunched his mouth a bit. "This should be a simple witness deposition, I'd imagine. In and out in less than an hour. Unless there's something you haven't told me…?"

I glanced at the pavement, choking a little on the words. "There's a bit. Not anything about me being guilty or anything like that, but…" I didn't know what else to say, so I just finished with "It's all just *complicated*."

Frank flashed his grin again, but it seemed tighter this time. "It usually is," he said. "Better fill me in…"

∾ ∾ ∾

"Just to be clear," Frank said once we'd ventured inside, met up with Detective Fallon, exchanged terse pleasantries, and ensconced ourselves in a bland conference room, "is my client a suspect, or being charged in any way, at this time?"

"No." Detective Fallon leaned her head at a nearly imperceptible angle toward the digital recorder on the table between us. I'm not sure if she did so unconsciously or as a sign to reassure me that she was being straight with us. I tried to find that gesture comforting. Nope, nope, nope. "This is a witness statement only," she went on, her voice soft yet formal, her eyes meeting mine, then Frank's, then mine again.

"I've been told that you *do* believe she might be a suspect in your investigation," Frank said, not letting her off the hook that easily.

Detective Fallon shot a tight smile across her face. "I may have made a dramatic overstatement in an earlier conversation." She looked at me. "I apologize for any confusions that might have caused. My bad."

"Noted," Frank said. "But for the record…?"

"For the record," she said with exquisite formality, "Jennifer Ioanna Shilling is not a suspect, nor is she being charged in any way at this time. No claim of custody is being made, and she is free to curtail this interview and leave anytime she wants." Detective Fallon gestured again toward the recorder on the table, with her hand, this time. "This interview is being recorded for official purposes, with counsel present. Should circumstances change at any time in this interview, both Miss Shilling and counsel will be informed of that change in status." She leaned back in her chair, spreading her hands toward us, palms up. "All I'm looking for here is information about a currently open case." Again, she looked both of us, one at a time, in the eyes. "Does that work for you both?"

I nodded. So did Frank. I glanced over at him. Frank nodded to me too. "Thank you, Detective Fallon. I believe it does."

I noticed that she'd said *interview*, not *interrogation*, and she'd said it twice. According to my earlier briefing with Frank, that was a good sign.

"So, how *are* you, Genét?" Detective Fallon's formal manner dropped like a novice toon's hit points. "This has been quite a week for you. I'm sorry."

"Thanks." I just stared at the yellow legal pad, untouched at that point, by her hand. After a few seconds, I added, "Thank, you Detective Fallon."

The stifling air of formality behind my words surprised even me.

I hadn't been much more talkative before that point, either. My usual double-barreled snark attack had dwindled to monosyllables, terse nods, and an obsessive attention to details. The conference room itself: drop-ceiling acoustical tile; no obvious two-way mirrors; a plywood table edged with rubber that had been pulled at by nervous fingernails; slingback chairs, black-framed with green /gold /black checkerboard patterns; the room's color divided at just above waist-height between forest green and faded gold; the faint buzzing of florescent lights; the industrial-cleaner scent wrapped around old seat and fast-food odors with hints of nicotine for flavor; Detective Fallon's black blazer and slacks, her bright white blouse contrasting with tanned or olive skin, the stylishly ragged chop of her hair (naturally black, it seemed to me), the bright yellow of the pad and the black Bic pen beside it; my weight in that chair and the stronger, thicker weight of the last week pressing down on me in that goddamned place. In my head, puzzle pieces kept morphing into chess pieces, checkers pieces, *Minecraft* pieces...

And y'know what? I didn't *get* it! I mean, *I hadn't done anything wrong*. I sat there in that chair, in that room, in front of Detective Fallon and Frank my lawyer like a sullen perp, and I hadn't even done anything illegal. Well, nothing they knew about, anyway.

Nothing I was being charged with. As far as I could tell, this wasn't even an interrogation room – it was a conference room set aside for our private conversation. I could walk out anytime I wanted to. And yet, sitting there in that room, all I felt was a cement overcoat of guilt.

God help me if I actually *had* done something wrong.

I felt a brief surge of sympathy for my rotten siblings and their many brushes with the law.

"I see Roland taught you that trick too, Genét."

"Huh?"

Detective Fallon smiled with all the warmth of skinny-dipping on an iceberg. "You're a quick study. I'm not surprised."

My mouth replied before my brain could process. "What trick?"

"The silent-treatment trick, of course. The one that keeps other people talking." She noted my dismay. "Don't worry about it, though – he's not nearly as good at it as he thinks he is, either."

Okay. So she was playing major-league ball while I was still looking for my Wiffle bat. No wonder she was the only officer in the room. She was the Good Cop, the Bad Cop, and every Cop in between.

"I can understand why you'd want to feel…" She nodded slightly in Frank's direction. "Protected. I get that. But unless there's something I don't know about, you're not in any trouble here." She leaned in slightly toward me, her hands on the table, her short nails shining slightly with clear protective polish. "Pretty much the opposite, really. I've watched the video, Genét. A lot. More than I wish I had. I don't envy you there. I'm guessing you probably play it back every night when you're trying to get to sleep, am I right?"

"Pretty much, yeah."

"I got statements from the other witnesses," she went on. "Everyone else just stood there trying to figure out what to do. Not you – you acted. The video's clear about that. I admire what you did. You were pretty heroic there."

"Thanks," I replied, not meeting her eyes. I felt the memory of charred skin ride the air-conditioned draft across the room. "I don't feel very heroic."

"That's obvious. Why not?"

Good question. I chewed that one over for a bit. "Because I couldn't save her."

"I know the feeling." Her sadness sounded genuine. "Every cop knows there are lots of people you can't save. It can eat you up inside."

I met her eyes on that one. If she was still playing games with me, it didn't show. "Yeah," I told her, trying to see past my paranoia. "It kinda does."

"It doesn't have to, though."

"No," I replied, getting my breathing under control. "It doesn't."

Frank watched us, quiet, as I eased the blast doors open and let myself cooperate.

∾ ∾ ∾

We talked trivia for a while. Simple questions, for the record: *How long did you know Monica Maria Randolph* (aka Blue), *how long had you been with the dance troupe, how did you first meet up*, that sort of thing. I answered as truthfully as I could without tipping over the applecart of weirdness that contained our lost weekend at the bottle. Although Detective Fallon had dropped his name in the middle of the table, I didn't mention Rol at all, or go into the details about why a couple of hours turned into a couple of days. Detective Fallon made notes on her yellow legal pad. Frank said almost nothing, just watched the two of us play hide-and-seek with facts. Finally, after what must have been fifteen or twenty minutes of this, she looked at the recorder, glanced up at me, glanced over at Frank with what looked sort of like a signal, put down her pen, and turned the recorder off.

"Genét," she said, tying some weight around the words and measuring that weight before tossing it out to us. "We all know there's stuff here we're not talking about. What you've been telling me is helpful, but it's not the stuff I really need to know." She spread her hands again – a disarmed gesture. "I'm not helping matters any by playing by the usual rules, so I'm willing to break a few."

Huh.

"Genét," she continued, "you are the very opposite of stupid. We all know that. I respect you, I think you respect me –"

"I do," I interrupted on a reflex. "Yes."

"So in order to save us all a lot of time, I'm going to share a few things with you that are Not To Leave This Room." She dropped in the cop-talk capital letters just to make sure I got the picture. I did.

Detective Fallon glanced over at Frank to check his reaction. He bent down one corner of his mouth, but then nodded at her to continue.

"Everything I know about you," she told me, "which, trust me, is more than you think you know I know, tells me that I can trust you with a greater level of honesty than most people ever receive from me on either side of this table, or any other one." She looked again in Frank's direction. "Frank Chambers, I know I can trust further than any other lawyer I'm aware of. The following is off the record as far as I'm concerned. It needs to be the same way with both of you."

Frank finally spoke up. "We both know those are dangerous waters, Detective."

"They are," she agreed. "Which is why I'm emphasizing *trust* here, between us, now." She gestured to the rest of the room. "We're in a conference room. Not an office or interrogation room. No cameras, I promise you."

I clamped my lips over an echo of Frank's earlier observation about *I promise*. The mental pieces of this particular puzzle tossed themselves in the air and hovered there, waiting to see how they'd fall together next time.

"If it turns out," she said, looking back at me, "that my trust has been misplaced, you will both lose my trust and all the associated goodwill that comes with it..." She brought back the cop-talk capital letters: "And that is a thing *You Do Not Want*."

Then she smiled, dissipating the sternness. "Is that clear?"

I checked with Frank. He nodded.

"Yes, Detective Fallon," I said. "It is. And thank you for that trust. I really appreciate that from you."

"So," she told us. "To start with, we're aware that you and several... friends... spent the weekend at the Bottle."

My guts froze up and dropped twenty stories or so before hitting the ground and shattering somewhere in the vicinity of my ankles.

Frank glanced over at me, but said nothing.

"And yes," she continued, "we're already aware of the temporal anomalies around that firetrap, so it's my guess that the length of time you spent there wasn't exactly your choice."

I caught the invitation to a response at the end of that remark. After checking in with Frank, who nodded, I shook my head.

"I didn't think so," Detective Fallon said. "So anyway, we're also aware that Caroline and Ashley are involved with a drug called Red Shoes, which is the same drug involved in Blue's overdose last week."

"*Overdose?*" The words shot out of my mouth before I could stop 'em, which had probably been the point. "*She caught FIRE.*"

The detective shrugged. "Like I said, overdose. The official story is that Blue attempted an unauthorized fire trick while under the influence of drugs, and that trick went bad." She looked both of us over. "But I think we all know by now that's not what happened."

"So," I asked her, "what *did?*"

"We know the *what*," she continued. "We're still trying to figure out the *why*."

I took her up on the implied question: "Why some Red Shoes users catch fire and others don't."

"Exactly."

Frank's face looked like a question too smart to ask itself.

"And," I added, "why most don't."

"Again, exactly. If everyone who used Red Shoes caught fire, this city would look like Sherman's ghost had come back around for a lookie-loo and decided to set up shop again."

I thought of the Burn, tried not to shudder, and failed.

"But," she said, learning in toward me in a conspiratorial sort of way, "I'm guessing you figured that out too."

I looked toward Frank again. This time, he shook his head. Once. Firm. I kept my mouth shut.

"I'm not accusing you, Genét." Detective Fallon leaned back in her chair, conciliatory. "My guess is, that wasn't consensual on your part. Still, there's a certain look that comes with Red Shoes use. And you have it."

I said nada.

"We're also aware," she continued, "that the Bottle has kind of a relationship with Red Shoes. You might call it a 'base-line' relationship. It's not the only source of that damn drug, but around here, at any rate, it's a significant one. We know that much."

"So why," I asked, my curiosity overriding Frank's better judgment, "is it still in business, then? Why haven't you…?" I trailed off, aware that I might have said too much.

"Why haven't we shut it down, Genét? For the same reason that every other meth lab, crack house and pot farm in existence is allowed to stay in business until a certain threshold is crossed. You've been there," she added, waving one hand with helpless dismissal. "What do *you* think would happen if I took a SWAT team down into that basement?"

A gargantuan icicle seemed to bust in through the top of my skull and slide all the way down to my toes. "You'd get slaughtered."

"At the very least, there'd be a very ugly, very public, very risky, very expensive fiasco on my hands." She sighed. "If we bust a squatter-artist colony, especially one filled with slumming rich white kids, every media outlet on God's green earth would be calling for my head on a platter. And right now, it's just not worth it. Not with a single OD, no matter how theatrical it might have been, and please pardon the pun right there – I didn't mean it. Hell, Seattle loses more kids to heroin in one slow weekend than we've lost to Red Shoes in a year."

"Oh."

"Besides all that," she added, "Red Shoes is not illegal."

"It's *not?*"

"Not really, no." She shook her head and spread her hands. "There's no ingredient in Red Shoes that violates the law. It's not illegal to sell it, take it or make it. *Stupid*, maybe, but not illegal."

"It takes a lot," Frank added, "to put something on the 'controlled substances' list. Public attention, outcry, testing, lobbying, studies… A lot of drugs just fall through the cracks."

I nodded, getting it. "The whole 'bath salts' thing."

Frank nodded back. "The whole 'bath salts' thing. Exactly."

Dammit.

I looked down at the table again. "So you're gonna do nothing?"

She panned her head between Frank and me before she answered me. This time, her voice sounded low and sad. "Genét, there's something I call 'the implacable arithmetic.' Life, death, the law – they all run according to it. People die. That's life. How *many* people die, *how* they die, what it's worth to *stop* some people from dying… well, that's part of the arithmetic. Every cop has to work out those odds in his or her head, usually right there in the moment when things are going to shit. And right now – and I'm sorry here, but it's true – one dumb kid using the wrong drugs isn't worth our time."

Rainbows of ugly feelings replaced the icicle, shimmering around inside me as I stared at the tabletop again.

No one spoke for a while.

Finally, I muttered, "I get that. So why am I here, then?"

She reached across the table to place her fingers on the top of my hand. "Because I still want to get that poison out of my city. I don't want anyone else to die because of it, but I have to be smart and realistic and come at things from a different direction. Kicking down doors won't work here. I want to find another way to come at this thing, and you might be able to help me there."

Frank looked as if he was about to say something, so I said it for him. "Are you asking me to go back in there and be a stealth agent or something for you?"

Detective Fallon laughed loud and rocked back in her chair as her laughter barked back at us from the walls. "Hell *no*, kid. I want you to *stay the hell away from there*." She shook her head at me. "Jeeze, God knows what would happen to you next time. And I don't want any of us to find out the hard way."

I smiled, embarrassed, like I'd sorta been half-kidding and was in on the joke with her. "Me neither. That was…" I left the statement unfinished when I realized there weren't words for what it was.

"And stay away from those friends of yours too," she added.

"Ash and Caroline?"

"Yeah, them. Those two are two ticks short of an explosion. Don't get blown up along with them."

"I won't." Right about then, neither of them was looking to be on my next Christmas list. "You've talked to them already, right?"

She nodded. "Several times, with Ashley. First on the night of the… accident, twice since then. She's twitchy, that one. But she hasn't admitted to anything I can use."

"But you know she's involved with Red Shoes." Frank looked at me, but said nothing.

"It was an educated guess until now. But yes, I figure she's involved. Not just using it, but selling it too."

That would explain a lot. "Do you know that for sure?" I asked.

"That's not something I can tell you. And obviously, this all stays between us here." She offered me one of those patented cop glares.

"Yeah," I assured her. "I've got no reason to want to be on her good side after what happened last weekend. Not anymore."

"I get that." She nodded. "Like I said, stay clear of her. Of both of them, if you can. They're in further than either one of them realizes, and I'm not the only one who's watching for their next slip."

The thought of one of those things in the Bottle passed through me like a low-grade shock.

"You okay?" Detective Fallon asked. I must have flinched hard enough for her to see. Frank was looking at me too, curious.

"I'm fine," I told them. "This is all just really wearing on me."

"That makes sense," she said. She looked at her notes, giving me a chance to let the goosebumps go down.

"Maybe we could call it for today?"

"If you want, Genét." She looked disappointed. I couldn't blame her. She'd just pulled back the curtain on some stuff, and I hadn't given her much in return. "Maybe a few more minutes? Or a short break?"

"Okay," I said. I'd started to get up, but sat back down. "I'm not sure what I can add to what you already know, but I'll see what I can do…"

∾ ∾ ∾

It took a bit more than "a few more minutes," and we didn't take a break. Once I'd opened up the floodgates, I told them both a lot of stuff. About the "troupe meeting" that turned out to just be Caroline, Ash and me. About how we'd drank to Blue's memory, and how somebody'd spiked the drink. About how Rol had been my backup, but he'd been dosed by the mead as well. I left out the weirdness in the basement, in part because I didn't know how much of it to believe myself. I *did* fill them in about the "temporal anomaly," though, which led to me and Detective Fallon giving Frank a brief rundown on warped physics and the nature of time and space dilation. I learned a few things myself from Detective Fallon's end of that conversation, and made a few mental notes to add to my research into that sort of thing when I got home.

For his part, Frank looked a bit dazed.

Although she never flat-out told me about the special cops and their special cases, I was able to fit together the things she did, and didn't, say. Like I mentioned earlier, police officers see things they'll never admit to in public. The Big Blue Brotherhood keeps its secrets well, and it has ways of dealing with those secrets if they start to bite. I couldn't give you specifics, but if – as Detective Fallon said – I had the look of someone who'd gone dancing with Red Shoes, she had the look of someone who'd looked behind the curtain of the everyday world, and now carried the weight of what she'd seen.

She and I both knew throughout that conversation that we weren't saying everything we knew. We couldn't have. It was too big, too scary, too much of... well, *TOO MUCH*. I *did* tell her about Rol and the lost-time effect; I did *not* tell her about the transdimensional inviso-thingies. I told her about how my cell phone had lost its signal until we wound up in the parking lot.

I kept quiet about the fight Rol and I had had, in which he might or might not have tried to punch my face in. I admitted that I'd seen some weird shit, but kept the exact impressions up in my mental lockbox with the biohazard sticker across the front. I'd given Detective Fallon plenty to chew on by that point, and her yellow legal pad was as covered with notes as my mental puzzle-board was covered in pieces that had begun falling together at last.

"Be careful, Genét," she said like every movie cliché ever. "Like I said, there's an explosion right around the corner. I don't want you anywhere near it when it blows."

"Don't worry," I told her, painting a different *Kick Me* sign right smack on my butt for God. "I don't want anything more to do with all this shit."

Yeah, we'd loosened up a bit by then but weren't exactly slapping high-fives in the cop-shop hallway. The place still felt like a tacky bright dungeon, and I was ready to find the exit.

Detective Fallen took out a business card, wrote an email address on it, and handed it off to me. "Put this address into your phone," she told me. "If you find anything that could help me out here, send it to this address."

"If I find anything," I told her, "I will." I made a point of not saying *I promise*.

Frank walked me to my car. I was sorta talked-out by then. All the same, I thanked him. A lot. "So," I asked him when we reached my car. "What's your opinion, counselor?"

"Oh, Genét," he said, shaking his head. "You Shilling kids certainly give your parents their money's worth."

TILL THE WHEELS
FALL OFF

∿ ∿ ∿

I had planned to go take my frustrations out on some
punching bags at the gym. As it turned out, I was so
exhausted by playing Show-and-Tell with Detective Fallon that
I headed home and took a much-needed nap. Thanks to my
unexpected (but welcome) break from work, I was able to scoop up
about four hours of quality crash-time before waking up in a more
centered state of mind.

One heavy-duty snoozeathon later, I woke up in a sizzle of
late-afternoon sunshine, Inanna curled up alongside my legs.
Stretching the kinks out and treating myself to a hedonistic
late-afternoon shower, I puzzled over the aftermath of our little
powwow in the conference room. Detective Fallon wanted me
to stay clear of her investigation? Fine by me. I had no plans to
face off with Hentai McMonsterface in the Bottle again, and
the thought of Caroline and Ash made me itch for a nice firm
punching bag. Okay, I was still curious, sure, and I can't pretend
that the idea of sitting back and letting the cops handle the hero
stuff didn't make my inner Blood Elf twitch. Still, if I could avoid

ever taking a tour of a police station again, that would be just fine with me. So I decided to cool my jets and let the pros handle the heavy lifting. Besides, I had a life to live, and the idea of losing any more time than I already *had* lost to burning friends and time-dilating temporal bullshit with tentacles and drugs was not my idea of a plan.

My phone started singing shortly after that, as I chowed down on an especially yummy slice of Garlic Meat Deluxe. I considered not answering it, but given that the song was "Dance Motherfucker Dance," I figured it was probably important.

"Hey, Vivienne." I pitched my voice with the sympathy I figured she would need.

"Hey, Genét." Vivienne's heavy tone showed that I'd been right to take the call. "I figured I should let you know personally: I've dropped out of Arcana Darque."

That surprised me. "I thought you *were* Arcana Darque, love."

Her shrug was more or less audible over the phone. "I formed the troupe, but it was never all about me. And now, well…"

"I'm sorry, Vivienne." My voice hugged her as much as possible. "Really. I know the troupe has meant a lot to you."

"After Blue…" She trailed off a moment. "I just couldn't. Not anymore. And Ash and Caroline still want to continue with it, so…"

Of course they did.

"So you resigned?" I tried not to sound angry. Not angry with Vivienne, anyhow.

"Well…" I could hear her trying to paste the prettiest mask over the face of what had to have been a very ugly conversation. "I met with them earlier today, planning to break up the troupe. Inky's already out, and I knew you were on the fence, and I really have no…" I noticed dark undercurrents beneath her words: "…no desire to do this anymore."

"I get that, Vivienne," I told her. And I *did*. This had to have been seriously rough road to her to be dragged along. "Anything I can do to help?"

"Thanks," she said. "But no. I just wanted out, and they didn't, so I ceded the company over to them."

It hadn't involved much, really. I found myself wondering, as Vivienne told me the details, if this had been Caroline's plan all along. Or Ashley's. The idea that they had maybe killed Blue in order to… No, that didn't seem logical. Still, I'd be lying if I said the thought didn't cross my mind as Vivienne laid the transfer out for me.

"How are you feeling about all this?" I asked when she'd finished.

"Kinda raw," she admitted. "But my heart really isn't in the game anymore. Not since last week. I just can't imagine doing this again after what happened to Blue."

I thought of the contrast between my snarky ringtone for her and the defeated voice I heard on the other end of the line. "I get that," I repeated. "But Blue's accident had nothing to do with you, or with dance, or with the troupe."

Thing is, for as much as I was insisting that there was no connection between dance, Arcana Darque, Vivienne's leadership, and Blue's faerie-tale demise, the pieces of this mess kept rearranging themselves in my mind. And the picture they formed was beginning to bother me.

Vivienne clearly knew more about Red Shoes than she was willing to admit to me. That much was clear from the pauses between words, the things she didn't say, and the guilt-tinged way she said them when she spoke. She knew they were doing the drug, and had probably been doing it herself. I was beginning to feel like one of those folks who twigs to the fact that she's the only person in her community that *doesn't* do meth, right about the time everybody's teeth start falling out and the fumes come drifting in from right next door.

Could it have been a dancer from another troupe? Maybe Chalice or someone else who wanted to take over? Had someone slipped Blue a flaming roofie in order to force Vivienne out and take over our troupe? All the pieces kept spinning around in my head, falling into patterns that didn't make much sense before flying apart all over again.

"What about you?"

"Huh? Sorry, Vivienne – I lost you for a second." *Lost* was right.

"Are you planning to stay with the troupe?"

"Nah," I told her. "I enjoy dancing and all, but I think… I think I've had enough of it…" (I'd almost said *them*.) "For a while, anyway."

Vivienne's tight voice relaxed a bit. "Yeah, I kind of figured that."

At somewhere way past 30, Vivienne was by far the oldest of us, with a home and a kid and two partners in an open relationship.

I think maybe she'd felt responsible for us, the designated grown-up in a bunch of silly Goth girls. Vivienne just loved dancing, and refused to get old like society said she was supposed to do. Kinda like my parents, that way – *adult*, I mean, but not *old*. On the phone, though, she sounded ten years older than the Vivienne I'd known before. It's all fun and games, I guess, until the wheels fall off.

As if I needed one more thing to throw on the bonfire of my feelings for Ash and Caroline, it was the way it seemed they'd guilted Vivienne into turning over the keys to Arcana Darque. I mean, it probably *had* been her decision, but I was willing to bet they'd helped.

We spent the last few minutes lightening up the conversation. When we hit the graceful-dismount part, she was laughing and we assured each other that we'd catch up in person soon. Maybe even go out dancing or something. This was the Vivienne I liked, the one I wanted to keep in my head no matter what else happened to us.

Outside my window, the rain had started up again. Inanna had demanded my attention about halfway through the phone call, and now she purred in a warm pool of cute on my stomach, the two of us sprawled out across my bed. For a few seconds, I felt my mind drift toward the computer and the familiar *World of Warcraft* start-up menu. A year or so ago, that would have been my default escape hatch from Cray-Cray Town. Now, it didn't appeal to me the way it used to. Mimosatia ran around her pixilated landscape in my memory, but the call to adventure echoed from a long way off. Instead, I lay back under our furry goddess of the Underworld, stretched out, and let my thoughts go wander in the rain.

THINK OF A NICE
THING TO SAY

∾ ∾ ∾

*I*T *FUCKIGN FIGURES!* The all-caps typo from Caroline
went out to me, Inky, Ash and Vivienne, topping off a
Facebook link.

Just when I thought things could not possibly suck worse, they
showed how wrong I was.

My social media connection to Blue came from the name Blue
Palisade, not from her legal name, Monica Randolph. Turns out
she had two Facebook pages, one for her friends, and one for her
family.

And her family had left her friends a message:

*Monica has been returned to her family. Because of the depth of
our loss and the tragic circumstances of her death, Monica's services and
funeral are to be private affairs. No public announcement will be made.
Her family requests that all non-invited parties respect their privacy in
this time of loss. Thank you for your friendship to her in this life. She is
with her Lord and her family now.*

TL/DR: *Friends of Blue, fuck off.*

I had to turn my phone off and close my eyes and breathe deep until the pounding in my ears and the urge to punch the entire world in the face finally faded away.

SEE ME HIT YOU,
YOU FALL DOWN

∾ ∾ ∾

The next day or two seemed pretty mundane. I got a few more texts from Ash and Caroline, venting about the funeral and asking me to stick with "their" troupe. I declined with the sort of polite firmness any halfway attractive girl learns by the time she hits puberty. My own texts to Rol, offering to spring for a *Fast & Furious* marathon at our place were likewise turned down, though with a bit less politeness than I had used on Ash and Caroline. Ouch. Before our adventure in time-space physics, I'd always been able to charm Rol out of his moods. The old charm wasn't working this time, though. I wondered if we'd be able to patch things up at all.

No further contact with Detective Fallon, which I took as a good sign. Meghan and I caught up, Kristen and I binge-watched *Fast & Furious* films, and I went back to Crash the day after my conversation with Vivienne. Life, for whatever that was worth, kinda returned to normal.

Having decided to take Detective Fallon's advice, I got my heroine fix by beating the living crap out of heavy bags at Warrior Fitness. Or rather, I got my fix by bruising the living crap out of my knuckles, shins, elbows and insteps on those bags while the bags themselves laughed silently at my efforts. Okay, I was finally starting to make *some* progress, if only because my redirected hero-quest pushed me into more squats, push-ups, pull-ups and crunches than I'd ever thought were possible. The sweat-drenched apparition glaring back at me from the mirror was starting to get kinda cut, and I liked the look. Hurt like a sonofabitch, but I couldn't argue with the results. By the end of that week, even the bags had begun to respect mah *authorit-tay.*

Eric Childers, of course, did not. "Smarter, not harder, Shilling," he advised near the tail-end of an especially sweaty volley of punches between me and the heavy bag. "You're gonna hurt yourself doing that."

"I swear," I gritted back at him, refusing to dignify Childers with an actual glance. *Eyes on the bag*, Genét, I told myself. *Don't give him the satisfaction of breaking your rhythm.* "If you give me some crack about 'breaking a nail,' I'm replacing this bag with your face."

"It'd be fun to spar with you sometime," he replied. "I'd like to see what you could do."

"I'll bet you would."

"Hey, I'm complimenting you, Jenny. You should…"

"Don't you *DARE* say I should *smile.*"

He threw his hands up in wounded mock-despair. "This is hopeless," he said to someone else nearby. "I'm just trying to be nice."

"Then go try to be elsewhere." Next to Childers, I heard some girl laugh, then heard him stalk off to go pester someone else. At least I had upped my verbal game with regards to Childers. That counted for something. As he walked off, I realized I hadn't lost either my rhythm or the upper hand.

"Nicely handled." Jacqueline's voice sounded close by behind me, but not close enough to startle me out of my routine.

"Boys suck," I shot back. "That's why we hit them with rocks."

"Or fists. Or feet."

"Or that, yeah." I just kept my head ducked in and my arms and legs moving.

"As annoying as he is, though, he's not *entirely* wrong, you know."

"How so?" I stopped punching. Jacqueline motioned me to resume, though, so I did.

"About going smarter, not harder. You're toughening up, Genét, and it looks good, but you're a thinker, not a tank." She motioned me to stop and step aside, which I did. Gloveless, she hit a stance and started throwing a series of rapid jabs, feints and kicks into the bag, all at different locations. Most of my shots had been aimed in a tight grouping of impact points. She aimed low, then high, then at a dozen impact points or more, all in barely enough time to blink more than once or twice.

"Holy crap," I breathed, my lungs working harder than her hands seemed to work.

"I'm not going to tell you not to practice hitting for strength and power," she said as she stepped back from the quivering bag. "You need to know how to hit hard, and you'll need to build more strength before you're in a position to do damage when you hit. But wearing yourself out isn't smart fighting. In fact, the smartest tactic, especially for a woman, is to let your opponent wear himself out trying to hit you, and then clean his clock once he's winded."

I cut eyes over at Childers, who was bro-ing it up with Joe Sanderson, Ricardo, and that guy whose name I can never remember because it sounds like the moniker equivalent of dish soap. In a gym dedicated to serious training, these guys hadn't quite graduated from clown school. Still, Childers had muscle and moves, Sanderson was a brick with legs, Ricardo was small and fast, and I think they kept the other guy around as sort of the ugly girl to make the pretty girls look better.

Speaking of girls, Childers had begun – for reasons beyond my apparently feeble powers of comprehension – hanging around with Chalice. Or she was hanging around with him. Or something. I could not wrap my head around why one of the hottest dancers in Riverhaven was swapping spit with a 'roided-out man-boy like Childers. As she leaned against him and ran her pale fingers down his sweaty back, I felt my skin do a crawling little dance up my scalp. Some girls have zero taste in men.

I can't say I really knew much about Chalice other than her reputation. I'd never talked with her or anything, and aside from her YouTube channel and a fairly bland Facebook page, she kept herself apart from the dance community even though she was kind of our resident superstar. I'd seen her dance once or twice, though, and regardless of her appalling taste in boyfriends, she'd earned her sterling rep among the other dancers. The girl moved like a liquid serpent, tight muscles undulating under heavily tattooed skin. Never put a finger or a foot wrong, either, so far as I could see. Red yarn hair-extensions wound their way through a mess of crimson white-girl dreadlocks, and the bindi stuck to her forehead would have looked like she was trying too hard for that whole Madonna '90s-retro thing except that on her it just sorta *worked*. Now, here, in the gym, she wore tight red yoga pants, a red scarf, and a not-quite-matching sports bra. Her hair hung loose, too long and messy for any kind of workout except the kind you get on a dance floor or between the sheets. Whatever she was here for, it didn't involve punching heavy bags.

I admit, I was tempted to slide up to her and talk some bellydance shop... y'know, maybe wedge her away from Eric and the Loser Boys. But watching her run her fingers through his chopped jock-hair, I figured it wasn't worth the effort. She certainly hadn't tried to approach *me* or anything, and given that she'd seen me at dance performances before – including the one where my friend died while I was trying to put her out – I kinda figured that *Chalice* should be the one making an effort to say hello to *me* instead. Y'know, if for no other reason than to say something like, "Hey, wow, I'm sorry about your friend." Instead, she was not-so-sneaking kisses off her boy-toy in the gym, hanging out instead of throwing down.

I couldn't say why right then, but just the sight of them together made me want punch Eric's balls into the sun. If I wanted to spar with him, though, and not make a total ass of myself, I was gonna need to up my game even further than before.

Did I want to spar with him? If so, why? Beating someone's ass over some nicked-up pride really wasn't my style. That day, though, the urge to do it felt stronger than usual.

As I stood there trying, and failing, not to notice Chalice and Childers, she glanced my way. At first, I thought maybe she was going to invite me over or say hello or something like that. But that's not how it felt when our eyes met. A cold flash jumped through me, and I may have taken a step back before I broke eye-contact and looked down at the floor. When I glanced back up, Chalice was locking lips with Childers again, like I had imagined the whole thing. Maybe I *had*. The Red Shoes affair was really getting to me.

"You okay?" Jacqueline asked.

"Yeah. Sorry. Just tired. And I've got work tonight, too."

"Well, *that* sucks."

"Yeah." I still felt that weird chill. "Kind of a *lot* sucks lately, to be honest."

Ignoring the Chalice-Childers Show, I thanked Jacqueline for the heads-up, asked her for tips, and practiced the moves she showed me – slowed down, of course, at the usual training pace, then gradually speeded up as she watched, commented, and adjusted my form. She put sparring pads on over her hands, and I threw increasingly complex patterns of blows into the pads until she finally said, "That's enough for today." My fists throbbed inside my gloves, and my shins and instep ached on a molecular level as Jacqueline told me to step off and shower up. "Hitting the bags like that," she reminded me, "creates microfractures in your bones. They'll toughen up as they heal, but you can overtrain and wind up breaking everything." Worse still, she pointed out as she walked me toward the locker room, is *rhabdo*, or rhabdomyolysis, when overstressed muscles literally explode from the inside out. "Leave that stupidity for the cross-trainers," she warned. "It's hard to come back from that level of damage, so don't get there in the first place."

I ran over the pattern-drills in my mind as I headed home to rest up before going in to work. Hmmmm... If I looked at the human body like a puzzle, I could envision each blow as removing a piece of that puzzle until the picture collapsed into chaos. Jenga, maybe – pull the right stick and your opponent falls down. Okay, sure – real bodies don't work that way. The mental images gave me something to work with, though, and that was a lot more entertaining than the other images that kept creeping in around my mental barriers whenever I gave 'em a chance to mess with me.

It bothered me to realize how easily I'd become accustomed to things I really shouldn't have become accustomed to. Death was one thing, even a death as bad as Blue's had been. Getting wasted? Been there, done that. Wanting to punch people? Sure, occasionally, even if I'd never really done that before. But the undeniable existence of Rapey McTentaclepants opened doors in reality itself, especially when coupled with that little time-slip that resisted sane explanations. Hell, Detective Fallon herself knew those "temporal anomalies" were real, so what did that say about the slippery state of everyday delusions? When the *cops* admit that time slides out of joint sometimes, then nothing's really certain, is it?

Time certainly seemed to creep at my job. The stuff in my head kept trying to crawl out all through my shift, and my Warrior workout had turned me into a shambling Pain Elemental who still needed to look perky and smile for the customers. I was so glad when my shift finally ended that night that I almost cried with relief. Heading home in yet another rainstorm, I consoled myself with the thought of a hot bath full of Epsom salts, a bowl of popcorn, a lapful of Inanna, and the most fucked-up horror film I could find.

Said hot bath was quickly enjoyed upon my return, with a purring goddess-kitty perched on the toilet nearby. Kristen came home just as the water was starting to cool, soaked and aching and grouchy as hell, so rather than Bogart the bathroom, I drained the tub and toweled dry as we exchanged hellos and updates. Popcorn was soon popped, streaming video was established, and Bruce Campbell's godlike countenance was faithfully ensconced on our TV screen when Inanna suddenly leapt up, bristling, and shot into Kristen's bedroom.

"Huh," Kris said. "That's weird."

"She doesn't usually have problems with what we're watching," I said.

Kris uncurled from the couch and headed toward her room. "Inanna? Honey, it's okay. It's all right – just a TV show. You don't have to…"

I got a sudden tingle of high-octane *WRONG*. "Kris?" I ventured.

Kristen turned just as something thumped outside our front door. Loud.

Kris and I both froze.

Oh shit.

In my head, Cthulhukid Jr. lurched just outside the door, filling the hallway and spilling down the stairs, warping time into an awkward instant just before everything goes eternally to hell.

Then we both heard another dull thud outside our door.

Y'know that feeling you get when something bad is right out of sight and you know you can't avoid it and you can't see it but every other sense you've got tells you it's right there?

Yeah, that feeling. It buzzed through both of us.

I uncoiled from the couch and began to stand, measuring the distance between our positions and the kitchen knives.

BANGBANGBANGBANG

"POLICE! WE HAVE A WARRANT! OPEN UP – NOW."

FEED YOU PAIN

∿ ∿ ∿

W_HAT?_

Kristen froze as we both felt the unseen weight of heavily armed cops on the other side of that steel fire door. I tried to speak, but the words locked up. _How the fuck had this happened?_

My cop-shop paranoia suddenly seemed justified. I'd been honest. I'd trusted Detective Fallon. I'd told the truth. I wasn't a suspect, she'd said, so _what the shivering fuck was THIS shit?_ Rage surged up over terror, washing over me with cold electric waves.

"Who _what?_" Kristen forced the words out in a cracked-throat whisper.

The TV screamed.

BANGBANGBANGBANG

The steel door boomed in its frame.

Kristen screamed.

Our back door exploded, showering the kitchen with wooden shards.

"*STOP!*" My own scream disappeared in thunder as a battering ram smashed our front door in.

The TV threw our screams back at us as a million wet cops busted in.

Kristen freaked.

Throwing herself at the first cop through the door, she hit Feral Survivor mode and clawed at his face. I screamed, she screamed, the cops screamed, the TV screamed, we all fucking screamed for fucking ice cream as a wave of real-life stormtroopers knocked our rebel asses to the floor.

The paralyzed instant between the first command and the busted doors became a storm. My face was on the floor, my arms yanked hard behind my back, the sore muscles and sockets howling louder than the voices everywhere. The quiet night home blurred into handheld-camera chaos edited into jump-cut incoherence. Stomping boots and smashing stuff drowned out anything rational Kristen or I might have said. I even tried a few escape maneuvers from my Warrior Fitness classes, but I was essentially slugging a heavy bag filled with lead, with both arms tied tight behind my back.

It's not like what you seen in movies or games. That was the closest thing to a rational thought in my head at the time.

Kris was a fucking firecat, thrashing through a sea of arms and bodies that held but couldn't stop her. She and the cops who held her smashed into the couch, the wall, the TV stand, knocking the screen into a death-fall that dented our hardwood floor. Arms and legs flailed out from a sea of heavy armor. Someone pulled my hair back hard and slammed me face-first into the wall. Behind me, out of sight, I heard something like a lawn-sprinkler, then even louder screams from Kris. "*She's got fucking PTSD, you stupid fucks!*" I heard myself screaming over the storm. "*She's an abuse survivor, goddammit. You're just making her worse!*"

"You need to be quiet now." This from the cop with her hand in my hair. "You're both under arrest. We have a warrant."

"*For fucking WHAT?*"

"*Go limp*, ma'am." This from a male cop on my arms. "Stop fighting us."

"*We didn't fucking DO anything.*"

"Stop fighting."

"*Let my friend GO!*"

Cop radios and codes, more smashing, the floor shaking, voices everywhere, Kris shrieking, and all I could see was the wall.

Somewhere behind me, a dog was barking. Oh, no – Inanna! "*We have a CAT, dammit. Get that dog outta here.*"

"*Stop fighting us, ma'am.*"

"*Got weapons in this room!*" Oh, great – the cops had found my collection of knives and swords. No one seemed to have noticed the baseball bat we kept behind the door, but that was probably just as well.

A second K9 officer shoved in through the crowded doorway, bundled in riot gear, her dog sniffing and searching. Outside the door, cops shouted down the neighbors. From Kris's room, the first dog barked up a storm. Poor Inanna! "*Drugs in here*," the first K9 cop declared. This just kept getting worse.

I got the TV-mantra Miranda treatment as the dog barked and Kris's screams subsided into sobbing. Voices in the hall, voices everywhere. By the time they turned me around again to face the wreckage, our living room was trashed and at least a dozen cops were searching the place. Two dogs in sight, no Inanna as far as I could see. Kristen was a limp mess covered in restraining cops. Inside, I felt lava boil through a hollowed-out shell of cold-hot fury. And, of course, a bunch of people in the hall had phones out as the cops tried to block their view.

Some view: two barefoot girls in sweatshirts, robes and underwear, pinned by SWAT cops trashing what was left of our home.

"I have no fucking clue what this is about," I snarled through the gravel in my throat, "but the lawsuit's gonna be *EPIC*."

THROUGH THE COLD

∾ ∾ ∾

Frank and his cop escort swept into the interrogation room a few hours later. *How many* hours later, I couldn't tell you – time did that endless-instant thing again. Could have been one hour, could have been twelve. One of the funny tricks time pulls on you when lighting changes and you can't find any sort of clock is that your mind enters a sort of trance where the only thing that matters is each moment itself.

I found myself wondering if that's what Blue felt like as she caught fire in the literal heat of that moment.

For me, the moments had blurred into a kaleidoscope of cold pain and colder rage. I was still handcuffed, still barefoot, still wearing a sweatshirt and panties – now wet, thank you, rainstorm – in a room where the AC had dropped the temperature somewhere in the terminal-goose bumps range. My robe had gotten torn in the scuffle and soaked by rain, so they'd taken it from me when we arrived at the station during my intake processing. So there I was: wet, shivering, achy as hell, handcuffed to a steel desk, and refusing to talk until my lawyer arrived.

"For God's sake," Frank snapped at Officer Williamson, the Office In Charge who'd been trying to grill me – unsuccessfully – for however long I'd been in that room. "Isn't someone going to at least get my client a blanket?" No conference room for me this time, oh no. We were in full-blown interrogation-room territory now, with a steel desk, steel chairs, a single bright light, and an obvious two-way mirror. My throat hurt and my arms throbbed and my whole body had been shivering with cold, fury and adrenaline since they'd hauled me into a cop car and Kristen toward an ambulance. It'd been raining hard, of course, so all of us had taken a nice thorough shower. In my case, they'd hustled me to the Ashford U precinct. I hadn't seen Kristen since they'd driven off with her, and the images of where she might be and what she might be going through kept me colder than the room did.

Officer Williamson glanced from Frank to me and back again. "This your lawyer, kid?" he asked. Dude was built like a Harley Ultraglide decked out in cop-suit blue, with buzzcut hair and skin a few shades darker than Frank's. I nodded. "About time," he said, as if he hadn't been the one who took for-fucking-ever to even offer me a phone call. Pro tip, kiddies: That whole "one phone call" thing is crap. Sure, you can make a call once you're in police custody; *when* you get to call someone, though, is entirely at the officers' discretion, and Officer Williamson was no friend of mine that night.

We'd gone round and round for what had to have been hours, him trying to get me to admit to having a meth lab or something set up somewhere other than our apartment, me refusing to say anything other than my name and my refusal to talk without my lawyer present. Oh, yeah – and I'd kept asking him where Kristen was and how she was being treated… questions he answered with a firm refrain of "I don't know, but she hit some cops and so wherever she is, it isn't good."

Helpful.

"Hey, Morrison," he said to the cop escorting Frank – a tall, tired-looking woman with bench-press shoulders and a fuck-you frown. "You get this girl a blanket, please?"

"Sure thing, Jake," she cut back at him in a tone as flat as the desk. "I'll just get right on that now."

Thing I noticed that night: Cops working the late shift give zero fucks, especially if they're stationed near a college campus. I was just one more spoiled little rich bitch who was probably waiting for Daddy's high-powered lawyer to breeze in and go Hollywood shyster on everybody's ass. The fact that this impression wasn't entirely wrong – Frank's not like that, but the rest was more accurate than I would have liked – did not help the officers' attitude toward me at all.

The one cop who'd been remotely civil had been the lady cop supervising my body-search when I'd first been brought to the lockup. Thankfully, they didn't do the cavity-checkup thing on me. Instead, a second lady cop ran a metal detector over me, patted me down (hard), pulled my underwear up and my sweatshirt down, and then told me to stand on an airport-security sorta pad while they scanned me with an X-ray machine. "Here, kid," the supervising officer had said after they finished scanning me. She handed a towel to the officer who searched me, who told me close my eyes and then scrubbed me (again, pretty hard) down with the towel before sending me off with a third officer – a guy, this time – to get the obligatory mug-shot, fingerprints, and name /rank /serial number shit. Finally, he'd dropped me off… well, escorted me in and then handcuffed me to the cold steel desk… to stew for a while in my wet not-quite-clothes until Officer Williamson came in a while later and started trying to wear me down.

Aside from asking about my roommate, and giving them the bare answers to the questions on their forms, I locked my mouth shut until Officer Williamson finally opened his cell phone, looked up Frank's number, and held the phone next to my head while I left Frank a message. That had been hours ago. Very long, very cold, very angry hours ago.

I can't tell you if I'd maybe gotten used to things by then, or if I was in shock, or if I was just so goddamned pissed off about everything to even *let* myself feel fear. But the gut-shut terror I had felt a few days earlier when I wasn't even in trouble was pretty much submerged that night beneath a sea of white-hot rage. Some motherfucker had set me up. Worse, they'd hurt Kristen and Inanna, and I had no idea how *badly* my roommates been hurt, either... just that it *was* badly. So no matter what it took, no matter what it cost, no matter what I had to do in the process, I was gonna find out who'd done what to us, and then I would cook them like a fucking steak.

That fury kept the fear down where I wouldn't have to deal with it quite yet.

If Frank had been called out of bed, it didn't show. Under his wet raincoat, he looked ready to go toe-to-toe in court. "Officer," he said to the guy in charge, "why is my client sitting here in her underwear, shaking wet and chained to a desk?"

Officer Williamson glared back at him. "They tell you why she's here?"

"An anonymous call, active shooter with pipe bombs and a lab in her apartment," Frank replied. "Which is obviously nonsense. Or haven't they told you yet there's not a damn thing in her apartment that substantiates that call?"

Top Cop grimaced. "Drugs, weapons, her roommate assaulted officers…"

"*Her roommate*," I snarled, breaking my oath of silence for the first time since I'd left the message at Frank's office, "is a rape-and-abuse trauma survivor who went into frenzy mode when a bunch of people *busted down her goddamned door.*"

"Genét," Frank warned, "I've got this."

"Sorry."

"And," Officer Williamson added, "your client resisted arrest."

"You busted our door down and *Tasered my roommate…*"

"*Genét.*"

I slumped back down and locked my lips shut, biting the bottom one to keep from going full-blown psychobitch on smug Officer Williamson. He'd been trying to get under my skin for hours, and now, with Frank standing there, he'd finally managed to do it.

"Where," Frank asked Officer Williamson, "is…" He looked to me: "Kristen?" I nodded. "Now?"

"I'm not sure," the cop replied. "And since you're not her lawyer, I don't have to tell you that."

"She doesn't *have* a lawyer…" I managed to keep from adding *asshole.* "She's just a college kid. And not a rich one, either."

"Not my problem," said Officer Friendly.

"Frank?" I kept my eyes locked on the handcuffed hands in front of me. "Would it be a conflict of interest if…?"

"Not at all," he said to me. "Officer Williamson, pending any further developments, I am offering to represent Miss…" He looked to me again.

"Woodrow," I told him. "Kristen Ellen Woodrow."

"Unless Miss Woodrow does not want me to represent her, I will be providing her legal counsel, and in that capacity I need to know where she is and how to contact her so I can consult with her as soon as possible."

My eyes blurred a little at the corners. "Thank you, Frank."

Officer Morrison showed up with a police blanket and was dutifully sent off to inquire about Kristen's status. "I think," Frank said as he wrapped the blanket around my shoulders and hooded it over my hair, "that we've established by now that my clients do not pose active threats to the community." His voice was soft, but his eyes could have peeled paint off the walls. "Have you learned anything that says otherwise, Officer… Williamson?"

"Just that she's got a temper and an attitude. And a smartass lawyer."

When Frank grinned, I saw why so many people call lawyers *sharks.* "Yes, she does."

"Her father's got a record too," added Officer Williamson. "I saw that much." He leaned in my direction, but I kept my gaze on my hands and the cuffs. "Her brother and sister too. Quite a family, that one. They must keep you busy."

Frank chuckled. "Yes," he admitted. "I guess they do."

The two men shared a laugh at the expense of the cold, wet college girl chained to the desk in her underwear.

"Okay, Officer," Frank said in a more friendly tone of voice. "I need time to consult with my client now."

"Suit yourself, brother. Have a ball."

"I think we can remove the handcuffs," Frank added. "She's not going anywhere."

"I don't imagine she will be, no." Top Cop rustled through some keys, unlocked me, looked me over like I was a cockroach, and left.

I waited till the door clattered shut before I let the tears out.

Hell, I didn't mean to cry, but it'd been a long day, and a long night, too. Sitting there shivering my ass off and boiling with rage and wondering what poor Kris was going through… and whether or not Inanna was okay… and envisioning cops trashing our apartment, and then leaving up a bit of crime-scene tape across the doors so that the anyone who wanted to could just go in and take whatever else they wanted from us while we sat in the fucking cop shop and… well, it was a lot to deal with and nothing I felt safe enough to think about until after Officer Friendly had left the room. I knew someone was still watching and probably videoing me through the mirror, but with Officer Williamson gone and Frank finally there, I quietly let myself go for a minute or two until I stopped wanting to kill everything in sight.

Frank stood off to the side and said nothing until I whispered, "Do you by any chance have a Kleenex or something, Frank?"

"Yep," he said, pulling out a pocket-sized tissue package. "I never leave home without 'em."

"Sorry to be such a girl about this." My hands, after hours in the handcuffs, didn't work right. I couldn't wipe my face, so Frank helped me.

"Don't kid yourself," he said. "Boys cry too, and usually after a lot less than what you've been through."

"How long have I been here?"

"Four or five hours, I'm guessing."

"Holy shit." My throat closed up behind the words. I swallowed a few times. "That long?"

"I'm not sure yet. My answering service reached me about an hour-and-a-half ago. I had to get up, get dressed, find out whatever I could find out about your situation, and then drive out here." He shook his head. "It took a while."

"Thank you for coming out. It's gotta be close to dawn or something, right?"

"Close enough." He sat down in the other chair. "Do you want to stretch your legs?"

"I do, yeah." So I did. "Why was that cop being such a butthole? I didn't do anything wrong."

"Third-shift officers get grumpy. It's generally the worst shift to work, especially if you're right off campus. Far as he knows, you're a college brat cooking up drugs in your dorm room and waiting to skate out on Daddy's money. Plus, you resisted arrest, and your roommate decked a few cops. That's not going to make you popular."

I rubbed my wrists, pacing the cold floor. "She didn't 'deck' them – they were all over her. Kris has PTSD something fierce. They smashed the doors in, and she went feral."

"Be that as it may," he said, rubbing his face, "that's not something police feel terribly understanding about. Your family's history doesn't help matters much."

"I'll bet." I'd known about Rick and Lisa, of course, but the fact that dad had an actual record was sort of news to me. I thought Frank had insulated him from that, but apparently Dad was more colorful than I'd thought.

"So what's this about drugs and weapons, Genét?"

My face tightened. "The pot is Kristen's. She smokes it when her anxiety kicks up."

"She have a medical card for that?"

"Do you know how hard those things are to get?"

"Okay." He sighed. "So is there anything else I should know about?"

"Not that I know of, no." Suddenly, I was *really* glad I hadn't gone poking around the dark net in search of Red Shoes recipes.

"And the weapons?"

It was my turn to sigh. "I've got a few knives, a fencing foil, epéé and sabre from the classes I was taking, plus a tai chi jian and a few replica swords. Oh, yeah – I've got a stun-gun, too. A self-defense one. But that's not *illegal* or anything, right? I mean, second amendment and so forth."

"Rights are relative, Genét." Yeah, I'm guessing if anyone would know that, it'd be a Black southern lawyer. "So," he continued, "did you wave any of them at the police or anything?"

"Hell, *no!* They weren't even in the same room we were in – they were in my bedroom. We were in the living room watching TV."

"Okay." Frank took a minute to chew that over. "The swords are probably a non-issue, the pot less so. And then there's the call itself. You were accused of some pretty nasty things."

"It's all bullshit." I felt the fury rising up again. "We *didn't DO anything.*"

"The police can't afford to take the chance that you *might*, Genét. Whoever called this in knew all the right buttons to push."

"What buttons?"

"I don't know the details yet," he admitted. "But I'll find out. Have they charged you yet?"

"Not that I know of." I let the anger walk itself all over the room. If nothing else, it helped me feel less cold. "How do they do that?"

"If you were being formally charged, they'd tell you. So if Officer Williamson or some other officer didn't say that you were, then you haven't been. Which means…" He looked at me and waited until I stopped pacing. "That they didn't find much evidence they can hold you on. Beyond the pot and the part where you and Kristen resisted arrest and assaulted peace officers, anyway. And that's not nothing, Genét. Your friend could be in trouble here."

"*She was SCARED!*" My shout bounced off the walls. "Kris gets *night-terrors* and shit." I felt tears start back up in my eyes. My words snarled up through my raw throat. "Her grandparents were really fucked up, and they used to beat on her when she was a kid, and then when she was in ninth grade or something, some other girls got mad at her and they… they…" I couldn't say it. It hurt to even *think* it. Anyone who thinks that boys hold a monopoly on cruelty haven't seen what girls can do when they set their minds to it. "She's haunted. Seriously haunted. The doors busted in, and she just went off."

"I'll probably be able to make some psychiatric arguments, then," Frank said, his voice bringing me back down to Planet Earth. "I'll need to get her medical records, but…"

"There's legal records, too," I added. "The girls who did that… they went to juvie for it."

"That's going to be a headache, I think." Frank looked like he had one too. "The records are probably sealed by now, though I won't need to know so much about *who* did what as long as I can find out *what* was done and what effects it had on her."

I didn't envy Frank or Kristen that conversation. At all.

"We were just *watching TV*, Frank! Just watching a fucking show when a million wet cops busted in our doors…" I stopped. "Oh, shit. Inanna. Kris's cat. Holy shit, I hope she's okay. I hope she didn't…" Every scenario I imagined looked worse than the one before.

"Shhhh…" Frank stood up and – after checking in with me – took my shoulders and faced me, his eyes warm, his voice soft. "It's okay, Genét. It's all right. We'll get to that when we get to that. Cats are smart. She's probably hiding as far back in the apartment as she can get."

"Yeah." I let myself breathe again. "Inanna *is* smart. She's probably still under Kris's bed. Poor kitty." Our little Goddess of the Underworld was on a new journey, and I hoped it didn't take her out of our apartment. "Can I make another call?" I asked. "If I can call Kris's girlfriend Celeste, maybe Celeste can come over and get Inanna and take her over to her place until all this gets sorted out."

"You probably can," Frank agreed. "But we should wait until Officer Williamson or someone else comes back in to talk. It's not wise to make requests until we can start hammering out the answers that the police will want from you."

"I don't know what to *tell* them." My voice started rising again. I pulled away from Frank. Whoever was on the other side of that mirror must be having a field day with the show. "We *didn't fucking DO ANYTHING.*"

Frank held his hands out to calm me. "I know that, Genét. And we can get to that. Right now, we need to take things step by step. They don't call in SWAT teams for just anything, and there were some pretty serious accusations made against you…"

"SWAT teams…" I stopped up short. The light blinked on in my head. "Holy shit, *some little fucker SWATTED me.*"

One of the cuter tricks in the arsenal of obnoxious creepy dudes on the internet involves calling in SWAT-team raids on people you don't like. It's like doxxing, but with bigger teeth – the better to shoot you with, my dear. It started off as a prank teenage boys used to play on their gaming rivals online; they tricked cops into showing up at your door expecting you to go all Kleibold-Harris on the neighborhood. After all that Gamegate crap a few years back, some folks started using it as a weapon against people they wanted to shut down and scare off. I used to worry about it back in my heavy gaming days. And now… now that I'd seriously *cut back* on my gaming… someone had used it on me.

And worse, on Kristen and Inanna.

I thought I couldn't get any madder than I already was. Turns out I was wrong.

Okay, I admit it. I kinda lost my shit, which did not exactly make Frank's life any easier or make me look better as far as the cops were concerned. After I'd screamed my head off for a few seconds, Officer Williamson, Officer Morrison, and a couple other officers came through the door.

"Girl," Officer Morrison growled. "You will sit your ass down in that chair and be quiet *right NOW*, or you will be taken to a holding cell and you can scream all you want in there."

I shut up.

"Or," she added, "I can have you restrained again, right here in this room, and send your lawyer home. Do you want that?"

"No, ma'am," I said, suddenly quiet. "I'm sorry, officers. No."

Officer Williamson shook his head at Frank. "Doesn't look like you're having a lot of luck with your client, counselor."

Frank returned the cop's attitude with a chilly look of his own. "Girl was watching TV when a SWAT team busted down her door and Tased her friend, all because some little snot wanted to get his jollies on the internet. How calm would *you* be about that, brother?"

"Oh." Officer Williamson's face got a very complicated mix of expressions. "Yeah, maybe not very." He said that like he'd already known we were innocent.

If I had been expecting apologies for the way I'd been treated (which I wasn't, but it would have been nice), I would have wound up disappointed. Instead, the other officers left the room while Officer Williamson asked if we needed more time to consult before we all got down to business together.

"A few more minutes would be fine," Frank said, giving me a *You good now?* look.

I nodded. "Five more minutes or so?"

"I'm going to get some coffee," Officer Williamson said, heading through the door without turning his back on us. "Anyone else want some?"

"Could I please get some water?" I asked him. I hated how little-girl I sounded then, but it had been a long fucking night and the last thing I was concerned about, after five hours or so in my underwear, was my sense of dignity.

BENEATH THE MOUNTAIN TOP

~ ~ ~

Y ou're free to go."

Okay, so it wasn't quite that easy. Or that simple. Or that quick. By the time Detective Fallon announced that I could be "released on my own recognizance," I'd spent nearly seven hours in the Ashland U police station, the majority of it in wet sweats and underwear. Officer Williamson eventually got me a dry T-shirt, and Frank had given me his jacket, but I still felt like damp cat in an icebox when Detective Fallon arrived to sort out the whys and wherefores with me, establish that I was not being charged with anything (not *yet*, at least) and could finally go home.

A few phone calls established that Kristen still faced a potential possession charge. Given the circumstances, though, our assault and resisting charges were written off. Inanna was in Celeste's care – the poor girl had, in fact, been hiding under the bed, and it took Celeste almost half an hour, some dried fish flakes, a bowl of food and lots of coaxing before our goddess decided to leave her personal underworld. Celeste, Dad and Mom put up the money to bail Kris out, and Celeste picked her up and took Kris over to Celeste's place. I wasn't sure I'd have a roommate after that fiasco went down, but at least Kris and Inanna were safe.

By the time Detective Fallon showed up, Frank and I had been conferring with Officer Williamson, the much more reasonable Sgt. Yamaguchi, Officer Blake – the woman who arrested me – and a dude from Internal Affairs whose name I can't remember offhand. The simple breakdown was this: I'd been set up by someone who knew how the system worked – someone who'd done this sort of thing before, and who knew which phrases to throw around in order to mobilize a home invasion courtesy of the Riverhaven PD. Given my family's sketchy history, the equally sketchy history of pretty much every off-campus college neighborhood ever, and the fact that a friend of mine died in a drug-related accident roughly a week earlier, *and* that two other friends of mine had been arrested in connection with that incident, they decided to take no chances with me.

Oh, yeah – I found out that Caroline and Ashley had been busted, too. Unlike mine, their charges were probably gonna stick. That's how we knew it wasn't them who ordered the little party at my place: both of them had been in custody at the time, Ashley was still in jail, and Caroline wasn't bailed out until several hours after the shitshow went down at our apartment. The cops questioned both of them about me after my arrest, and seemed pretty sure that it came as a big surprise to them, as well.

Also, the 911 caller had been a man. I couldn't imagine why Rol would do that to me. I mean, he was pissed at me and all, but Rol hated cops and he hadn't been all *that* pissed off at me. I hadn't been gaming in weeks by that point, so that ruled out a grudge-hit from some online asshole. Hell, I hadn't even gotten into a blowout

with anyone online recently, which meant this was a targeted hit
from someone who knew where I lived and wanted to fuck up my
life in a very big way.

And whoever it was also knew that I'd spoken to Detective
Fallon, too… and claimed that I'd lied to her when I did. Hence
the heavy artillery.

"You never know," Officer Blake had said, "what's waiting
for you on the other side of that door. I've been shot at, bitten by
attack dogs, one lady even stabbed me with a butcher knife, and
we're talking about this skinny old grandma-type with a meth lab
in her greenhouse." Officer Blake showed me the scar on her arm.
When she didn't have me by the hair and wasn't bouncing my face
off the floor and walls of my apartment, she was a pretty cool cop,
all things considered. I can't say I was in a very forgiving mood
when all was said and done, but I more-or-less understood where
they'd been coming from.

Detective Fallon arrived maybe an hour after Frank did, and
under her pro-cop mask she seemed unspeakably pissed. I had to
read between a lot of lines, but my guess is that she'd been hauling
people over the coals about all this. She'd been asleep when my
arrest warrant made the rounds and the raid had been planned and
executed. From what I learned, it's not unusual to have left her out
of the loop on something like this, but she seemed furious that
they had. "A few phone calls," she told me, "to the right people"
(meaning her) "would have kept this anonymous tip from blowing
up the way it did." It wasn't totally the fault of the police, though –
the guy who'd phoned the tip in had known exactly which notes to
play.

And man, cops do *not* like to be played. At all.

On top of all the other messes, the video from the raid had gone viral. Some of my neighbors put it online, and if there's one thing that'll make people scream louder than videos of innocent Black people being beaten by cops in the street, it's a video of two cute white chicks getting beaten by cops in their own home. I mean, we weren't actually *beaten* per se, but I saw the video afterward, and it made the cops look totally Gestapo. The Internal Affairs guy said an investigation was going to be underway soon, and I kinda felt bad for whoever it landed on. Not *too* bad, though, considering what the cops had done to us.

"So it's vital," Detective Fallon said, "that we figure out who did this, and why. If there's anything you can think of that might suggest an answer, that would help. A lot."

"What did he call me?" I asked her. "On the phone, I mean."

Her expression perked up. "How so?"

"What name did he use on the call?" I said. "Did he refer to me as *Genét* or *Jennifer*? The name he used might tell you something about who he is. Most people know me as Genét. If he said *Jennifer*, he's either someone from one of my classes or somebody who got my name from ID theft or an online database."

"That is an excellent idea," she said, writing it down. "I haven't heard the 911 call recording yet, but I will."

"I'll need to hear it too," Frank added.

"In due time, Frank," she assured him.

It was well into morning by the time we finished up and Detective Fallon confirmed there were no charges being brought against me... "at this time." So, Sword of Damocles, anyone? On top of that, my apartment had two busted-in doors and an unknown amount of wreckage waiting for my still-barefoot self to deal with.

"I can take you home, Genét," Frank offered as we left the station and stepped into the humid morning air. "Do you want me to drop you off at your family's place? You don't need to go back to your place just yet. No one would blame you for wanting to get clean clothes and some sleep."

I sighed what had to have been the millionth heavy sigh of the day. "Thanks, Frank, but I should probably just go home and see what the damage is. If I go back to my parents' place..." (and didn't it just speak volumes that I called it that instead of calling it *home?*) "...I'll just toss and turn in bed wondering how bad things are and envisioning people going through mine and Kristen's stuff seeing what they can take." The though hit me then. "You don't think someone could have called this in so that they'd know we'd be gone and the doors would be smashed in so they could rob us or something, right?"

"I doubt it," Frank said, opening his car door for me: a steel-gray Lexus with all the trimmings. Maybe I needed to become a lawyer. "First off, crooks tend to be allergic to police presence. Just the sight of yellow crime-scene tape scares off most would-be thieves under average circumstances. Especially these days, there's no way to know the site isn't still being watched, and few thieves will risk the possibility that it might be. Second, your neighbors seem to be watching out for you two. They not only videoed the raid – which in itself can get someone in trouble with the police – they slapped it up online, which is taking a serious gamble with the authorities." He started the car, which purred like a well-fed cat. Huh – I probably *should* become a lawyer. After backing out of the parking space and heading toward the road to my place, he added: "Most of all, though, swatting is a heavy-duty offense. Most of the kids who do that kind of stuff *are* kids, not really aware of the legal consequences if they get caught. Adult criminals, especially ones who make a habit of robbing places, are very much aware of the penalties for various offenses, the odds of getting caught, and the likelihood that they'll be able to walk away if they do. The penalty for calling down something like a SWAT raid – making false reports, misusing 911, et cetera and so on – are a lot stiffer than the penalties for robbery. No thief in his right mind would risk that kind of heat on the chance that he'd be able to steal some goodies from a pair of college girls. It's not worth it."

"So," I said, "either we're dealing with a kid, a grudge, or somebody really fucking stupid."

"Genét," he said, turning to look at me. "'*We*' are not dealing with anything. You're going home and staying away from all this Red Shoes crap. You're already in about as deep as I can get you out of as it is. Help Detective Fallon get what she needs to know, and otherwise stay the hell away. You got me?"

That stung. "I was *already* staying away, Frank," I muttered, crossing my arms like a cliché mad girl. "I backed off and let the cops handle things. I did what they told me. And look where that got me. And got my roommate and our cat, too, for that matter."

Frank looked me over hard for a second, then busted out laughing. "God," he said, shaking his head. "You sound just like him. You really *are* your father's kid."

I laughed harder than the situation called for. After the last day or so, I needed to laugh to go crazy. "Yeah," I finally said when we finished sharing a big ol' ha-ha, "I guess I kinda am."

Thing is, Dad and I can get pretty hard to shake when we get it in our minds to do a certain thing. And while I wasn't planning to hitting the Bottle again, so to speak, I had no plan to sit at home while somebody dropped another anvil on my head.

"Uh oh," Frank said, reading my expression. "I know *that* look."

"What look?"

"The one you and your father both get just before y'all do something stupid."

I snorted. "Frank," I told him, "you don't know me well enough to see how I look before I do something stupid."

"True enough. I know your father, though. And that look of his is one I've gotten used to seeing over the years." He let a chuckle escape his mock-stern face. "Have to admit, that expression has done good things for my bank account over the years. I'd rather, though, that it didn't get you into more trouble than you've already got."

"You and me both, Frank." I thought about wrecked doors, a busted TV, and the nightmares Kristen was gonna have from now on, and whatever was left of my smile disappeared.

We drove for a while in silence.

"Look," Frank said, breaking it at last. "I know a thing or two about how far you can and cannot trust the cops when you need them on your side." Again, he left it unsaid, but I got it. "And I won't tell you not to watch your back and hit whoever's coming at it with a knife in his hand… and hit 'em *hard* if you have to. Hard enough so that they never think of messing with you again." Frank's lawyer face slid down a little bit, and I saw the man underneath it – the man who'd gone to law school for reasons other than a steel-gray Lexus. "Just be careful you don't trip yourself up in the process, girl, and wind up in much further over your head."

"I won't," I told him. "And I won't say 'I promise' about it, either."

Frank chuckled. "That's wise. Just say this for me, though, will you?"

"Say what?"

He turned to face me again as we waited at a red light a block or so from my apartment. "Tell me in advance if you're planning to do something stupid, so I don't get any more 2:00 a.m. phone calls."

"I can do that. Sorry, Frank, and thank you."

"Just doing my job," he said, as the light went green. "Even if your family's turning that into a full-time occupation."

I half-laughed. "We *so* are not!"

"Not yet, anyway. Let's keep things from coming to that, shall we?"

"You got it."

I refused Frank's offer of breakfast. "It's not like I'm dressed to go anywhere," I told him. I've got food at home."

"We'll hit a drive-through," he insisted. "You need to eat *something*, Genét."

"I'm fine."

"After what you've been through, 'fine' is the last thing anyone should be."

"Point taken," I admitted. "But please, let's make it fast."

We hit a Wendy's on the way home, and the steamy burger-smell got me salivating. "Okay," I conceded, "you were right. Thanks, Frank."

"Just doing my job," he said, handing me the food. "I'd be a lousy lawyer if I wasn't making sure my client was of sound mind and body, right?"

"Just add it to my bill."

"Nah," he said. "This one's on me. Your family might be my clients, but your parents are my friends."

The messy meal reminded me how hungry I had been. We both ate silently in the parking lot. Once we'd scarfed down and cleaned up, we headed back toward the apartment. Again, he offered to take me to my parent's place, and again I politely but firmly refused.

As we pulled up at my place, I started to take off Frank's jacket and hand it back to him. "Keep it for now," he told me. "Give it back the next time we see each other. It's not like that's going to be a long time from now." Especially since he'd probably be representing my roommate in a minor drugs-charge case, that would probably be sooner rather than later. Frank jerked his chin up towards the apartment. "You want some moral support going up there?"

"Thanks, Frank," I told him. "But no. If I can't face it now, on my own, I'm always gonna wonder if I could have, later."

Frank looked at me as if he was considering how to answer that, then just said, "You make your father proud. Really proud. He ever tell you that?"

"It hasn't come up in conversation much."

"Well, he tells me."

That was good to know, but I didn't know how to respond to that. Especially since I suddenly realized that my front-door key was still in my apartment... I hoped.

"Oh, shit," I told him. "I don't have my key. It's inside. That is, if the cops didn't take it in as evidence." They had taken a bunch of my stuff in, and Kristen's, too. Our computers, our cell phones, my blade collection, God knows what else. They'd given me back my cell phone at the station, but the rest of it was still in evidence until either they checked it over or Frank got it out.

"Well, damn," he said. "Are you sure you don't want to go back home? I can take you there if you want, and I know your parents would be glad to see you safe."

"This *is* home now." Yet another sigh. It was that kind of day. "Or it will be if I can get inside again…"

LIVING ROOM'S LIKE
A BATTLEFIELD

∾ ∾ ∾

Fuck, what a mess.

I'd already known the back door was smashed in. That part was hard to miss. God, had it only been the night before? I was so tired by that point I could have fallen asleep on the back stairs if I'd let myself do it. Instead, I hauled myself up the wood-and-metal framework which ranges up the side of the building, back doors blossoming along its expanse, till I reached the second story. Our floor.

And just stopped.

I hadn't seen the damage first hand, just heard the door exploding across our kitchen, cracked under the battering ram and kicked aside by armored cops. Now, crossed by bright yellow police tape, the doorway stood open, with our kitchen naked behind a G-sting of yellow crime-scene tape.

Naked and trashed. Plates, glasses, shelves shattered and scattered by the force of the ram, the door, and the cops.

Muddy bootprints smearing the linoleum. An obstacle course of glittering fragments, damp splinters, and razor-sharp shards of broken everything. And me still without my shoes. Meghan probably would have waltzed barefoot right through that mess, but I'm not Meghan and such stunts weren't high on my list of ever-wanna-do-thats.

Why hadn't I taken Frank up on his offer, again? Oh, yeah – pride or something. Too proud to go home in this condition, all too much like my brother and half-sister and the hangdog looks they wore whenever they'd been bailed out of jail again. Pride, wheee. Fat lot of good it did me now.

I just stared at the ruins for god-knows-how-long.

When I closed my eyes, I felt myself shaking.

Oh, sure – lack of food, lack of sleep, yesterday's workout, the raid, the whole nine yards, that had me shaking. Worst of all, though, was the raw fucking *violation* of it all. The sight of my home, *OUR* home, busted open and smashed in and tromped over and left wide open like a wound, our dishes and mugs and *just everything we ate and drank with* tossed aside and stomped to pieces and the grated boot-patterns etched in mud and the sheer shining ruin of our intimate safe space… it shook me, hard. There's no way I can convey the ripped-up sense of atrocity that rooted me on that landing, staring in the broken-toothed mouth of what used to be our apartment's back door.

At least I'm the first one to see it, I thought. *I can clean this mess up before Kristen has to come home again.* She'd already suffered enough, and the woods still stretched out in front of her and even with Frank and Celeste and Inanna and me at her side, there was a long way to go before she was out of them. Before either one of us was out of them, for that matter.

My chest ached with hollow punches of raw-edged lost-kid rage.

If and when I found out who'd done this to us, I was gonna cut his world into puzzle pieces and mess them up so badly he'd never put that puzzle back together again.

A few deep breaths later, I tiptoed through the wreckage as carefully as I could. Managed to get through the mess with only a small cut or two and a few bits of broken dish lodged in my calluses. The rest of the apartment, thank god, wasn't nearly as bad as the kitchen. I'd expected worse, I guess, so the mess that greeted me when I returned to the scene of the crime was… I don't know, *less*-worse than what I'd expected? The TV was a loss, of course, and at least some considerate soul had turned it off after we'd been hauled outside in handcuffs. The furniture cushions had been flipped, the drawers opened, the furniture was shoved around, and cop-boot prints were *everywhere*, but at least no one had smashed holes in our walls or anything.

The cold hand of memory slapped me on the back as I looked over the room where Kris and I had been watching Bruce Campbell rage against the Evil Dead until we landed in a horror movie of our own. I shook my head to ease the shaking. Our bedroom doors stood open, and I wasn't sure what I'd find on the other side of them. By that point, I was hoping my bed would be in sleepable condition, because doors or no doors, I wanted to sleep about a year before tackling that clean-up job.

Oh, fuck… job. I needed to call out again. Hell, after the arrest, I wasn't sure I'd even *have* a job left. Guilty or not, stores don't usually want YouTube celebrities on the payroll if the fame in question came from being busted on-camera by the cops.

That's when I spotted the note on our busted-in front door.

I didn't need to read the text below them to understand the big red letters at the top: *EVICTION NOTICE.*

Grand.

Apparently, our landlords had been so upset about having a police raid in their building that they were kicking us out even though we'd been innocent. Showers of emotion ran through me as I read the note: Shame, rage, fear, embarrassment... I couldn't process them all right then. I could probably hire Frank to fight this, but would it be worth the trouble and the money? Jesus, what a train wreck this all was.

I tried the door to see if it would still close without falling off the hinges. It did. Not totally shut, but well enough to block out the boot-printed hallway, anyhow. Good. There wasn't much I could do about the back door, but at least our home felt... *I* felt... a little less naked with the front door closed.

I checked Kristen's room first. The bed had been freshly made, the drawers shut, the room straightened out. That puzzled me for a second, until I remembered that Celeste had come by the apartment while I was still talking to the cops. She must have straightened things up so Kristen wouldn't come home to a totally ransacked room. Okay, I've gotta admit I felt a little bit jealous right then – I mean, it must have been nice to have someone who cared enough about you to clean up your cop-trashed bedroom before bringing you your cat and taking you home when you got out of jail. I realized that was self-pity talking then... hey, I'd had someone to *get me* out of jail! To be honest, though, I sorta missed having a significant other at that moment.

Then again, the last three guys I'd dated wouldn't have done that sort of thing for me either. Hence why I wasn't dating them anymore.

My bedroom had not, shall we say, enjoyed a visit from the clean-up fairy. My mattress was still flipped over, my sheets and blankets and pillows tossed aside. My drawers were still open, my stuff shoved aside though not actually tossed all over the room. My computer was gone – big shock there, right? – and my books had been pulled off the shelves and pawed through. The cops still had my blades, too; even though I was innocent of the things that'd been told about me, those weapons were still evidence if they found some other reason to bring me in again. *"You'll get them back,"* Detective Fallon had assured me, *"once we've settled the dust and made sure the accusations against you weren't true."* That meant that on the very off-chance that Tentacle McRapeyface showed up in my living room, I was going to be depending on kitchen cutlery or Warrior Fitness moves that hadn't worked so well when I'd really needed them… which, while it had been a good thing with regards to the police, wasn't a great realization from a self-defense perspective. My clothes had been pulled out of the closet and left on my de-sheeted bed. My shoes and boots were scattered across the floor.

Well, if nothing else, I could put on some clothes and boots and feel more like *me* again. Which, from a sanity perspective, was pretty much my top priority at that point. The muddy boot-prints on my rug, the casual disarray of my stuff everywhere… my room, my stuff, *my LIFE* had been rummaged through by strangers who'd thought I was a weapon-toting drug fiend.

My bedroom had been turned into a 3-D jigsaw puzzle. So after slipping on some clean clothes and buckling up my New Rocks, I started piecing it back together.

Figuring that I was gonna need to crash sooner rather than later, I fixed my bed up first. Then arranged my clothes back in the drawers and closet, trying not to think about the hands that had taken them from their rightful place and left them on my bed. I began keeping a mental tally-sheet of the things I noticed missing, then took out a pad and began writing them down. If and when I needed to go to the cops… or to court… with a list of missing items, I wanted something more reliable than just my sleep-deprived mind. Plus, the act of writing things down in a legible fashion forced me to steady the shaking in my hands. Every so often, I'd let loose with some heartfelt profanity. I kept it quiet, though – like someone might be in the apartment with me. That's a thing I noticed that day and on the days after it: Once strangers have muscled their way into your private space, it never feels like *your* space, private or otherwise, again. For as big a pain in the ass as moving to a new home would be, the eviction notice was beginning to look like a favor to us.

Us? Oh, yeah – like Kristen would want to live with me again after *this* shit went down. That thought stopped me cold, and even though I was feeling pretty much cried out by that point, my eyes still burned at the thought their our friendship, our *home*, could be broken up so easily by a stranger with a grudge.

So yeah. About that "stranger." As I went back to work, my mind started piecing together another puzzle: the identity of our little benefactor, the reasons behind what he did, and the way I could figure out who he was so that I could pay him back in kind.

To begin with, he knew my address – my apartment address, not the address I grew up at. His information, then, was fairly current and not easily accessible. Most databases, from what I had learned from Dad, would contain my parents' address, not the address I had lived in for a little less than a year. My phone was still on their plan, too, so again it would have listed that location, not this one. Being a student, I used my parents' place as my permanent address for things like school, taxes and employment. Of course, to have my employment information, the swatter would have to know that I worked at Crash… and now *that* was a creepy thought to add to all the other ones in my head. My bank information listed this location, but if he could hack bank data I was in even bigger trouble than it seemed. My gaming subscriptions still listed my parents' address too, so this guy hadn't hacked those sources. I'd hardly even *been* gaming this summer, and once classes started up again, I'd be gaming even less. The Arcana Darque troupe info listed this address and phone number, though, which suggested a tie to Caroline, Ashley, Inky, Vivienne, or even poor dead Blue. That stuff wasn't listed in any publicly accessible database, so Laughing Boy was either involved with one or more of them, or had access to their computers and knew what he was looking for on them. A neighbor, maybe? Nah – neither Kristen nor I had pissed anyone in the building off that badly as far as I was aware of, and a SWAT raid in the building could go badly in too many ways and spill over into neighboring apartments. Besides, as far as I could tell, the neighbors had been on our sides last night. That left the gym… and I wasn't sure which information Warrior Fitness had for me on file. I'd originally signed up with them while I was still living at home with Mom and Dad, but I seemed to remember something about updating my info after I'd moved in here…

My ruminations got lost in the ringing of my phone… or, more accurately, under the sound of Dad's ringtone. Oh, yeah – I'd kinda forgotten to call them when I got out of jail. Some "good kid" I was turning out to be. "Hi, Daddy," I said once I'd dug my phone out of Frank's jacket pocket. "Sorry I was–"

"Are you all right, Jennifer?" Wow – *Jennifer*, yet. He *must* have been worried. "Frank told me you were out, but we hadn't heard…"

"I'm sorry," I repeated. "I kinda got lost in my head when I came back home and found my door smashed in." My voice started shaking on the precipice between *Big Girl's a Grown-Up Now* and *Little Girl Wants To Be Taken Care Of Again*. "I'm sorry," I said for the third time, "I should have called and let you know I was home safe."

"Why didn't you just come back here?" Dad's voice held a tense note I wasn't used to hearing from him – not when he was speaking to me, anyhow. My siblings, sometimes, but rarely me. "You know you can," he said. "Any time."

"I know, Dad," I said, trying to pull my inner Big Girl back from the edge. "And thank you. Really, I mean it. I just needed to see what the damage was back here. And after a night in an interrogation room…" I tried to make it sound light and humorous. "I just needed some quiet space."

He laughed a little, which was a good sign. "That's what your mother said. 'She needs her space, Bob. She'll call us when she's ready.'"

I laughed too. "Mom's been spying at the inside of my head again." I felt a little throb in my chest, but it was a good kind of pain.

"She *is* worried, though. She's not good at admitting that, but she is."

"I know," I said, guilty of Parent Worrying in the First Degree. "Does it make sense if I say that I was embarrassed to come home like Rick or Lisa did all those times?"

"It does." He signed. "Frank told me the family history has become something of an issue with the police, for you."

"Yeah." I sighed too. "It sorta did, yeah."

"Your infamous siblings?" he asked, going for a lighter tone as well. "Or your desperado dad?"

"Both, actually. And thank you for sending Frank in like the cavalry."

"We've certainly kept him in practice for that."

"Much as I love you, Daddy, I plan to make this a first-time/ last-time sort of thing." I shook my head at the thought of a younger him in an interrogation room or cell. "I have no intentions of carrying on the family tradition."

He laughed at that one. A nervous sort of laugh. "Good. Your mother would have to sell the house or something if you did."

"Just to pay the legal bills?"

"Just to keep Frank from firing us as clients."

"Jeeze, Daddy – you make it sound like we're the Mafia or something."

"I'm not Italian enough."

"Seriously, though," I brought my voice back in line with Big Girl. "Thank you. I really appreciate it."

"No problem. Just don't make a habit of it."

That part hit a nerve. "Dad, I didn't *DO* anything! I was *innocent.*" My voice headed into Bitchville USA, but I think it was entitled to go there just then. "As I keep telling everybody, Kris and I *did not DO anything.* We were *watching a fucking TV show* when a SWAT team kicked our doors in." I don't cuss a lot in front of my parents, but the moment sort of demanded emphasis.

"I know, Jen… Genét." Even under pressure, Dad speaks fluent Conciliatory. "I know. I was just making a joke. Kind of bad timing, though, right?"

"Right," I agreed. "And I'm sorry for going all bitchface on you, Daddy. It's just…" I felt the edge creeping back toward me. "It's just been a *seriously* long day. I haven't even slept yet since… jeeze." Suddenly, my remade bed looked really inviting.

"Didn't get any sleep last night? No, no I guess you wouldn't have."

"I was handcuffed to a desk. Sleep wasn't really an option."

"God," Dad's voice took on what Meghan calls his Old Man on the Mountain Voice, "I remember the first time I was arrested. I wound up in a cell with 20 or 30 other guys, half of whom were drunk off their asses, and I was wearing a Black Flag T-shirt with the sleeves torn off, and one of the guys was up in my face going, 'Hey, faggot,' and I was still pretty angry form the arrest and so…"

I yawned. Not intentionally, I swear.

The nervous laugh came back across the phone. "That boring, huh?"

"*No!* No, really, Daddy… it's just been…"

"Exhausting. It would be, yes. Go get yourself some sleep, kiddo."

"Yeah." Suddenly, my cell phone felt like the heaviest weight I could arm-curl at the gym. "Yeah, I need to do that."

"Call us if you need us," he said. "Any time."

"I will, Daddy. Thank you." Another yawn – wider this time – made my jaw crack.

"Ouch," he said. "I heard that."

"That's my cue to hit the bed, Dad. Thank you again."

"Much love to you, Jen… Genét. Sorry. I should be used to that by now."

Something nagged at the back of my mind when he said that, but I was too tired to know what it was just then.

"Love you too, old dude. Love to Mom as well."

After signing off, I shoved the remaining clothes aside, unbuckled my boots and pulled myself under the covers pretty much fully dressed. Warm daylight drew me further into Sleepy Country as the nagging puzzle piece circled around and around in my head, then disappeared without falling into place.

INTO

NO STRANGER'S FEET
WILL ENTER ME

∾ ∾ ∾

*S*omeone's in my bedroom.

Adrenaline slammed me awake. My eyes flew open.

And no one was there.

Believe me, I checked.

With a heavy boot in each hand (the cops had taken our baseball bat after all), I stalked around the apartment, looking for whoever had dared to walk in on me.

I noticed a faint smell of cinnamon, as if someone was baking cookies next door. It wasn't strongest in the kitchen, though. It smelled strongest in my bedroom. The bedroom whose door I'd closed and locked when I'd gone to bed.

I'd heard a tiny chiming sound, too, as if something had broken loose in our air-conditioning unit. I turned it off, but the chiming was still there. Distant. Faint. But present anyway.

No one was in our apartment, though, except me.

After a minute or two, I turned the AC back on, went back to my room, and made sure the door was locked this time. Even shoved my computer chair in front of the door before falling back into bed.

The lack of trespassers didn't alleviate that prickly feeling of being watched, however, and it seemed like forever before I was able to sleep again.

Eventually, my heart stopped trying to beat itself to death against my ribcage. The adrenaline surge still sent cold fire through my veins until radical fatigue dropped me back into Sleepytown, my brain scrabbling at loose puzzle pieces that slid through my fingers and scattered on the dream-dark floor.

GETTING UP HAS NEVER BEEN EASY

∾ ∾ ∾

I woke up again several hours later, still warmed by mid-afternoon sunshine. That in itself was sorta disorienting – I'm not used to crashing out from exhaustion – but while I felt like I'd been run over a few times with a moving van, the rest had done me good. Climbing up from the depths of sleep, I half-expected to find Inanna curled up around my legs. When I noticed her absence, my missing computer, and the remaining disarray my room had been left in by the cops, I felt that tide of violated anger rise up inside me again.

People have this mental image of women as passive vessels of acceptance and love. What most guys don't realize is that most of us are like the Hulk: always angry. What we *do* with that anger tends to be more subtle than the raging roidism guys display, if for no other reason than that we can't get away with acting that way most of the time. Oh, but we *do* get angry, and stay angry, and do things with that anger when we can. Detective Fallon, in her way, was working with her anger. So was Officer Blake, and every other cop on the force who's got too much vag to be accepted as one of the boys and too much rage to work behind a desk.

What was I gonna do with my anger, then? Good question. All I knew, as that red tide climbed back into my brain, was that Swatter Boy was going to pay the Iron Price when I found out who he was.

Oddly enough, my phone hadn't woken me out of that much-needed slumber. When I reached for it, I found out why. *"Dammit,"* I growled to myself. I'd let the charge run down. Given the state of ruin my room was in, it took me a few minutes to find the recharger. When I plugged it in, the rush of texts and phone messages came in.

I checked them: Meghan, of course, who was frantic over the video of my bust online. Ditto that for a few other friends of mine. Rose, my boss, checking in to see if I was okay, and for the same reason; that video had made the rounds in a big way. Caroline, frantic, wanting to see me *NOW*. Fuck her. The next message was much more important.

"Genét, this is Detective Fallon. I checked the recording of that 911 call. I thought at first that the caller referred to you as 'Jen-*ay* Shilling,' but when I re-listened to it a couple of times, I realized he was actually saying '*Jenny* Shilling.' Does that ring any bells for you? If it does, call me back and let me know."

Jenny.

Did it ring any bells for me?

Damn right it did.

That disappearing puzzle piece reappeared in my mind and dropped into place. This time out, it had a name attached to it… and a face. I face I suddenly wanted, more than anything else in the world, to kick through the back of his skull.

Finger shaking, I brought up the number for Archer, Chambers. Dialed it. Breathed in deep to steady my voice.

"Archer, Chambers Law Group," Peggy answered. "How may I direct your call?"

"Peggy," I told her, "it's Genét Shilling."

"Hi, Genét! Are you trying to reach Mr. Chambers?"

I took a deep breath, held it, let it out. "Yes, thank you. I am. Is he available?"

"He's not right now, I'm afraid," she said. "He's in court." Oh, jeeze, poor Frank. He'd been up since forever o'clock this morning, and he'd known he needed to be in court that afternoon. Wow.

The red tide rose even higher in my head.

"Did you need to leave a message for him?" she asked, apparently unaware that he'd just gotten me out of jail a few hours earlier.

"Yes, please, Peggy," I told her. "Please tell Fran... Mr. Chambers... that I'm about to go do something really stupid."

And then, before she could stop me, I hung up to go do it.

WHEN MY FIST HITS YOUR FACE, AND YOUR FACE HITS THE FLOOR

∾ ∾ ∾

"Hey, Eric. Still wanna spar?"

Okay, it wasn't one of my smarter ideas. But in my defense, I not only wanted to kick Eric Childers' teeth into the Atlantic Ocean, I also needed to know, for more-or-less certain, that he *had* been the one who called 911 on me and turned my home into a true crime episode. Oh, I had every intention of telling Detective Fallon who she could pin to the wall for that little party; before I subjected him to the resulting chaos, though, I felt I had to assure myself that Childers *was* the guilty party. That I wasn't just doing this because he looked like a good target for my bad mood.

"Um…" Eric's face went slack when he saw me standing in front of him. His eyes didn't quite pop out cartoon-style, but they were, let's say, very surprised to see me in our gym instead of in jail.

"You said you wanted to spar," I said, pouring a nice thick coat of innocence all over my words. "So I thought, hey, I'm kinda feeling up for it today. Let's go for it."

Physically, I was feeling pretty much the opposite of "up for it." Everything, and I mean *everything*, hurt. I was in a mood to share that hurt, though, so I figured Eric Childers was a good place to start sharing.

As far as I could remember, Childers was the only person since elementary school who called me "Jenny" more than once. That in itself was enough to wrap his neck in my noose. Until that afternoon, I might have thought he'd be too smart to use such a distinctive quirk if he'd wanted to remain anonymous... not that *smart* and *Eric Childers* shared the same page in my mental encyclopedia, but he had to have been not *entirely* stupid if he'd played the cops so well. My conversion with Dad reminded me, though, as he'd been fumbling over my name in our earlier phone call, that tension has a way of messing with a clear thought-process, tripping us up when we know the stakes are high. Unless Childers was a total idiot – which, granted, was pretty much a given, but I wanted to give him the benefit of the doubt – he knew that calling in a SWAT team is serious juju. That shit might be small potatoes when you're a spoiled rich kid, but it's a whole other ball game once you've reached legal age. Maybe he knew that, maybe not. Maybe he just said "Jenny" out of habit. All I knew then is that I had to find out for sure before I brought the cops down on his neck... but if I *did*, then I *would*.

"Hey... um, Jenny, you sure about that?" Childers looked like I'd just taken a mallet to his favorite toy. "I mean, uh, you might get hurt or something."

I shrugged. "We're just sparring, pretty boy. 'Contact, not impact,' remember?"

"Kick her *ass*, bro!" Ricardo wasn't normally the biggest misogynist in their little clique, but a hungry glow behind his eyes told me he'd wanted to see some blood that day, even if the blood in question was social, not physical.

"Hey, Shilling." Joe the Brick-Wall Tank added his own voice to the chorus. Good – I was sorta counting on the brute squad to help me out in a roundabout sort of way. If there's one thing I've learned about male egos, it's how badly they need an audience and how stupid they can make a guy when his pride is on the line. My plan counted on getting Eric riled up in public, and his bros would make handy tools in that regard. "I saw you get busted online. Daddy bail you out of jail?"

"Gee," I said with a hot fresh topping of innocent-sauce. "That video really made the rounds, didn't it? I mean, it seems like *everybody's* seen it." I stared Childers in the face as I said it, and his guilty look did not disappoint me.

Overhead, the gym's sound system pumped pounding metalboy tunes. Warrior tends to play that adrenaline-pumping stuff to keep us feeling warriorish or something – heavy beats, heavy bass, bragging lyrics, you know the drill. "Funny thing, Joe," I said, still eyeing Eric, "the cops let you go when it turns out you're innocent."

Ricardo snorted a bitter little laugh.

"So whadda ya think, Childers?" I tossed him a pair of sparring gloves. I held a second set in my other hand. "I wanna see if you can hang, or if all that muscle's just for showing off."

"*Dooooooode!*" Joe didn't disappoint me either. I meant to throw down the gauntlet in front of Childers' friends, and they bit the bait like starving dogs.

More pieces of my newest mental puzzle fell into place.

I'd laid it out in my head on my way to the gym. Rather than changing out in the locker room, I'd suited up at home, warmed up in the living room, grabbed my gloves and mouth guard, and headed off to Warrior Fitness. If Childers and his bros were there, I figured, I'd lurk a bit while I warmed up a bit more, hang back where they probably wouldn't see me, step up at a dramatic moment, take him up on his offer, and watch his reaction. Every piece in this particular puzzle suggested that Eric was my little SWAT buddy, but I wanted to trick him into admitting it before I acted on the hunch that he was. Hell, I'd even run around the block a few times before walking into the gym, both to get my heart-rate up and to take the edge off my anger. If I wanted to make Eric mad enough to set him off his game, I had to be clear-headed myself.

Yeahhhh… I wasn't really in what you'd call my right mind. Who *would* be under those circumstances? But after the last 24 hours, I was done being a chew-toy. Maybe the plan would work, maybe not. If nothing else, tagging Childers a few times would help me feel like I'd accomplished something worthwhile.

"So, Eric," I said, glancing at his boys. "Let's do this."

"*Damn*, dude," Joe said. "I think the chick's scalp-hunting you, bro."

Now, technically we're not supposed to work out grudges in the ring. As our trainers made clear, Warrior Fitness is a reputable gym, with no scalp-hunting allowed. If the trainers got wind we were really pissed at one another, they'd send us home to cool off. With that in mind, I set my voice on Max Innocent and my face on Playful Mean Girl – Just Kidding. Hey, if Childers and his buddies wanted to act like we were still in high school, I'd play that game too.

As expected, Eric's face went all Bro-Magnon. "Sure, *Jenny*," he said, putting an extra twist on that hated name. "Yeah, *let's* do this."

Point One scored before we even hit the ring.

The Warrior ring is a square around twenty feet per side – minimum size for a regulation MMA exhibition ring – with thick red-and-white vinyl padding over a steel-and-wood structure. Padded steel poles in each corner, and a heavily padded Ensolite form floor. Thick black bungee-like ropes on all sides, also padded and four rows high. Our ring sits near the front window so that folks walking by the gym can see what we do here. Let's be honest – it's as much a stage as a fight-zone. A space roughly seven feet wide separates the ring from the nearest wall, with roughly ten feet between the ring and the floor-to-ceiling window. Warrior smells like sweat and vinyl, but despite the testosterone atmosphere – or maybe, as in my case, because of it – the club's membership is about least one-third women, maybe as much as a half, with three cut-muscled ladies on staff. Warrior's a place where grace and power make out like sweaty young monsters: slick, stylish, and ready to kick your ass for fun.

Eric unfolded to his lanky height – almost foot taller than me. "Sure, Jenny" he said with a little bully laugh. "This'll be fun."

Deep inside, I heard a little voice call out *What the fuck are you THINKING, girl?* Panic kicked me in the belly as I realized I was about to get what I wanted whether I still wanted it or not. Crazy as it was, though, I needed this. My "*Let's do this*" wasn't just for Eric's benefit. It was for mine as well.

∾ ∾ ∾

"Are you *sure?*" Jacqueline looked doubtful. Childers and I had strapped on the shin guards and were heading toward the ring when I got clearance from the staff to video the match. I handed my phone off to Jacqueline, nodding. "Yeah, yeah," I assured her. "We're cool." *Cool* is pretty much the last thing I felt like inside, but no girl gets through her teens without learning how to throw up shields over how we really feel. Under the surface, I was seriously boiling and determined to use that to my advantage.

Going head-to-head with Eric would be suicide for me. I knew that going in. Some girls might trade head-shots with a dude, but not me and especially not with the size difference between us. Childers was better at this game than I was, too – he'd been training a lot longer than I had, and he had that whole roughhouse-boy thing going for him. He'd played basketball in school, not football like his friend Joe, but he was no pushover. Unless I wanted to wind up on my ass, I needed to play smart, fast and dirty. So I would.

Eric had height, skill and endurance on me. I'm smarter, faster, and more flexible. I could wear him down if I managed to keep from getting tagged too badly, but I had to watch my own energy level, or *I'd* be the one gasping for air at the whole time. I need to play him mentally – turn his pride against him and keep him overconfident. Fake high shots and then go for low ones. Watch the joints for openings, and lead him into traps where I could use his mass and height against him. Use Muay Thai kicks and Brazilian jiu-jitsu lock techniques. Work him like a puzzle as I took all the necessary pieces away. Make sure everything I did stayed gym-legal. Oh, and keep Eric from taking my head off in the process. Yeah, I was mad in the British sense of that word. If I'd been sane, I would never have done this.

But here we were, on our way to the cage.

Overhead, Limp Bizkit was urging us to break stuff. I hoped the stuff in question wasn't gonna be me.

Sane Brain Genét was throwing hissie kittens as we climbed into the ring. The foam floor sponged beneath our feet. That sweat-and-vinyl smell rose to surreal proportions, my senses sharpening to combat-level clarity. My heart, which had slowed down following my run around the block, kicked up speed again. I bounced around on the balls of my feet. I shook my head to toss off the stress, cracking my neck out and limbering my spine as Eric slapped high-fives with his bros, rolled his shoulders, and otherwise peacocked around the ring. Vanity or no vanity, I could tell he wasn't gonna fuck around. It's not like we'd be throwing full-force blows at each other, but Childers certainly didn't plan to go easy on me. Which was fair, because I wasn't planning to go easy on him either.

"You want a face guard, Jenny?" He held out a bright red form mask.

"I'm good," I told him, shaking my head again. "You wearing one?"

He laughed. "You think you can even *reach* my face, Jenny?"

As a reply, I snapped up a *bata loop pak* kick that would have connected with his nose had he been within closing distance. Yeah, that was showing off, but from the hoots among the gathering audience, it seemed to have had the desired effect.

By this point, we'd kind of attracted a crowd. Joe and Ricardo, of course, plus Jacqueline and two other trainers, Jack and Rayvon. Willow and Rue, cheering for me. Benny, Rak and Charles on

Childers' side. No Chalice this time out, which was too bad, really – it would have been fun to kick his ass while his girlfriend watched me do it. A few other folks I didn't take the time to recognize, guys and girls both, most of whom didn't seem to be taking sides. Jacqueline wasn't the only one holding up a cell phone, either. Whatever happened, it was gonna be on video. Which is exactly what I had in mind. It's not like Childers was gonna confess on camera to swatting me, especially not with a mouth guard across his teeth. Still, if I managed to rattle him hard enough, he might say something stupid. If that wound up online too, I'd count that as a win.

Jacqueline climbed up into the ring with us, to referee. "Okay if I hand this off?" she asked me, waving my cell phone.

"Sure," I told her. "Hey, Willow – you cool with filming this?" Willow agreed, so Jacqueline gave her my phone and guided us toward the center of the ring.

Before slipping in my mouth guard, I stepped in close to Childers and said, just loud enough for him alone, "So, did you hear she's in the hospital now?"

"Huh?" He seemed confused. "Who is?"

"My roommate. She got Tasered. You see that part in the video too?"

He shook his head and tried to say something, but his mouth wouldn't work right. That's okay – his eyes said everything I needed to know.

"God, Childers," I said. "I hope you don't play poker with that face." Then I slid my trusty ShockDoctor up over my top teeth and worked my lips around the edges. Pulled on my gloves, and

Velcroed 'em tight. Breathing through my nose, I moved my mind into pattern-sensing mode as I shifted my center of gravity to just above my hips. Our soundtrack shifted into something that sounded like Metallica as I rolled my shoulders and dropped my chin.

Childers secured his mouth guard and gloves. "Hey, Jenny," he said, his words slurred by the mouth guard, "you maybe wanna do this some other time, when you're not mad at somethin'?"

"Nope," I assured him. "I'm good. I'm fine."

"Cool," he said. "So'm I."

We touched gloves, and there we went.

I opened with an axe kick, dropping my foot toward his face. He blocked it, of course – that was the plan. I wanted to sucker him into blocking high. Childers slid in and fired off a fast volley of punches at my face in return; as I blocked 'em, I felt his leg shoot out and try to hook mine. I evaded that shot with just enough time to realize that he wasn't quite as stupid as I'd been hoping he would be.

That's where things became a blur.

As I'd learned the hard way the night before, there's a world of difference between the named techniques we practice in class and the brutal storm of sensations that erupt when you're fighting for real. Reflexes take over, muscle memory over planned strategy, and Childers had a lot more practice at this sort of thing than I did. My blow-by-blow mental breakdown of our fight went totally to hell once arms and legs started flying. I found myself looking at the world from behind my raised gloves as Childers pressed in with fists, elbows and knees. *Fuck*, I thought as the shocks busted my stance and guards, *this was a really bad idea.* He wasn't hitting *hard*, but he kept hitting *fast*, with sure balance and an anger of his own.

A bright flash impacted with my face. I found myself slamming to the mat, my jaw bursting with dull pain that ran up the side of my skull. My ears rang. *So that's what it means*, I caught myself thinking, *about someone ringing your bell.*

Childers jumped on me, his right glove headed for my nose. I took the blow on the side of my head, sending up another flare of white pain. A moaning roar loomed up over the ringing in my ears.

"*Break! Break!*" Jacqueline towered over me, close in on Eric's personal space.

Childers hopped back off of me. His grin cut through the stink of feet-sweaty vinyl.

Jacqueline leaned in. "You okay, Genét?"

I grinned around the mouth guard and the pain in my face. *You're a poet and you don't know it*, I tried to say, but it came out mush.

"What?"

"Nemmermind," I mumbled. "Ahm ghud."

I got back up under my own power, bounced a few times, shook my head clear, and hit a ready-stance again. We touched gloves a second time, and Eric fired a barrage into my gloves before I managed to make an opening move.

I threw a couple kicks and punches, but he blocked all of them.

Again, he rained me with punches and kicks. Didn't take me down, but he came close. My ears continued to ring. Instead of wearing off, the ringing got louder.

I was getting creamed out here.

I *so* needed to change the equation.

So far, Childers had me on defense. A couple of blows slipped past and tagged my shoulders. He blasted me another shot or two in the face, busting my vision with white bursts and thick concussions. He threw fast combos of leg- and hand-strikes, then jabbed me with elbows underneath my guard. Adrenaline warded off the worst of the effects, but I knew I was gonna feel this workout, and feel it soon.

I found myself retreating across the ring as he whaled in on me. My shins began to ache from the shock of blocking his kicks. If I'd been thinking straight strategy when I cooked up this plan, I would have waited until my body had recovered from yesterday's workout and my endless night. As it was, I was in zero condition to fight. But hey – I'd stepped up, so this was all on me.

Willow was still filming it all. Joy.

I dodged a clinch attempt, then wound up bang on my ass as Childers kicked my back leg out from under me. *Watch your guard,* I kept telling myself, but he was pretty much everywhere and I couldn't block it all without cringing against the ropes, which I was not about to do.

A blur of sound roared in from outside the ring as I slid from defense into offense. *Sound!* That was it. The pounding macho-music rocked a tempo I could ride. Firing off my own volley of punches and kicks, I locked in to the sound and let it guide me. I was a dancer? Then I would fucking *dance!*

I closed my eyes and dropped toward the beating trance-state I found when the music took me in.

Music surged into strength, into purpose, into righteous rage – not hot, but blizzard-blast cold, rolled up and pushed out in a bright red musical tide.

It's not like I went blind. I just got out of my own way and let my body do the thinking.

A cascade of punches and elbow-strikes lashed into Childers' gloves, his sides, his shoulders, his face. I wasn't making 'em hard, but I was making 'em count. He tried to loop me into clinches, but I ducked and swerved and evaded them all. Sure, he tagged me a few more good shots here and there, but my shoulders and gloves took the brunt of them, and the rest I couldn't even feel. Now I had Eric on the run, dodging, blocking, evading when he could as I pushed and chased him around the ring.

The song poured into me, lent me strength. The pounding beat melted into my pulse. Heavy chords filled my muscles, energizing me, throwing each power chord behind each punch, kick and block. My heart beat in time with the music.

It was glorious.

He took a few more shots at me, and I turned them back against him, angling a punch off my glove and into his shoulder, blocking a kick and knocking him off-balance. He threw a sharp extension at my face, but I snagged him up in it. Catching Childers' arm, I hooked my instep around his ankle, then shoved hard up and let gravity do the heavy lifting. *BOOM!* He hit the mat face-first, and I wrapped around him, rolled him over, and unleashed a hail of punches – real punches – at his face.

"*BREAK! BREAK!*" Jacqueline's voice cut through the roar.

I sprang back off of Eric, who had a new kind of fear stamped on his face. A little blood there, too.

"*Shilling*," my trainer barked. "There a problem?"

"No," I tried to say. My mouth guard slurred it into "*Raow.*"

"Contact, not impact," she reminded me. "If you can't control your blows, get out of the ring."

"Orrie," I said. Or, in Mouth-GuardSpeak *Sorry*.

"*Doooooode!*" I was starting to wonder if Joe's vocabulary had ever acquired synonyms. "Ricky, she was kickin' your *ass*, man!"

Willow kept filming. Rue was jumping around, cheering me on. A lot of folks simply looked stunned. I kinda felt that way myself. Meanwhile, the music pulsed and throbbed, kicking me to a higher level of awareness and ferocity. My skin felt hot, and the heat pulsated under my skin, down to my bones. Sweat shined in the sunlight through the window, but my breathing was steady and my muscles jumped with adrenaline joy. Holy shit – *I took him down!*

Scanning the crowd, I noticed a girl I hadn't seen in the gym before. Even so, she seemed familiar. Black hair, dark skin, she looked kinda Middle Eastern. Gorgeous, and I mean *GOR-JUS*, face, with lush lips, a strong nose, and thunderstorm eyes. Dressed in tribal dance garb, she wore a shimmering red veil wrapped across the top of her head. Beneath that veil, white pearls and gold coins gleamed on an ornate headdress. Long dark hair spilled out around the edges and fell past her shoulders. Her eyes flickered between Childers and me, as if she was watching us for something we hadn't *done* yet but probably were *supposed* to do. A lacy gold necklace ran down from her throat to the upper levels of her cleavage, which rose up out of a red dancer's bra decked out in a mesh of gold coins. The coins rustled and chimed as she glided around the edges of the ring. I couldn't see below her ribcage, but she moved like she wore a skirt, like she was barefoot, like a dancer.

What the fuck was a garbed-out bellydancer doing in the gym?

A subtle yet insistent chiming sound echoed underneath the pumping workout music, the voices in the gym, and the ringing in my ears. No one else appeared to notice.

Eric and I headed off to opposite corner so we could cool down before Round Two. Jacqueline leaned in toward me. "I'm not sure you should be doing this right now, Genét," she told me. "You looked good out there, don't get me wrong, but I'm getting the impression you're a little *too* invested in this, and you need to show better control than you just did."

I took out the mouth guard. "Sorry," I said. "I'll watch it next time."

"You better, or I'm wrapping this up and sending you home."

Jacqueline praised me on a few moves, offered some corrections, and made sure I was hydrating enough. Across the ring, Rayvon was checking in with Eric. Childers waved him back, glaring at me. His nose and lower lip puffed with swelling, though the blood from both had stopped. He looked mad too, now. Good. That made two of us.

The music pumped in my bones and brain, muscles and heart. I shook sweaty hair out of my eyes and glared back at Childers. "Ready for more?"

"More than," he replied.

"Good."

We put in our mouth guards and went back to work.

Again, we touched gloves, me bringing mine down softly on top of his. We jumped apart and I noticed the reddish tinge on Eric's skin. Like me, he was shining with sweat. That's to be expected. As the music pounded deep into my core, though, I felt my pulse jump with it… and the flush on Eric's skin seemed to throb with it as well.

Red Shoes.

Oh, *shit*. So that's why he'd swatted me. Eric Childers had been doing Red Shoes. A lot more of it, I was willing to bet, than I'd been dosed with.

A handful of puzzle pieces fell into place as he lunged at me. Motivation. Timing. Ash and Caroline's arrest. Why he'd made it personal. *Jeeze*, I remember thinking. *No wonder he's mad at me – he thinks I narced out Ash and Caroline to the cops.*

I hadn't, really, but he wouldn't know that. Nor, for that matter, would they. All three of them probably thought I *had* informed on my pretty-much-former friends. Which meant I could expect similar fun times from Ash and Caroline, assuming they got out of jail. Oh, this just kept getting better and better.

Well, at least that realization gave me some new ammunition to hit Childers with. If and when I got a chance to hit him again, that is.

Heat bloomed in the ring, thick and furious. My bones throbbed with pulsating fever. Music wrapped itself around the ringing in my ears. I could tell that we were moving fast, but every moment painted itself across a high-definition TV screen in my skull.

Childers was flowing with the beat, but didn't seem to be riding it the way I was. Kinda like he *felt* it but didn't *understand* it. He had internalized the pulse of the music, and it was fueling his angry energy. Unlike me, though, Eric didn't appear to know how to dance with that pulse, or how to use the energy it fed him.

That gave me an edge.

Blocking his attack, I let Eric have the lead while I timed his blows and openings by the music boiling through us both. I let him build up a good head of steam, too; the energy was driving *him* – he wasn't in control of the energy. Sweat sprayed from his face and hair every time he moved – I watched everything slow down as I caught the beat and rode it. As I felt the heat rise under my skin, brightening from blue fire into red, I felt us both slide into super-slow-motion. An angelic choir of chiming voices swelled up under the thunderous beat and muscular chords of rock. As each blow pounded into my gloves and guards, I puzzled out not only where Childers *was* hitting me but where he *planned to* hit me. And because I could sense the blows before they landed, I could block them too.

Childers came in at me for a clinch. I caught his lunge and spun my weight on the balls of my feet, letting his weight carry him down. He hit the mat and rolled up as I tried to loop him into a hold. Still, I caught his sweaty head in my sweaty arms and leaned in close to his ear. "Did you think I wouldn't find out?" I growled around my mouth guard.

He slid out of my grip. "Finna wha?"

I let him go. Confessions wouldn't play in Mouth-Guard-Ese. If I was gonna get Eric to admit something, I had to do it when we didn't have our mouths full.

Around us, the gym blurred. Sounds and colors whirled. The rest of the world flooded into distant sensory slurs.

We danced.

Launching a series of fake-out punches at his face and chest, I belted Eric in the thigh with my shin. He staggered but kept his feet. Again, I aimed high, he blocked high, and I went low with a few solid kicks at his legs. That's a wear-down tactic, one that's especially effective when a smaller person's fighting a larger opponent. MMA fighting's all about legwork. Tag someone in the thighs a few times and you slow 'em down. Best of all, they don't feel the worst effects for a minute or two… but when those kicks add up, they can take a person out of a match. After all, you can't fight if you can't walk.

Childers' skin flushed deeper red. Mine did too. Both of us were going for broke now, throwing harder, right on the edge of gym-legal blows. The hot core of energy began to sizzle up inside me – and, if the flush on his skin was any indication, inside of Eric too.

We danced hard in our Red Shoes haze, neither one of us remembering where that could lead.

I caught sight of that Middle Eastern dancer again, watching us both as we circled and struck. Unlike everything else I could see beyond Eric and our fight, she seemed perfectly clear to me. Her eyes darted from my face to Eric's back.

I saw him almost imperceptibly turn, as if he'd sensed someone coming up behind him.

So I plastered him right in the mouth.

BOOM.

I hadn't put my full strength into the punch. He staggered as if I had. His eyes rolled for an instant, unfocused, glazed. Childers rocked back from my punch and started to fall.

Then he caught himself and rolled up into a full-force blow to my face.

If that blow connected, it would take my fucking head off.

So I ducked it.

Swept in down under his extended arm.

And slammed him with a full-force liver punch.

Time froze.

The chiming music swelled around us.

Childers dropped hard to his knees.

Took a breath. And collapsed.

He tried to stand, and couldn't.

"*BREAK!*" Jacqueline exploded. "Shilling, what the *hell?*"

I glanced up at Willow. Her mouth hung open, but she held my phone like she was filming us. I spat out the ShockDoctor. "Still recording?" I called out. Willow nodded.

"Shilling," Jacqueline snapped, "you're done."

I ignored my trainer. "Did you think I wouldn't find out?" I repeated, clearly this time.

Jacqueline bent down over Childers. "What's your *problem*, Genét? What is *wrong* with you?"

I still felt the heat inside. "She's in the *hospital*, Eric. And when she gets out, she could go to *jail. Because of you!*" Okay, I was bending the truth a little. My roommate was out on bail. But Eric wouldn't know that. My plan, meanwhile, had gone completely shitsward. I guess I got my revenge but I didn't feel great about it. The fire pounded with the music in my ears, under my skin, at the edges of my sight. I was still raging, still wanting to dance, still wanting to hurt him until there was nothing left to hurt.

"*What the fuck are you talking about, Genét?*" Jacqueline turned on me. "And Willow, turn that damn thing off. Show's over. Stop recording. It's done."

The Middle Eastern girl watched from beyond the ring, her eyes bright and dark and wide. She still seemed clearer to me than anyone or anything else in the gym.

Rayvon and Jack climbed into the ring as Jacqueline leaned in toward me. They kneeled down next to Eric. "Hey, buddy," Rayvon asked him. "You okay in there?"

Eric groaned, tried to stand, and still couldn't get up.

"You're done too, Genét." Jacqueline peeled my skin off with her eyes. "Get your shit and get out. You're done here."

"*It's his fault!*"

"*We don't work it out in the ring.* This is a gym, not an alley. Get your gear. You're out."

Fuck.

Rayvon helped Childers spit out his mouth guard. Eric was hurting. I didn't care. "You shouldn't have called me 'Jenny,'" I told him as I leaned in to pick my ShockDoctor up off the mat.

Eric was out of it, still lost in Painsville. "Called you Jenny *when?*" he asked me.

"On the recording, Eric." Rayvon and Jack helped him to his feet. I leaned in. "*On the 911 call.* The one where *you fucking swatted me.*"

That got him.

"Oh," he said. "I did?"

"Yeah, asshole," I snarled. "You did." Score one for little victories.

"Someone got hurt?"

"Yeah, Eric. My roommate, Kristen. My friend." I nodded, hard. "Yeah, she got hurt."

"Genét," said Jacqueline. "I said you're done." This time, though, her voice was softer. Her expression as she looked at Eric's face, however, was pretty much the opposite.

"Oh, jeeze," he mumbled. "Hey, I didn't mean to hurt anybody."

And there it was.

"Well," I told him, "you did."

"Dude," Jack said, "you need to be quiet now." He and Rayvon were looking hard at Eric too.

Eyes bleary, Eric stared at us glaring at him. His friends stayed put outside the ring.

Time stood still around us all.

I glanced up at Willow. And yeah, she was recording it.

"Aw, man," said Eric Childers. "Shit."

NOT SO STRONG
WITHOUT THESE
OPEN ARMS

∾ ∾ ∾

"You should've let the police handle it."

"From here on out, I am," I told Jacqueline. "I just had to make sure first that it was him. Now I know."

Jacqueline had walked me to my car. Joe'd looked ready to murder me, and most of the other guys, even Jack, had shut down tight as I gathered up my gear and headed out the door. I'd heard Rayvon advising Childers to call a lawyer. Eric still seemed foggy in the head. I've heard a lot about the power of a liver punch, but Childers was only half-there by the time I left the gym. I don't know how much of his dazed expression came from my punch, the kicks to his thighs, or the Red Shoes high we'd both been on, but all the cock had gone out of his walk and I guess the realization that he was about to get his own visit from the cops was beginning to dawn in his twisted little brain. My Warrior Fitness membership was still scorched earth, but at least something good had come of it.

"It's not that I'm not sympathetic, Genét," she said. "I am. But you broke a lot of rules in there, and you abused what's supposed to be a safe environment. You abused my trust too, and I'm probably in trouble for letting things get as far as they did."

"I'm sorry, Jacqueline," I shook my head. "Stuff just kinda took over."

"If you actually damaged Eric's liver, I have to tell you, you'll probably get another visit from the cops. We'll need to file a report regardless. We'd do the same for him if he'd hit you that hard."

"I get that," I said. Man, Frank was gonna hate me. "Well," I added, "If the cops *do* show up at my place again, at least this time they won't Tase my roommate."

"That happened, huh?"

I frowned, thinking of Kristen's screams. "Yeah," I said. "It happened."

"How is she?"

"She's been better. But I lied a little bit in there. She's out of the hospital. At her girlfriend's place now. Still in legal trouble, though, and it messed with her head to have cops busting in her door." I grimaced. "Messed with *my* head too."

"I'm sorry," she said. It had begun to rain again, and I felt a little bad for keeping Jacqueline outside. Thing is, she could have gone inside again if she'd wanted to. I'd started shaking from the adrenaline comedown, and I think she was shaking too. "If it's any consolation, Eric will probably lose his membership too. After what happened…" Her blue eyes went cold. "I don't think he'll be welcome here anymore."

"No doubt," I said with what felt like a little smile.

Silence did the awkward dance in the air between us. I kept hoping to see the Middle Eastern girl come out of the gym, but I was beginning to think maybe she already had… and that no one but me and maybe Eric Childers had seen her to begin with. If even *he* had seen her.

I was beginning to understand Meghan's strange little world, and how that felt to her.

"For what it's worth," Jacqueline said at last, "you looked really good out there. I didn't know you could do some of the things you did."

I laughed at that one – the nervous kind of laugh. "For what it's worth, I didn't either."

"Look," she said, not looking at me as she said it, "if nothing bigger comes out of this, and if you still want to train some time, we can maybe set up some lessons or something at a different gym."

"I'd like that," I said. "I'm sorry I blew things at this one. It's a good place."

"It *is* a good place, yeah."

"I'll miss it," I said, and meant it.

Jacqueline shot me a tight little smile. "After what just happened in there, I don't think it'll miss you. But I kinda will."

"Yeah, I'll miss you too."

We shared a clumsy hug before she headed inside.

Once I'd driven my car a few safe blocks away from the gym, I pulled over to check out the videos Willow had shot with my phone. The girl in the ring handled herself like Ronda Rousey in her best days, not like an awkward kid who'd gotten herself way in over her head. She *was* me but *not* me, if you know what I mean. It was kinda awesome and sorta scary at the same time, and while I'm not gonna deny the roles of anger, motivation and hard practice, Red Shoes definitely had a hand in the fight I saw. As we fought, the crimson flush spread across us both – deeper on Eric but still noticeable on me. How close had we come to combusting like Blue?

I shuddered. Hard.

We could have died in there.

My liver punch did us both a favor. Even Eric. He was better off hurting than dead.

I looked for the dancer in those videos. She wasn't there. No big surprise, really, but that chilled me anyhow. Who *was* she, and how deep was this rabbit hole gonna go? Every time I thought I'd found the bottom, it kept getting deeper, with weirder things at every level.

The gamer in me shuddered again to think of what the boss level might be like.

I checked the final video, and there it was: Eric Childers admitting in public that he had swatted me. I doubted the video would be admissible as evidence, but I had what I needed for Detective Fallon's investigation. I called her number, got a message, and left a message of my own:

"Hi, Detective Fallon. This is Genét Shilling. I got your message, and yeah – I know who sent that 911 call. His name is Eric Childers, and I'm sending you the proof." I brought up her email address on my phone, attached the video, and sent it off to her, then headed home for a cold shower, some food, and my much-needed bed. The adrenaline was wearing off, and I felt sore and tired in an elemental way.

MAKE THE MOVES
UP AS I GO

∿ ∿ ∿

The shakes hit me on my way home, so bad I had to pull over for a few minutes on Prophet's Walk Drive in order to let 'em pass. Adrenaline burnoff, the after-thrill of violence, the realization that I'd been kicked out of a gym because I'd decked a dude in the liver because that dude – who I'd known since frikkin' *grade school* – had called in a police raid and hurt one of my best friends… Yeah, it was a lot to take in. So I gripped the steering wheel and let music wash over me until I felt human again.

When my hands had stopped shaking, I took out my phone and checked my messages. I'd had the phone set to vibrate, not ring, while I was in the gym. No reply yet from Detective Fallon. A text from Frank, and another from Meghan, both essentially saying *CALL ME NOW*. Another from Rol. Huh – that one surprised me. I checked it.

Sorry I was being a dick

Oh, good. So we were back on speaking terms again. That helped loosen the tightness in my chest. I hate fighting with people who matter to me, and Rol mattered to me more than either of us was willing to admit out loud.

I texted him back:

Sorry I was being a cunt.

That word's not usually part of my vocabulary, but I figured it'd give Rol a laugh.

Meghan's message was almost as direct, if less profane. Frank's message seemed a bit more important, if only because you don't wanna piss off your lawyer when you're in as deep as I was at that time. Feeling the shakes come back around for a second pass, I called his office back.

"Hello, Genét," Peggy's voice sounded somewhere between wary and weary.

"Hi, Peggy. I got Frank's message. Is he still around?"

"Back in court. He got your message during recess." She sounded annoyed, too.

"Sorry," I said. "I hope that doesn't mess up anything for him in court."

She laughed. "It'd take a lot more than a stubborn client doing something stupid to throw Frank off his game." She paused. "*So…*" She drew the word out. "What stupid thing *did* you do?"

"Got myself kicked out of my gym. Possible assault-and-battery charge, but I doubt it. I figured out who'd swatted me, and I more or less beat a confession out of him."

"Impressive." Peggy sounded like she meant it, too. "So why aren't you in handcuffs again? Or are you, and they're just being nice enough to let you use your own phone?"

"No handcuffs this time. I belong to… *belonged* to… a martial arts gym. The guy had challenged me the other day. I took him up on it."

"Didn't go the way he wanted to, I gather?"

I laughed that time. "Not so much. He's probably puking his guts up in the men's room if they haven't kicked him out too by now."

"God, girl – what did you *do?*"

I grinned. "Liver punch. Not gym-legal at full force. He's gonna be feeling that for quite a while. And by the time the pain fades, the cops will be inviting him in for a little chat. I got him on video admitting he was the one who called them on me. And given what Detective Fallon told me about how the caller knew all the right buttons to push in order to bring in a full-scale raid, I'm willing to bet that wasn't his first time doing that." Again, I saw pieces falling into place. Guys like Childers love doxing girls like me. And stalking us. Sometimes even swatting us. I was willing to be Eric had been doing all three, and doing them for a while. If there was now one less douchebro using the internet as Misogyny Central, I'd check off a box on my Good Me list and reward myself with something nice.

Like maybe a new apartment.

Ugh. So much for my grin.

"Hey, Peggy," I asked. "Who at your firm handles fighting evictions?" Landlord-tenant stuff isn't Frank's department. You need a different sort of lawyer for that kind of mess. And maybe a civil-case lawyer for suing Childers, too – I'd be damned if he was getting off with just a liver-punch from me. This whole thing was becoming seriously expensive. How did people afford stuff like this when they didn't have rich parents? Oh, yeah… that's right, they *couldn't* afford stuff like this. Meghan's friendship had taught me that. No wonder she's always so pissed off.

"Yeah," Peggy said. "Jackie Lee Logan does. Want me to check in and see if he's available?"

"Yes, please. Thanks, Peggy." I rolled the name around in my head. "Jackie Lee Logan? A name like that and he's a *lawyer?*" Sounded more like a country singer or NASCAR driver to me.

Peggy chuckled. "He started off in varsity football, but busted his knee in college and changed fields. He's good. I'll set him up with you. What's the problem?"

"My landlords don't appreciate police raids on the premises. Go figure."

"I can post a note to Frank about that. He may be able to talk them out of the eviction without going to court over it."

"Thanks, Peggy. That would rawk." As the adrenaline wore off, the aches set in, along with the realization that I'd been pushing myself hard and not eating nearly enough to keep me going. "Hey, Peggy," I said. "I need to go get something to eat, as in now. Do you need anything else from me?"

"That should be fine, Genét. I'm glad you're all right. I'll get the rest to Frank when he's available, and let him know you won't be needing him to get you off the hook again."

I thanked her again, restarted my car, and headed off to Crow Creek Tavern for the biggest burger I could eat.

LET ME BE THE ONE
TO LEAD YOU HOME

∾ ∾ ∾

We're on our way back."

Not *home*, but *back*. Her phrasing didn't surprise me, but still I found it revealing.

"Meg," I protested, "I thought you had more shows to do on the tour."

A rude, dismissive noise buzzed through my phone. "Fuck the shows. We called ahead and cancelled at the venues. Even called in some favors to make sure that folks we know got the gigs. Happens all the time. We're good."

"Meghan, I'm fine. Y'all don't have to…"

"I just saw my best friend get body-slammed by the po-po." Vehemence burned through the miles between us. "We're coming home. Done deal. I'm not leaving you alone down there."

That time, she'd said *home*. I didn't cry, but I thought about it.

I'd called Meghan back once I'd finished my burger and felt fatter than a tick on a racehorse's flank. My server was cute and kinda flirtatious, and in a better mood I might have flirted back with him. Instead, I'd flicked a smile in his direction from behind my phone as I checked my texts and decided who to call back. Still nothing from Detective Fallon, another text from Dad, three from Caroline (fuck *that*), and two more from Ash (ditto), plus the message from Meghan I responded to with a call. Especially at times like these, a good friend's voice beats pixels on a screen.

"When do you think you'll be back?" I asked her. "Aren't you like at the other end of the country or something?"

"Nah. We played Kansas City last night, and voted to turn back just before we did the show." She laughed. "It wasn't just me who decided to come home after we saw the video. It was pretty much unanimous."

I heard Max and Tucker shout something like "*Hi, Genét*" in the background.

"We'll probably be back by tomorrow if we drive straight through and have good luck with the traffic."

"Meg, seriously…"

"I don't wanna hear it, Genét. If we flip the script on this, you'd be there for me in a heartbeat."

"That's true. I would." My voice felt tight. My chest, too. I guess I'd been scared I would lose her to the road, but that didn't seem to be happening just yet.

She asked for an update, and I filled her in the scene at Warrior Fitness. The pavement may have curled from the barrage of cuss words she threw down when I told her about Eric Childers;

she'd known him in school too; he used to call her "Troll Doll" on account of her long hair and bare feet. "I hope he limps for a fucking year," she said. "Asshole."

"*I* hope his family doesn't sue me."

"Fuck *that*. *You* should be suing *him*. You *are*, aren't you?"

"Pretty much."

"Good."

She got quiet when I'd told her about the Middle Eastern woman who didn't seem to fit in at the gym. Meghan's had a little experience with stuff most people don't see. "Did she look like she was real?"

"Well, *yeah*. Real how?"

"Real as in, 'not like a ghost or hallucination or something.'"

"Oh, yeah. She looked as real as anybody else in the gym."

"Anyone else notice her?"

"I really wasn't paying attention. Too busy kicking Eric's ass." The server was back, I guess to check on whether I wanted anything else to eat or drink. His flirty smile had gone a little lopsided. I grinned at him. He mouthed *sorry*, ducked his head with embarrassment, and backed away with amusing care. I laughed. "And now I just scared the waiter."

After we shared a chuckle or three, Meg returned to the dancer in the gym. "You said you heard music, too? I mean, not just corporate metal crap, but like a bell or something?"

"Yeah. Like… kinda like the rustling of a coin-belt, ankle-bells, and zils – those little finger-cymbals bellydancers use. Except she wasn't dancing or playing any instruments, just walking around."

"And you could hear this over blaring cock rock."

"Exactly."

"And you've never seen her before today?"

I thought about it. "Not that I remember."

"Not even during that night at the Bottle?"

That *weekend* at the Bottle, more like. Suddenly, the whole thing made a lot more sense.

"I'm not sure," I told her. "I might have, but if I did, I don't remember. There's a lot I don't remember from that… that whole thing."

Oh, yeah. That whole vortex running through the middle of my everyday life and sucking it down the rabbit hole to Wonderland in Hell.

Realizing this was probably not a conversation I needed to be having in public, I asked Meghan to hold off the heavy stuff for a few minutes, then paid my check, smiled at the server, and headed back toward my car. Warm sunlight bathed the street and turned my car into a sauna. At the edges of the sky, I spotted dark hints of another storm.

Once I'd secured my Bluetooth and edged out of the parking lot, I steered our conversation back to phantom dancers and other strangeness. "You think I'm seeing this girl now because I got dosed with Red Shoes?"

"Probably."

"Great. So, does that mean she's really there, or she's in my head?"

"I dunno. Maybe both." Meghan took a deep breath, and I could practically see a scale weighing out the words she was about to use.

"Okay," she finally said, "this is probably something we should talk about more when I get back there. For now, though, I'll say that it sounds like you're dealing with some sort of manifestation – a presence, an entity, whatever you wanna call it – that's taking on a shape in your perceptions because it's something your perceptions expect to see. Does that make sense?"

"Not entirely." I was beginning to feel a refrigerated centipede creep along the back of my neck.

She blew out a long breath. "Okay, so this girl? The dancer you saw?"

"Yeah?"

"You might be seeing her as a dancer because this whole thing centers on your dance troupe and that friend who… who died while dancing."

"Like a ghost?" I asked. "But she doesn't *look* like Blue. She doesn't look like anyone I've ever seen before."

"Not like a ghost," Meghan said. "Unless she *is* a ghost. But she doesn't sound like one, from what you just told me. Real ghosts don't tend to walk around crowded gyms during broad daylight, for starters."

"I don't believe we're even having this conversation, Meg."

She laughed, then said, very seriously, "Time to start believing, bitch."

"Yeah. I'm getting that impression." I'd gotten it a long time ago. But there's remembering some crazy shit your best friend said back when you were kids, and then there's dealing with crazy shit that's going down right now in front of you.

"So," I repeated, "is this woman real, or in my head?"

Meghan repeated herself, more certain this time: "Both. I think she's probably both. I mean, there's *something* really there, but the way you're seeing it is shaped by your perceptions. Make sense now?"

"Kinda." I felt my face squinch up. "Yeah. Yes, it does."

On one hand, this creeped me out. On the other hand, it was sort of cool to have a backstage pass on the stuff normal people can't see. I was beginning to see why people liked this stuff. And *that* realization was scarier than anything Meghan had actually said.

"From what I've heard," she went on, "Red Shoes is kind of like acid mixed with ecstasy and popped up with a little coke to keep the party running all night."

"Or all weekend."

"Exactly."

And so if it could make you fight like Eric and I had fought…

"It's hero juice," I said. "Instant fantasy-hero juice."

"Maybe, yeah."

And the only drawback was that you might catch fire from the inside out. "That," I told my best friend, "is sort of unsettling."

"Yep."

"Because really, if it wasn't for the whole maybe-burn-alive thing… well, I've had worse results from the average beer. I could get used to that sort of thing really fast."

"Crap, Genét." Meg's voice growled in her throat. "Don't *even* joke about shit like that." Meghan's a musician, but she's no big fan of getting wasted. Lots of bad examples in her family. In mine too, for that matter.

"I *was* just joking," I assured her. "I'm not gonna strap on my bright Red Shoes again."

"Good. Don't." She paused, asked someone a question in the background, then came back to me. "It's possible," she said, "that you saw the spirit of Red Shoes itself. Or a manifestation of it, anyway."

"Really? Drugs can do that?"

"Send out manifestations of themselves? Totally." She chuckled. "You ever hear about the Green Fairy?"

Of course I had. "C'mon, Meg – I took my nickname from *Jean Genét*, right? Absinthe."

"Right. And Mary Jane, pink elephants, 'hair of the dog that bit you,' all that stuff. People get fucked up, and then they see manifestations of the drug they're on at the time. Filtered through the mind of the person who's seeing them – that whole 'eye of the beholder' thing – but yeah, more often than not the thing they're seeing is really there."

"Wow." The image hit me then, of crack-zombies haunting rundown houses, runny-nosed specters drifting through celebrity parties, grunge-'90s rock stars sharing an eternal nod while boozy ghosts crouched on barstools and dreamed of better days...

Sunlight or no sunlight, I felt distinctly cold.

To shake it off, I asked, "If this girl is a manifestation of Red Shoes, shouldn't she be like an old-school Danish peasant or something?"

"You mean like in the original story?" Meghan replied. "Maybe, maybe not. The shape you see has more to do with *you* than it has to do with *them*, if that makes sense."

"Yeah, I guess it does." Mentally, I set out yet another collection of puzzle-pieces and a nice clean table to connect them on. The Middle-Eastern dancer. The Red Shoes in my system (*how long does this stuff LAST in your system, anyway?*). Arcana Darque. The fight at Warrior Fitness. "So how," I asked Meghan, "does what's in my head influence what I see when I'm seeing something that's really there?"

"Uh, wow." Meghan kinda laughed. "That's pretty much *always* happening, Genét. I mean, everything you see or hear or feel or whatever gets processed through electrons and chemicals that your brain interprets through your consciousness. That's the way our senses work: we take a bunch of electronic data and perceive it through our memories and expectations and hopes and fears and all that stuff. The way Dervish puts it, reality's a big shared hallucination; we agree on a lot of details, but there's still a lot of gray area where we experience totally different worlds."

Different worlds was right. Mine kept getting stranger, and Meghan's had been stranger than I'd realized for longer than I'd thought. Hell, if Eric Childers had known the right ways to sic riot cops on innocent people, then there was a lot more *different worlds* stuff going on than even *I* had realized. As I slowed down at the traffic light ahead, I found myself scanning the other cars, the crowds on the sidewalks, the people I could see in the windows of the stores along Boleshire Lane… all those people, each one a reality unto themselves. A wave of vertigo swept over me as I realized how deep and wide the spaces between us all really are.

"Hey," Meghan said. "You still there?"

I'd been quiet longer than I'd realized.

"Oh, yeah. Sorry." The light changed and we all moved forward. "Just thinking. It's a lot to process."

"Yeah," she said. "I know what you mean."

"I kinda get the impression that you do." My laugh came more from nerves than from humor. "Thank you," I told her, meaning it. "Thanks for helping me out with all this."

"No problem. I just wish it was happening when I was actually *there*. But I'll be back in a day or so."

Friends rock.

"Okay." I brought us back on track. "This girl, this 'manifestation' or whatever. Why's she following *me* around? I mean, I've only done Red Shoes once. By accident. Why isn't she bugging Vivienne or Caroline?"

"Maybe she *is*." Meghan laughed. "Why not ask her?"

"Can you *do* that? How?"

"Depends on the entity. Some of 'em just talk, like we do. Most of 'em, though… you have to *read* them. Like with a cat or a dog. Read the ways they move, the way they look at you, the stuff it seems like they *might* say. You can have conversations – kinda limited ones, but still communication – if you focus on them and they focus on you and y'all try an understand each other."

I slowed down to let a little kid cross the street in front of me, "Okay," I said. "That makes sense. Focus *how?*"

"From what you've been saying, I'd say it's music. Or dance. Maybe both."

"But I'm not a dancer. Not really. I mean, I do it for fun – I'm not serious into it or anything. And music is *your* gig, not mine."

"You're hearing music when you see her, right?"

"Right."

"And you saw her looking at you?"

"Yeah."

"So she's trying to communicate with you, I think. Something about you's on her wavelength, or she's on yours."

Wavelength. Vibrations.

"Like with alchemy, right?" Traffic sped up, so I did too, my voice rising with excitement. "Sublime musical frequencies, that primal-sound stuff we talked about last week?"

"Exactly. Right."

"Okay, so if I understand what I think you're saying, I need to hit a trance-state that resonates with her vibrational frequency or something, right?"

"Pretty much."

"By dancing?"

"Worth a shot."

"Huh." I began brainstorming, laying out a potential playlist and envisioning the moves I might make…

…which is when a loud car-horn reminded me I was supposed to be driving.

I cut hard to the right as some asshole in an SUV blew past me on my left. An incoming car blasted his horn too, and I honked back and cursed, on reflex, at both of them but really at myself.

"Shit," Meghan spat. "You okay?"

"Sorry, Meg. Some dude just tried to run me off the road."

"You're *driving* and talking about this stuff?" Her voice was half-laugh, half-yell. "*And* you just got booted out of your gym after kicking the ass of some dude who called the cops on you and got you thrown in jail and stuff and *now you're talking metaphysics on the phone while you're DRIVING?*" She was laughing now. I could hear the others laughing too. "Hang up the *phone*, girlfriend! Call me when you get back home and *don't* have a fucking accident."

"Point taken," I told her. "Talk to ya soon. *Love you.*"

"Love you too, you crazy bitch."

I thought about cuing up some music, but drove home in silence instead, sorting out the implications of what she'd been saying, what I'd seen, and maybe what I had to do next.

YOU ARE SAFE
WITHIN THE DANCE

∾ ∾ ∾

The blot on the edges of the horizon had begun throwing rain at my windows by the time I got home, hashed out my plans, and laid out the living room for our little conversation. Sunlight had gone bye-bye in that way it does with Southern storms. I'd swept up the living room, clearing away the glass and splinters and other stuff as much as I could manage. Mentally apologizing to the folks downstairs, I'd clonked around in my New Rocks until I was sure the floor was clean. I secured the busted front door with a bungee cord, and shoved the back door into its frame as far as I could wedge it. I'd called Kristen to see if she planned to come home that night, but her calls still went to voicemail and I didn't blame her a bit.

I did *not* want witnesses for what I planned to do next.

The cops still had my computer, but I still had my phone. And so, I laid out a playlist in the cloud, arranging tracks from Dead Can Dance, Vas, Solace and so on, then let my brain ride the waves of sound and feelings as my body cleaned the room. Intuition, not analysis, chose the tracks and their order for me. If Meghan was right – and I knew she was – then this wasn't something I could think through. I had to *feel* it, deep outside my conscious mind, or else nothing would happen at all.

I'd tried to reach her again after I got home, but the call went to voice-mail and the messages went unanswered. No signal, probably; that happens a lot when you're talking from the road. No problem. I thought I had what I needed in order to do this thing, and if I pondered it too much I was liable to write the whole deal off.

As I swept the floors to within a molecule of their raw-wood surfaces, I focused on the image of the woman I had seen. Her eyes. The planes of her face. The wavy flow of her hair. Red veil, white pearls, gold coins, the sound of her zils. The strong, sure beauty of the way she moved. I closed my eyes and let Geno Valle's "Hair of the Gods" draw me into a space between the worlds. Zen monks turn housework into meditations, so I let myself do that too.

The apartment darkened as the storm came in, its drops and gusts a symphony on glass and groaning wood. Outside in the halls, I sensed neighbors pass, their footsteps creaking on the floors. It may have been my imagination, but I swear I heard their heartbeats underneath the music and the floors, beating back at mine with simpatico recognition. I *felt* them more than *heard* them, the way you feel objects in a room where it's too dark to see, the way you feel eyes watching you when there's no one in sight but someone's clearly *there*. Dropping from everyday perceptions into trance-awareness, I sensed the building open up and let me in.

Gene Valle blended into "Invocatio," a short vocal track from Irfan that Vivienne sometimes used to get us in the mood. I'd selected the playlist from a range of songs we used in the troupe, choosing – again, more by instinct than by strategy – to follow a wave of sound and emotions, building to a peak after a long, percussive drone of voices and drums, accentuated by chimes and synthesizers until everything merged into a vast temple of sound. It was all modern stuff, not traditional culture music; it sounded right, though, for what I had in mind.

I'm not usually an incense kind of girl, but I'd stopped by Matrix on my way home, grabbing a few packages of frankincense, a brass incense burner, and a tiny bell. On impulse, I'd also grabbed a statue of some goddess I'd never heard of until then. *Genét, love*, I told myself, *Meghan's right. You really ARE being a crazy bitch.* With how cray-cray my life already was by that point, though, I figured Crazy was the order of the day.

Crazy or not-crazy, I was taking precautions. Two pans of cold water rested on either side of the space I'd cleared on the floor for the dance. Our coffee table got smashed during the raid, but I propped a TV tray off in the dining area, within reach of where I planned to dance. I put out three more glasses of cold water on that tray, figuring that if anything would dispel a pending case of Genét flambé, it would be cold water and lots of it. I'd bought a package of chalk at Matrix too, looked up some designs on my phone, and drawn what I hoped would be a passable circle on the living room floor. Honestly, I don't know shit about magic rituals, but if nothing else, ten years of gaming (give or take) will teach you to ward your space if you plan to summon something not-quite-human. If I'd had time and my computer handy, I would have done more serious research before attempting something this insane; better yet, I'd have gotten Meghan, Max and Dervish to do it for me. They certainly knew more about this metaphysical crap than I ever did. That afternoon's appearance of the Red Shoe Faerie, though – or whatever the hell she was – had me feeling like a clock was ticking somewhere, and that chat with Meghan had me thinking this was something I had to do myself.

So I improvised like mad and hoped that wouldn't get me killed.

It occurred to me, as the sky went dark, that the preparation itself was a dance – an improvised one, but one with steps, a beat, and a flow. When you dance, if you're doing it right, you let the music take you over and guide the way you place your steps. Serious dance demands serious practice and training. Really, it's a lot like martial arts that way. And in both disciplines, there's a time to surrender to the moment and the flow – to let your body, mind, and what I was quickly beginning to recognize as spirit guide you *beyond* your training, to a place beyond conscious thought. I've always been analytical by nature; I'm good at puzzles because I process data well. Even in puzzles, though, you need to see past the pieces – the data, the practice, the conscious thoughts – and perceive the bigger picture that *can* become real once you bring imagination into play.

"Find the meaning in your movements," Vivienne used to say. "Let the feeling of the movement guide what you think it means." So I did.

After I'd cleaned the room and "set the space," as Vivienne often did before practice sessions began, I unbuckled my New Rocks and changed into some dance gear. In place of the bra and skirt I'd worn the night Blue died, I pulled on a black skirt and a violet *choli* blouse. Coin belt, coin bra, ankle bells, the whole bit. Oh yeah – plus zils, of course. I figured if anything would get the spirit's attention, it would be the sound of zils. I switched out the light and let the music move me. As I warmed up and stretched to the sound of DCD's "De Profundis," faint rumbles of distant thunder resonated through the soles of my feet.

I felt the everyday world fall away, and prayed to whatever might be out there that I had enough sense to catch myself before I fell too far with it.

When Vas's song "In the Garden of Souls" began, I bowed to the room, eyes closed, my palms pressed together in front of me. Raising my hands and rising from the waist, I swept my fingers out into the darkness, following the flow of the notes. My toes reached out and skimmed across the floor. Eyes still shut, I drifted into tides of energy, floating with them as I stamped percussive counterpoints to the beat.

Isolations of my shoulders. Isolations of my hips. I folded, clenched and undulated stomach muscles, feeling the warm bite of adrenaline wash the soreness from my limbs. As my body woke up and began to flow, I surrendered to the pulse, the beat, the chime, the drone.

When I'd first joined Arcana Darque, I'd just wanted good times and killer abs. Once I'd gotten past my self-consciousness and adjusted myself to the movements and exercise, I'd begun to realize how much deeper this whole "lose yourself in the dance" thing could go. We had choreography, sure, and it was important to remember the moves. But just like the training at Warrior Fitness, there's a place you reach – when you really want to reach it – where dance stops being exercise and starts being communion. Religion has never been much of a thing in my house or with me. Knowing Meghan, though, taught me there's a lot more to life than the material stuff we see, and dancing with Arcana Darque showed me how to let go and become magical.

When you spend as much time as I do parsing things out with logic and analysis, it felt really fucking good to let my body do the thinking and put my mind on hold.

Practice becomes reflex. Reflex becomes instinct. Instinct can save your life. Rayvon taught us that in self-defense class at Warrior Fitness. He was talking about fighting, but it's true of dancing too.

I kept my eyes shut as rain and thunder rolled in beneath the beat. In my mind's eye, colored trails followed the path of my hands and feet. I wove patterns in the air, arcane designs that *felt* mystical even if they meant nothing more than the movement of skin through space. The texture of the wood under my feet warmed and shift beneath me as I danced. I moved outside the circle, but by then I didn't care. Whatever was going to happen was going to happen anyway.

For a time, time went away. Everything was music, movement, energy and breath.

Even with my eyes closed, I sensed the edges of the furniture and walls, the edges of my dancing space. Awareness spread outward in a fan, brushing obstacles and letting me know they were there. "Toward the Within" from Dead Can Dance kicked in. Its drumbeats echoed inside my chest. Music swelled up and drew me in, currents of sound pulling me in strange directions. Each time stray thoughts poked up, the current pulled them down and washed them away.

Then I felt her enter the room.

She didn't use the door or windows. She was simply *there* where she hadn't been a second before. A blur of heat in the darkness beyond my eyes. A sense of weight on the creaking hardwood floor. That familiar scent of cinnamon. Her zils chimed and her coins rustled perfectly in time with the music. As horns blared the intro to a new song, I felt her slide in close to me. My breath caught in my chest. My eyelids twitched, but I kept them shut. I wanted to see her, but I didn't want to look. The moment crackled with holy danger. My skin flushed with the familiar spicy heat of Red Shoes, and I thought *If I open my eyes now, I'm burning up like Blue.* So I kept them shut like Indy and Marion in *Raiders of the Lost Ark*. Whatever happened in that dark and sacred room, I wouldn't see it with open eyes.

Her skirt brushed my legs as she glided beside me, taking up the rhythm of our dance. Her feet thumped the wood near mine. This wasn't some ephemeral ghost-girl, but a woman as solid and alive as I am. I felt her body heat radiate through the air conditioned room, and heard her breathing through her nose as she danced close to me. I was tempted to open my eyes and find out, but that scene in *Raiders* overrode my curiosity and – not wanting my face to melt off – I kept them shut.

I stuck the tip of my tongue up behind my front teeth, and opened my lips slightly to take in breath. Up my spine, the bright blaze of energy uncoiled from the base toward my head. Protesting muscles warmed, stretched, flowed like snakes. Spicy frankincense settled in my nose and tickled across the bottom of my tongue. Metal coins and weighted silk waved a dance between gravity and inertia. And alongside me, another woman danced, her clothes rippling and her coins rustling and our zils *ting-tin-ting-tinging* away in unison. Wood creaked and skin shushed its way across the floor.

Red Shoes... or, as I was beginning to think of her now, *Zil...* slid her dry palms into mine. I damn near opened my eyes in shock, but squeezed them tight until light crackled across the darkness under my lids. Her weight guided me into a twist, a spin, a wave as we raised our hands and sent that wave rolling through our bodies from end to end. She led the dance and I followed – not the way you'd do with a guy who's trying to show off, but the way you might if you shared a dance between equals, the energy passing between you both without conscious thought. The tiny cymbals on our fingers clashed and sang and rode like awkward metal cowboys strapped to our fingers and hanging on for dear life.

As the music slid into DCD's "Saltarello," I felt my awareness of space expand beyond the confines of our apartment and the hall outside. The walls and furniture seemed to fade, replaced by a sense of monumental openness. The wood floor beneath our feet – warm from our heat – remained, but the area we danced in had no walls, no furniture, no sense of confinement at all. It felt like a dark ballroom in the middle of nowhere, with music echoing through empty space and a faint hiss of rain on distant windows. Again, I nearly opened my eyes. Again, I kept them shut.

Zil spun me out in an impossible arc. Nothing tangled my legs or bashed against my toes. I rode the spin and turned it into a dervish twirl, throwing my head back and letting momentum shred my remaining conscious thoughts. Everything was reflex now, with a small outpost of my rational mind caught up in a primal storm.

I couldn't tell you how long we spun and leaped and stretched our bodies past their limits. Songs wrapped their way through endless space. Zil moved and I moved with her, our bodies connected by streams of elemental essence. Gradually, I felt heat rising under my skin; this time, though, there was no bite or suffocating press of fever. The sweat on our bodies dampened our clothes, slicked our flesh, slid stickiness across the floor and sent tiny drops of moisture flying. When we touched, that slickness passed from skin to skin. Whatever sort of "entity" she might be, Zil felt as human as any dancer in the troupe.

Neither of us spoke. Music and footsteps and breath and distant rain were the only sounds I heard.

Music is a conversation. Meghan told me that once, I think. Musicians, their instruments, the audience if there is one, even the space in which they play – they all share that conversation. Waves vibrate through space in frequencies, changing everything they touch even as they change themselves through contact and dispersion. I felt myself changing in the conversation of that dance, my snarky comfort-zone transforming in poetic metamorphosis.

I began to see where Meghan got that her ability to go from grumpy kid to goddess in a single turn of phrase.

My dance with Zil became the opposite of my fight with Eric Childers. We weren't competing, she and I – we were complimenting one another. Instead of looking for openings and guarding against blows, we flowed like a warm river over every obstacle and block. I'd say it was like sex, but it was better than any sex I've ever had. The music blended Zil and I into a single spirit in two skins, and those skins kept blending into one another and then separating out again.

Then it changed.

Zil slid one palm across my belly. A cramp reached inside my guts and pulled. Hard. The shock almost wrenched my eyes open, and I heard myself shout in betrayed surprise. Thrown off-step, I reeled into a crouch, lost my balance, and fell.

My knees took the worst of it, and I cried out again as I leaned into the pain and bashed my head into the floor.

Another cramp. Another twist in that familiar location. I felt a rush of sticky heat, and found my voice: "*Why?*"

Zil said nothing, but circled in around me.

Now she felt hotter – not quite fire, but a blast-of-furnace warmth.

Oh, fuck, I thought. *I'm gonna fucking burn.*

TOWARD THE WITHIN

∿ ∿ ∿

My eyelids flickered open. The view revealed a vast darkness, from horizon to horizon without a wall in sight. My playlist still played, but the sound carried on thin air, coming from nowhere I could see. The hardwood floor remained, the lines of my awkward chalk circle glowing in near-total night. Rain rattled against the windows somewhere out of sight, with little licks of thunder rumbling the wood under my palms and legs. My living room, though, was gone, and the circle glowed huge in the endless black.

Fucking spirits. If they could bend time, it made sense they could bend space as well.

Zil's feet slid across the sweat-damp floor behind me. I closed my eyes before she crossed into view.

"What the *hell?*" My voice grated against the pain. "Why'd you *do* that to me?"

Instead of words, I heard the *ting-ting-ting* of her zils, the rustle of her coins, the faint jingle of the ankle-bells.

I felt her lean in toward me again, and pulled back out of reach. "No," I told her. "You lost your touching privileges. I won't let you hurt me again."

Where was the damned water? It had been within reach before I started out, but it had vanished to wherever the rest of our apartment had gone. I scrambled around on the floor, but found nothing. Zil's chimes rang out as she circled around me, her arms waving unseen arcs that I could feel. My guts pulsed in a tangled knot of sticky pain.

Blind, hurting, drenched in sweat in the middle of Bellydance Limbo Hell, I was feeling kinda fucked.

"What do you want?" My voice held more steadiness than I'd expected. "I don't know what to call you, and don't even really know who you are, although I think I have an idea about that last part. I just wanted to talk. I saw you watching me, and I wanted to make contact and find out what you want."

Ting-tikka-ting-ting. Ting-tikka-ting-ting. Zil's... um, zils... clashed in a beckoning rhythm, drawing me back up and to dance. I felt her urging me up to my feet, encouraging me with gestures and nods. Hurt and angry as I was, the invisible bonds between us remained. I couldn't see Zil with physical sight, but my mind's eye saw her perfectly.

She wanted me to get up and dance some more.

With unsteady grace, I rose to my feet. My belly rippled with dull spasms. Imitating the image I held of Zil in my head, I began contracting and releasing my abs, focusing on literal *belly*-dance in the ways that gave that dance its name. I still refused to open my eyes, but I could feel us both mirroring one another, our bellies arching snakelike in rolling waves of skin. The coins on my belt rustled soothing rhythms. Their weight across my hips lent power to the wave. Tender warmth bloomed across my skin – not the harsh heat of Zil's approach, or the crackling fury I'd felt at Warrior Fitness, but a soothing ease to my twisted guts.

You can open your eyes. It's safe.

My ears didn't hear her words. My mind did. After that little trick with the cramps, though, I wasn't feeling safe with Zil quite yet. I turned the shake of my head into part of the dance but kept my eyes pressed shut.

Our muscles rolled like steady waves, accentuated by the clash of zils and the throbbing pump of drums. Collaboration, not conflict, two bodies with a single purpose.

The warmth spread, became bliss and then euphoria. Pain eased away, replaced by soothing calm.

It's medicine, I realized. *Red Shoes is medicine… or at least it's supposed to be.*

Then I understood.

Bellydance didn't start out as showing off for men. It began in the rituals of women, as dances and exercises they shared between themselves. Those rituals included easing menstrual cramps and childbirth. Their undulations and contractions strengthened belly-muscles, soothed labor-pains, and gave women a place to go in their bodies where the pain couldn't reach them. Trances. Bodies. Music. Flow. Ritual became play; play became communion; communion became performance, and performance grew larger than its initial mysteries. Vivienne had told us all about it but the whole picture hadn't made itself clear in my head until that moment. *Find the meaning in your movements.* I did.

That picture I'd been searching for suddenly became clear.

Red Shoes wasn't supposed to be a party drug – it was supposed to be sacred medicine. And like bellydance, it had mutated into something else. Something that could be abused. Someone was abusing it. Abusing them both. Hurting people with them both. And Zil didn't like that part. At all.

"So," I asked her silence, "you want me to become your instrument?"

Her hands took mine as she guided my dance.

Her way, I guess, of saying *Yes*.

"But why me," I whispered, my voice quiet even in my own ears. "Why *me?*"

No reply.

Perhaps Zil was just making do with whatever she had to work with. If so, that said some sorry things about the state of our local bellydance scene.

My playlist cycled over and began again. Still we danced, the rain drumming on distant windows in another world untouched by our presence as we moved.

The warmth in my belly spread throughout my body, lending energy to my arms and legs. Sweat stuck my clothing to my skin. Zil pressed in close to me again, then whipped back into a spin so frantic I could feel the breeze from her skirt as she spun. Up on my toes, I followed suit, the breeze rushing outward in a gentle storm.

The song slowed, faded, and stopped at the end of the track.

No other song followed it.

The music ended.

The dance was done.

I heard my breath whistle in my throat. Blood drummed behind my ears. My heart thumped a tight red cadence behind my ribs. The pain was gone. My head floated on bright euphoric waves.

Zil stilled, motionless. Again, I followed her example. I felt her bow to me, and so I did the same to her.

The air between us burned with frankincense, cinnamon and sweat.

Coins and fabric rustled as she reached out and draped light silk, damp with perspiration, across my shoulders.

She leaned in close. I didn't move. Her soft lips touched my sweaty forehead.

"Open your eyes," she said in words. "It's okay now." Her voice held a gilded melody of accents. A little Indian, a bit of Arabic, rounded with a touch of BBC English. Those few words spoke of a bigger world.

Shivering, I opened my eyes.

The intensity of her eyes almost made me shut mine again.

Masked out in thick black khol, Zil's eyes shifted from black to warm brown to glowing hazel and deep green and resonating blue and back to black again. Her dark skin sparkled in the faint light from the living-room window. We stood again in my apartment, still standing in the circle I had drawn across the floor. Her face and head were bare; she'd draped her veil across my shoulders.

"You see the weave," she said. "Not many do."

I realized then that I'd seen something else, too.

I'd seen her in the Bottle that night.

Not dancing like she enjoyed it, but dancing like she was trapped.

Like she'd been imprisoned there until something... or someone... set her free.

Were you...? I tried to speak but the words wouldn't come together.

And then she disappeared.

Not suddenly, but in a Cheshire Cat fade. Zil's eyes were the last parts of her I saw.

My knees wobbled, but I didn't fall.

Gradually, my breath and heartbeat slowed down. I didn't move. The light-headed warmth inside me lingered, pulsating in time with my heartbeat.

Holy shit.

Except not *shit*. Just *holy*.

Wow.

Our apartment seemed totally unchanged except for a coat of sweat on the hardwood floor. The floor beyond the circle remained dry. The water waited where I'd left it, rippling slightly as I arched myself in a yoga stretch, looked around, and stepped carefully out of the circle.

Nothing happened. She was gone.

Running my fingers across her veil, I stepped first one foot and then the other into the cool trays of water on the floor. I reached for the table and realized that two of the three glasses of water were empty. The third one – the center one, of course – remained full, but the water had turned red and glowed with warm, familiar light.

Red Shoes. A glass of it.

Ah, jeeze. *Now* what?

Trembling with the strain of the craziest week I'd ever known, I reached for the center glass. Picked it up. Looked it over. Swirled the liquid around and examined it in the ghost of streetlights outside. Little flecks of sparkling grit cast bright flashes in the glowing crimson fluid. As the warmth inside me ebbed, I shivered. My hands shook. My feet throbbed in the cool water-pans. Heaviness set in – the weight of everything I'd done and everything I figured I still had to do.

You see the weave, she'd said.

She wasn't wrong. I did.

I eyed the glass again. *It's medicine when you use it properly.*

And I still had shit to do.

Ah, fuck it, I thought. The trembling in my hand went still.

I closed my eyes, tilted back my head, and drank the fucking drink.

A FEELING YOU
CAN'T OUTSOURCE

~ ~ ~

S o I figured," I said, my voice higher and faster than usual, "that if this was my boost for the final boss-fight, then the clock is ticking and I need to gather up a group for the boss level!"

If Dervish was puzzled by my babbling Geekspeak, she didn't show it. Her gaze remained resolutely peeved, and her aura blazed with bright intensity. Around us, the Silver Key sparkled, its walls and instruments glowing bluish-white. The smell of cinnamon, frankincense and dancer-sweat wrestled with the scent of old instruments, oil, and musicians. The "musicians" part probably smelled the worst, but the olfactory overflow would have given me a headache if I hadn't felt so energized.

Oh, yeah – *energized.* I was flying so high on Red Shoes by that point that Dr. Frankenstein could have hooked me up to steampunk generators and the resulting shock treatment would have felt like nothing. My hair wasn't actually on end, but it certainly seemed that way to me.

"So you came to me," she said. "To be what – your cleric or something?" Okay, so she understood at least a bit of Geekspeak, but her tone and expression didn't seem especially enthusiastic.

"Something like that, maybe. I'm not sure yet. What do you think you'd be?"

"I think I'd be *working*, thanks. At my job. Which is what I'm doing right now, if you don't mind. Please take your dungeon crawl elsewhere."

This was gonna be harder than I'd thought.

Zil's little *Drink Me* boost had lit me up like Christmas. Soreness and fatigue? Gone. History. Where I should have been dragging ass, I was flying. Unfortunately, the red blast of energy had thrown my coherence to shit. I was wide awake but blabbing like a fool.

The ticking clock in my head didn't help matters at all. Sure, I was bouncing off the walls, but for how long? When would the crash hit me, and how bad would I flame out when it did? Would I flame out *literally*, like Blue did? I had no clue. By the time I'd hit the Silver Key, though, I was running a mental timer and every ticking second put my victory in doubt.

Back when I was a kid who'd just discovered her love-affair with puzzles, Dad showed me how to up the stakes. Once I'd mastered the basics, he would set a timer and see if I could finish the puzzle before the buzzer went off. If I beat the clock, he'd take me out to go buy something cool; if not, he'd give me a hug, say "Well, you did good anyway," and ask me if I wanted him to set the timer and try again. I got good enough at the game to win more often than not. Now I felt like the timer was running and I still had missing pieces and I doubted that Zil would come give me a hug and let me try again if I failed that first time out.

That glass of Red Shoes hit me like a truck when I first threw it back. For I-don't-know-how-long, I stood there with my feet in pans of water, feeling the universe Big Banging in my head. This wasn't a small dose snuck into my drink when I wasn't looking – it was a freight train I had *chosen* to drink, high-octane Red Shoes straight from the source. The rush blew out all the cobwebs in my head, replacing them with clarity. It was pretty much the opposite of intoxication. Instead of foggy, I felt free.

Once the rush passed, I laid out the puzzle in my head again. A few pieces were still missing. Up till that point, I'd felt like I was fitting together bits of some mysterious whole without knowing what the final result should be. Once the Red Shoes kicked in, though, I began to see what the puzzle would look like when completed. As Zil said, I'd begun to see the weave.

Problem was, I realized, the pieces had been moving too. And some of them were moving *me*.

And that's when I realized I was playing a game. Or at least, that I should start *thinking* of things like I was playing a game.

Up to the point when I'd decided to kick Eric Childers' ass, I'd been dragged along for the ride without even seeing what that ride looked like. I'd viewed the whole thing like a puzzle – static, passive, unmoving – until the moment I stopped trying to fit things together. But this wasn't a puzzle after all – it was a dungeon quest. A raid. It always had been. And now the clock was ticking and I'd leveled up and it was time to stop *being* played and become the player instead.

… which brought me to the Silver Key, face-to-face with a rather peeved Dervish.

"Oh, God *dammit*," she'd snapped when I walked in the store, my eyes dazzled by the bright latticework inside. "You're on that shit now, too. I can smell it on you."

"That's sweat," I'd replied, giggling like a sorority chick. "Dance sweat. Sorry, I didn't take time to shower up before I came in. I need to talk to you."

"Get out," she snarled. "I don't need this shit." All former friendliness disappeared. "You've got it oozing out your pores, for crying out loud. Can't you even *see* yourself now?"

Oh, I'd seen myself, all right. In the windows. In the mirror. I was glowing like a red neon Christmas angel.

Dervish glowed too, but her halo wasn't Red Shoes red. The crackling field around her shimmered deep violet, with snaps of angry red shooting through it when she looked at me. "God…" She shook her head. "I can't believe *you're* doing that shit now too."

"I'm not…" I began.

"And don't fucking *lie* to me," she growled. "That's just making you look even worse. Now get *out*. I have customers here. I've got no time for this."

Yeah, she had customers: two middle-aged dudes off in one corner trading blues licks on guitar and bass. Neither of 'em paid any attention to us.

"Look," I said, leaning on the counter, "I can explain all this. But time is one thing I do *not* have right now, so please just hear me out."

"Fine." She crossed her arms. "Explain."

Nearly whispering, I did: The dosing, the Bottle, the loss of time and weird-ass entities, the swatting, Kristen's freakout, our arrest, the fight at Warrior, Meghan's phone-call and impending return, the dance with Zil and the resulting glass of shiny red goodness. "Which is why I'm here," I concluded. "You know stuff I don't know, and I need to know it *now* because I don't know what will happen when this stuff wears off or what shape I'll be in when it does."

"Holy fuckwow," she muttered. Dervish no longer looked quite as pissed, and her aura eased down to a bright violet sheen. "Man, Genét, you don't do half-measures, do you?"

"Not my strong suit right now." I tried not to giggle again. Emphasis on *tried*.

"Okay..." She looked over at the Blues Brothers, who didn't seem to have heard a thing we'd said. "Yeah, maybe, okay. But fuck up any further and we are so *very* done here."

After sending the boys home with a sob-story about her sister (me) having a crisis, Dervish locked up the store and got down to business. "Okay," she said, still wary and annoyed. "When you look around in here, what do you see?"

"The instruments are glowing," I told her. "Do you sell *magic* instruments?"

"Not exactly. It's not the instruments that are magical. It's the energy of the people who play them." She picked up an acoustic guitar, fretted it, and strummed a few chords. The violet glow around her made the strings shine purple for a moment, then they faded to faint blue.

"Holy shit," I said. "Does it always do that? I mean, whenever people play music?"

"Not really," she said. "It's just certain people – the ones who have a gift for *more* than just music, if you know what I mean."

"Meghan and I have been best friends since we were kids. I know what you mean."

"Figured you would. Still, I have to be careful about who I say this stuff to. Most people would think I've done too many drugs… no offense. Much. And the ones who actually thought they *understood* magic would never leave me alone."

"I've been realizing a lot lately," I told her, recalling my off-the-record chat with Detective Fallon, "just how *much* stuff people don't talk about because of the way other people would take it if they heard what's being said."

"Got *that* right." Dervish's fingers hammered across the strings, speaking her anger for her. Each chord sent up shivers of purple glow. *If that's what a few strums from Dervish would do*, I thought, *then Meghan's guitar must outshine Las Vegas.*

"So," Dervish asked me. "How much do *you* know about this stuff?"

"I'm sort of getting a crash-course in the real thing. I mean, I've been into fantasy and stuff since I was old enough to watch *Lord of the Rings*, but this is…" I flashed back to Blue's burning dance. "It's different."

"It is," she said. "Yeah. More subtle. Less theatrical. And really, more dangerous in certain ways because you don't usually see it coming."

I closed my eyes, shaking my head to clear out the memory of burning Blue. "You really *don't* see it coming, do you?"

"Meghan didn't." Dervish looked me over before saying more. "How much do you know about that?"

"I was there for some of it."

"And this still seems new to you?"

"There's a lot I didn't want to see."

"That's a pretty common reaction, actually. Most people default to '*I did NOT just see that*' when the moment passes. These days they do, anyway. I guess it was different back when more people believed in magic." She snorted. "Then again, considering how well that turned out for a lot of so-called 'witches' in the old days, I think denial is probably an improvement."

I flashed back to Kristen's screams during the raid, the sound of doors being smashed in and our whole life going to hell. "I'm gonna go with you on that one. Given my last experience with the cops, I'd really rather not have witch-hunters showing up at my door."

"Now you know why I was so short with you when you first came in." She reached out and gave my shoulder a sympathy squeeze. "Sorry about that, but when I saw Red Shoes all over you, I just wanted you out of the store before something worse showed up."

"Something worse like *what?* Like those things at the Bottle?"

She nodded. "Maybe. Or cops. Like I said, they love to hassle us. Or maybe just the freaks who make that shit."

"*Which* freaks?" I leaned in on the counter again. "Sorry, but that's part of what I need to know: *Who makes this stuff?* I mean, I figure it's being made in the basement of the Bottle – the local stuff is, anyway. I think that's probably part of what I saw down there that I don't remember. But who's doing it?"

She barked a bitter little laugh. "I thought you knew *that* part already; it's your friends, Ash and Caroline."

My belly did a cold drop. "So it *is* them, then?"

"Pretty much. They're selling it now, anyway. Them and that pathetic dude who thinks he's still in high school or something."

"Eric." Well, that took care of *that* little mystery, too.

"I think so. Probably him, yeah."

"What about Chalice? Her too?"

Dervish quirked her mouth like a question mark. "The dancer? The really good one?"

"Yeah."

She thought about it. "Not that I know of, no. Why?"

I shook my head, which was starting to feel a bit spinny from… well, *everything*. "I dunno. I've just seen her hanging off Eric at the gym, so I thought she might have something to do with it too."

"Ugh," Dervish said. "Gross. But no, as far as I'm aware of, she's not involved with that stuff. I mean, I don't know her *well* or anything, but I personally haven't seen or heard anything linking her with that Red Shoes shit."

"Just gross taste in guys."

"Well, yeah." Her sad smile held a hundred stories behind her lips. "But then, she wouldn't be the only girl-artist with awful taste in men. Or *boy*-artist with awful taste in men, for that matter. Sometimes that seems to be a job requirement."

I laid out the puzzle in my mind, fighting the urge to just flip my mental table and go home to bed. "Dammit," I finally sighed, again. "What a *mess*."

"Yeah." She put a hand on my shoulder. "I'm sorry. Like I said, I thought you knew about them."

"I sorta did," I admitted. "I was just hoping to be wrong."

"Sometimes the big mysteries aren't really that mysterious."

"I guess." The light seemed to leak out of the room. Or maybe it was just me. Now what? "Dammit."

"I know. It really sucks when people you like turn out to be assholes. I knew that story pretty well myself." She spread her arms. "Sorry I've been kind of a bitch tonight myself. Hug?"

"Yeah," I said. "I could probably use one."

Her aura seemed to hum as she gathered me up in a hug. My skin hummed too. In a really nice way.

"Does it always do this?" I asked her. "I mean, not trying to be rude or anything, but…"

"Does what do what?" She looked around. "Oh…" she realized what I was referring to. "You can see it, huh? Or feel it?"

"How does anybody *not*?" Then again, I hadn't seen it either until I'd downed that glass of Red Shoes. I settled into her arms, marveling at the crackle of her energy against my skin. I closed my eyes and I think I might have purred a bit.

Dervish stiffened a little. "Ummm…" she said, "Not that this doesn't feel good or anything like that, but I don't think we've *talked* about this yet."

"Like what?" I asked her, opening my eyes to find that my hand had somehow wandered up right below Dervish's left boob.

"Oh, *jeeze.*" I jerked my hand back from her chest like it was stove. My palm was still humming. "Crap! Aw, man… I am *so* sorry. I didn't mean to…" I squeezed my eyes shut. "*ARRRG!* I am *such* a dipshit."

Dervish laughed but stepped back out of the hug. I let her go, maybe a bit more slowly than I had intended to. "It's okay," she said. "I guess… just, y'know, consent is sexy, right?"

I tried to apologize some more, garbled it, and just said, "Right. God, I can't believe I *did* that."

"Hey," she told me, "it wasn't *entirely* unwelcome, okay. Just ask next time, okay?"

"Right," I repeated. We were both kinda doing that thing where you keep saying the same words over and over because you're not quite sure what you *should* say.

So then, we didn't say anything else.

Silence crept in – the kind of silence where, as Rol had told me, people talk just because it beats the awkwardness of *not* talking.

"Like I said," Dervish told me, her voice light again, "most people don't see this sort of energy thing to begin with. And even the ones who *do* don't always see it the same way. Some people hear it – not as a color, but as a hum. Or feel it."

"It's a vibration."

"Exactly. That's exactly what it is."

"That's why Blue caught fire." I couldn't stop looking at Dervish's aura. "She changed her vibration so badly it became unstable."

Dervish grimaced. "Probably. Sort of like metaphysical feedback. Resonating instability past the pain threshold, to the point where things break down."

"Jesus." Vibrations. Alchemy. The glow around the instruments seemed obvious to me then. My own glow too. Red Shoes shifts your relationship to those metaphysical vibrations. The more of it I had in my system, the more I sensed what was there all along. And with a more honest version of that medicine, I didn't feel sick or unstable, like I had before. "But this is the way it's supposed to be," I said aloud.

"Huh?"

"Sorry – I was just thinking. The way I feel now – it's the way the medicine was *supposed* to make you feel. The original medicine. Not the way it feels when it's been... well, corrupted, really, into Red Shoes." I gestured at the guitar. "When I was at the Bottle, I felt sick. I threw up all over the place, it was pretty awful. And when I felt it back in my system during my fight with Eric... I mean, it was exhilarating and all, but it was still *wrong*, y'know?"

"I know," she said. "I tried some of that shit myself. Red Shoes, I mean, back a while ago. To be honest, I think I'm kind of jealous of you right now. Of what you're getting to feel and see."

"Can't you see... y'know, *deeper* too?"

"Yes and no. I mean, I'm aware of it, but it's more of a sensory awareness then actual sight." She touched the guitar and rested her fingers on the neck. "For me, it's really *tactile*, if that makes sense. I feel it more than I see it." She smiled. "Meghan does too. She ever tell you that's why she goes barefoot all the time?"

I laughed. "I thought she was just being contrary."

Dervish laughed too. "Meghan *is* contrary. There's just more to this than that."

I nodded. "Lots more."

"That's part of why I got into dance myself, you know? And why I learned to play guitar. Because I could feel the vibrations through my hands and feet – vibrations that weren't just *sound* waves but like waves of the universe talking to me in code." Dervish stopped and laughed again shaking her head. "Wow. Listen to me. No wonder I don't talk about this stuff where the customers can hear it."

"I get that. God, it's a relief to be able to talk about it now. I mean, I'm still playing catch-up on all of this, but at least I don't feel like I'm running blind anymore."

But one piece still didn't fit quite right.

"Wait up," I said. "You said they're *selling* it. But who's *making* it?" I found myself staring at the guitar Dervish touched, watching the faint sparkle of her energy on the neck. "Okay, I realize I am, like, *way* late to the party with all this magic stuff, but unless I'm being more clueless than usual, Ash and Caroline aren't… well, y'know, like you and Meghan are."

"Not that I know of, they're not. No." She got up and checked the door, making sure it was locked. She'd already turned the lights down to "we're closed" o'clock, but even in the half-dark her anxious expression still looked clear to me in that shining violet aura.

"So…" I pressed, sensing the answer she wasn't giving me. "Who *is*? Who's in charge of those time-warping hentai things and running the endless party in the Bottle's basement?"

"I don't know the answer to that one. Like I said, I tried Red Shoes once, and now I stay as far away from it as I can get. As for the Bottle itself, I'm not a fan. There's all kinds of sketchy stuff going on there, and I don't need the grief."

"I'm not a fan either." I found myself staring at the guitar she had played. Purple light still flickered around the strings. "I tried to stay away from all this. I really did. But after all the stuff that's gone down these past few days – even before Zil showed up and gave me a big glass of power-up juice – it's pretty obvious that I can't just walk away from this mess no matter what I *want* to do. I tried leaving it alone already, and… well, look where *that* got me."

She nodded. "Yeah. Sometimes running away really *isn't* an option. I'm sorry that's where this has all gone for you."

"Thanks."

I'm not sure how much the impression of fading light had to do with my mood, the late hour, the diminishing effects of Zil's gift, or a combination of them all. The feeling that I was losing time and would not get another chance to set things right, though, was starting to freak me out a bit. How long did I have before the boost in my system ran down and I crashed. How bad would that crash be when I *did*?

Dervish noticed me grinding my fingernails together. "You okay?"

"Yeah," I replied. "I guess." I tried not to sigh like a teenage brat, but… well damn, I did it anyway. "Thing is, what do I do *now?*"

Dervish looked at me for a second, squeezed my hand, and said, "No. What do *we* do now?"

And then we started to plan.

DRUMS OF THE
STREET CABARET

∾ ∾ ∾

Nothing.

That's what we found when we did an internet search for the weird party in the basement of the Bottle. Nada. Not a single video, picture, blog post or tweet about it. Oh, sure, there was plenty of material about the Bottle itself, and the work people were doing in the studios. But when Dervish and I tried to figure out a strategy for dealing with whatever was in the basement – something we really needed to do, and *fast*, if all our suppositions about Red Shoes and the Bottle were correct – we came up with a big fat zero. And I can't speak for Dervish here, but I'm usually pretty good at that sort of thing.

"Doesn't that strike you as odd?" Dervish said as the evening dragged on and even *I* began to feel the passing of time. "I mean, not even a *whoo-girl* selfie taken down there."

"Yeah, pretty strange."

By this point, I expected to find Chalice neck-deep in the Red Shoes mess. I checked her Facebook and YouTube channel, but aside from some a few mentions of the Bottle in her comment threads – which wasn't especially unusual considering that my troupe practiced there as well – I came up nada on that score.

My phone battery, I noticed, was running down, and I'd left my recharging cord at home. We'd been using the store computer, but my battery wasn't the only thing in the Silver Key that was running out of energy.

Dervish yawned a jaw-cracking yawn. "Look, I am all in favor of helping out and all, but I've been here since noon, and… holy shit." She looked at the time. "I need to go. Not all of us gulped goddess gogo juice today."

We gave the store a final shut-down tour, then headed out to our respective cars. As the Silver Key fell into silent near-darkness, I swore I heard a faint echo of rustling coins, chiming ankle-bells, and zils.

Dervish gave me another hard-muscled hug as we stood by her car. Her energy crackled against my skin, and I breathed in a little hint of oranges underneath girl-sweat and music shop.

The hum of our bodies, our energies, went straight to my bones. I felt breath catch in my throat as my chest tightened and my skin sang.

That sweat-and-oranges smell blossomed around me.

I felt myself settle in close to her, breathing her in, my eyes closed, and…

"Hey, hey, *hey*." Dervish half-pulled, half-pushed me away. "Ease up there, cowboy."

Oh, shit.

I jerked back from her. "Oh shit," I repeated, this time out loud. "Oh, *shhhhhit.*" I shook my head to clear the haze. My skin flushed redder than Red Shoes itself. "Ah, *fuck* – sorry, Dervish, I didn't mean…"

"Yeahhhh, I think you kinda *did.*"

"I don't…" Words spiraled away in a cyclone of embarrassment. I shook myself again. "I don't know what I was thinking… except, y'know, I'm just… just…"

"Just tripping your ovaries off on psychotropic joy-juice, which is sorta messing with your boundaries. And mine."

"Yeah." I hugged myself tight, squeezing my eyes shut so I didn't have to look at her. Hurt, embarrassment, whining hunger and little dots of rage tossed themselves around in my interior tornado, swamped out by surges of frustrated girl-lust. "I'm sorry. Yeah, I guess I am."

"It's not that you're not attractive or anything," she said, her voice softer but still posting *No Trespassing* signs around the premises. "Pretty much the opposite of that. But unless I miss my guess, and I don't think I do, you're not normally into girls and you're pretty far from your right mind right now."

"You're right." The words rasped out of one corner of my mouth. I still couldn't look at her. "About the 'right mind' part, anyway. The other part I'm not sure about. I mean, I haven't really *thought* about it much but…" I let that line of inquiry drop. "I'm sorry I was… I made… I read everything all wrong."

"Go get some sleep, Genét. Be careful driving home, and let me know what we're doing, if we're doing it, as soon as you know more, okay?"

This time, I was able to look at her. "You're not mad at me or anything?"

It was her turn to sigh. "I'm not mad at you, no. You just need to get your head on strai… um… bad choice of words, okay?" She blew out something sort of like a laugh. "You just need to know *what* you want, *who* you want, *if* you want, when you're not flying high on that shit. And if you still want to figure out the rest of the confusing stuff, then we can talk more later about that. But right now, stick to the mission, okay?"

"Okay."

She didn't close the space between us this time. "You all right to drive?"

I nodded. I was. "Yeah."

Dervish looked me over, then probably decided that as tired as she was, and as badly as I'd just kinda fucked things up, she'd already done enough for me. "Okay, I trust you. No going off on any quests until we sort out what we're gonna do here, right?"

"Right," I agreed, and I meant it. Some dungeons will kill you dead as soon as you walk in the door if you try to solo them without a group. I had a feeling this was one of them.

That realization didn't keep me from cruising down to scope the place out from a distance.

The idea hit me as I watched Dervish drive away. Walking back to my car, I was struck by the radiance of the lights down Archer Street, near the music shop. Sure, I'd driven past them many times before, but in the deepness of night the streetlights and storefronts took on a faerie-tale sheen. Like the hush of a snowy night, when every sound seems muffled and every surface seems to glow, the deserted expanse of Archer Street felt like a world outside the everyday realm. Like someplace magical and still, hidden from the eyes of boring normal people. I've never felt like one of those people myself… but really, does *anyone?* That night, as the sound of Dervish's car echoed off the walls and faded in the dark, I felt as though I could walk through walls and jog down the street to my own private Narnia.

The concrete seemed to pulse under the soles of my New Rocks. The breeze picked at the ends of my hair. I hadn't changed when I left our place, so my skirt rippled softly against my legs. Coins jingled. My skin prickled up. The ghostly memory of Zil's presence sent shivers up my arms and tingled at the back of my scalp. I leaned against my car, unstrapped my boots, rolled off my socks, and felt the city sing underneath my feet.

Meghan and Dervish sensed sublime vibrations through their skin. Maybe I was starting to feel things that way too.

Rain-damp pavement hummed with the vitality of a city more or less at rest but still very much awake. That deceptive stillness guarded the rush of water in secret pipes, the electric tremor of power lines, the life force of people asleep behind windows or gazing bleary-eyed at screens that crackled in the dark. Electric sunshine illuminated office windows and cast thick shadows in the corners of the streets. Wind creaked the cables of phone wires overhead. Closing my eyes, I noted the distant rumble of thunder in the mountains and the cold air rushing ahead of the storm. Broken beats of music bounced around the empty streets, their sources hidden by buildings and the dark. Pizza vapors drifted past my nose, accenting the tang of oily rain puddles and wet cement. Branches clacked. Leaves rustled. Spectral voices curled around the night like ghosts. I soaked the whole night in.

Why hadn't I noticed all this before?

Sure, the Red Shoes or whatever it was had a lot to do with my sensitivity to it all. The bigger answer, though, was simple: I'd never stopped to pay attention like this before. We're always rushing around, ears full, eyes on our phone-screens, cybernetically sealed in our little private worlds. You have to stop moving and turn off all the chaos before your senses reach out and remind you how close real magic is – the magic of the breeze and the pavement and the thousand little miracles right in front of our faces.

Stillness, I remember Vivienne telling us one night at practice, is one of the Five Rhythms of Life. A dancer named Gabrielle Roth identified them as something like *flowing*, *staccato*, *chaos*, *lyrical*, and *stillness*. I remember thinking at the time that those five qualities don't really fit together well as words – I mean, *flowing* and *lyrical* are verbs, *staccato* and *stillness* are adjectives, and *chaos* is a noun. When Vivienne showed us what those five rhythms worked like in practice, though, I had to admit Roth was right about the way they *felt*.

And so, I danced in stillness.

I let the breeze wash over me, sensations of that magic night creeping in past mental preconceptions of computer screens and puzzle pieces. I slowed my breath down to a faint rise and fall, breathing with my diaphragm not my lungs. Weariness tugged at my muscles, but Zil's gift kept the tiredness from crashing down on me. So I breathed, and I listened, and I danced without moving a step.

I felt the city move.

Unseen cars cruising with deliberate slowness on incomprehensible errands. Loose papers and plastic bags jousting with the wind. Electric currents washing through the night.

Surging sewers and sleeping birds. Bats skimming bugs from the air. Ghosts of voices spoken hours ago whispered on the breeze as it ruffled my hair and slid through the folds of my skirt. Life in infinite forms hovered around me, and I realized it was always there, always *would* be there. All I had to do was stop and listen and let myself feel it.

Death was there too, squirming bugs and rotting bodies and the scent of decay from the Dumpsters nearby. Somewhere someone was breathing their final breaths, and although I couldn't smell them that awareness made me cold. Back when I was a little emo kid, I was fascinated by the beauty of what I thought darkness was. Seeing one friend burn alive and another get stomped on by the cops had left me feeling kinda raw about the things we tell ourselves are "dark" when we're too young to know any better. Still, there's a kind of beauty in knowing you're gonna die someday, if only because it makes living in the moment feel so much sweeter when you stop moving long enough to realize that's what you're doing... what we're *all* doing. "From the moment you are born," I remember reading someone say somewhere, "you are dying." When I was younger, I curled up with that saying like it was a warm blanket to hide me from the world. Now – still kinda young, I guess, but a little older and a lot wiser than I was back then – I realized that saying wasn't an escape or a shield. It's a call to arms, a slogan for living your ass off while you still had an ass to live with.

That realization pulled me down like cold hands in colder water, grabbing my ankles and yanking me to places where I couldn't breathe. The night closed over my head and I felt myself sinking in it, drowning in it, my chest crushed by sudden mortal dread.

So I opened my eyes.

And I saw the weave.

Thin threads of radiant energy shimmered in the breeze, luminous spider webs humming with life. What I saw that night, though, was *the* web – the Web of Life, if you want to get poetic about it. It's not like the web was wrapped around everything I saw; it's that everything I saw was *made* of Web, pulsing and glowing and everywhere *alive*. All around me, I heard the gentle rustle of Zil's presence. The rustle of my own skirt and coins echoed that sound, blended in and became one with it. My breath, released from the crush of that invisible sea, rushed down my throat and filled my lungs and sent my head spinning with sudden ecstasy.

I looked down at my hands, glowing golden-green, throbbing with my heartbeat, etched from light – not skin and bone, but pure pulsating light. The breath in my lungs sank into my belly and then rose again up my spine, crackling serpent lightning that rose to the top of my head, expanded to a crown, and got breathed back down my throat to start the whole journey over again.

World of Warcraft was never like this.

This wasn't a pretense of magic, buffed with CGI and arcane-sounding names. This was the essence of magic, the show behind the curtain that we pull across the truth just so we can go on living day-to-day in our lies.

"Zil," I heard myself say in words that sent my throat humming like Meghan's guitars strings. "Are *you* doing this, or am *I?*"

No answer. Just the rustle of coins and tiny bells.

I stared at the shimmering landscape until my eyes began to burn. Tears welled up in the corners of my eyes, and when I blinked them away the landscape blurred. One blink, blur. Two blinks, blurrier. Three blinks, and my eyes stayed shut, pressed tight while ghostly afterimages sent little lightning storms through the darkness behind my eyelids. I felt my body sway in that darkness, falling into myself without moving my body at all. *I'm still dancing in stillness*, I thought as vertigo caught hold. I shook myself hard and opened my eyes, and all I saw then was a perfectly normal city-street night.

Damn, I whispered. And I think I'm the only one who heard.

It took me a while before I convinced myself I wouldn't have some kind of flashback behind the wheel.

When I checked my phone, it said 4:18. Hints of dawn had started coloring the sky. "I need to get home," I told myself as morning-shift commuters started revving their engines and crawling through the streets. I'd had practically *no* sleep in several days now, but Zil's energy drink kept me flying. When I crashed, I realized, I'd crash so hard I'd sleep for a week and still feel tired for a month or so afterwards. For now, though, I remained wide awake, and so I pulled on my socks and strapped on my Rocks. Dawn pinked the sky by the time I popped the Power button on my Prius and eased her into the early morning street.

I meant to go home. That was the plan, honestly. A few minutes, later, though, I found myself on autopilot, heading toward Shady Creek and that elite piece of real estate known as the Bottle.

Yeah, that night I was just *full* of good ideas.

PULL IT TOGETHER,
YOU'LL BE FINE

~ ~ ~

The pumping thunder of the Bottle's everlasting party boomed across the parking lot as I guided my car through the early morning gloom. Slivers of red cloud appeared along the edges, but the sky was still dark with rainclouds and departing night. I'd been listening to an Arcana Darque practice playlist in an effort to keep my head in Zil-space. By the time I hit the parking lot, though, fatigue nibbled at my Red Shoes buzz. With two or three days of little or no sleep under my dance-belt, I was bound for Dreamland once the stuff wore off. *Well, then,* I told myself, *I'd better get this taken care of soon, shouldn't I?*

This time out, I wasn't taking any chances. I rode up to the edge of the building with exactly zero intentions of getting out and going inside. As far as I could tell, the resident Bottleites were inside sleeping or fucking or partying or whatever else you do around dawn when you live in a place like this. I admit, I'd always found the place kind of cool and fun until the night of Blue's wake and the weekend-long blackout it had become. Now, just the *sight* of it creeped me out. The nearer I drove, the more disconcerted I felt. By the time I reached the edge of the building, the hair on my arms stuck straight up out of my goose-pimpled skin.

I didn't need Red Shoes to feel the vibration of that beat or the prickling uneasiness it brought out in me. Mental images of blurred faces and leering things slammed through my skull, conjuring ghosts of red vomit up my throat. I squeezed my eyes tight to lock the memories down, shook my head out, and opened my eyes again.

The rotting bricks of the Bottle's walls danced with faint electric currents, invisible to normal sight but obvious to mine. Trickles of energy coursed along the surface of the bricks, seeping through the mortar in between. Those currents – one moment electric, the next moment liquid – pulsed in time with the music underground, that Underhill beat that ate up time and spat out people too dazed by ecstasy to care. Somewhere in that throbbing mass, someone was turning Red Shoes from a medicine to a drug. That someone had killed my friend, or at least given her the tools to kill herself. And despite my fear of the things downstairs, I felt that beat pulling at my bones, urging me out of the car and in through those doors into God-knows-what.

Although I couldn't see anyone else outside, I didn't feel *alone*, exactly. The building had a presence of its own. The longer I sat there, staring at the trickles of energy across the walls, feeling the thump of electric rhythms underground, the more I wanted to go inside.

My skin shivered with the kiss of forbidden pleasures. Back when I'd dated Charles Ecké – the fashionably bi ex-boyfriend who'd introduced me to the work of Jean Genét during his successful campaign to get my pants off – we made out in all those places you're not supposed to make out in. Charles sometimes ran his lips and the furs of his chin up the back of my arms, causing me to shake with pent-up lust. He didn't even need to kiss me to drive me mindless back then; he got that kind of reaction just by using the sort of gentleness you almost never find in teenage boys… or in teenage girls either, for that matter. I'm not sure where he learned that delicacy, but his bedroom chops could've made college boys cry with envy. There are worse ways to lose your virginity, and Charles probably racked up quite a score by the time we graduated. I hadn't thought of him in years, though, until that tricking energy and pulsating beat called me back to the Age of Charles, when *what you shouldn't do* and *what you want to do* mingled in a cloud of panty-wetting lust.

Stay in the goddamned car, my better self said.

So of course I didn't.

Silly girl.

I found myself opening the car door. My boots crunched on gritty pavement. Scattered flecks of glass gleamed with micro-starlight in the rising glow of approaching dawn. Pleasure-shivers ran through me, head to foot and every spot in between, as I stepped out of the car and softly closed the door. The pumping beat from down below called me toward the Bottle's doors, so I locked my car and headed toward the building's entrance, caught in a tug-of-war between my body and my brain. *Don't do this*, my brain insisted. *Really, seriously, don't do this*. My body, though, kept moving toward the door, entranced by memories of Charles Ecké's lips.

Entranced. That was it. The word broke through my hormore haze. Entranced. That's what was going on in the Bottle's basement.

Like Underhill, it entranced the participants of its wild party until they lost all connection to the world outside.

That's when I realized that the Bottle's aura of cool might come from more than just a bohemian rebel vibe. It was *literally* a vibe that drew and held people here – a vibe I felt more strongly under the influence of clarified Red Shoes. A metaphysical vibration as well as the physical sensation of pounding beats and chords. The combination drew us in, held us there, and made everything else important disappear. Time. Hunger. Common sense. Consent to be part of that party at all.

Consent is sexy, dervish had said. What, though, was sex without consent?

Seduction.

Intoxication.

Rape.

Let's be honest, that's what it was.

Metaphysical rape.

I recoiled from that door like it'd slapped me in the face.

That trickling energy suddenly looked like rape-drug cascades. I stepped back from the door and headed toward my car again, my skin bristling with terror-raised hair. Charles' phantom lips skittered like cockroaches up my arms. I dashed to my car, turned her on, and floored it right the fuck out of there.

I was still shaking by the time I got home. By then, all reservations I'd had about shutting the damned thing down for good were gone.

Phantom faces followed me all the way home: people, and whatever the hell else they were down there, all locked in an endless dance where whoever they were and whatever they had been before got lost in a time-skewed pounding haze. It wasn't a party down there – not anymore, if it ever had been to begin with. It *was* Underhill, a trap, a sundew or pitcher plant where the sweet taste of a lure attracts prey and drains it of… well, whatever it was that the Bottle drained people of. I was guessing it was life force, and the fact that Rol and I had almost gotten lost down there ourselves changed those shivers of desire into shakes of fearful rage.

This wasn't about Blue anymore. It wasn't about me. It wasn't about Ash and Caroline and whatever they hell they were making in or around that basement trap. It wasn't even about Childers and the shit he'd done to me and Kristen. This was bigger than a drug, or the death of one girl stupid enough to die from it. *You can see the weave*, Zil had said, and now I'd seen a lot more than I'd bargained for.

I hugged myself tight as I boomed up the stairs, heavy boot-stomps echoing through my apartment building's halls. I eased my front door open, ducked under the police tape, and found myself face-to-face with yet another fun surprise.

So, read the note in Kristen's handwriting, set next to the dancing circle I had chalked out the night before, *do I WANT to know why there's a summoning circle in the middle of our living room floor?*

SO SPIT IT OUT NOW

∿ ∿ ∿

H ey, Kristen."

"*Hiiiiiiiiiii…*" Her drawn-out syllable and uplifted
tone at the end asked the question without having to actually ask it.

Kris isn't real-life magick-people. Not the way Meghan
or Dervish are. She *has* watched a lot of *Fullmetal Alchemist*,
though, so it's not like she didn't have a pretty good idea what
I'd been doing in our living room. After making sure my phone
was recharged, I called Kristen in order to sort things out. As I'd
figured, she and Inanna were still over at Celeste's place. I guess
they'd come back over to collect a few things and had seen a new
reason why Kris should stay with her girlfriend, as away as far away
from me as possible.

By the time I called Kris, morning had washed our living
room in warm shades of post-rain sunshine. Southern humidity
spread its sticky wet blanket across town, and so I'd turned on the
AC back on. Zil's pick-me-up was fading from my system and
my entire body felt like a rusty robot about to topple over. A text
message on my phone let me know that Meghan and her band had
arrived back in town sometime around 7:00 a.m. and were crashed

out at Thunderdome's place. In order to hear Kris better, I headed toward the kitchen. "So…" I began, trying to think up a good way to sum up the insanity of the last few hours, "about that circle in the middle of our floor…"

"Yeah," she said, "I was gonna remind you that *I'm* the one with the little black cat, not you." Okay, so Kris making jokes was a good sign to start with.

I gave her a strained little laugh. "I guess the best answer to your question is that I decided to stop playing by the rules of rationality because the current situation isn't exactly rational."

"Judging by the evidence, I'm gonna agree." I heard her tell Celeste that I was the one on the phone. "So," she said, coming back to me, "you gonna educate me or not, Rumi?"

Still making jokes. Good.

Briefly as I could, I filled Kris in about Eric Childers and the beatdown I'd inflicted on him back at Warrior Fitness.

"Had. It. Coming," she said when I was done. "And by the way, dear, before we talk about anything illegal, how 'bout you come over and have some tea?"

"Over to Celeste's?" After the last few days, I wasn't sure how well that would go over.

"We can meet up over at Von Mox if you want."

"That'd be good," I told her. "Lemmie just get cleaned up and I'll be right there."

∾ ∾ ∾

"Okay," Kris said. "Not judging. What are you on?"

"It's that obvious?"

"Hon," she said, "I *live* with you. I know you. This *is* you, but it's like you to the thousandth power. So what's going on?"

I told her.

Von Mox is a sweet little geek-café about three blocks from our apartment. They've got awesome scones, free wi-fi, and the best hot chocolate in town. The couches are kinda ratty, and the tables and chairs have seen better days, but Von Mox has been our go-to hangout since Kristen and I moved into the Aberdeen. As an extra bonus for this particular conversation, Von Mox hosts gamers, artists, writers, and all sorts of fantasy geeks. Weird conversations are pretty much standard practice there, and so we could talk about crazy shit without seeming out of place.

Celeste sat beside her girlfriend, radiating Mama Bear energy without actually being rude. Honestly, I couldn't blame her. I'd made a mess, and Celeste had just spent a ton of time and money cleaning it up. She held Kristen's hand with deceptive firmness, her fingertips curling over the tops of Kristen's fingers. Tall, elfish, and blessed with a spectacular long blonde mop, Celeste doesn't fit any of the usual stereotypes… but then again, most folks don't. That morning, she wore a black pin-striped vest over a white tank top and skinny Wrangler jeans, and greeted me with more coolness than usual. Celeste's eyes narrowed when Kris mentioned drugs, but although her fingers tightened a bit, she kept her mouth shut.

Kris herself looked kinda haggard. Her strawberry birthmark stood out bold on her unusually pale face, and the bags under her eyes suggested that Celeste had been pulling heavy night-terrors duty these past two days. *Fuck*, I hated Eric Childers even more than ever.

Kris brightened up a bit when I dished up a heaping helping of my "so then I beat the shit out of him" review, and even Celeste let a smile prick the corners of her mouth. Still, I was clearly on Celeste's shit list, and all the crazy-talk about Red Shoes and Zil was not helping matters at all.

I tried to keep my voice down, but the bright edges of the Red Shoes high were beginning to feel pretty sharp, too. My fingers trembled as I gripped my cup and sipped that marvelous Von Mox chocolate. The taste helped steady my nerves. I told Kris and Celeste about the strange woman I'd spotted in Warrior Fitness during the beatdown, but then pulled up short once the words were out of my mouth. Okay, sure – I could trust *Kristen* with the weird story about dancing with a spirit in our living room... but Celeste? I kinda doubted she'd be receptive.

Crap.

"You okay, hon?" Kristen asked.

"Yeah." The word sighed out of me from deep in my chest. "Yeah, I'm just tired. It's been a long few days."

Kris put her free hand over mine. Celeste offered me a sympathetic smile that I read as a sneer. Maybe I was just tired. In any case, I was not ready to talk about dancing with spirits in front of Celeste. "I get that," Kristen said.

Celeste added, "I think we all do."

We sipped more chocolate in the silence that followed.

"So, Kristen said. "Continue."

I did.

Up to the part where Meghan and I had been talking about manifestations. "Um," I said, "I'm not sure where to go from here. The story gets seriously weird now, and…" I glanced back and forth between them, then looked down at the table. Fuck. "And…"

"And," Celeste said, "you're not sure I'll understand."

"Kinda, yeah. That."

She took a deep breath. "I know you don't know me well, so I'm not going to force you into saying something you're not sure you can say in front of me." She squeezed Kristen's hand and stood up. "So I'm going to go get myself a brownie or something, and you two can talk about it without worrying what I'm going to think."

I squeezed my eyes shut, then forced myself to look up into hers. "Thank you, Celeste."

"Thank you, baby," Kristen said, reaching for Celeste's hand again and squeezing it back. "I appreciate it."

"Just remember this much," Celeste said, giving me a *I will kill your entire family if you fuck with me* glare. "This bullshit has hurt someone I care about… someone we *both* care about, and love very deeply. Whatever else you're doing, whatever else is going on here, you leave Kristen the hell out of it from here in. I am serious as a heart attack. Leave her out."

I couldn't help smiling. Yeah, maybe I *did* need to get a girlfriend. One like Celeste, anyway. "I will," I told her. "And thank you. Thanks for looking out for Kris."

She bent down to kiss her girlfriend's hair. "Someone has to, right?"

"*Hey*," Kristen mock-protested. "Still sitting here, remember?"

Celeste hugged Kristen and went to go kill time over at the counter. "Okay," Kris said once Celeste had more or less moved out of earshot. "So what about the rest?"

I told her everything.

"Wow," she said once I'd reached the point where I'd come back home and got her note. "Um. Just... *wow*. So... yeah." She shook her head. "I've gotta give it to ya, Genét. I really don't know what to say to that."

"I can't believe I just said it. And I lived it. And I'm *still* having a hard time believing it."

"So, you decide, in your infinite wisdom, to down a glass of magic 'Drink me' shit. From a spirit. I'm gonna sound slightly maternal here: So what do we *know* about this spirit that's handing you spiked drinks? Other than, y'know, she's probably a 'manifestation' of a drug?"

"She's not a party-drug, though," I said. "She's medicine. And I think she's more than that, too. She's healing, She's dance. She's... okay, this is gonna sound all Women's Studies class and stuff, but she's a women's secret. Like bellydance used to be before it became a public performance art."

"Okay," Kris said. "Granted. Okay. Still, it's not like you to go swigging roofies like freshman sorority sister. What gives?"

"You know, I'm not sure." I glanced around Von Mox as though I could read the answer on the walls. Celeste was sitting in one of the couches, thumbing through an old video gaming magazine like she couldn't be less interested in the contents. She caught me looking her way and cocked her head in a *You done yet?* sort of way. I shook my head. I had to wrap this up soon, before things got more awkward than they already felt to me. "I felt like I could trust her," I told Kristen. "Like, she was trusting me with something huge, so I had to trust her back."

"I'd say that summoning a spirit in your living room is pretty damn trusting, wouldn't you?" Kris glanceded over at Celeste and smiled. "And you let her take you somewhere... I dunno, *else*, while you were at it, too."

This was a morning for sighs, I guess. I let another one float to the surface. "It all sounds pretty crazy, doesn't it?"

"Hon, *life* is crazy. I learned that a long time ago."

I thought about her night-terrors. "Yeah."

"What you've just told me isn't any less insane than stuff I've seen and experienced myself. So I'm not judging you or dismissing what you say." She gave me the proverbial long hard look. "What I *am* doing is making sure you don't disappear on me. Or get arrested again. Or get *me* arrested again. Or hurt my girlfriend. Or my cat. Or do any of the other crazy-ass things that can happen when things get as deep as it looks like they have." She put her hand over mine. "Hon, I just want you to be careful. More careful than you have been being these last few days. Because I don't want anything to happen to you, okay? And whenever all this stuff is over, I want us to still be friends or roommates or whatever, and go back to watching TV with Inanna in our laps and a bunch of cold pizza in the fridge."

I swallowed and closed my eyes against what felt like they might be tears. "I was so afraid," I choked up over the boulder that had somehow lodged itself in my throat, "that I was gonna lose you over all this."

"I'm not going anywhere," she said, "except back to Celeste's place until you figure out how to finish up whatever the hell this is."

"And until we find another place to live," I added. "There's still that eviction notice too."

"Yeahhhhhh, there's that."

"I asked them over at my lawyer… *our* lawyer's office to see if they had someone who could help us sort that out. Maybe they can, maybe not." I tossed a little shoulder-shrug. "Worst case, my mom's in real estate. She can help us find another living space."

"I'd like that."

I ducked in and dropped my voice. "So you're not thinking of moving in permanently with Celeste?"

Kristen squinched her face a bit. "Not yet, no. Her place is kind of small, and we're still a little new for moving in together yet, I think. Don't get me wrong," she added, making sure we didn't look conspiratorial to Celeste, "she's being awesome, and I love her a lot. She treats me really well – better than anyone else I've dated. But after Gary and Charles…" She grimaced at the two ex-boyfiends' names, and I seconded said grimace. "I'm not quite ready to move into a permanent situation with anyone I'm involved with as anything more than friends. Not yet, anyway."

I nodded understanding. "Have you told her yet?"

"Yeah, we've had the talk. I think Cel's hoping I'll change my mind, and I probably will. Eventually. But not right now. Right now, as great as she is, I'm looking forward to getting my own bed back." She smiled. "And Inanna is going crazy in that little apartment. She keeps looking at me like, 'Mom, where's the *rest* of it?'"

We laughed, and I felt a lot better about everything.

Celeste looked up at us with the *Is it safe for me to come back now?* question plain on her face. I think that may have been the moment when I appreciated her most of all. Whatever Kristen's girlfriend thought of me personally, she respected Kris and that meant everything to me. "We should let your girlfriend know she can stop trying to be interested in four-year-old issues of Inside Gaming," I said.

"We should." Kris waved Celeste back over to our table. "One last thing, though."

"Yes?"

"What are you planning to do about this?"

As Celeste ambled back to our table, trying not to look to anxious about it, I told her that too.

"Ohhhhhkayyyyy…" Kris said as Celeste reached the table and glanced at both of us. Kristen beckoned Celeste to lean down. "C'mere, you."

Celeste leaned in, and Kristen kissed her with as much affection as I've ever seen anyone kiss somebody. A wave of yearning hit me. Yeah, I was really thinking I *should* try this whole girlfriend thing myself. When I was able to touch someone again without fucking everything up. "Thank you, honey," Kristen told Celeste. "I really appreciate that."

"Me too," I added. "I'll leave the kissing to Kristen, though."

Once we'd finished our *break the tension* laugh, they headed back to Celeste's place, leaving me with a cup of cooling dregs and a looming sense of loneliness and dread.

A HEAVY HEART
TO CARRY

~ ~ ~

The crash kicked in soon afterward.

By the time I got back home, I was fading hard and my feel-good energy had run out. My heroic determination had crashed, burned, and departed too.

Aside from the hum of our air conditioner, the apartment felt too still, too quiet. No Inanna, no Kristen. Y'know how a place feels different when someone who's supposed to be there *isn't?* That's how it felt in our apartment. Even knowing that Kristen planned to come home soon, and that she'd be bringing Inanna with her when she did, the place just wouldn't feel like "home" until they came back to it again.

I just wanted everything to stop spinning and return to the way things had been before.

In the bright light of day, the entire situation seemed like a bad dream that kept unfolding like an Escher print on crack. My missing swords and computer, the sheer *violation* of our kicked-in doors and busted-up kitchen, all drove home just how costly this crusade of mine had been.

The more I thought about the situation, the more I realized the entire idea was batshit cazypants and suicidal to boot.

There's a line in the film *Serenity*: *You know what the definition of a hero is? Someone who gets other people killed.*

I didn't want to be that kind of hero.

I almost gave up right then and there.

Days without sleep. A night spent more-or-less in jail. The fight, getting kicked out of Warrior Fitness, acting like some drunken frat boy with Dervish in the music shop... it all just piled up on me then. I suddenly felt a million years old and all I wanted to do was sleep.

So I hauled my leaden ass to bed, through the partly-straightened wreckage of our home.

Unbuckling my boots, I fell into bed fully clothed. Faint voices from outside drifted underneath the air conditioner's hum. Eyes closed, I settled into sun-warm sheets, feeling the weight of the last several days press down on me. *Just let it go*, I kept telling myself. *You can't win this. Stop.*

In the stillness, I drifted.

I can't call it *dreaming*, exactly. No matter how much I wanted to, I just couldn't fall asleep. The sun warmed my skin and lit up the insides of my eyelids. The whooshing coolness of conditioned air brushed along the tiny hairs on the backs of my arms and raised little goosebumps where the sunlight didn't reach. I rolled over to block out the brightness of that light, and ran my cheek across the sheets. So tired I physically hurt, I pulled the pillow over my head and tried to block out the world.

Still, I couldn't sleep.

Twisted. Growled. Wound myself up in the sheets, but could not fall asleep.

That empty-room feeling receded from a subtle presence. I'd closed my door, but the room suddenly held the unseen mass of someone else. Under the AC's purr, I caught the soft pad of soles across the hardwood floor, muffled then by the rug around my bed. A faint rustle of skirts, and the chime of ankle-bells and coins. The creak of the floor beneath her feet.

My breath stopped short in my lungs. Chills chased each other across my back.

"Zil?"

The pillow muffled my whispered voice.

My fingers dug into the sheets. The invisible weight on top of me pressed down. My heartbeat thudded through the mattress, to my ears. My pulse beat quicker. My muscles tensed.

Through the pillow on my head, I heard a soft *clink*, like a full glass set down on my nightstand.

"*Zil?*" Again. Louder this time. "Is that you?"

I've seen enough horror movies to know I should look, and enough of them to know I didn't want to see her.

"Dammit, Zil," I snarled into my pillow. "Quit fucking around and leave me be."

That unseen presence disappeared.

Again, the room felt void of everyone but me.

This seemed to be the day for heavy sighs. "Tell me," I informed my pillow, "that I just dreamed all that."

But the cup of liquid on my nightstand was no dream.

If you see it in bright sunlight, Red Shoes shines an incandescent crimson glow. Darker particles waltz slowly in their sluggish dance. The now-familiar cinnamon scent teases your nose as it hangs, impossible, in the light of a waking day.

"No," I whispered. "Not more of this stuff. *No.*"

But I picked the glass up anyway.

Zil's frankincense-and-sweat perfume hovered in the air above my bed. The glass felt warm beneath my fingertips, slightly heavier than water would have been. I inhaled the warm aroma of the drug, prickling my nose-hairs and raising shivers up my arms.

"No," I repeated.

The glass in my hand kept edging toward my mouth.

It was a bad idea. This whole thing, this whole plan. I knew I should just dump the red stuff down the drain and go the fuck back to bed and sleep for a week and then apologize to everyone because, for crying out loud, I didn't need to be a hero.

But Meghan and Tucker and Thunderdome and Max had driven halfway across the country to help me now, and what was I gonna do? Tell 'em, "Hey, guys, thanks for coming back and all, but I decided to wuss out and stick to my own side of the street. Sorry about all those shows you missed, but hey – at least I didn't do anything *stupid*, right?"

Dervish was right. I didn't need this shit messing up my head.

But my arms trembled and my heart beat faster and the weight of days without sleep and the bruises from fists and feet and handcuffs and the floor... it all pushed in on me.

Just a sip. Just a little. Just enough to get you through tonight.

I was up on my feet, unsteady but heading toward the bathroom sink.

No. I was not gonna play this game again. I was *not.*

And then the glass was tipping and the red sparkly stuff was pouring down the drain and I couldn't help myself, I just had to stop and take another sip.

The rush hit me full-blast, blowing my nerve-endings wide open and blasting away fatigue. My mouth burned with holy fire. My throat expanded to drink it down.

NO.

The glass exploded into bright red slivers, splattering Red Shoes like blood across the sink and floor and me and pretty much everything else in sight.

I stood there, panting, senses sharp enough to cut, gleaming like the shattered glass in the sink where I'd thrown it, the Red Shoes bleeding its scent and color everywhere.

"I'm gonna regret this, aren't I?" I said out loud.

The problem was, I wasn't sure *which* decision I was going to regret more.

THE CHALLENGE
OF OUR RIVAL

~ ~ ~

All thoughts of sleep and remaining doubts blew out like birthday candles in a storm. For better and worse, the taste of Red Shoes lit fires in my veins. *Fuck it*, I decided. If I was gonna be a hero, than I'd best start acting like a hero. And so, I got to work.

First I called a decidedly sleepy Meghan and outlined my plan to her. She agreed it sounded good. "We'll be there," she told me. "There's no fucking way I wouldn't *not* be."

"You mean no way you *wouldn't* be?" I teased.

"And fuck you too. I'm going back to bed. You suck."

I laughed. "Love you too."

Then I called a decidedly sleepy Dervish and did the same thing. I stumbled through the plan with her, not certain how she'd respond after last night's little misadventures. To my profound relief, she said, "Give me a few more hours, and I'm there."

After that, I pinged Inky, then Vivienne. `We need to talk`, I texted each of them. I gave them a time and a place, and separately they agreed.

Rol was a bit harder to convince. When I told him Meg was back in town, though, and filled him in on the plan, he grunted. "Fine, okay. I'm in."

Checking Facebook from my phone, I got a message too. From Chalice. Posted on my wall: *Can we talk?* She'd misspelled it, though: *Can we takl?*

That was it. No explanation. Hmmmmm… Nice timing, girlfriend. Thank you, but no. I thumbed the X on my screen and shut Facebook down before I could change my mind.

I thought about calling Detective Fallon. Thought about it a lot, actually. In the end, though, I decided that forgiveness would be easier to ask for than permission, and I didn't know what she, as a cop, would be legally obligated to say or do if I told her what was going down.

It *was* going down, too. Once I made the decision, a new burst of energy picked me up and sent me flying high again. I started cleaning house as I talked to Rol, made my other calls, thought through the whole Detective Fallon thing, and fielded a call from Archer, Chambers Law Group: "Hi, Peggy."

"Mister Chambers needs you to come in and meet him at the office this morning, Miss Shilling," Peggy said, all business this time. None of her usual friendliness. I might actually be in trouble this time out. Shit.

"Um, okay," I said. "No problem. Sure. What time?"

Less than an hour later, I was sitting in the firm's waiting room, praying that the chills I felt came from the air conditioning and not from fear, another Red Shoes crash, or both.

"Miss Shilling." Peggy remained all-business, cloaking her usual disposition under a brisk officiality. "Mister Chambers will see you now."

I got up and headed towards the door of his office, my guts doing the cold-fall dance you get when the principal calls you in to bitch you out.

Frank... Mister Chambers... sat behind his thick red cherry wood desk. His stern face and clasped hands glared up at me from the clean glass overlay. I couldn't quite meet his eyes. "Have a seat, Miss Shilling," he said with ominous finality.

Ah, hell, I thought. *I'm gonna get fired as a client or something, right?*

Penitence was definitely the way to play this round. I sat down as demurely as I could in the thick red-leather client seat in front of his desk. "Yes sir, Mister Chambers. Thank you for seeing me."

"You haven't been giving me much choice in the matter lately, young lady. I began my day earlier than usual, again, at the police station, again, because of your activities. Again."

"I'm sorry, Mister Chambers." I gave him my best puppy-dog apology eyes. "I appreciate all the work you've been doing on my behalf."

"I doubt you'll appreciate my bill when you see it."

"Probably not."

"Now then. I am officially furious with you, Miss Shilling." Frank's typical friendly face had disappeared behind a righteous angry cloud. I cringed a bit in my chair. "Your actions," he continued, "were reckless, risky, against gym policy, and illegal. You could be charged with felonious assault and then some, and because you challenged Eric Childers in the boxing ring, you could not plead self-defense even though he clearly was trying to send you to the morgue." Frank hit me with a witness-cracking glare. "That was an *extremely* foolish thing to do, and I would be within my rights to dismiss you as a client. It's not as though I don't already have my hands full, and family friendship – even in your case – goes only so far."

I nodded. "I'm sorry, sir. You're right."

"You understand just how serious all of this could be?"

"I do."

"Good."

He glared at me for what seemed like ever, then added, "Unofficially, I wish I'd been there to see it. That little asshole is a Class-A scumbucket, and it was a pleasure seeing you deck him."

He grinned. I grinned back at him. "You saw it?"

"Let's not get ahead of ourselves just yet."

According to Frank, Eric's daddy had been champing at the bit to charge me with every crime applicable *and* sue the shit out of me for good measure. His darling boy had been a basket case, and with the fury of entitled douchebags everywhere, Eric Daddy Senior had decided that I was the party at fault for our little altercation.

"I see where Eric gets his attitude," Frank said. "Eric Pére is as big a shitheel as I have encountered in these-here parts, which for a Black attorney practicing law in the South is, I assure you, quite an accomplishment. Now, in my sympathetic heart-of-hearts, I'd be willing to bet that boy has a legitimately tragic tale of woe. Being the son of such a man, regardless of how favored he might be otherwise, is no picnic."

"I'll bet." A part of me actually *did* feel kinda sorry for Eric then. Not much, but a little.

"Eric's father was breathing fire like a veritable dragon at Detective Fallon and myself. We let him. It seemed best not to interrupt." He quirked an eyebrow at me, and I laughed. "When he had finally unleashed every cliché in his formidable arsenal of threats, I took the liberty of showing him his son's handiwork."

How...? I prepared to ask. Then it dawned on me. "The video."

"The video." He grinned. "The video of two little college girls being Tasered and perp-walked in the comfort of their own home. Apartment. Anyway, I showed it to both of them without comment, and then when it was over, I read them a few of the comments on it too. I thought Mr. Childers might strangle his bouncing baby boy right then and there."

"Ugh." I wasn't sure I wanted to know what people had said. Actually, I was really sure I never wanted to know. *Ever.*

Frank noted my discomfort. "Oh, naturally, the usual trolls came out to play... and yes, Genét, I *do* know what trolls are. I'm not *that* old. The majority of the comments, though, were in your favor. And not, I might add, friendly to the officers in question. Quite *un*friendly, truth be told. The real venom, however, was aimed at one Eric Childers, esquire. People were *really* not happy with him."

"Um… but how did they know?" I asked. "I mean, how would a bunch of people on YouTube know that Eric swatted us? Or even that we'd been swatted at all?"

"That," he said, turning his laptop around so I could see the screen, "is the other reason I called you in this morning. Detective Fallon and I thought you might want to see this in person."

He hit Play on a cued-up video.

A police body-cam video.

Of a no-knock SWAT raid.

On Eric Childers.

Who apparently still lived with Mom and Dad.

It was glorious.

"Oh my God." I couldn't stop laughing. "Oh my *God!*"

Frank's righteous grin made the show even more vindicating. "Have you seen the news yet this morning, Genét?"

"No computer. The cops still have it. And our TV got demolished in the raid. Not that I watch the news on it anyway."

"Dating myself again, I see," Frank said. "To save us both time, let's just say that Mr. Childers' arrest made the morning news as well. Hence the more supportive comments on the video where you and Kristen get arrested." He paused the video as Eric's pained face filled the screen. Again, I felt a flash of pity for him. A really *quick* flash, though. Nothing serious. "That video, of course, is already online. This one is not. Let's keep it between ourselves, shall we? Detective Fallon may have bent protocol a bit when sending it to me."

"Understood."

"When she received your video last evening," Frank went on, "Detective Fallon obtained a no-knock warrant for Eric's arrest. And since it's likely that such suspects, when confronted with an arrest, tend to destroy all of the associated evidence, warrants in such circumstances tend to involve SWAT teams at inconvenient hours. I understand you have experience with similar situations."

"Just a little, yeah."

"Detective Fallon did not lead the raid. That's not really her jurisdiction. The officer in charge, one Detective Owens, is very happy with the results, however."

"He's been doing this for a while, hasn't he?" I envisioned the nightmare Eric had unleashed on Kristen, and on me, happening to other people too. Girls, mostly, I guessed. Maybe some guys too. I felt sick.

"For obvious legal reasons, I can't go into the details as I've heard them so far. The short answer, though, is yes. Yes he has. Since high school, apparently. And, as Eric and his father are being reminded the hard way, Mister Childers Junior is no longer a minor, and thus is facing some rather unpleasant consequences. Beyond the bruised liver you gave him, that is."

"Really? I hit him that hard?"

"You did some damage, Genét. I won't lie to you here, if the circumstances were any less in your favor, you would probably be in handcuffs by now." He sat back, that stern look planted back on his face. "Eric's father certainly wanted that to happen, and he made a rather... vocal... point about it. Repeatedly. His lawyer did as well."

My chill was back. "So what happened?"

"Detective Fallon told them both, in as many words, that any judge in the country would give you a medal for decking the little shit."

I laughed. "That sounds like her, all right."

"How is your friend?"

"I just saw her a few hours ago. She's staying with her…" I hesitated for a second, not really sure how cool Frank was with the whole queer thing. "Her girlfriend," I finished. Frank was too sharp to *not* notice my hesitation, and I didn't want him to have any reason to doubt my being truthful here.

Frank just nodded. If he had any objections to Kristen's sexuality, he didn't show it. "I'm glad she's safe. I hear you're having some trouble with your landlords over this?"

"A bit, yeah."

"I'll make some calls. See what we can do."

"Thank you."

"Billable hours, Genét. Billable hours. And speaking of which, does Kristen wish to retain me as counsel?"

"It's my impression that she does, yeah."

"Good. I'll call her once we're done here."

Frank and I went over a few more details before I left. I hadn't been sure my video would be admissible in court, but Frank assured me that what he called "profound utterances" – that is, as far as I understood it, stupid things people say that turn out to be important when you're charging them with a crime – are perfectly acceptable as evidence. "Now, if *Detective Fallon* had hit him," he told me. "That would be another matter. But you had clear circumstances, and witnesses who have corroborated your story, and a perfectly reasonable reason to be angry with him. Eric slipped up, but that's on him. You didn't beat a confession out of him, much as the Childers' lawyer might like to argue otherwise. Eric admitted to the swatting himself, and..." He paused to smile with predatory glee. "Well, I was fortunate enough to witness the interrogation, thanks to Detective Fallon, who called me as a courtesy at a *dis*courteous hour of the morning to come in and see it. A criminal mastermind, Mister Eric Childers certainly is not."

"So he folded."

"Like a pack of cards at prayer."

Once we'd covered all remaining concerns, Frank shooed me out of his office, with a warning: "Be *careful*, Genét. Luck has been on your side so far, and that's mostly because Eric Childers is remarkably stupid even for a spoiled rich white boy. I can't help you if you decide to keep playing Nancy Drew with a mean right hook. Whatever you're up to – and yes, I know you're up to something, I can smell it on you – you're better off leaving it to the police. Right now, you have a friend in Detective Fallon. As much as a police detective *can* be friends with anyone, that is. If you keep pretending this is some sort of action movie, though, you're liable to lose that friendship, and possibly my help as well. Understood?"

"Yes, sir," I told him. "Understood."

The shakes hit me again once I'd left the office. But by that point, it was way too late to turn back.

I GUESS THIS IS
GROWING UP

ᔕ ᔕ ᔕ

I tried to reach Mom and Dad on their phones just before heading off to face whatever it was that we were gonna face down there in the Bottle's basement.

In both cases, I got their voice mails.

I guess it's a sign that you're growing up when Mom and Dad respect you enough to let your calls go to voice mail. A sign that they're growing past you, too. That you're no longer the center of their world or something. That life goes on. That kind of thing. Whatever. Right.

I half-wanted them to pick up, and half-wanted to not have to explain what the hell I was about to do.

I wanted someone to talk me out of it, and knew I couldn't let them if they tried.

So I wimped out and just left "I love you" messages on their phones, then set my own phone to go to voice mail before I changed my mind.

PLACE

YOU DON'T WANNA MESS
WITH ME TONIGHT

∿ ∿ ∿

"ONCE WE GET DOWN THERE," MEGHAN ASKED, "*THEN* WHAT?"

"I wish I had a better answer than 'I'm not sure yet,'" I replied. Meghan, Dervish, Rol, Inky, and the rest of Black Swan looked back at me, and I felt the shakes begin again. Jeeze, this party-leadership thing was hard, especially when it was lives, not pixels, at stake. A bunch of my friends were trusting me with God-knows-what, and I had to make sure I didn't get them killed… or worse yet, locked up in a time-loop or swallowed by Mr. Happy Hentai and his buds. "So far as I can see," I told my crew, "the biggest problem now is, I still have no idea who or what we're up against here. And I'll be honest – that kinda scares me. But I *have* to do something, and it has to be now."

It took the rest of the day to set all the pieces in motion, have the necessary sit-downs with everyone involved, grab the party favors, and hash out the introductions so that everyone involved knew everybody else. By the time the sun dipped over the edge of the mountains and the shadows made their slow crawl across Riverhaven City, we'd figured things out about as far as they *could* be figured, given the time and personalities involved.

Inky had been glad to help. "I'm sorry to have been so absent lately," she'd told me when we'd met up. "Fucking brain-weasels have been eating me alive since the night Blue died, and I just really haven't been ready to deal with anybody or anything since then." She'd been staring at the floor up to that point, then looked up at me with an expression of pure determination. "But I am now. So let's do this. Whatever needs to be done, I'm in."

Vivienne had not been so forthcoming, but I really wasn't surprised. No answers to my calls, no answers to my texts. She had a lot to sort out, I guess, so I gave her space to do it. *Cleaning up the mess at the Bottle*, I'd texted her. *You know where we'll be if you want to find us there.*

"You've *been* in the basement, right?" This from Thunderdome, Meghan's drummer and one of the biggest dudes I know this side of Rol. He's got that whole retro-'90s Rollins Band thing going on, too: cropped hair, bike shorts, no shirt, no shoes, and tattoos for days. Over six feet tall, almost pretty, and possessed of a truly amazing set of abs, guns, pects, and pretty much every other muscle group you could count, Thunderdome, along with Rol, was our life-insurance policy. If things actually came to blows in the basement, this pair of berserkers could tank for us while Max, Meghan, Dervish and I handled the magic shit.

Yeah, I had pretty much come to terms with it by that point. *Magic.* After the last few days, how could I not? Every last doubt I'd had about this stuff went running for the door when that second glass of Red Shoes manifested on my nightstand.

"I have, yes. Rol's been there too. Trouble is, I don't remember much about it up till the point where Rol slung me over his shoulder and I wound up puking up my guts."

"How much of that do you think came from the Red Shoes in your system," asked Max, "and how much came from the place itself?" Probably the oldest member of our crew, Max was sort of Meghan's mentor when it came to matters metaphysical. Slender, short-haired, and just a shade taller than Meghan, Max wore a top hat and steampunky gunslinger's duster coat despite the summer heat.

"I wish I knew," I answered. "Rol? Any clues about that?"

Rol's not the most sociable guy under the best circumstances, and was even edgier than usual. I was picking up a lot of tamped-down fear under his façade, and I really couldn't blame him for that. "Not really," Rol muttered. "I wasn't paying attention to much except getting out of there without getting spewed on."

Our little group had gathered in a cluster of cars, vans and SUVs in the Bottle's parking lot, a few yards off from the main entrance. Those vehicles were filled with music-making gear, and covered in band decals, Pagan and geek-culture bumper stickers, and a few shout-outs for the local NPR and college radio stations. We huddled on the side of Meghan's van, our faces lit by cell phone screens and Rol's cigarettes as the sun disappeared and the darkness moved in. Although we hadn't noticed anyone else coming or going from the building, several windows glowed with light, and the thumping techno bass-beat from the basement shook our cars and vibrated through our shoes and feet. Meghan was her usual barefoot self, of course. Dervish and Thunderdome were, too. How they could stand there like that on busted pavement and glass-scattered gravel was one of the great mysteries of the universe.

As for me, I felt myself starting to fade. Magic or no magic, three or four days with several beatings and no sleep to speak of was seriously kicking my ass. I glanced down at my shaking hand, and hoped my voice wasn't shaking like that too.

Some fearless leader *I* was.

"I've been down there," said Inky – one of the first times she'd spoken since we all gathered together in the parking lot. We'd talked earlier, of course, but she tended to be quiet in a group. "It's not really that different than any other outlaw rave-space. The makeup's a little weirder, and the vibe is…" She squinched her face up. "Off-putting, really, which is why I didn't stay. But it's not like there are trolls in plate armor there or anything. It's just kinda… *meh*. Loud music, crazy people, not much else. It felt *blurry*, actually. Like it was moving in slow-motion, or like maybe *I* was." She shook her head. "And the sound system *sucked*."

"Sucked *how*, exactly?" We'd been over it already one-on-one, but I wanted to get the rest of the team up to speed as well. Inky's a sound-tech who I think toured with VNV Nation back in the day. A bit older than me… maybe a *lot* older, not that she looked it or anything… Inky had stories for every occasion, and most of them were true. *No shit, there I was* was kind of Inky's Guide to Life, and in the few times I'd actually talked to her outside of Arcana Darque I'd learned that if she told you that she'd done something, then she'd probably done it at least twice. Purple-haired and tattoo-covered, Inky had introduced me to my favorite brand of boots. And so we figured that if Inky had scoped out the sound system in the basement, then she might be able to shut it down, take it over, or drown it out.

"It was *loud*, yeah," she said, "but really badly wired. Shitty components. My guess is a bunch of garbage from a pawn shop. Beat-up as fuck. It had all seen better days, and so had the guy behind the mixer."

"What'd he look like?" Meghan asked. "Anything... y'know, weird?"

Inky shrugged. "Typical guy. Burnt-out-looking, really old for a DJ in a rave club. Y'know how Iggy Pop kind of looks like the Mummy's dead grandfather...?"

"Hey," Meghan warned. "No shade on the Iggster!"

"No shade thrown." Inky shrugged again. "Iggy's awesome. The Death Valley diet plan, though? Not a good look for him. Or for anybody else, either. And the DJ looked like that, only worse."

Maybe like he'd been leeching the life out of other people while getting his own life leeched out too. Another piece of the puzzle fitted itself into place. "I wonder if it's still the same guy," I said out loud. "Rol, do you remember anyone behind the mixing board, or playing instruments?"

"Not really, no."

"The big thing I remember," Inky continued, "were these two dudes in robes. Sitting cross-legged, kind of like Buddhas, if Buddhas were thin and creepy with long stringy hair and weird, ornate tattoos. Oh, yeah – and that Chalice chick. The really great dancer. She was there too."

"Thought so." *That* puzzle piece finally fell into place, too.

"It's not too surprising," Inky said. "I mean hey – party, dancer, you know." She thought about it a second. "Kind of the center of attention, too, come to think of it. Not that *that's* surprising either."

"Oh," was all I had to say to that.

Chalice. Eric. Caroline. Ash. Red Shoes.

Dammit.

The muggy night suddenly seemed colder.

Well, I finally knew who'd been pulling all the strings here. And who to blame for everything, too. I was willing to bet the DJ was not the top of this particular food-chain. Chalice was. Lovely. No wonder she'd wanted to "talk." Good thing I'd skirted *that* particular land mine.

"Why are we even *here*, again?" Tucker, Meghan's lanky bass-player boyfriend lit up a new cigarette of his own. How Meghan could stand the smell of them was another one of those things I'd never understand about my friend. Okay, Tucker's cute enough, I guess, in a hippie-puppy sort of way with just enough bad-boy smirk to seem compelling. Meghan says he kisses like a god, and he *must* because honestly I don't get the attraction otherwise. But whatever – that's her deal. And he was here, when he could have been sleeping off their trip back home, so I guess that was worth a few points in the Good Guy column. The tone in his voice, though, scraped up the back of my last nerve. "I mean, hey I *get* it," he went on. "Your friend died of some bad drugs your other friends were selling her. They dosed you and Rol…" Tucker indicated his old friend, who he'd known since early high school. "And that's *absolutely* bad, and I don't blame you for having them arrested…"

"I *didn't* have them arrested," I replied. "They managed that part on their own. I just got blamed for doing it."

"Okay, sorry. You're right." Tucker waved the hand with his cigarette in a sort-of-conciliatory-but-really-not sort of way. Points of light danced across the mirrored sunglasses he almost always wears. "But I get that. And you kicked that one guy's ass… which, by the way, was *awesome*." We both smiled at that one, but my smile felt pretty tense. It was Other Shoe to Drop O'Clock, and Tucker was setting up to drop that particular shoe on me.

I saved him the trouble: "But you don't know why we're all here right now."

"Right." He took a drag.

No one else said anything. They just looked between us both.

Meghan's mouth tightened like she was trying not to go off on him.

"Why," I said, not making it a question. "Is because *this*..." I waved my shaking hand at the brick walls, still coursing with an energy I knew Tucker couldn't see. "This is *rape*."

"Um," Tucker said. "Genét, it's a *wall*."

"It's *energy*," I insisted. "I can understand if you don't feel it, Tucker, but *I* feel it. Meghan feels it too, right?"

Meghan, glaring at her boyfriend, nodded. "Yeah. Yeah, I feel it."

"I think Dervish and Inky feel it..."

Dervish nodded as Inky added, "I wasn't sure until now that *that's* what I felt going on here, but yeah – yeah, I feel it too, and it makes me fucking sick to my stomach." She stared at the walls. "I don't know how we spent all those months in this building rehearsing with the troupe when..." She shook herself. "*UGH*."

"I didn't figure it out myself until this morning," I said. "When I could actually, y'know, *see* it. So I can see why you don't realize what's really going on here, Tucker." I realized then that the shaking in my body, and increasingly in my words, was *fury*. White-hot motherfucking rage. "But this is bigger than a party or a rave or drugs or whatever else is going on down there."

I slapped the brick wall. My palm stung. "This is rape, Tucker. *Rape. Energy*-rape. Taking people's life force without their consent, without them even *realizing* it, and then channeling that energy into or out of God only *knows* what." I heard myself getting ranty, and I didn't fucking care. "It's rape of *medicine*, too. Zil showed me that the drug they're making and selling and taking in there and dosing people with…" My hands were shaking. My voice too. "It's supposed to *help* people. To help *women*, specifically. It was originally created to ease childbirth and soothe pain and now it's being turned into something that fucks people up. That set my friend on *fire*. That made me and Rol lose an entire *weekend* and that's trapped the people down in that party into losing… I dunno, maybe everything they ever *had* or *thought* or *cared about* or *were*."

I realized I had gotten right up in Tucker's face without even noticing that I had moved. His cigarette burned bright spots in my vision, and the tobacco smell slid up my nose and down my tongue. "It's not just about drugs anymore," I said, my voice calming though my hands still shook. "Don't you see that, Tucker? It's not even about Blue. It's about realizing there's something here I just can't walk away from and pretend doesn't exist, because I know now that it *does* exist and if the cops won't do anything about it – and they *won't*, I know, because I already asked, and besides this sort of thing isn't even on their radar except maybe for a few of them who are doing everything they can just to deal with the little bit they know about…" I heard myself getting kinda ranty again, so I stepped back and took a breath.

"I have to fix this because it needs to be fixed," I said at last. "I need to fix it, and fix it *now*, because I can't live like this anymore. Not now. Knowing what's going on down there, I just can't walk away."

Tucker looked at me from behind his mirrored sunglasses. I saw myself looking back at him. "Okay," he said, nodding. "Then let's shut this damn thing down."

SKY HIGH, BONE DRY

~ ~ ~

It was worse than I thought.

Once we got inside the building, the vibrations slid over my skin like a slick legion of pervo slugs. The ghost of Charles' kisses was back, but this time the sensations skeezed me to my soul. I wasn't the only one who noticed it, either; pretty much my entire crew looked dazed, then excited, then disgusted as we moved down the hall toward the doors that led down. Meghan and Dervish, in particular, shuddered with distaste.

"Holy shit," Meghan hissed. "Has it always been like this?"

"So you can feel it too?" I asked her.

"How could anyone *not?*" She wiped her feet on the wooden floor, as if to scrape invisible sewage off her soles.

"I don't feel anything," Tucker said. "Well, except for 'Wow, this place is kind of a mess.'"

"Remind me again why I love you," Meghan said.

"I play bass pretty well, and I'm told I'm a good kisser."

"And both are debatable."

I felt a fight coming on. "Not now, kids," I told them both. "I need you two with me here."

"Yes, Mom," Meghan said, with a much more joking tone. She *had* to be joking. She really hates her mom.

∾ ∾ ∾

The best way to get into someplace you're not supposed to be, as I learned long ago from some of my more questionable friends, is to act like you're totally supposed to be there. And so we trouped on down to the basement with Black Swan's gear like we owned the place, running a handcart filled with amps and drums down the cargo ramp, shielded from the worst effects of that creepy music by one of the little secret weapons we'd brought along with us: earplugs.

It really pays to pay attention in AP Lit class.

We'd worked out some hand-signals in the parking lot, and proceeded to use them as we skirted the crowd and set up our gear. Black Swan had the routine down to a science, and Rol had roadied enough for Meghan by that time to know where and how his strength and size could do the most good. I'd given Dervish money so she could rent us some monitors and speakers from the Silver Key – and trust me, that was *not* inexpensive! Thunderdome's drums took a few minutes to set up, but Inky, Dervish and Tucker made quick work of the amps and cables while Max hashed out a chalk circle on the stone floor and surrounded it with glyphs that kinda made my brain hurt.

While the rest of my crew set up our gear in the closest thing to a private space that we could find, I laid out my own set of preparations, scanning the crowd to see what I could see.

What I saw made me shake even worse. Not with fear or fatigue, but with flat-out, all-consuming, quiet-screaming rage.

Imagine a toga party at the grossest frat in town. Throw in bits of Caligula's Rome and then shower the place with roofie-juice. Yeah, this was kinda worse than that. I felt sick just looking at it.

Flickering strobes and colored floodlights washed the party in uncanny colors, obscuring details while blasting out microseconds of unspeakable clarity. Sound waves pounded off the walls and swept over us with physical and metaphysical brutality. I once had a boyfriend nicknamed Dragon, who was seriously into the rougher kinds of mosh pits and whose favorite sex games involved scratches, shoves, wrestling, and bites hard enough to leave both of us bruised and bleeding afterwards. He was fun, I'll admit, and exciting in crazy-making ways. I broke up with him for my own good, because it wasn't good for me to be with him for long. That basement was like Dragon on steroids: freakishly seductive and bloody dangerous.

I'd been in *that* mess? For *two days?* How had I made it out of there still dressed? And what had happened to me before I did?

No wonder I was shaking.

The basement stretched outward from that cluster of light and bodies. The walls seemed to absorb the light that bounced against their surfaces and got lost on the way out. In that darkness, I saw figures scattered along the walls or clumped up into little balls of skin and clothing. Some appeared to be sleeping, some were snuggling, and some were… well, doing more than that. A few appeared to be crying, and I wanted to go over and hug them and tell 'em it was all going to be all right. I didn't, though; I had to hold the center for my crew, and if I wandered off the whole thing would fall apart. Through that darkness, thin streams of rippling light – green mostly, some purple, a lot of red, and a fair amount of blue – drifted between those clusters of people and the booming intensity of the dancing crowd.

You see the weave, Zil had said. I sure as hell was seeing it now.

You'd think the place would smell like a sewer full of sweat. It didn't. It smelled, instead, like those cinnamon brooms that stores put out for sale around the time when summer turns fallish and the holiday season does its dance of retail-products – Halloween, Thanksgiving, Christmas, New Year's, you know the drill. Sure, I noticed stale sweat and body fluids and spilled booze and all the rest. The rich sharpness of cinnamon, though, overwhelmed it all. The basement, and everyone in it, smelled like Red Shoes.

I had to wonder how many people had burst into flame and burned to ashes down here like Blue had done. And then I had to *stop* wondering about that before I went insane.

And then, we had the topper on this shit-cake of craziness: The two creepy Buddha-dudes, meditating in occult circles and crackling halos of red life-energy...

...Chalice, literally haloed with pulsing crimson light, spinning barefoot and pale-skinned as death in the center of the mob, decked out in black, red, and silver Gothic tribal dance finery: chains, silks, coin belts and bras – the works...

...and Ash and Caroline, in full Arcana Darque regalia, who spun beside her, lost in the frenzy of their own demented dance.

I expected them to stop dancing and come our way, but they just kept dancing. Wherever their heads were at, they didn't seem to notice us.

Whiplashes of red-neon energy snapped between the five figures and sizzled in the grooves of those inscribed circles and wicked glyphs. Those glyphs circled the orgy-dance area, bordering the crowd with infernal energy. The hair on my arms pulled tight and pricked up as I watched the spectacle: Chalice, Ash, Caroline, and the two Buddha-dudes, drawing bright life out of the crowd and focusing it on the sound board and the DJ behind it.

As for the DJ, he jerked like an electric marionette, his gaunt hands dancing across the board. Inky had been right; the guy *did* look like a skeletal Iggy Pop, shirtless and glowing, black hair whipping around his sunken skull-face, his tattoos flaming like emerald cattle-brands.

Manifestations, Meghan had called them. But what kind of power manifested *him?*

I wish I could say he looked like a demon or satyr or something. The scariest part, though, was that he appeared to be a more-or-less normal dude – okay, yeah, tattooed and gaunt and shit like that, true. I've seen scarier people on campus any day of the week, though. It was less the way he *looked* than the way he *felt*. That guy, at more or less the center of his personal maelstrom, radiated a skin-shivering combination of raw charisma and hungry lust. The phrase *psychic vampire* ran through my head, but this DJ had about as much in common with Edward Cullen as a rabid wolf has to a teacup poodle: similar features but a totally different beast.

Which reminded me: Where was Tentacle McHentaiface? And did he have friends? In the light-splashed darkness of that basement rave, they could have been anywhere… or *everywhere*… around us. With that realization, I felt the darkness press in around us, and the feeling that we were just wasting our time here… or worse, that I had just put all my friends in danger over my stupid little crusade… crushed in on me.

For a second, all I saw was black.

And then the floor, at very close range.

And then I was being picked up off the floor by two sets of arms, one set on each of mine.

That damn booming techno pulse pounded off my body and turned my bones to mush. Behind the earplugs, my ears echoed a high-pitched squeal. My head thumped sudden blasts of pain, and a bolt of puke threatened to leap up my throat and all over everything.

"Genét?" Muffled voices strained to be heard inside my head. "Hey, Genét! Come on – we've got you."

"Meh *ruh?*" Passing out does not do wonders for one's ability to be articulate. Our voices blurred under that damned techno assault and buzzed against the earplugs we all wore. Meghan and Dervish were hauling me upright as I got my feet under me again and shook my head to clear out the mess. Said shaking made my headache worse, but I finally managed to get my bearings straight again.

They held me until I waved them off. "I'm good," I told them, my own voice muffled by the earplugs. "Thanks. Good now."

Meghan nodded, then indicated the cluster of drums, cables, mic stands and amps that had miraculously assembled itself thanks to Inky, Thunderdome and Rol.

I leaned in close to Meghan, emphasizing my words with gestures and over-enunciation: "Can *you* see that, too?"

"See *what?*"

"*That.*" I mimicked lightning with my fingers. "Over there?"

She gaped her mouth open in a silent *O*, then shook her head. "No, but I can feel it."

"Good," I replied. "At least I know I'm not going nuts all by myself."

"You good?" Dervish asked with the awkward redundancy we all get in those moments when we're not sure what else to say. I nodded, and my headache glared at me for it. Dervish reached for the box containing our other secret weapons, then looked a question at me.

I nodded again. "Yeah. I'm ready. Let's put 'em in."

We passed around the in-ear monitors (essentially a hearing aid that allows a musician to hear the mix from the sound board), swapped out one earplug apiece for a monitor, made a few adjustments, and checked the sound-balance, tunings, and in-ear volume levels. Meghan tweaked the soundboard channels as I looked over at the mess on the dance floor again. Inky pulled out her gear and made sure all the cues and connections were set properly.

"We ready?" I asked when it looked like they were done.

Nods all 'round.

I nodded back to each of them as I reached for the buckles on my boots. The idea of dancing barefoot again in this rotten place, especially under the present circumstances, made my guts churn.

If I was taking point on this little exorcism, though, I had to feel, as well as hear, the power we were bringing down.

From a jewelry box, I took out what I hoped would be my best and biggest secret weapon: Zil's red veil. Unfolding it with careful reverence, I spread it out between my hands, kissed it, and draped it loosely over my hair and shoulders.

Finally, I centered myself. Breathed deep, closed my eyes and reached out with every sense I had.

I'm not religious or anything. At that moment, though, with everything weighing down and obvious supernatural powers lined up against us, I did what maybe every human being has done when faced with such an obvious crisis of power and need.

I prayed.

Not to Jesus, or to Buddha, but to someone I knew existed and I figured was listening.

"Zil, Lady Zil, whoever or whatever you are, please help me out a little here."

∾ ∾ ∾

Inky, also bootless, slithered through the mass of bodies. At its edge, the DJ did his thing, bright energy swirling around his booth. Watching her, I slowed my breath to a three-part yoga technique

I'd learned was called *dirga pranayama*. I shifted my balance, and though I couldn't hear them rustle, I felt the coins and silks of my dancing gear shift with me as I closed my eyes again and reached out with all my senses for the ocean of energy on the dance floor nearby.

Sharp cinnamon spread across my tongue. The odor of that spice flowed up my nostrils as I breathed. In my ears, behind the plug and monitor, I caught the faint echo of zils and rustling coins. Breathing deep, eyes shut tight, I drew in a ball of coursing energy from the floor, through my feet, up my legs, into my belly, and into my chest, my arms, and finally my head.

There's a Hindu word called *Kundalini*, which refers to the primal energy that supposedly animates all things. In its highest form, Kundalini becomes *Shakti*, the essence of existence. Shakti is also a goddess… maybe even *THE* Goddess, if you believe in that sort of thing. I learned all this in my yoga classes, and although I'm kinda fuzzy about the details, and didn't really believe in goddesses until I'd met Zil, I know I felt *something* uncurl at the base of my spine as I pulled that energy from the dance floor into me. Something bright and red and powerful, flowing up my spine like electric water and washing away all the pain and tiredness I felt. In yoga, Kundalini is a serpent, reaching up from your spine to your head through a series of gates called *chakras*. Until that night, I'd thought of Kundalini as a metaphor. Standing there, though, in the circle Max had drawn, feeling the tide of energy rush through me, I swear I felt that serpent wake up, flick her tongue, and start to dance.

Even then, though, I stood perfectly still, all my movement on the inside except for the gentle rise and fall of breath.

A light tap on my shoulder. I opened up my eyes. Meghan stood close, checking in with me. *You okay?* she asked without a word. I nodded. Better than okay. *Lots* better, actually.

Meghan nodded with her chin toward the DJ booth. Inky danced in front of it, her body writhing like a snake. Inky had her own Kundalini action going on, and as she reached out toward the DJ, her hands slowly on pulling invisible ropes, I saw him look down at her and smile.

It was *on*.

Inky snaked her way up a few short steps between the dance floor and the booth, her tattooed skin shining with sweat. "I *have* to do this," she'd said as we planned our dance floor coup. "I stayed out of the game when you needed me before, so I have to make it right now. And besides," she had added, "who *else* is gonna know what the hell to do if and when you get up to the booth?" So this was her gig, and she scored it like a champ. The DJ leered like some kind of Gothic Pan statue as he stepped aside and let her up on the stage beside him.

Inky curled her limbs around him, sliding her fingers across his gaunt-corpse skin.

Shouldered his questing hands aside.

Turned her back on him and slid slowly down his chest.

Then elbowed him hard, right in the solar plexus.

The guy collapsed, and she shoved him off the stage. He lost his footing, bounced down the stairs, and disappeared into the dance floor's neon mob.

No one seemed to notice except us.

I glanced between the members of my crew as Inky popped her phone out of a pouch, hooked it up to the sound board, and eased the faders into place.

Inky glanced at me. I nodded.

Ready.

Set.

Go.

THE HOST OF SERAPHIM

∿ ∿ ∿

The bones-deep organ drone of "The Host of Seraphim" swelled up through the fading techno noise. As the booming beats subsided, Lisa Gerrard's voice soared. It's a majestic sad transcendence of the mundane world into the reaches of endless spiritual epiphany. Vivienne used the song as warm-up music for Arcana Darque, I used it to summon Zil in our living room, and now Inky cued it up and let it roar until the chaos on the dance floor stilled and the lights slowly faded down to darkness.

Although the strands of life energy continued to twist and glow, Inky brought the physical lighting down to almost nothing. The room deepened into shadows until only the indicator lights of the electronic gear still shone.

I felt the Kundalini snake rise inside my skin.

Warm energy surged up through the concrete floor, into my soles, up my legs, to my spine and higher still. It flowed upward into my arms, wrists, fingertips, and beyond. I gathered the energy into me and felt it lift me, like a kite on inner winds.

In the darkness, I began to dance.

Meghan, Max and Dervish raised their voices to join the song.

The amps and in-ear monitors blended their voices into the Dead Can Dance track, all four voices harmonizing in what Max had called a *Neopolitan chord*: a "flat major second," whatever that means, which is supposed to redirect harmonic frequencies toward a new goal... or, as Max had phrased it, "to seek and then expand the bounds of tragic uncertainty into sublime bliss." That had sounded like a plan to me, and as the three of them began to sing, each one standing at a point of a triangle Max had drawn around my dancing circle, their voices curled around one another like undulating limbs, weaving harmonies within the recorded music until my skin shivered and my hair pulled tight and stood on end.

I could see it. I saw the sounds they made. Strands of light cutting through the gloom. Purple, blue, green and silver threads of sound, rising from the speakers and weaving themselves into a gleaming tapestry. A net. A mesh of lace. A veil of sound-waves... I don't know how else to describe it. Sound and light and energy – they all appeared, at least to me, like a physical weave of rainbow essence.

It danced, and I danced with it.

The serpent inside me shook its coils and slithered up my spine. My fingertips and toes cut tiny gashes of light in the dark. My skirts flowed like extensions of my skin, all parts of me seeking and finding and holding on to ecstasy. My skull expanded with the surge of energy. The coins on my belt and ankles and bra glided across each other's surfaces, the sound of them lost in the rising music. Inky pushed the faders to the edge of distortion, yet held the music back just below that point. Sound and light and movement become one. I was part of it, and lost myself in the dance.

The recorded track receded. Thunderdome's kick-drum shook the air. Dancing in the circle in front of him, I felt the rush of air shaken by the sound. Thunderdome started with a heart-beat pulse, slow and thick with elemental life, amplified until it seemed like the whole room was a single giant heart. As Inky faded down the Dead Can Dance track, Max drew her bow across the strings of her electric cello. Tucker's bass guitar laid down rumbling notes. Meghan and Dervish pulled intricate chords from their guitars, the voices of their instruments growling toward orgasmic screams. The counterpoint of high notes and deep beats reverberated in my bones. The music moved me, and moved with me in return.

I closed my eyes to shut down what Vivienne calls "the monkey mind." Twisting in the darkness, I let myself glide on the flow of the moment, riding currents of energy and bliss to directions I couldn't *plan*, just *do*.

In the best collaborations, there's a sweet spot where all partners lock into a groove together. We found that groove and flowed together as a single song. My skin tingled and my heart sang and the Kundalini serpent shared our dance.

As time hung suspended in that liquid moment, I learned what true magic is. Magic's not fireballs and pixels; it's the point where a person meets the universe and moves it – and moves *with* it – to create something powerful and new.

Energized, I sped up the dance.

Behind me, the band picked up speed, and the energy flowing between us kicked into high gear.

That warm flush spread out into a glow around me, a halo of red heat illuminating nothing but casting energy out in waves. Thunderdome pounded his drums with primal intensity.

I heard Rol beating on a steel oil drum like it owed his whole *family* money. Dervish, Meghan and Tucker cranked their guitars to the brink of dementia. Max sawed deep rumbles of sound from her cello, and the voices of all three singers cut a wordless wail of harmonic ululation through the gloom. The storm of sound whirled me like a ragdoll.

Then wheels fell off.

The darkness at the walls reached out and caught the light. Our song slowed into a drone. My dance slowed with it. As if some mad god had remixed us to a sludge-metal pace, our frenzy became a sonic freeze, its thunder slowed to an uncanny crawl.

The void at the walls opened its eyes.

Dozens of them.

Tentacles whipped out with implacable speed.

Grabbed Inky.

And threw her into the mob.

Inky fell by inches, slowed by impossible currents of time.

Temporal anomalies.

The things I'd feared in the hallways were here.

They'd probably been here all along.

And we were right where they'd wanted us to be.

WAKE ME UP

∽ ∽ ∽

*Z*il, where the fuck ARE you?

AROUND THE
CROSSROADS INTO
THE STORM

~ ~ ~

It seemed like a good plan at the time: Stop their music, start our own, and use it to summon Zil so she could sort out the fiasco in the basement. Trouble was, that last part counted on Zil showing up to help us, and as my plan slid sideways into a temporal freeze-zone, the spirit who'd quested me was nowhere to be found.

My friends' voiced slowed to a molasses drone. Thunderdome and Rol still pounded on their drums but the beats rumbled like distant lazy thunder. Vibrations shivered through my feet and propelled me, with aching slowness, though my dance. Hands reached up from the mob as Inky fell, her body disappearing into a hazy sway of bodies and limbs. Red arcs of energy crackled like frozen lightning, the time around them compressed until each spark and snap stood out bright against the shadows.

Everything except those tentacles by the walls moved at the pace of a snail on Quaaludes. The tentacles coiled at the edges of the light, flickering with restless urgency and snapping at frozen bolts of energy, absorbing them into their bottomless void.

Dancing bodies rolled aside. In the center of the mob, all eyes on me, three figures turned in my direction: Chalice, Ash and Caroline.

Oh, yeah, they saw us *now*, all right.

And Chalice, I noticed, no longer wore the red scarf I had seen her wearing at Warrior Fitness.

She didn't have it anymore.

I did.

No wonder she'd wanted to "talk."

The three of them moved at normal speed – slower than usual but faster than everybody else. As the crowd blurred to a slo-mo background fog, my former friends and the hot-shit dance star regarded me, their eyes bright with coruscating life-force.

I couldn't stop dancing, though. My mind worked at normal speed. My body dragged behind my thoughts. I could see what was happening but not respond to what I saw.

Shit Creek just kept getting deeper.

Red light burned Chalice's hair into a crimson waterfall, tumbling over her shoulders and highlighting her pale skin. Black tattoos cut dark spaces where her body ought to be. "Oh, good," she said, her voice clear despite my earplugs. "You *did* bring it back to me." Then she grinned. "You're awesome. Thanks, Genét."

Ash and Caroline held their hands out to me. Neither said a word. Ash's face held a frozen sort of horror, as if she'd been hoping I wouldn't come back. Caroline opened her mouth without speaking, looking like that friend at the prom in some stupid '80s teen-flick who's glad to see the heroine show up on the arm of her longtime crush. If I could have laughed, I would have. Nothing about them looked real, but everything about them *was*.

All I could do was dance as though trapped underwater in slowly-freezing ice.

Pure high-octane nightmare fuel.

"Jen-*ayyyyyyyy*." Chalice drew out the second syllable of my name. Behind her, I saw Inky raised high on a sea of hands. Those hands pulled at her clothing, her hair, her skin. Inky's mouth gaped in a soundless scream. Drumbeats pulsed. Voices and guitars shrieked in sluggish banshee wails. Faces glimmered in the crowd, blasted into sharp relief by the light before vanishing in shadows again. Chalice glided toward me, Ash and Caroline close behind her.

I tried to pull back.

Could not.

Behind them, the DJ and his Buddha dudes grinned, dark smiles creeping out underneath their lank long hair. Red light seethed in the glyphs, life-force lava in the concrete floor. The crowd surged slower as the DJ, Chalice, the Buddha-dudes, Ash and Caroline moved at normal speed. Music hung heavy in my ears, feet, muscles, bones.

And there was not one damned thing I could do about any of it.

Zil, I thought, *if you're out there, this'd be a great time to show up.*

Chalice stopped at the edge of the circle Max had drawn on the basement floor. Undulating her arms, she beckoned me to cross the circle.

Oh, HELL, no, I thought. I still danced, but on my side of that barrier.

"You're an awesome dancer." Chalice spoke like we were hanging out at a bar instead of stuck time-sidewide in Underhill. "Really. I mean it. I've always wanted to dance with you."

Yeah, I'll bet, I tried to say. My mouth was frozen shut.

Sweeping her arms out toward Ash and Caroline, she gestured for them to flank me.

Like stubborn puppets, my ex-troupemates danced toward me.

Straight up to me.

Around me.

Cutting me apart from Meghan, Dervish and the band.

Reflexively, I fell into step with them. We *had* been troupe-mates, after all.

As the three of us danced together, months of practice and bonds of friendship wove us together as one again.

Our arms snaked through the spaces between each other. Our feet arced through intricate steps. Beats and sound broke down all divisions between us. My slowness fell away as we picked up speed to match each other. Time's gravity eased. Ash and Caroline engulfed me in their energy.

We merged together, a sisterhood of dance, vibrating on a single plane.

Up close, I saw terror in their eyes, frozen faces locked into rigid masks of bliss. Caroline's mouth moved, but whatever it was she'd tried to say got swallowed up somewhere between her brain and my ear.

We twined around each other as slow drums pounded and voices soared.

And then Caroline reached out and slowly drew the veil off of my head.

Tendrils of darkness, glowing with eyes, reached out toward Meghan, Dervish and the band. I watched them howl, helpless, unable to stop the music. Their hands and mouths handly seemed to move at all. The air around them shivered with displaced time as black tentacles hovered beside them, shivering with pandimensional glee.

We.

Were.

So.

Very.

Deeply.

Fucked.

The sea of hands tugged at Inky, clutched her hair, yanked her jewelry, tug-o-warred with her in the clearing on the dance floor. Bursts of light illuminated ashes, glittering beneath their feet. The ashes, I was sure, of others who had burnt to death in Red Shoes ecstasy.

An ecstasy I felt myself.

That hot familiar flush began along the path of the serpent, pulsating at the base of my spine and pumping with each heartbeat up my back and into my chest and limbs. The cinnamon scent of Red Shoes filled my lungs. Its sharp taste pushed up my throat. Hot sweat burned my pores. My feet flew across the concrete floor with impossible abandon, my fingers slashing hot arcs through the air as my arms flailed the darkness and cut it apart with light.

Ashe and Caroline led me through the dance.

We glided over the edge of the circle, toward Chalice's waiting hands. She danced too, flowing with impossible grace. My skin rippled. My hair pulled tight against my scalp. My bones and organs shivered as liquid fire blasted through my veins.

As if in a ritual, Caroline held out the veil to Chalice. Bowing to the three of us, Chalice slid the veil through her fingers and draped it across her shoulders like a shawl. The red haze around her darkened. Her skin glowed brighter. She seemed to burn with a terrible kind of beauty. The kind that gods command.

Chalice's fingertips brushed my own. A humming surge leaped between our fingers, jetting straight through me like a dirty lightning strike. My bad-boy ex Dragon could do things with his tongue that left me shuddering breathless on the bed, but Dragon had *nothing* on those fingertips. Chalice touched me, and a kick of unwanted pleasure blasted me rigid.

I did not consent to this!

Terror, pain, and screaming ecstasy wrapped themselves in a barbed-wire ball ricocheting through my guts. I writhed, sickened, conscious thought blown to hell by that single, violating touch.

I've been lucky, my me-too moments stopping short of physical rape. This was… there are not *words* for what this was. It was everything I'd come back the Bottle to stop. And when Chalice touched me, it shook me like a fucking chew toy in a Pit Bull's mouth.

I could not, in that moment, have possibly hated her more.

They danced around me, then, circling me, sister sharks in Gothic drag. I tried to break their spell but twisted in shocked, relentless rapture, pulled by tides of crimson energy. Together, we danced out of the circle Max had drawn, my mind shrieking, my body lost in spasms.

The room spun. Faces, bodies, darkness, limbs fuzzed in a sensory tide.

Heat in my bones. Heat on my skin. Sheened sweat flying off like raindrops.

Time seized, stuck between worlds.

Underhill.

Enchanted.

Damned.

Chalice caught my fingers and spun me around. Bolts of rapture sizzled through me. My mind screamed. My body danced. Ecstasy seizures took control. Around us both, red halos blazed. Chiming zils echoed through my mind.

"Thank you," she whispered, her voice clear despite the din. "For coming here. For joining us. For bringing them to me."

Bringing *them* to me?

Oh.

Dervish, who blazed with energy.

Meghan and Max, the magic bards.

Thunderdome and Rol. And Inky too, for that matter. Hell, even Tucker was probably good for a little pick-me-up.

And then, of course, there was me.

I'd brought Chalice a gift-basket of energetic goodies wrapped with Zil's red veil.

Just. Fucking. Brilliant.

Chalice leaned in close. "Thank you," she repeated. "Genét, I love you."

But nothing about this all said "love."

Lust, yeah. Desire. Bottomless hunger. But not love.

She was too hungry, I guess, to know the difference.

Hungry like the DJ. Like the Buddhas. Ash and Caroline. The mob.

Hungry like Blue had been hungry. Too much but never enough.

Chalice swept me up. Ash and Caroline whirled around us. Chalice wrapped us all in a web of vital energies.

She was draining me. Draining all of us. Soon, we'd all be ashes on the floor as her dance went on and on and on.

I was gonna get us all killed.

I THROW IT ALL AWAY

~ ~ ~

I was missing something vital here, but *what?*

I clamped my eyes shut so I could see with my mind. Searching for that missing piece.

Red pieces. Blue pieces. Gray. White. Black. Edges fitting, edges not fitting, patterns, chaos. People who died. Showers of shit. Hot chocolate and chalk.

It all added up to something. But *what?*

Chalice leaned over and kissed my forehead. Cold chills flashed through me. Cold and heat. It felt good. Too good.

I opened my eyes to get out of my head.

Everything blurred but Chalice's face. Her pale eyes and pale skin. Her fingers wrapped around mine.

Around us, time smeared the room to finger-paint designs.

That was it.

Finger-paint. Smeared designs. Colored chaos.

Embrace the chaos.

That's what I had to do.

Chaos has its own flow. Its own energy.

You can't fight *against* it – you have to flow *with* it.

I'd been trying to fit clear pieces into chaoic designs.

If the pieces don't fit, you're trying too hard.

Pieces don't always have to fit. Sometimes, in life, they just are what they are.

I'd learned that much from Blue.

Blue was the person she'd made herself to be. She was chaos, sometimes, but it was *her* chaos, not the chaos imposed by others. Family drama. Abuse. Neglect. She'd made the girl she was from the pieces her life had given her.

And really – don't we *all?*

Through the chaos, I saw Chalice. The person she had made herself to be. She wanted me and my friends and Zil and the dancing mob to feed *her* crazy little world at the expense of our own.

Yeah, *no.* Fuck that.

Chalice grinned. I grinned back.

Then I closed my eyes, gave myself to chaos, and threw my puzzle in the air.

FIGHT FOR ONE
MORE BREATH

∾ ∾ ∾

I snatched Zil's veil, pulled free, and spun back toward the band.

Away from Chalice, into Max's magic circle, and toward the cables on the ground.

Toward the pedals between the instruments and amps.

It all came down to vibrations: The music, the dance, time-displacement, Red Shoes. As GnosticWarrior said, and Meghan and Dervish confirmed, Red Shoes changes your vibrational state. Down there, Underhill, Chalice and her monk-buds had altered our vibrations.

To break that spell, I had to alter them again.

With chaos.

Meghan, Tucker, Max and Dervish each had effects petals out in front of them. Most of those pedals had names embossed across their tops: *FUZZ. OVERDRIVE. ECHOPLEX. THE SCREAMER.*

Electric instruments turn vibrations into electronic impulses. Effects pedals alter those impulses and distort the vibrations. The musician steps on them, and the sounds transform.

I whirled across the space, reached the pedals, and slammed my feet down on them.

Kaboom.

The wall of sound buzzed, screamed, exploded. Amps poured out hyper-loud fuzz.

Time bent, bowed, and blew the fuck out.

Chalice smashed into an invisible wall.

Ash and Caroline stomped across the pedals too. Sounds jangled, tangled, churned. Meghan screamed a full-lunged shriek. Amps blasted it into a storm giant's roar. Dervish shook the time-molasses off. Rol and Thunderdome bolted up to speed, their drumsticks pounding out the beat.

Behind us, Chalice shrieked – a primal cry of furious command.

It blasted past my eardrums and into my skull.

I reeled, spun, and slammed to the floor.

Ash and Caroline went flying. Ash smashed into Tucker. Caroline plastered into Rol. Ash and Tucker fell back into writhing walls of tentacles. Caroline bounced off Rol and collided with the floor.

Stuck at the edge of Max's circle, Chalice raged. "*You fucking CUNT,*" she howled, all loving pretense gone. "*Give her back to me!*"

Not *it. Her.*

Zil's veil. Zil's power.

The final missing piece.

You see the weave. Yep. And now I wore it, too.

Not Chalice. Me.

Zil had given me, *freely* given me, herself.

Chalice and her buddies had stolen Zil. Misused her power. Turned her into something terrible.

But I'd brought Zil home to herself. Now she could take back what rightfully was hers.

"You *want* her, Chalice?" I snarled. "*Fine.*"

I reached out toward a pedal. The one marked *LOOPER.*

Slammed my hand down on it.

Distortion. Echoes.

Feedback City.

Noise screamed from every amp.

Signals and sounds and shrieking dissonance.

Chalice grabbed her ears.

Dervish pulled free.

Rol punched the darkness in whatever passed for its face.

And Inky howled "*MOSH PIT!*"

Chaos, baby.

Chaos.

LAY DOWN YOUR SOUL

～ ～ ～

The place exploded. Bodies everywhere. Solid walls of sound. Thunderdome tore strips of noise from his drums and beat the room to death with them. Dervish slammed her fingers across the strings of her guitar as Meghan threw back her head and bellowed with the loudest voice I've ever heard her use: "*BLACK METAHHHHHL!*"

I guess that's a song she does with Black Swan.

It was the worst piece of shit I've ever heard, but I don't think they meant it to sound *good*.

The pedals shat every sound into sonic sludge. Thunderdome kept pounding away. I yanked my hand back as Dervish, aura blazing, stomped her foot on the looper pedal over and over and over, sending up squalls of overlapping noise.

In the mob, Inky threw herself at everything in sight. She smashed one Buddha-dude off his pedestal. Kicked the other in the nuts. Meghan roared, her voice blown past the pain point by shrieking feedbacked amps. Rol heaved an oil drum at the wall. It bounced off the blackness. The darkness cowered. So Rol picked up the drum and threw it at the darkness again, and again, and again.

Chalice was on her knees, eyes wide, hands over both ears, screams lost in battlefields of sound. Whatever spell she'd had on me was gone.

Oh, yeah, I thought, *I should probably DO something, shouldn't I?*

Meghan screamed chord changes like a cheerleader gone mad. Black Swan ripped into a song I almost sort of recognized. Sheer demented intensity kept the sonic texture ragged, too unpredictable to hold. If anything, the music sped time *up*. The mob, meanwhile, had turned into a grinder storm of flesh. I'd seen mosh pit "walls of death" before, and this was a wall of death on crack.

I shoved myself up and ripped the monitor out of my ear. Ash and Caroline, dazed, tired to push themselves up from the floor. With no idea where their loyalties lay, I spread my arms, took a deep breath, and threw myself into a dance.

Not a bellydance of any kind. This was raw chaos wrapped in sweat and fire.

I body-surfed on waves of sound.

We tore the dark to shreds.

Chalice tried to stand. I body-slammed her. We busted into the mob and everything went red.

Total. Fucking. Glorious. *Chaos.*

We the concrete floor again, pounded by bodies, legs and feet. We rolled in bloody ashes, my fingers locked around Chalice's arm. Limbs hammered us through walls of black and red. Wave after wave of sonic catastrophe smashed into the mob. "Pain," as Inky says, "is a flavor," and I felt that flavor on my tongue.

Next thing I knew, Chalice was gone and Inky was hauling me out of the mob. Everything, and I mean *everything*, hurt. "*Where's Chalice?*" I yelled, but my voice got swallowed by the roar.

One Buddha-dude lay bleeding in the corner. The other Buddha-dude was being pounded against the stage while bodies smashed the gear to ruin. A smear on the floor looked vaguely like the DJ.

This was *too much* chaos. It had to stop.

I reached for Zil's veil. Fuck. It was gone.

Inky yelled in my face: "*You okay?*" I didn't have an answer so I just nodded *yes*.

Back in the circle, Black Swan busted through a scream of death-metal fire. Their auras burned brighter than the lights. The walls glowed like neon smoke. Chalice stood at the edge of the circle, face bleeding, legs shaking, hands held high.

She wore Zil's veil again.

Smoke boiled around her. Red veils of smoke, chiming above the noise.

Zil.

I must have heard her in my head, because nothing less than exploding jet engines could cut through that wall of sound. I know what I heard, though, and I heard Zil, her bells and coins and cymbals clashing.

I pointed at Chalice. "*You see that?*" I screamed in Inky's ear.

"*See what?*"

"*On Chalice?*"

"*Let's clock that bitch.*"

"*Not HER!*" I grabbed Inky's arm. "*Around* her."

She looked. "No. *What?*"

Red Shoes in my system: The gift that keeps on giving.

Chalice, arms raised, began to dance along the edge of the circle – not a frantic mosh, but a slow-motion glide. She spun her hands in lazy circles, gathering energy between them in a pulsing ball of light.

That much, Inky saw. "Oh, *fuck* this."

Inky launched herself at Chalice and body-slammed her past the circle's edge.

Chalice screamed as impact tore the chiming cloud of smoke away.

Zil's red veil floated free.

Inky grabbed Chalice in a headlock.

Meghan jerked her hand up in the air.

The music slammed to a halt.

The chaos stilled.

My turn now.

In the sudden silence, I scooped up Zil's veil, draped it across my shoulders, and stepped up to the runes cut into the floor. Bowing down from my waist, hands outstretched, I ran my fingertips across the runes.

The runes glowed with bubbling light.

I brushed my fingertips across them. Cold, they tingled but did not burn.

As I slid my fingertips over the runes, the light shimmered on my sweat, bled into my pores, and disappeared.

The heat inside me faded into warmth.

Energy no longer crackled in the air. In its place, a fog of fading essence hung. I waved my hand through it, cupping the essence in my palm. Cool relief washed over me. I closed my eyes and gathered more.

Pain faded, replaced by bliss. Not that forced ecstasy of energetic rape, but the soothing calm of stillness – the final movement of life itself.

Stillness: Both the beginning and the ending of a dance. The eternal origin and end. A snake or a dragon eating its own tail.

In the alchemy stuff I'd read, that snake or dragon is called *Oroboros*: introspection, "one that is all," the eternal cycle of life and death and rebirth in which nothing really dies, only gets transformed.

As chaos became silence, I began with stillness and started to move.

I reached my hands out toward the edges of the room, those thick walls lost in writhing dark. My fingers climbed up toward the light, shining, sweaty, smudged with ash.

I breathed deep, expanding, infinite. Energy surged outward from my core. My toes slid across the runes and ashes. Zils chimed inside my ears.

Thunderdome began a slow, thudding, kick-drum pulse. I glanced across the circle at him and shook my head. He stopped. Sliding into a leftward wave, I caught Meghan's eye. She understood. Her hand stayed high. No one played a note.

Silence replaced the storm of sound.

And in that calm, I danced.

I'd never considered myself an artist until then. Art, I though, was for other folks, not me. I was a poseur, a performer, a kid trying to live out the fantasies in my head. But in that stillness, as I moved, I felt life flow through me in a stream. I was the weeping boy with goat's horns, the bright-eyed girl covered in tattoos. I was Meghan and Rol and Dervish and Max. I became the ashes and the blood. All women, all men, and none of us but all between.

I even became Chalice, the dancer who had danced too far. I felt her hunger, her needs, the aspirations she had held and the deals she'd made in order to become this Underhill Queen of Dance. I felt thick dark woods with crossroads and bones. I read bargains etched with undecipherable runes, their terms more awful than any mortal law. I felt hot stones beneath her feet, weaves of ecstasy shaped from pain. I realized, as I danced her path, that patterns which seemed plain to me remained broken in her mind. Scattered pieces she couldn't read, they didn't fit until she forced them into place.

She never saw the weave, only moving fragments of the greater whole

She was crying. Sobbing up her guts. Red lights caught rivulets of tears. The shine, the power, the fearsome majesty of her was gone. Really, she was just a kid – my age, maybe, but not really more than that. Her hands were stained with ashes and her face was smeared with blood. Inky kept her in a headlock, but Chalice didn't fight. All she did was cry.

I didn't blame her. I'd cry too if I had done what she had done.

The deals she'd made had price-tags, and they cost more than I would ever want to pay.

For second there, I wanted to hug Chalice and tell her it would be all right.

But it wouldn't be, and I wasn't gonna lie.

Many people think compassion involves sympathy and forgiveness – "bygones be bygones" and all that crap. I disagree. Compassion, my mom says, involves seeing a person for who they are, honestly, warts and all. It doesn't mean *forgiving* them, exactly. If the things they've done are terrible, then accept that they *are* terrible. Compassion means acknowledgement, not giving in. "Sometimes," Mom told me once, "the most compassionate thing you can do for someone is let them experience the consequences of what they do." And so, as I stood over Chalice, ashes on our hands and blood on our skins, I saw her, and accepted her, and mirrored what I saw.

Chalice looked away, so I reached out – gently but without remorse – took her face between my fingertips, looked her in the eyes, and whispered, "This is your mess, Chalice. Own it. Make it right."

And then I let her go.

No one moved.

So I moved for all of us.

I danced the lives that had been lost and stolen, the ashes beneath my feet and the tears in the eyes of the dancers who still lived. I felt their lives, and let them go. It wasn't my place to hold or keep them. All I could do was move and be moved by them in turn.

I danced to the sound of Zils in my head, their sound-waves silent to everyone but me.

I felt Zil near me, but could not see her.

So I closed my eyes, and in the dark we danced.

Time fell away again.

Each moment became eternity.

And in time, the chiming slowed.

Then stopped.

And so did we.

From stillness I had moved. To stillness we returned.

Oroboros in a silent dance.

"Open your eyes," Zil whispered.

So I did.

And she was gone.

IN THIS SILENCE

~ ~ ~

If this had been a movie, the cops would have busted in right then. Detective Fallon, badge held high, would lead a charge of SWAT team dudes down the basement stairs, round up all the bad guys, and put everything right again.

That's not what happened, though.

Instead, we all just stood there. Motionless, until someone found the switches and turned on the basement lights.

Blocks of greenish light started at the far side of the room, advancing until everything was foggy and bright. In the stark glare of industrial lighting, we stood exposed, all of us, revealed for who and what we were.

Just people. Everyone down there was just people.

No monsters. No goat-headed freaks. The whipping tentacles of time and space were gone. No trace of the DJ, whatever he had been. The Buddha-dudes? With the lights up, they were just *dudes*. Everyone else? As human as I am.

Sure, the battered and confused club-kids were covered in blood, sweat, tattoos, and other stuff I didn't want to speculate about too much. But if there had been faerie beasts or alien horrors, they had all disappeared. More likely, the Red Shoes in my system had finally run its course, and I saw things then the way I'd seen things before I'd ever touched that shit. The way most people see the world, I guess, when our eyes are closed to greater mysteries. Or maybe this *was* the greater mystery: That underneath the carnage and special effects, we're all just people after all.

No one said a word. Chalice had stopped sobbing. In place of that Queen of Underhill, I saw a pale-skinned, broken girl, smeared makeup on her face, eyes haunted by all the things she'd done. I think I might have hugged her then, if only because she looked so sad. But she'd done too much and gone too far, so I just let her suffer whatever was going on inside.

I shook my head at Inky. Inky let Chalice go. Chalice started to open her mouth, so I shook my head again. She closed her mouth, looked down at the floor, and cried.

The revelers blinked and stared. Most covered their eyes. Many covered other parts of their anatomies. Without the darkness, haze and music, everyone stood naked no matter what we wore.

Never get caught dancing when the house-lights come back up. It's an old nightclub saying, and it shows just how ridiculous the whole thing seems when the colored lights give way to industrial brightness and the magic falls back into normalcy. In that basement, our former Underhill, we'd been caught by the house-lights at last.

For a long time, we just stood there, shielding our eyes, covering ourselves, silent in the sheer absurdity of it all.

The ashes on the floor were still there. Had they been people once? I didn't want to know. Someone else could hash out all the details later. Me, I was tired. The lights were on. Show's over. Time to tear down our gear and go back home.

I wish it had been that simple.

It took *forever*. Even in the bright light, with all our experience combined, packing all that gear up took a ridiculous amount of time.

Ash and Caroline helped us out, of course. I said nothing to them. They said nothing to me.

The others, we left alone. I mean, legally, what else could we do? We weren't cops or doctors, just dancers and musicians. I wanted to fix it, but there wasn't anything more I *could* fix. Whatever awful things had gone down in that screaming darkness between worlds, they had to be sorted out on a case-by-case basis by the people who'd been there.

I'm glad I wasn't really one of them. I had my own demons to chase and my own baggage to sort through when all was said and done.

No one said a word. Not one of us. To anyone.

What happens in Underhill, stays in Underhill. Unless it happened to you. And then you have to live with yourself.

SHATTERED INTO ASH

∾ ∾ ∾

Daylight burned the morning sky by the time we finally emerged. I wasn't sure I wanted to know what day it was. Time, I've learned, is an abstract design forced into the arbitrary puzzle people think it is.

We loaded the gear back in our respective vehicles, hugged each other's sweaty bods, and went our separate ways. What we'd experienced went so far beyond words that none of us had words to say. We'd talk about it plenty after that. That morning, though, no words fit and so none were said.

I went to hug Rol. He was shaking hard. When I reached for him, though, Rol shook his head *No*. I respected that, but it hurt. Meghan wrapped her arm around his waist. He let her. One-handed, they hugged. He bent down to kiss the top of her head. She craned her neck up to look at him, and whispered the first words any of us had said in hours: "Thank you."

They went their ways. I went mine.

I pretty much broke down on my way home. Pulled over to the side of the road and let the shudders pass. I didn't cry, though.

Not a drop. Didn't throw up either, though, honestly, I'd had the *right* to. I just shivered and trembled and felt all those things people feel when adrenaline passes and the crisis ends. Shock? Maybe. The biggest thing I know I felt, when all was said and done, was relief. I had stuff to process, yeah – kind of a lifetime's worth. That stuff could wait till later, though. I just needed to get some sleep.

Oh, yeah – there *was* one other big thing we'd done before we left.

After we'd packed up the gear, while Thunderdome and Dervish kept an eye on our stuff, Max, Meghan, Inky, Rol and I went looking for the Red Shoes lab. We found it, too, in a back room behind where the DJ booth had been, decked out with some steampunk combination of modern tech and old-school alchemy. Like Doctors Jekyll, Frankenstein and Strange had tripped their balls off watching *Full Metal Alchemist* with a high-school chemistry set and some junk from Macklemore's favorite thrift shop.

We smashed everything that even *looked* important, and let Red Shoes soak into the dusty concrete floor.

Max snagged a few notebooks and some other stuff, but we turned Chalice's computer – some old PC with a yellowing CRT monitor – into wreckage. I'm sure the hard drive had some interesting data on it, but certain puzzles are best left in pieces on the floor, so that's what we did.

The cinnamon smell hung heavy in that room when we were done, but whatever magic had once had been there was gone.

NO ONE WANTS TO
BE NAMELESS

∿ ∿ ∿

I should have been there," Vivienne said to me later that week. "I'm sorry I never showed."

"To be honest," I replied, "I'm not sure what you could have done."

We were sitting in the Hearthstone, back where the whole thing had begun, sun on our faces and the scent of hot chocolate in the air. The roundabout nature of Vivienne wanting to meet me there, where this whole mess started, seemed too perfect for me to pass up, so when she'd suggested that, I agreed. Besides, Tabi makes some fucking great hot chocolate. Not as good as the stuff at Von Mox but good enough for a Tuesday afternoon.

I'd slept for what seemed like forever once I finally got home from Underhill. It had only been one day, thank God – one dusk-to-dawn throwdown in the basement of that fucking place. I'd awoken feeling raw, quieter than usual. That night had left its mark on me, and to be honest it's never really healed.

I don't have Kristen-style night-terrors, but I don't sleep well anymore. Sure, I got to be the hero after all, that night, but the problem with real-life boss-fights is that they leave scars behind. You can level up in real life, yeah. Hell, it's not life if you *don't* level up occasionally. Unlike a game, though, life changes you when you live it. Our time in Underhill had changed me. Changed all of us. I haven't seen all those changes yet, and I'm not sure I ever will. They're *there*, though, and they'll always be a part of me.

I still haven't tried the whole girlfriend thing yet. To be honest, the idea of touching *anyone* intimately kinda turns my stomach right now. I'll sort that out eventually, but in the aftermath of the whole Red Shoes thing, I just wanted to be left alone. Even so, when Vivienne finally called me, I'd agreed to meet with her. Arcana Darque had unfinished business, and I wanted to sort it out and lay it to rest.

"You're quieter than usual," she'd said after some awkward stabs at conversation.

"Less smart-ass, anyway," I said. I smiled, but the grin felt tight. Oh yeah, I've still got my snarky side. After that night at the Bottle, though, I've been a bit less flip about deploying it unless I really feel the need.

We stumbled around some pleasantries before we hit the heart of the matter: Her role in the Red Shoes situation.

"Chalice was one of my original dance partners," Vivienne said, picking at a bit of goop stuck to the table in front of her. "Back then, she went by 'Cadence,' though her real name was Candace or something like that. Anyway, she really wasn't very good. Enthusiastic, but she had no head for choreography. I think she was dyslexic but I'm not really sure. I brought it up a few times…

I mean, I was just trying to get her to practice more. But that just pissed her off. She got frustrated easily and wasn't that good about practicing."

"I think you're right," I added. "About the dyslexia thing." That fit the misspelled post Chalice had written on my wall. During my brief head-bond with her, I'd realized Chalice didn't see patterns the way I did. Where I saw order, she saw chaos. To get free, I'd needed to see things that way too.

Vivienne took a deep breath and looked at something in her past I could not see. "When I formed Arcana Darque," she told me, "Cadence wanted to be part of it. I told her she needed to get better first. I thought it would encourage her. It didn't. We had a big fight, and that was kind of it for us."

"I'm sorry." I reached out my hand to hers. This wasn't one of those situations where I felt like it was right to *not* comfort someone who'd kinda screwed up. After all, Vivienne hadn't been wrong. No matter how guilty Vivienne might feel about what went down, Chalice made her own decisions. Vivienne never forced Chalice to become what she'd been or to do what she did.

We talked for a while after that, sipping on hot chocolate and trying not to think too much about what had happened or what it cost. "You didn't do this," I finally told Vivienne. "Don't try to carry it. It's not your fault."

"I know." She let out a leaden sigh, and nodded. "I know that intellectually." Vivienne's a big ol' mama bear – tall and solid and charismatic as hell. Most times, she radiates vitality. That morning, she just looked old and sad. "But I should have said something sooner, or been there when it all come down. I left that one your plate, Genét, and I shouldn't have. That all happened years before you joined the troupe. My mess should not have been your problem."

"So what *happened* to you? I mean, after Blue died…" I glanced at the stage without really meaning to. "Up there?"

Vivienne took another deep breath, then looked me in the face. "I freaked out. Let's be real here – I have kids, and my husband's got kind of a precarious position at his job…" Her big eyes went bright behind her glasses. "And suddenly there were cops and dead people and… and… and I just didn't want to risk all that might me mean for my family and me."

I used Rol's old silence trick.

"And so I didn't say anything. I just pulled back and hoped it would all go away."

"Well," I said at last, "eventually, it sorta did."

I hadn't meant it to sound cruel but I guess scars show up when you least expect them to.

After Vivienne left, with big hugs and some promises we both knew we wouldn't keep, I nursed what was left of my hot chocolate. Late-morning sunlight turned to afternoon. Tabi checked in on me. After some small talk, though, I waved her off. Extrovert Genét wanted to be left alone.

The room was full of those people that day – students like me, older folks, some people with little kids, a pair of guys who looked to be about my father's age but whose shy glances and calculated body language had First Date written all over them. I thought about Rol, who I hadn't seen since that night at the Bottle, and suddenly felt very old myself.

Rol made it clear that night that he wanted me to keep my distance. I did, but like I said, it hurt. I fumbled out my phone, thought about texting him, decided not to, and put it back again.

Life went on around me.

The dragon chewing on his tail.

FIND YOUR PEACE OF MIND

∾ ∾ ∾

By mutual agreement, I didn't go back to Crash. I'd let Rose down and we both knew it. That had been a good job and all, but Red Shoes took a toll on me and I needed time to get my head as back together as it's gonna get. Besides, I don't think Rose is quite ready to have an employee on her sales floor who got hauled off by the cops in her underwear. That damn video's still online, and I'm just not ready to talk much more about that night than I already have.

Red Shoes is still out there. Not in Riverhaven, as far as I can tell, but I still find hints about it online. Somewhere, I imagine, that creepy DJ and a new batch of acolytes are spinning magic out of life force and drinking it down. I don't know who Zil's instrument is these days, but I hope it's never me again.

Kris and I decided to relocate and start fresh. Even though Frank got the eviction notice revoked, Mom found us a pretty sweet place off Chamberlain Avenue, close to campus but far from the Aberdeen. That's the way we like it. Our old building has too many ghosts.

Inky, Dervish, Celeste and Black Swan helped us move our stuff into the new place. Meghan and Celeste hit it off like college roommates in a sorority house from hell. Yes, that's a good thing, although you'd probably have to know both of them to understand why it is. The two of 'em spent half the day flying punk-rock purity flags, and the other half staging Ani DiFranco sing-alongs. They both knew all the words. By the end of that day, so did we.

It was, of course, the hottest day of summer when we moved, so the new place got baptized with beer, musician sweat, and enough Garlic Jim's pizza to feed Sicily with leftovers to spare.

"You find anything in those old notebooks?" I'd asked Max while the others were singing their heads off.

"Yeah-uh." Max has a way of stretching certain words, like *yeah*, into two syllables or sometimes three. "Your friend Chalice wasn't exactly an occult mastermind."

"She wasn't my friend. I mean, I knew *who* she was, but I never met her until that night."

"She kept notes on you. Like a *lot* of notes."

"Weird. Like what?"

"Well, that's kind of the problem. I'm not really sure. She had *teh-reh-ble* handwriting…" Again, Max stretched the word out past its normal length. "And I can't read much of what I have from her."

"I heard something about her being dyslexic."

"That would do it, I guess. Lot of misspellings, scratch-outs, the works."

"Makes sense," I said. "But what I'm wondering, though, is did she have anything in there about who or what Zil is? Or was. Or whatever." I still had Zil's veil, but hadn't had the nerve to do anything more with it but stick it in my closet and hope I didn't wake up somewhere *else* with a big glass of Red Shoes near my head.

"Zil is what you made her," Max answered with a shrug. "An essence given form by a mind. Chalice didn't see her the same way you did. I wouldn't see her that way either. She's got a core truth at the center of her identity – which, I *gh-ha-ther* from what you've told me, is the Red Shoes medicine – but her outward form is different for everyone who sees her, because she's not bound by the same rules we are."

"But she *does* have rules, right?"

"Genét," Max told me, taking a swig of cider, "*everything* has rules. Even chaos has rules."

I'd kinda gotten that memo. Everything's got a pattern. Even the most chaotic phenomena create fractals of mathematical precision. If you stare too long at them, though, those patterns fall back into chaos again.

So, do we make the patterns because we expect them to be there? Or is the chaos in our minds the real illusion?

I honestly can't say. But I don't plan to wear that veil again anytime soon if I can help it.

∾ ∾ ∾

Meghan stuck around town for about a week or so, just to make sure I was okay. Then Black Swan hit the road again.

"Thanks for coming back for me," I told her as we hugged outside the van. Thunderdome had the motor running. Max was going over a checklist of their gear. I think Tucker may have already been asleep.

Meghan snorted. "As if I'd leave you to deal with this shit alone."

I hugged my rock star bestie tight. "Friends are *for*."

She hugged me back tighter. "Friends are *for*."

Rol never showed up to see her off... but then, I never asked him to. He'd done enough to deserve some privacy. Still, I missed the guy.

We all have our chaos, ghosts, and nightmares.

After Frank tore strips off me in his office, he and I had a come-clean session with Detective Fallon. At his insistence, I did *not* mention trashing the alchemy lab. She knew about it anyway, and I can't say she was happy about the way I'd handled things. "I really wish you've saved some samples from that lab," she complained. "Legal or not, we really could have used that stuff."

"That," I replied, "is why we trashed it." I thought about ashes and blood and living walls. "*Somebody* would have used it. And nobody *should*."

She really couldn't argue with my logic there.

I got most of my stuff back eventually, though Kristen's not quite out of the woods yet in terms of her possession charge.

As for Frank… well, let's just say I now understand how he affords that Lexus.

Knew you'd want to see this, Caroline posted on my Facebook wall a few days after everything went down. It was a cell phone photo of a grave marker with *Monica Maria Randolph* on the stone. In cobalt lipstick, someone had crossed out the name and written *Blue.* The post also listed the address of a cemetery near Charlotte, North Carolina. I thought about visiting. Maybe someday I will.

I've heard Ash tried to restart Arcane Darque. That went nowhere, and gee I can't possibly understand why. Inky and I have been talking about starting up a new troupe, though. "This time," I told her, "I want to make sure we do things right. No more shortcuts and half-assing around." No more troupes full of just white chicks, either. Sure, dance fusion is bigger than any single ethnicity, but the mess with Chalice – or whatever her name is this week – showed me what can happen when you assume it's your right to take other people's stuff as your own.

After some inquires around town, I found Adìle: a classically trained Turkish dancer who gives lessons in the more traditional forms of bellydance. Inky and I enrolled in her class, and we're making a point of learning more than just the moves. As Zil showed me, good intentions aren't really good enough when you play in someone else's cultural sandbox. There's more to dance than moving. Lots, lots more. We've been talking with some friends from the local drum circle, and at least one of Adìle's students, Mahin, has expressed an interest in joining us if we do. It's all up the air, I guess. The whole Red Shoes thing taught me not to make too many plans, and to stay… well, flexible about a lot of things that used to seem secure.

A week or so after we moved into our new place, I was practicing some of Adile's isolation exercises in our new living room when I got a text from Rol:

Hey you moved

I felt something unlock underneath my ribs. Smiling, I texted him back:

Yeah. Shitty neighborhood. Too many cops.

where you now?

I told him, and about a half-hour later, I heard Rol's big boots clomping up the stairs.

"Hey, you," I said when I'd opened up the door.

Rol glanced around our new living room. "It's an improvement."

"Yeah." I nodded. "About 300% less broken glass and a lot less nightmare fuel."

Inanna padded up to see what all the fuss was about. She stared up at Rol and mewed.

"The household goddess gives her blessing," I told him. "So you'd better get your ass in here before she changes her mind."

"Fuck you, Genét," he replied as he bent down to skritch underneath Inanna's chin. But I knew what he meant.

"Yeah, you asshole," I said, herding him inside. "I missed you, too."

ACKNOWLEDGEMENTS

Big shout-outs to my editor Laura Anne Gilman, my audiobook collaborator Ivy Tara Blair, our cover artist Cora Ocean, our graphic designer Sherry Baker, and to the various friends and contacts who've provided information, feedback and inspiration for *Red Shoes*: Robbie Barnabee, Annalisee "Fox" Brasil, Kate Bullock, Jessica and Victoria Buskirk, Daniel Clark, Danielle Curry, Stephen Cree, Ryan Elliot, Francesca Gentille, Merav Hoffman, Seanan McGuire, Ted Pertzborn, Clary Lucretia Pollack, Emily Siskin, Ann Lenore Taylor, S.J. Tucker, and Shan Wolf; plus the Asheville Movement Collective, Dance Underground, and Seattle's Dance Free Form Dance Dance, and to the folks – especially Lauren and Grant – at the late, lamented UFC Gym Seattle.

Thanks most especially to Inky Grrl, Christopher Sloan, Bryan Syme, Kristen Leigh Wood, and my Belovedest mate, spouse and partner, Sandra Damiana Swan.

Much Love to all y'all!

THE SET LIST

Wax Audio /Iron Maiden /*Dhoom 2*, "Maiden Goes to Bollywood"

Ani DiFranco, "Two Little Girls"

Billie Eilish, "Strange Addiction"

Neko Case, "This Tornado Loves You"

The Smashing Pumpkins, "Bullet with Butterfly Wings"

S.J. Tucker, "Lady Vagabond"

Violent Femmes, "Dance, Motherfucker, Dance"

The Jim Carroll Band, "People Who Died"

Elvis Costello, "Red Shoes"

The Nails, "I Dig Myself a Hole"

Kate Bush, "The Morning Fog"

Social Distortion, "Reach for the Sky"

Concrete Blonde, "Caroline"

Nina Simone, "In the Dark"

L7, "Shove"

The Rocky Horror Picture Show OST, "The Time Warp"

Nickelback, "Flat on the Floor"

S.J. Tucker, "Black Swan Blues"

Japandroids, "Adrenaline Nightshift"

Ayo, "Life is Real"

L7, "Till the Wheels Fall Off"

Archive, "Fuck U"

Guns 'N' Roses, "It's so Easy"

Soundgarden, "Jesus Christ Pose"

Jessie J, "Flashlight"

Theory of a Dead Man, "In Ruins"

Kate Bush, "Get Out of My House"

Elastica, "Waking Up"

Sick Puppies, "You're Going Down"

Yeah Yeah Yeahs, "Runaway"

Taylor Swift, "Shake it Off"

Gamma Ray, "Real World"

S.J. Tucker, "In the Name of the Dance"

Dead Can Dance, "Toward the Within"

The Guild, "Game On"

Thea Gilmore, "And We'll Dance"

Lady Gaga, "Till it Happens to You"

Joss Stone, "Tell Me 'Bout it"

Florence + the Machine, "Heavy in Your Arms"

Survivor, "Eye of the Tiger"

Blink-182, "Dammit"

P!nk, "U + Ur Hand"

The Beloved, "Falling on My Face"

Dead Can Dance, "The Host of Seraphim (Trisagion remix version)"

Jess and the Ancient Ones, "Crossroads Lightning"

Brandi Carlile, "Throw it All Away"

I Prevail, "Chaos"

Venom, "Black Metal"

Delerium and Sarah McLachlan, "Silence"

Bastille, "Things We Lost in the Fire"

Dizzie Rascal and Florence Welsh, "You've Got the Dirtee Love"

Taylor Swift, "We are Never, Ever Getting Back Together"

Songs Cited in the Text

Hallucinogen, "Jiggle of the Sphinx"

Kate Bush, "The Red Shoes"

Bob Marley, "No Woman, No Cry"

Patti Smith, "Gimmie Shelter"

Jonathan Coulton, "Code Monkey"

The Ramones, "We Want the Airwaves"

Dead Kennedys, "Holiday in Cambodia"

Oingo Boingo, "Wake Up (it's 1984)"

Florence + the Machine, "What the Water Gave Me"

The Jim Carroll Band, "People Who Died"

Niyaz, "Shah Sanam"

Rollins Band, "On My Way to the Cage"

Limp Bizkit, "Break Stuff"

Avenged Sevenfold, "Hail to the King" *

Clint Mansell, "Requiem for a Tower (remix of Lux Aeterna)"

Geno Valle, "Hair of the Gods"

Irfan, "Invocatio"

Dead Can Dance, "De Profundis"

Vas, "In the Garden of Souls"

Solace, "Peng Heng"

Dead Can Dance, "Saltarello"

Macklemore and Ryan Lewis, "Thrift Shop"

* *Genét is wrong; it's not Metallica that's playing when she and Childers square off — it's Avenged Sevenfold.*

AUTHOR'S NOTES

THE ROOTS OF RED SHOES

The drug Red Shoes made its first appearance in my 2005 book *Everyday Heroes: Adventures of the Rest of Us*. The roots of this novel, though, run much deeper than that idea.

In 2002, my then-roommate Danielle Curry joined a bellydance troupe and introduced me to her friend Asha – the best bellydancer in Atlanta at that time. Classically trained in India and Turkey, Asha herself had no patience for what she called "stupid little white stripper-girls who take off their clothes and call it bellydance." Despite being a petite white girl herself, Asha worked hard to hone her craft, earning a fair degree of respect in the global dance community. Asha and I got to be good friends too, and I learned a lot about the politics of bellydance communities from her... including the very valid arguments about cultural appropriation involved in that form of dance.

Originating in a conflux of Turkish, Lebanese, Greek, Egyptian and Indian dance traditions, plus waves of immigration from those regions into the United States, combined with the American entertainment industry and a fascination with "exotic" cultural stereotypes (especially sexy ones), the modern belly dance / bellydance style is more-or-less a creation of 20th century popular culture. Many dancers treat this form of dance with respect, while others just strap on coin bras and wiggle their hips a bit.

The subject of cultural appropriation and the modern form of bellydance is a hot-button topic for certain folks. Some people feel white folks should just keep their grubby paws away from it, while others believe that bellydance, like other art forms, should be accessible to anyone who shows a proper respect for the origins and meanings of that form. Most practitioners I know personally go out of their way to distinguish between American fusion dance and the authentic styles of their appropriate cultures. Genét's perception of Zil stems from her desire to be respectful while, as she puts it, "playing in somebody else's cultural sandbox." Being half-Greek herself, Genét has a degree of claim over the tradition herself; even so, the end of the book finds her realizing that a greater degree of cultural knowledge and respect is in order.

On that note, I want to credit authors Rosina-Fawzia Al-Rawi and Monique Arav for their book *Grandmother's Secrets: The Ancient Rituals and Healing Powers of Belly Dancing*. That book provided a foundation for many of the themes, plots and ideas that went into *Red Shoes*.

My friends Asha, Jenn Kellem, and Laura Tempest Zakroff, among other members of various bellydance communities in Atlanta, San Francisco, Asheville, Portland and Seattle, also deserve credit for inspiring and informing elements of the book in your hands.

I love to dance, too. Although my 30-some-odd-year career in mosh pits ended at a 2011 Motörhead gig (middle-aged knees do not take well to dislocation), I still love to go out dancing. That love was born from a community workshop in Afro-Caribbean dance I took when I was 16, and was nurtured in the punk and New Wave scenes of the early 1980s. I took four years of ballet, jazz, and modern fusion classes during college, too, but I found those disciplines extremely frustrating to learn.

As I later discovered, I have dyslexia and dyscalculia: related sensory-processing conditions that mess with pattern recognition, mind-body coordination, consistent perception of external phenomena (especially letters and numbers), and one's ability to process stimuli – especially stimuli involving mathematical patterns. Because music *is* innately mathematical, and choreographed dance techniques demand intense mind-body coordination, dance class drove me batshit despite my love for the physical sensations of dance. Dancing in clubs, however, was my jam, and sometimes it still is. I was a regular feature in punk, metal, and Goth /industrial clubs between the early 1980s and the early 2000s, while freeform ecstatic dance – which I discovered in 2002 by way of my friend and then-sweetheart Francesca Gentile – allowed me to explore my love of dance without the frustrations of choreography. Soon, I became a DJ and facilitator for dance communities in Asheville, NC, and Seattle, WA, where I still dance whenever time, money and physical limitations allow. Genét's impressions of dance are drawn directly from my own.

(Francesca also introduced me to my longtime fascination with the saga of Innana's descent into the Underworld. I had heard the story long before we met, but Francesca's dedication to that goddess and her journey brought a personal resonance to an ancient myth.)

On a much darker note, *Red Shoes* also draws heavily from my experiences with abuse perpetrated against me and mine. I'm not going into details here, but let's just say that certain elements of this novel (notably the screaming night-terrors and the reasons behind them) come from real life. In case it isn't obvious, *Red Shoes* is a book about abuse; about addiction, music, and other stuff as well, but especially about abuse. Sure, it involves the abuse of drugs, but this book deals even more extensively in abuses of power, sexuality, trust, and even wealth. In that regard, it deals with privilege, too, and with what happens when a person who holds privilege recognizes abuses all around her. Part of Genét's journey through *Red Shoes* involves seeing the ways in which people around her have been – and still *are* being – abused, and then acting to stop it whenever she can.

At the end of these Author's Notes, I've included a number of contact-points for abuse intervention, counseling and aid. If you have been abused, please get help. If you notice abuse, please help others. You could change a life. You could save one, too.

DYSLEXIA, ARPEGGIO, AND REAL-LIFE HEROES

My dyslexia, and its attendant frustrations, inspired the idea that the character Chalice – who's far more dyslexic than I am – would seek shortcuts in order to become the dancer she envisioned in her head. One of the reasons people (especially children) with sensory-processing conditions like dyslexia, synesthesia, and the Autistic Spectrum can get temperamental, even irrational, about things that seem like no big deal to anybody else is because of the disconnect between what we see in our heads, as opposed to the world we're trying to interact with... which feels... well, *off* in unpredictable and uncontrollable ways. Even now, in my 50s, that sense of disconnection gets seriously frustrating. When I was a kid, my frustration occasionally boiled into violence. And so, despite her abusive behavior, I feel sorry for Chalice. She does terrible things, but most of them come about because her mind and body would not cooperate with the visions in her head.

Genét herself is a product of dyslexia. When artist Bryan
Syme and I created our now-defunct webcomic *Arpeggio*, Bryan
drew up character designs based on my written notes. In *Arpeggio*,
Meghan Susan Green was the central character; her best friend was
initially envisioned as a Goth-kid named Jenni, aka "Seraphim."
I had initially envisioned Seraphim as a long-haired languorous
Goth chick; Bryan dutifully drew the character I'd described,
but then added a lanky, short-haired embodiment of fashionable
punk-attude with a miniskirt, big boots, and a sly grin that felt
immediately more appealing than the rather mopey character
I'd originally conceived. I immediately loved Bryan's take on the
character, and the whole Seraphim thing was shelved. Thanks to
his own dyslexia, Bryan had labeled her as *Genni*. Having been
introduced to the work of Jean Genet by my high-school drama
teacher Dorothy Kogleman, I latched onto the idea of a smart,
snarky girl who'd turned her hated nickname, "Jenny," into the
suave, subversive *Genét…* complete with accent, because why the
fuck not? That character intrigued me far more than my initial
conception had, and so our Genét was born.

The idea of a 21st-century teenager who turned her all-too-common name into a reference to Jean Génet immediately made for a far more interesting character, and so I scripted Génet as a smart, fun, and rather popular young woman whose unlikely bond with moody Meghan created a delightful tension. The counterpoint between them mirrored the rather unconventional relationships we often find ourselves in real life, especially during our teenage years, when some of us proclaim "Fuck it" to the usual cliques and make friends with whomever we want. The fact that low-rent Meghan and well-heeled Génet defy the usual divides of class and culture spoke volumes about their attitudes. These were girls who broke rules on general principle – not because they had to act like rebels, but because those rules felt especially stupid and limiting. So yes, thank you, Bryan. Your decision to follow your own creative impulse turned Ms. Shilling from a background cliché to a vibrant protagonist in her own right.

(The Jenny /Genét reversal provided an appropriately snarky plot-point in *Red Shoes*, too. Oh, and the stuff about Genét's father being a college-radio DJ in the '80s is based on my gig doing the same thing in those days.)

Meghan herself, as well the comic *Arpeggio* and the band Black Swan, originated in a conversation with our friend, the indie-musician powerhouse S.J. Tucker. Sooj and I had been chatting about our lives as hypercreative teenage misfits in the South. A few months later, after meeting and hitting it off with Bryan Syme, I conceived the idea of an urban fantasy webcomic inspired by that conversation with Sooj. Meghan is *not* Sooj, obviously – she's really more of a younger female version of me. That magic barefoot bard fuses elements of our personalities (including my own rather militant distaste for shoes) into a fictional embodiment of our best and worst aspects.

"Black Swan Blues" is a song whose lyrics I wrote for *Arpeggio*. Sooj later added more lyrics, composed music for them, and recorded the song for her album *Stolen Season*. Because that song, in the comic, was composed and performed by Meghan Susan Green, I named her band after that song. Sooj herself lived in an SUV for six years or so, touring the country before settling down with her husband Ryan. She still tours several months per year, and if you haven't heard of her already, go check her out on YouTube, Bandcamp, and other music venues. I learned a lot about music's magical potential from my long friendship with Sooj. In a perfect world, girls everywhere would have S.J. Tucker posters on their walls, and so anything I can do to bring such a world to pass is a win as far as I'm concerned.

S.J. also introduced me to my beloved wife and frequent collaborator Sandra Damiana Swan. We met while I was working as roadie for Sooj, and our chemistry ignited when we began dancing with each other the following day. Sandi created the character Dervish for a roleplaying game I ran and designed: *Deliria: Faerie Tales for a New Millennium*. Dervish later became a supporting character in *Arpeggio*, and while (once again) Dervish is not Damiana, the influence of my Belovedest comes through in Dervish's manic, joyful charisma.

Max, Tucker and Rol appeared in *Arpeggio* too, although Rol's origins go back to a story I first wrote in 1991 and then rewrote and published in 1995 under the title "Special Guest." (That first Rol differs considerably from Roland Castile, but his basic temperament is similar.) Max is *very* loosely inspired by a fusion of Sooj and her best friend and longtime collaborator Betsy Tinney, and Tucker is largely fiction although my concept for him came from some friends I had in high school who should probably remain nameless. Thunderdome originated from a cross between

Sooj's buddy and occasional drummer Trainwreck, my buddies Ogre and Troll, and my longtime fascination with Henry Fucking Rollins, while the Silver Key is a fictionalized fusion of two Seattle music stores: Dusty Strings in Fremont, and The Trading Musician on Roosevelt Avenue. If you're a musician in Seattle, I urge you to go there and buy their stuff.

On that note, the Warrior Fitness subplots originated with a now-vanished Ultimate Fighting Gym that was also based on Roosevelt, across the street from Wayward Coffeehouse, where I often go to redline manuscripts and meet with friends and collaborators. Although my body was in no condition to begin that sport at my age, I used to take martial arts classes and spar with padded weapons during my 20s. The number of young women I saw training in UFC Gym Seattle nearly equaled the number of men I saw there, and if I'd been even 10 years younger and a few thousand bucks richer, I'd have probably joined that gym myself. Genét, being young, well-off, and idealistically heroic would have loved such a place. I had no idea, when I first wrote UFC Seattle into the book, where that element of the plot was headed; when I reached that point, though, I spent a few hours with the staff and some members, hashing out the details I needed for those scenes. Sadly, the place went under while *Red Shoes* was in revisions. I keep looking for it when I go past its location, but that bit of local magic is gone.

Both Genét's athletic inclinations and her fascination with puzzles come from my longtime friend and former partner Ann Lenore Taylor, aka Lady Snow Leopard. The stuff about those puzzles on Genét's walls? That's Ann, and those were our walls. Genét's puzzle-solving methods were inspired by Ann, and her mother's jock-to-real-estate-agent trajectory was inspired by Ann's mom. Ann loves to dance as well, and like her mother and father, she has remained in great physical shape by combining mental gymnastics with constant physical exercise.

Genét's martial prowess was also inspired in part by my stepdaughter Jessica Buskirk, who's been training in various forms since her early teens; and by my best friend on earth, Inky Grrl: fire-spinner, sound-tech, model, retired pole-dancer, and near-rabid UFC fighting fan. Jessie and Inky helped me plot out the strategies Genét would use against Eric Childers, with Inky supplying the liver-punch kill-strike. On Inky's recommendation, I YouTubed a ton of UFC and kickboxing matches between opponents of various (and occasionally mixed) genders, watching who did what to whom and noting the effects it had. Childers' failed attempt to stand was based directly on a fighter whose physical size dwarfed his opponent until the liver-punch ended his ability to move.

My other superhero stepdaughter, Victoria, helped me comb some excess snark out of Genét's personality. Although I'd intended it as defensive sarcasm used to ward off shock, Genét's narration made her come across, in Vicki's words, "abrasive and really fucking unsympathetic." Several other beta-readers agreed, so I toned down the sarcasm and amped up the shock… to, I feel, far better effect. Thanks, Vicki!

By the way, if it seems like *Red Shoes* features a lot of people who do amazingly cool shit, it's because my real life is filled with such people too.

Those amazingly cool people include my old friends Jennifer Kellem and Kristen Leigh Wood. Jenn, an old dancing-partner of mine and a longtime bellydance artist, provided the foundation for Vivienne, though Jenn would never have bailed on the troupe the way Vivienne does. Kristen has had my back in almost every situation for almost 20 years, and both of them were alpha-readers for this book. Although the characters who were inspired by them are, once again, *not* those people in real life, the presence of Jenn and Kristen in my life provided many elements of the story at hand. Kristen even provided some of her namesake's dialog in the coffeehouse scene, while Jenn answered many of my questions regarding the feeding and caring of a modern American bellydance troupe. With Kris' approval, I also immortalized her late feline companion Inanna; the fictional cat combines Kristen's companion with my own four-footed officemate Cupid, but her name comes from the real Inanna. Rest well, little goddess.

Thanks also go out to my friend Robbie Barnabee, who brought me into *World of Warcraft* when I realized that having a WoW-head protagonist meant I finally had to play that fucking game. I'd successfully avoided doing so for over a decade, dammit…

Robbie put up with my constant complaints of "But how do you *do* this?" and even got me to kind of enjoy it. Along with our friend Abie Eke, we terrorized our way through various dungeons for several months during the early writing-stages of this book. No, I haven't played again in ages, and if I did, I would not make my handle public. That's just asking for trouble.

SWATTING, COPS, & NO-KNOCK RAIDS

The swatting subplot came from the harassment and doxxing several of my friends have endured in recent years. Again, my research for this topic involved watching videos of actual SWAT raids, and let's just say that anyone who would aim such a thing at someone else as a "joke" deserves a hell of a lot worse than a liver-punch and jail.

Thanks go out as well to several folks in various police departments, and to some friends of mine who've been on the opposite end of the arrest-and-interrogation process. I plotted out the interview, the raid, the interrogation, and their aftermath through hours upon hours of conversations and reviews. Most of those sources have requested anonymity, for totally understandable reasons. My friend Clary Lucretia Pollack, however, deserves mega-credit for being my longtime go-to source for paralegal questions of the writerly kind. Thank you, Clary!

I confess my attitude toward police forces has become less than sympathetic in the years since I finished writing *Red Shoes*. This story obviously predates the COVID-19 pandemic and the related civil unrests of 2020. Although *Red Shoes* was written and edited before the killing of Breonna Taylor, I find it unnerving just how relevant that element of this novel became in light of her real-life murder.

And yes, I did say *murder*. Given what I learned about the protocols and procedures involved in no-knock raids – rules which protect police officers as well as civilians – I don't accept the "Oopsie" shrug that constitutes the police response to that killing as of the time this book heads toward press. Rules were ignored and broken by the police, with what our laws refer to as *depraved indifference*. Breonna Taylor was killed as a result, and other lives have been altered and scarred in turn. Although *Red Shoes* touches on the ways in which white Americans (especially wealthy ones) are treated better under the law than non-white Americans are, Breonna Taylor's death highlights that subject more than my words ever could.

No-knock raids, though sometimes necessary in extreme circumstances, constitute significant threats to the public welfare, the safety and conduct of police officers, and the assurances granted by Amendments 4 and 5 of the United States Constitution. Such extraordinary tactics must be handled carefully, with stringent policies involved and strict punishments for violating those policies. I hope to see such punishments eventually handed down to every one of the perpetrators and facilitators of Taylor's murder; as of this time, however, such consequences are nowhere to be found. And that, by every measurable definition of the word, is wrong.

MUSIC, DRUGS & FAERIE TALES

As you've probably noticed, the chapters throughout this novel draw their names from song titles and lyrics. Feel free to read deeper significances into *those* choices too – the significances are there, although they're not often obvious. If nothing else, enjoy the playlist provided at the end of this book. While you've probably heard a number of those songs before, I'm willing to bet you haven't heard them all.

On a more serious note, *Red Shoes* has been inspired by my experiences and observations in and around various subcultures over the years.

The Bottle came from a now-defunct "outlaw" art-space in Richmond, Virginia, where I used to model for artists during and after college. The band Gwar used to practice there too, and there *were*, in fact, awful things going on in the basement. As my late classmate Dave Brockie notes in his ironically titled blog "GWAR, Me, and the Onrushing Grip of Death," the basement of the real-life building was occupied by a meth-and-crack lab that supplied untold amounts of the "product" sold in and around Richmond during the '80s and '90s. Dave himself died from an overdose of heroin in 2014, and the tight proximity of drugs and creativity is a fact of life that any artist knows from personal experience. Although, like Génet, I'm no prude or virgin with regards to various psychotropic substances, I'm not an idiot either. However, too many of my friends, acquaintances, and in some cases relatives have made terrible choices with regards to drugs and alcohol, and although I have thankfully never endured chemical addictions myself, I have more second-and third-hand experience with them than I would like to admit.

Now, while I'm not gonna go all Nancy Reagan here – that would be not only hypocritical, but dishonest – I *DO* caution you to *stay the fuck away* from certain substances, especially those with a known propensity for killing people: coke, crack, heroin, meth, speed, PCP, and so forth. Sure, you never think that *you'll* wind up among the casualties. Those casualties didn't think they would either. And if you *do* think you'll wind up among them, and you think that's some cool, glamorous way to off yourself, *FUCKING STOP*. It's not glamorous, it's not cool, and it's sure as hell not painless. Drug abuse is a miserable, wretched, scary, embarrassing way to die, and it drags your loved ones through shit you can't even *begin* to imagine unless you've been there before yourself... and if you *have* been there yourself, then you probably know just how fucking stupid that mythology looks in comparison to day-to-day reality.

If that's *already* what your real life looks like, then please get help. I fucking mean it. Help is out there. Don't die that way, and don't take other people with you down that road.

Sermon over. But I'm serious about that. Really.

Faerie tales have an undeserved reputation as childish escapism. That's bullshit. As I wrote in *Deliria*, faerie tales aren't intended to help people *escape from* reality – they're to help people *deal with* reality. Sure, they're more entertaining than a lecture, but the symbols and themes within such tales reflect real-life concerns dressed up in archetypal garb. That's as true of modern fantasy (the good stuff, anyway) as it is of classical myth and lore. Elves and underworlds aren't just there to provide comfort-food for geeky masses. They also offer toolkits for everyday dilemmas and inspiration for those times when life just flat-out sucks.

Because, for artists and everyone else, life frequently *does* suck. And we don't need placebos to escape from that reality – we already know it's true. Instead, we need tools to help us face our dragons and emerge from our underworlds far stronger than we'd ever thought was possible.

Have a good one, folks.

Catch y'all on the flipside.

Take care, everyone.

ABUSE SURVIVAL AND
RECOVERY RESOURCES

Crash Override

http://www.crashoverridenetwork.com

The Cyberbullying Research Center

https://cyberbullying.org

The Mighty

https://themighty.com

The National Alliance on Mental Health (NAMI)

https://www.nami.org/Home

The National Domestic Violence Hotline

http://www.thehotline.org/resources

The Rape, Abuse & Incest National Network (RAINN)

https://www.rainn.org/
national-resources-sexual-assault-survivors-and-their-loved-ones

Surviving in Numbers

https://survivinginnumbers.org/resources-for-younger-
survivors

www.ingramcontent.com/pod-product-compliance
Lightning Source LLC
Chambersburg PA
CBHW022017050726
47499CB00004BA/1025